Keri Adams had lost ... Brian Michaels finally admitted he had seen the murdered woman on the day she died. He didn't seem to understand that, as his lawyer, she had to know *all* of the facts. They'd argued and Keri had stormed out of the restaurant.

Now, still angry with him and herself, Keri drove slowly down the streets of her gated community. She turned into the underground parking garage to find that only one dim light illuminated the way. Uncomfortable in the darkness, Keri hurriedly parked and got out. As she set her car's alarm, she heard sounds in the distance of a car accelerating.

Tomorrow, she thought, she would have to deal with Brian and apologize for walking out on him. The circumstantial evidence suggested her client had been framed and she couldn't mount an effective defense if Brian didn't tell her everything.

Without looking, Keri started across the drive. Suddenly aware that a car was speeding towards her, she ran. The car swerved, missing her by inches.

Keri stood shaking. There had been no lights on the car and the garage was practically pitch black. The realization dawned that the driver had been trying to hit her! She raced up the stairs to her townhouse, then carefully locked the door behind her. She went from window to window, checking to see that each was locked before setting the alarm for the night.

Who would want to kill her? Keri wondered as she made some tea to calm her nerves. The telephone interrupted her thoughts and she answered it quickly.

The line was quiet except for the sound of heavy breathing.

ER WITH HER CLIENT
D NOT GONE WELL

AMANDA HAZARD MYSTERIES
BY CONNIE FEDDERSEN

DEAD IN THE CELLAR   (0-8217-5245-6, $4.99)

DEAD IN THE DIRT   (1-57566-046-6, $4.99)

DEAD IN THE MELON PATCH   (0-8217-4872-6, $4.99)

DEAD IN THE WATER   (0-8217-5244-8, $4.99)

BEYOND A REASONABLE DOUBT

Toby Marlowe

Pinnacle Books
Kensington Publishing Corp.

http://www.pinnaclebooks.com

PINNACLE BOOKS are published by

Kensington Publishing Corp.
850 Third Avenue
New York, NY 10022

First Printing: November, 1997
10 9 8 7 6 5 4 3 2 1

Printed in the United States of America

Chapter One

"Objection!" Angry and belligerent, Louis Garcia sprang to his feet. "Your Honor. Defense is leading the witness."

"Sustained."

Keri Adams straightened the lapel of her navy pinstriped suit while she regarded the exasperated prosecutor with distaste. A noise echoed in the distant hall, making her aware of the strained silence in the small dim courtroom. Above the judge's bench a fluorescent ceiling tube flickered annoyingly, adding to Keri's mounting agitation.

Mentally rephrasing her question, Keri glanced at the witness watching her with detached insolence. Beneath long black lashes, her angry eyes swept disinterestedly over him, from the generous cut of his tweed sport coat to his greying hair and dark eyes.

A sudden chill permeated her body when she met his frigid stare. Here was a man with the outward appearance of respectability, but lurking just below the surface lay hostility and unresolved conflict.

Judge Harry Pennell sighed wearily and leaned back in his chair. He looked down at Keri, judiciously surveying her tall, shapely body and her soft blond hair, which fell in loose curls below her shoulders. She's beautiful, he thought, and threatening. She had changed since she first stood in his courtroom. Then she had been warm and outgoing. In the past three years since her husband's death, he had watched Keri throw herself into a world of conflict and competition. There she had honed her skills.

Until now.

Now, at thirty-one, she was a real presence in the courtroom: always business, always professional, always impersonal. Keri Adams could hold her own against the best. Her reputation as a criminal defense attorney was growing. At what cost to her personal life, he wondered as he shook his head impatiently and cleared his throat.

"Ms. Adams, it's been a trying day and we are going to adjourn. You may continue your cross examination of this witness on Monday morning."

The judge turned his gaze to the witness. "You may step down, Lt. Rodriguez. Bailiff, return the defendant to the custody of the sheriff." Judge Pennell glanced at the clock at the back of the courtroom. He had listened to enough bickering for one week. It was time to retreat to the privacy of his office where paperwork didn't talk back. "Court is adjourned until Monday morning at nine o'clock."

"Thank you, Your Honor." Keri turned back to the defense table. She had learned quickly not to press Judge Pennell when he wanted to break early. Maybe he was right; it had been a trying day and she was exhausted. Right now all she wanted was a hot shower, a cold drink, and a soft bed.

"All rise . . ." While the bailiff droned on, Keri threw her file on the table and whispered a few words of reassurance to her client before the sheriff took him away. As people filed out of the courtroom, she wearily began gathering her papers.

Weekends were getting harder and harder to face alone, she thought, but a fulfilling relationship was hard to find. Her marriage to Patrick had been comfortable and secure, yet he had never roused the passions which she sensed lay dormant within her. Since his death she had tried dating a couple of men, but there had been no magic. She was beginning to resign herself to the fact that the type of love and excitement she craved only existed in the minds of foolish dreamers.

Last year, a friend she had been dating proposed to her. When she turned him down, he became angry and accused her of being cold. She couldn't say that she was surprised, she had heard that before, not just from boyfriends, but from colleagues, from opponents, and even from her own husband. Patrick had used it like a tool to hurt her whenever she angered him. How easily the accusation had tripped from his mouth and undermined her confidence in her own femininity.

Truthfully, she admitted, she was afraid to fall in love again. What if she really was cold and aloof like most men thought? An empty marriage was not for her. No matter how lonesome she was, she didn't need another unsatisfying relationship. With her schedule it was very unlikely that she would have to worry about becoming involved; she just didn't have the time. Besides, she hadn't met a man that she found all that interesting anyway. She drew in a deep breath. *But there was one whose picture intrigued her . . .*

Looking up, she glared at Lt. Rodriguez who stood in a huddle with the prosecutor. His sport jacket had fallen open, exposing his spreading middle, which strained at the waistband of his trousers. With an absentminded gesture, he wiped at the beads of perspiration which had formed along his forehead. He looked all of his forty-eight years, Keri thought, studying the scowl on his face. Funny, she couldn't remember ever seeing the man smile.

Lt. Rodriguez had been the investigator on a number of cases she had defended in the past. From the first day his demeanor had been patronizing. He had always exhibited a complete lack of emotion and seemed to instinctively know how to irritate her even when her questions were merely routine. One day she was going to make that arrogance backfire on him in front of a jury. It was just a matter of time.

"Looks like you could use a drink!" A deep masculine voice interrupted her angry thoughts.

Keri wheeled around to see her partner, Roy Foxx, nonchalantly leaning against the end of the defense table. The long sleeves of his wrinkled white shirt were rolled back exposing his strong lean forearms. Wisps of his thinning brown hair had fallen across his forehead accentuating his disheveled appearance. With an impatient gesture, he threw his jacket over his shoulder and loosened his tie. An anxious expression left his face, replaced by a mocking smile.

"So you caught the last part of the hearing?" She flashed a smile back, quickly noting an undercurrent of excitement in his cold brown eyes.

"Just in time to see Hector Rodriguez, Miami's number one homicide detective, get you all hot and angry." His eyes narrowed suspiciously. "What is it between the two of you?"

Keri looked thoughtfully at him for a moment before answering. "Roy, I honestly don't know. The hostility has been between us since my first trial with him. I neither like him nor trust him." Her dark eyes once again filled with anger. "One of these days I'm going to send him back under that rock he crawled out from under."

"Back off, Keri, he can make life very unpleasant for you. Now pack up. I want you to come to jail with me." He straightened his tall frame. "We have a new client."

Without answering, Keri hurriedly stuffed loose papers into her file. For a brief moment Roy stood waiting. Annoyed that she appeared uninterested, he turned abruptly and with long strides, left her standing in the courtroom. Keri grabbed her briefcase and ran after Roy, her heels clicking loudly on the wooden floor. "Roy, wait! Who's the new client?"

Obviously pleased with himself that he finally had her attention, he handed her a newspaper. "Read the front page. I'll give you details over coffee."

Keri tucked the newspaper under her arm. The headlines could wait until they got to the courthouse coffee shop down the hall. She preferred to wait for a cup of coffee and a comfortable seat before trying to read. It had been a rough week and she felt fatigue setting in. Another crime was the last thing she really wanted to hear about. Still, it must be a very important one for Roy to seek her out in court on a Friday afternoon.

Then she glanced at his face with its odd expression and felt her interest come alive. His repressed excitement was contagious. What was going on?

As if he had anticipated her thoughts, Roy turned to her. "This one's big, Keri, really big!"

When they arrived, the coffee shop was empty of its usual array of attorneys, judges, and jurors. The small wrought-iron tables were clean and waiting for the late-afternoon rush. Roy led her past several empty tables before settling on a secluded table in the back corner of the coffee shop.

After they ordered coffee, she opened the newspaper—no longer able to contain her curiosity. Scanning the headlines, she looked at her partner in surprise. "It can't be, Roy. The police have arrested Brian Michaels for the murder of Emilia Martinez?"

"And we are defending him." Roy answered in a voice filled with self-importance and an arrogance that took Keri off guard.

Keri studied him with a troubled look. There was something different about Roy's demeanor. He was usually cool and calm. Today, though, he was excited. It was more than excitement—it almost seemed like fear. Keri sighed. Roy was so hard to read. Why waste time thinking about it?

Keri shrugged to herself. Whatever was bothering him could wait until he was ready to tell her. Anxious to read the article, she dismissed her thoughts and turned her attention to the newspaper. Excitement stirred within her. As much as she hated to admit it, she had more than a passing interest in Brian Michaels.

Baseball Star Brian Michaels Arrested for Murder

by Matthew West

Miami Stingrays' star hitter, Brian Michaels, was arrested late Thursday night at his home in Coral Gables. Michaels was charged with the murder of Emilia Martinez, wife of teammate Pablo Martinez. Mrs. Martinez was found floating in the family swimming pool by her husband and another team member on Tuesday, May 7, around 4:00 P.M. The police have refused to release information regarding her death pending the investigation, but sources close to the Martinez family have revealed that there were signs of a struggle. No motive has been established. Police state . . .

Keri leaned back leaving the article unfinished. At forty-one, Roy Foxx was a widely known and well-respected criminal attorney. He was also an avid baseball fan who socialized with a number of the team members. It was unbelievable. Defending Brian Michaels would attract national attention, and Roy was including her on the defense team. The realization swept over her: This was a great chance to prove herself and gain prestige as a criminal attorney.

"Is he guilty, Roy?" Keri's thoughts sobered. While it was a tremendous opportunity for her, if the case went to trial, the work would consume them for months. A man's life was at stake; they had to do their best even though it would drain them emotionally and physically.

"I don't know the extent of the evidence the police have yet. Presumably, they are treating the incident as a love affair gone bad." He paused for a moment to allow the waitress to serve the coffee. "You know my philosophy has always been that all my clients are innocent until they tell me otherwise. Keep that in mind, Keri. It can save you a lot of unnecessary compromise."

"What can you tell me about Brian Michaels?" Keri said as she reached for the sugar. "The scandal sheets present him as a romantic hunk that women chase after."

"Brian Michaels is very outgoing. Although he is gregarious, he isn't big on wild parties and that sort of thing. I suspect that he spends his free time going on fishing trips. He loves fishing so much that he wears fishing flies on his baseball cap for good luck. He's famous for that. As for women, I haven't seen any, so I guess he keeps a low profile."

"Low profile, my foot." Keri stirred her coffee. "I read a write-up about him two weeks ago in one of the tabloids linking him romantically to Emilia Martinez. The front page had a photograph of him with her hanging on his arm. She was in some skimpy little cocktail dress with cleavage to her navel!"

Keri knew about the twosome only too well. She had purchased the scandal sheet and rushed home to read it. Settling on the sofa she had sipped her Coke and read the article. *But . . . she kept looking back at the photograph.* The photographer had caught the two of them laughing. Emilia was looking at Brian Michaels as if he was the only man at the party.

He was.

He was tall and gorgeous. With light brown hair and brilliant blue eyes, he looked like a Viking prince. As if she knew what a Viking prince looked like. Mesmerized, Keri had no idea just how long she had been fascinated by him.

Keri remembered the photograph vividly. The muscles of

his broad shoulders were clearly defined beneath his ivory silk shirt. His throat was exposed and devoid of jewelry. His hips were slim and lean. And his devastating devil-may-care smile . . . She had felt herself melt as she responded to that rakish smile. A warm glow had crept over her, and before she realized it, she was imagining herself in bed with him.

Embarrassed, Keri had flung the tabloid down and jumped up. Damn. How many men did Emilia Martinez need for God's sake? She was hot. And the scandal sheets loved her.

Realizing she was jealous, Keri had laughed and silently chided herself, leaving the tabloid where it fell. Every day after that, the photo of Brian Michaels had smiled up at her with his bedroom eyes and arrogant self-assurance. Every day she had become more and more aware of her own passionless marriage with a husband who wanted nothing more than routine and stability.

Damn Brian Michaels, too!

Roy laughed. "Pull your claws in, pussycat. I was at that party. Emilia came and left with her husband, Pablo, who just happens to be a close friend of Brian's."

"Just remember, close friends have been known to be disloyal." A smile crossed her face. "Especially when the friend is six feet tall, has gorgeous blue eyes, and a body that women die for." Keri laughed. "Excuse the pun."

"Very funny," he responded before sipping his hot coffee.

Keri unbuttoned her jacket and leaned back to try to relax. It felt good just to sit and banter with Roy. Thanks to him, she had a comfortable life, but it hadn't always been this way. Her work as a public defender had left her unsatisfied and underpaid. Her husband had been unsympathetic. It wasn't long before the need to be independent had forced Keri to venture out on her own.

Even with a reputation for being a skilled attorney, the best cases had always seemed to go elsewhere. Eventually Keri had realized that she lacked the high-powered friends and money that so often bring in the more influential clients.

Keri had been flattered when the brilliant Roy Foxx asked her to work with him on one of his cases. He wasted no time in seeing her potential and, much to her surprise and delight, offered her a partnership in return for hard work and the readiness to be a team player.

Now he was giving her the chance of a lifetime. She would gain the respect and recognition of their legal community as well as national attention. Even in the infancy of this case, she sensed that her life would change drastically.

Her thoughts turned again to Brian Michaels. She wondered just how well Roy knew his new client. "Have you socialized much with Michaels?"

"No. But he took me along on a fishing trip to the Florida Keys with six of his team members one weekend." Roy smiled absently. "He has a beautiful custom Viking 58 Convertible."

"A sailboat?" Keri eyed him curiously.

"It's a fifty-eight-foot sport-fishing yacht that he docks at Dinner Key Marina. The first thing you notice is its tuna tower which reaches thirty-five feet above the water line. It's even got a four-berth fo'c'sle, which was designed to house a full tournament crew. I mean, you're talking serious sport fishing here!"

"You must have had a great weekend."

"We did." Roy smiled broadly.

"Were there any women along?"

Roy eyed Keri for a moment, anticipating her change in mood. "Keri, you have the wrong impression of Michaels. Before he made it to the major league, he was engaged to Rebecca Lawrence, the daughter of a wealthy Texas oilman. Two weeks before their wedding she ran off with some foreign guy with money and a title. Michaels was left with canceling all the wedding plans, returning the gifts, and explaining to their family and friends that she preferred another man to him."

A flood of sympathy and amazement washed over Keri. How could anyone leave Brian Michaels?

"To my knowledge, he hasn't been seriously involved with anyone since then. As a matter of fact, he ordinarily keeps his distance."

Keri sighed. "He'll probably never trust a woman again."

"I'm not so sure. Love is the strongest emotion a man can experience and sooner or later, he'll succumb. Don't feel too sorry for him. He's got it good!"

When Roy winked at her, his eyes alive with mischief, Keri laughed in spite of herself. He was right. Michaels didn't need her sympathy. With his rakish smile and drop-dead good looks, he could have any woman he wanted.

Keri sipped her coffee. She couldn't explain her attraction to him—she was drawn to his photograph like a moth to a flame. It was making her aware of the romance she was missing in her life.

Now she would not only get to meet him, she would help defend him. Keri wondered if he was really that handsome and sexy in person. Probably not. Photographs could be deceiving. No doubt he was also spoiled, selfish, and conceited—and maybe dangerous, Keri added mentally, trying to build up her resistance to him.

"He must have been impressed with you to call you to get him out of jail. Why did he wait until Friday afternoon?"

"Brian didn't call me. Jesse Davis did."

Seeing the questioning look on Keri's face, Roy explained. "Jesse is a friend of mine and a member of the team. I've defended him in some minor traffic infractions. He and Brian are pretty good friends."

"So why did he wait so long to call?"

"He didn't. Apparently Brian talked with one of our competitors who wanted Brian's earnings for the next ten years. Needless to say, their negotiations fell through. Jesse recommended me, so be on your best behavior."

"Roy!" Keri looked at him indignantly.

"I mean it, Keri. Don't let that hot little of temper of yours make me lose this client." Roy set his cup down hard. "You slip up this time, and you are off the case. I need your help, but I don't want him to change attorneys midstream."

Keri bit her tongue before she blurted out her retort. Even though her temper had already cost Roy one wealthy client, he was being unfair. The client had made a vulgar pass at her and she had lost her temper. It wouldn't serve any purpose to argue with him now. She was on the defense team and that was enough incentive to put up with Roy's testy demands.

Keri finished her coffee and stood up. "Don't worry Roy, I'll keep quiet. Let's get this interview over with before nightfall."

Keri grabbed her briefcase and wished she was on her way home. Brian Michaels was probably guilty, just like all of her clients. The police didn't go around charging people with crimes without good reason. She watched Roy finish his coffee before she walked out into the corridor.

Roy threw a couple of bills on the table and followed her out. Together they walked out the back entrance of the courthouse and paused at the head of the courthouse stairs. Keri looked up to the fifth floor where an enclosed corridor connected the courthouse to the jail across the street. "Prisoner's Walk" they called it. Only the prisoners and their guards used the corridor: a safeguard to keep the prisoners from escaping and the public from being endangered.

"Keri, there won't be enough time today to review the police files. However, I did make a few telephone calls before I came over." Roy was halfway down the stairs when Keri heard his comment. She rushed to catch up with him.

"Anything interesting?" she asked as they crossed the street and walked toward the jail.

"A few things. We should go to dinner tonight and discuss our impressions of the interview. We can go over the information I was able to get. How does Crystle's sound?"

"Great!"

"Here we are, Keri, adjust your boiling point," Roy teased when he opened the door to the jail. "Who knows? He may even like you. I hear he likes blondes."

Keri laughed and walked over to the security checkpoint. While Roy explained the purpose of their visit to the security officer, Keri thought about Emilia Martinez and her cruel murder. *What sort of man would make love to a woman and then kill her?* She would soon find out. She took in a breath and shivered at the thought of the interview.

Chapter Two

In the holding room Keri stood nervously by a tiny barred window where dirty panes filtered the light of the late-afternoon sun. She had never liked interviewing prisoners in jail. Jails were so bleak and foreboding. Every interview brought with it an uneasiness which bordered on being claustrophobic. And today that sense of confinement seemed stronger than ever.

Keri looked about her. The walls were yellowed with age and the room smelled musty. The linoleum floor was dirty and peeling. Large chunks of linoleum had been removed and never replaced. The heavy wooden table in the center of the room had been bolted to the floor to protect visitors should a prisoner get violent. The three straight-back chairs at the table didn't look stable.

Keri had never expected to meet Brian Michaels, and especially not inside a dark, dingy jail. Even though there was no alternative, she felt trapped—by her own provocative daydreams. What if she gave herself away? What if he could tell that he had been an object of her desires? Quickly she turned back to the window. She was upsetting herself for no good reason.

"What's keeping the guard? He could have brought in three prisoners by now!" Roy paced back and forth in front of the table not expecting an answer from Keri. With a quick motion, he took off his loosened tie and unbuttoned the top button of his shirt.

Keri looked at Roy in surprise. Where was the cool and calm man she had known for the past four years? His impatience was contagious. She could feel her agitation grow as she tried to calm herself. She didn't need his frustrations too.

Roy walked over to the window where Keri stood. "Don't forget, Keri, watch that temper."

Before Keri had time to respond, the door opened and a tall, handsome man walked in, followed by the guard. Whatever she had been expecting, this was not it. The magnetism and sex appeal Michaels radiated captivated her more than any photograph could. His peach sport shirt clung to his broad, muscular chest and his taupe slacks fit snugly on his lean hips. He looked thirty or thirty-one and in top physical condition.

With a stunned expression, he looked into her soft brown eyes, then rapidly glanced over her, taking note of her long shapely legs, her fitted suit and her full lips. He smiled a broad warm smile at her then turned his attention to Roy.

Incredible magic, that smile. Did he use it on every woman that he met? Well, it worked. Keri felt herself responding with an urgency that left her reeling, acutely aware that her traitorous body had dared to act independently of her mind.

"Roy, thanks for coming." His voice was filled with warmth and confidence.

"We got here as soon as we could." Roy rushed forward to shake his hand. "This is Keri Adams."

Keri nodded and took a deep breath trying to still her rapidly beating heart. Was this one of life's ironic moments? She had

just met the man of her dreams and he was taboo: a client—
a prisoner charged with murder.

"Wait outside." Roy's voice brought Keri back to reality
as he dismissed the guard.

Act professionally, Keri reminded herself. Don't look at him
as if you want him in bed. It was going to be tough, counseling
a client who evoked such an intense response from her. At
least she didn't have to worry about falling prey to his charm.
He would be locked up in jail the whole time.

Roy turned back to Michaels and continued. "Jesse Davis
called me this afternoon. He thought that I would be your best
bet since I know the team members and I have a lot of influence
in the community. I have been a criminal lawyer for close to
thirteen years.

"I wanted to get a copy of the police report and review it
before talking with you, but unfortunately, it was too late in
the day to obtain it. What I need are some basic facts." Roy
pulled out a chair and seated himself at the table. "Why don't
you tell me what happened on the day of the murder?"

Brian held out a chair for Keri, then sat down across from
her. He leaned forward and rested his powerful arms on the
table. For a moment his deep blue eyes held Keri's, then turned
to Roy.

"Before we discuss what happened, I want you to tell me
why Ms. Adams is here." He glanced at Keri appreciatively.
"Please excuse my rudeness, Ms. Adams, but my life is at
stake. I just spent the worst night of my life in a dark filthy
jail and I want out."

"Keri is my law partner and will be working with me on
your case." Roy explained.

"Why would a beautiful woman like you want to delve into
the world of criminals and crime?"

For the life of her, Keri had no earthly idea why. She quickly
found her wits. "I'm a good attorney, Mr. Michaels. However,
if you don't want me . . ."

"Don't be ridiculous, Keri," Roy interrupted, "I need you on my team. Keri has a good legal mind and extensive courtroom experience. Trust me on this one, Brian." Roy shifted in his chair. "I can't stress enough the importance of having a good defense team. We also have a good investigator, Tom Eaton, who you will meet soon. The three of us have worked together as a team in the past and we have been very successful."

"I didn't intend to offend you, Ms. Adams. But if I was your husband, you would never see the inside of a jail." Brian's voice seduced her with its gentleness.

Keri smiled and pushed herself away from the table. Her husband? Images of Brian's strong, lithe body lying next to her flashed through her mind. What kind of power did this man have to arouse her emotions so easily? She had never reacted this way to a man before and it was wonderful, unsettling, and frightening. She had to get away from him and regain control. She rose and walked to the window, unaware that Brian watched the movement of her hips as she retreated to safety.

"I managed to schedule an arraignment next Tuesday." Roy paused, noticing the distraction. "You've been charged with Murder One, which means premeditated murder. Usually there is no bail. However, the fact that you are a solid citizen and a public figure should help."

Keri turned from the window and added, "What it really comes down to is how much evidence the prosecutor has and what kind of evidence it is."

Her eyes caught his unguarded expression. Like a jolt of lightning, every fiber of her being responded to the passion smoldering in his hypnotic blue eyes. Keri looked away, fearful that he would see the need which threatened to destroy her composure and expose her. How was she going to handle being his attorney if she reacted to him this way every time she looked at him? And worse, did he realize his effect upon her?

During the ensuing silence, Roy scribbled a few notes on his legal pad before looking at Brian. "You're facing a death sentence. There is the possibility that we could plea bargain once we know what the evidence is.''

Brian shot out of the chair, knocking it over in his anger and haste. ''I didn't murder Emilia Martinez.'' His face reddened with repressed fury. ''I won't plea bargain.''

Keri looked at Roy in astonishment. Hadn't he just reminded her that he assumed all of his clients were innocent?

The door to the room swung open and the guard entered holding his hand on his holster. ''Is there a problem, Mr. Foxx?'' he asked while he watched Brian warily.

''No.'' Roy smiled and motioned to Keri to sit down. ''Everything is fine. Thanks.''

The police officer gave Roy a dubious look before closing the door behind him. The small room was silent, as Keri, feeling unnerved, walked over to the table and sat down. Brian set the chair upright, straddled it with his long legs and sat.

''Let's get to it,'' Brian commanded. ''What do you want to know?''

Brian waited for Roy to compose his thoughts. Keri smiled to herself. It was a rather perverse pleasure seeing someone control the egotistical Roy Foxx. That was a new twist. She looked at Roy. If they lost Brian as a client, Roy could certainly not blame her this time.

Keri studied Brian thoughtfully. He was no ordinary criminal. He was a pro baseball player who had probably never seen the inside of a jail before his shocking arrest yesterday. He had every right to be upset.

With an unconscious gesture Keri pulled at the hem of her skirt, aware of how easily her composure slipped whenever she focused on his broad shoulders and followed his rippling muscles down to the line of his slacks securely hugging his hips. Keri tried to still her thoughts of Brian's nearness. She reminded herself that if they were going to defend this man, they had better gain his confidence, not write him off as guilty.

"Where are you from, Brian?" Keri asked with a soft innocent voice.

"Fort Worth, Texas." Brian gave her a slightly puzzled look.

"Did you go to college there?"

"No. My skill at baseball earned me a scholarship at Texas A&M. I guess the rest is history." He smiled in spite of his anger.

Keri smiled at Brian. It might be history to a baseball fan, but she didn't have a clue. "Assume that we don't know anything about you and tell us a little bit about yourself."

"When I graduated from college, I signed a contract with the Texas Rangers. I played on their farm team for a couple of years and then went major league. It didn't take long to make a name for myself. My contract was traded to the Miami Stingrays and here I am." A look of pride crossed his features.

"Do you like being here in Miami?"

"There's no place like it." A broad smile warmed Brian's face. "I came to the Miami area three years ago when I joined the team. After six months I knew I wanted to stay, and some of my friends recommended Coral Gables. The city turned out to be unique with its old-world-style architecture. The homes have gable roofs, tiled floors, and open patios." Brian gave her an odd look as he continued. "I bought a five-bedroom Mediterranean home on Riviera Golf Course."

Unable to interpret the underlying meaning of the look that he gave her, Keri felt her excitement heighten. Was he inviting her into his bedroom or was it wishful thinking on her part? Keri flushed at her thoughts and glanced down to her legal pad before asking, "Was Pablo Martinez one of your friends who recommended living in Coral Gables?"

"Yes, he was. What made you ask?"

"I remembered seeing in the newspaper that Emilia Martinez had a home there."

The memory of the tabloid's erotic details of his feverish

love affair with Emilia was unsettling and Keri felt herself cooling off and calming down.

Roy pushed his chair out and leaned back with his hands clenched behind his head. "Did you know Emilia very well?"

"I knew Emilia almost as well as Pablo. When I moved, they spent a lot of time with me. They had me over for dinners and parties." Brian's vivid blue eyes fixed on Keri. "Emilia wasn't happy though; it wasn't hard to tell."

"Did she talk to you about the way she felt?" Roy asked.

"Not in the beginning. There was just something missing in the way they treated one another. They just didn't seem to care." A memory from his own past surfaced, and Brian grimaced inwardly.

As Keri studied the handsome man across from her, she found herself wondering if he had as much insight as he was projecting. She vaguely remembered reading an article about him recently that said he was an accomplished artist. Maybe he did possess those indefinable qualities of sensitivity and perception that added dimension and depth to the personality. Getting to know this man was going to be difficult and dangerous.

Reluctantly, Keri continued. "So did Emilia Martinez confide in you later on?" Of course she did. He had been her lover, hadn't he?

"Yes, she confided in me about a week before she was murdered. She told me that she was having an affair with someone and that she wanted to break it off. She wanted my advice on how to do it."

"Why would she ask you how to break off a romance?" Roy laughed mockingly. "From what I hear she had plenty of experience."

Brian ignored Roy's insinuation and continued. "Emilia told me her lover had a violent temper and had already hit her a couple of times. She was afraid of him and what he might do if he found out that she wanted to end the relationship. I advised her to tell Pablo and see if they couldn't work it out together. She didn't want Pablo to know.''

Roy's eyes narrowed. ''What did she tell you about this man? Was he a ball player?''

''Emilia didn't tell me anything about him that could help us identify him. She mainly focused on her fear and begged me not to say anything to Pablo.''

''Did you?''

''I did. Big mistake! He accused me of having an affair with her. We had a heated argument in the locker room. I was pretty upset when I left. I skipped practice and went jogging to work off the anger.''

''That was the day of the murder?''

''Yes.''

Keri felt chilled to the bone. Was he telling the truth? It was unlikely. Pablo must have confronted him regarding the affair. He could read scandal sheets, too. But had Brian killed her? Not only did he have the opportunity, he had just given them a motive for murder.

''Did anyone overhear you and Pablo arguing?'' Roy glanced unseeingly at the dusty clock hanging on the wall. ''Be specific.''

Brian slowly shook his head. ''I don't know. I tried to pick a time when no one else was in the locker room. It isn't the kind of information that should be made public.''

''Okay. Tell me when this occurred and when you went jogging. Do you have any witnesses to the jogging?''

''I talked with Pablo around noon. We argued and I left to go home about a half hour later. I showered, changed, and was out jogging around one-thirty. When I got back to the house, I showered again and went into the spa. After that, I grabbed a book and started reading. It must have been around four o'clock when I fell asleep on the bed.''

''Any witnesses?'' Roy sounded skeptical.

"I don't know." Brian sighed impatiently. "It was the middle of the day—surely somebody saw me."

"Don't worry, Brian," Keri said quietly. "We'll get the investigator on it." She tried not to respond to the feeling that he had killed Emilia after making love to her. However remote the possibility might be, he *could* be telling the truth. She glanced up from her notes and found herself looking deeply into his eyes. He was smiling at her with an appreciative look. Keri realized how lonely he must feel in jail, and again, her body came alive with feeling. She wanted to hold him in her arms, to comfort him, to reassure him. Brian's eyes flashed with a look of recognition, as if he knew her body craved the feel of him. Keri quickly lowered her lashes as a pale flush covered her cheeks.

Roy noticed the silent exchange. Still annoyed with himself for his comment on plea bargaining, he set his chair down hard and leaned forward on the table, ready to probe further. "You saw Emilia the afternoon of the murder?"

"No." Brian's voice was edged with anger as he turned to look at Roy.

"Good. Now, be objective. Is there any possibility that Pablo killed his wife?"

Brian hesitated before answering in a cool even tone. "I don't know. My best guess would be that he did not. There have been rumors in the past that Emilia had a couple of affairs. He knew. He didn't do anything about it then, so why bother now?"

"Well—" Roy glanced at Keri, who was busy taking notes. "—keep an open mind. If you remember anything—anything at all, tell me. Tell me no matter how insignificant you think it is."

"I will."

"You said there were rumors about Emilia's affairs. Who did she have affairs with and how long ago?"

"I don't remember the names." Brian paused. "They were

men that I didn't know." Brian shrugged his powerful shoulders indifferently. "It doesn't matter anyway. It's totally irrelevant."

"You're wrong!" Keri quickly contradicted him. "Any one of those men could be a suspect. Any one of them could have murdered her." Keri felt her voice choke in her throat. She realized that she desperately wanted him to be innocent.

"I am not going to defend myself by casting aspersions on everyone that I know," Brian answered. "Instead of worrying about Emilia's love affairs, why don't you concentrate on getting me out of this jail?"

"Take it easy, Brian." Roy unbuttoned another button of his shirt and leaned back in his chair again. "I'll see the police file on Monday. Your arraignment is on Tuesday morning. We'll meet later in the day and discuss strategy."

"Just get me out of here!" Brian rose from the chair like a panther ready to pounce.

Roy jumped to his feet. "Don't worry. We'll have you out of here Tuesday," he promised evenly.

Brian's jaw tightened. "Neither one of you believes me. I wonder if you will be able to give me a good defense." Ignoring Roy, Brian looked intently into Keri's eyes. A wave of disappointment washed over him as he saw reflections of fear and distrust. With a humorless smile, Brian turned and walked silently to the door. The door swung open and the guard walked in.

"Sorry to interrupt, Mr. Foxx, but it's closing time."

Chapter Three

Crystle's was crowded. Keri and Roy made their way through a standing-room-only crowd waiting to be seated. The maître d' recognized Roy as they approached and motioned to a waiter to take them to a table located in one of Crystle's small dining rooms.

Once seated, Keri looked about her and sighed. She always appreciated the elegance of the restaurant. The room was decorated in rich burgundy with gold accents. White linen table cloths adorned small dining tables filled with fine china and crystal. This was a meeting place for the affluent and a favorite spot for dining before attending the theater.

As she settled deeper into her chair, Keri thought about her physical response to Brian Michaels. She hadn't believed it possible. She had always wanted to respond that way sexually to a man, but not to a criminal, a murderer, a client.

It was her job to help represent and counsel this man. She would have to come to terms with her responses and with Michaels. The thought of seeing him again filled her with anticipation. She recalled his smoldering eyes probing hers right before he turned to leave, almost as if he could see into her soul. She wasn't willing to bare her soul to anyone, especially a man accused of murdering a woman he had seduced. Keri grew angry at herself for being attracted to him. She was afraid too, but her fear was more than a fear of violence or death, it was a fear of her own wild responses to him.

Deep in thought, she barely noticed as Roy ordered a light Chardonnay from the wine steward.

"You have been very quiet tonight," Roy commented. "What did you think of Brian Michaels?"

Keri took a sip of water before answering. What could she say that would sound noncommittal? She had better be careful around Roy.

"It is very difficult for me to form an opinion of the man," she lied. In her opinion, Michaels was incredibly handsome, incredibly sexy, and incredibly dangerous. But was he guilty? "He is obviously under a lot of stress and is a bit temperamental."

"A lot like yourself," Roy quipped.

"Very funny." Keri was in no mood for his teasing, but her protest died on her lips when she saw the wine steward heading for their table. Just ignore him—she reminded herself—he always laughs at his own failed attempts at humor.

After Roy tasted the Chardonnay, he nodded his approval to the steward to pour. He cast a wary glance at Keri before his guarded expression relaxed.

"A toast, partner." Roy held his glass up to meet Keri's. "To our success, Tuesday, and throughout the case."

Keri watched Roy intently as she sipped her wine. He had to have noticed her attraction to Michaels. Why didn't he criticize her for her behavior today and get it over with?

"The wine will help relax you and get you into a better mood, Keri." Roy smiled. "Did you believe Brian's story?"

"No. He's an athlete. I'm willing to bet that he could have

jogged over to Emilia's home, killed her, and jogged back home—with no one the wiser.'' Keri ran her finger along the edge of her wineglass. "Somehow, though, he doesn't strike me as a killer.'' It was useless to add that he did strike her as being Emilia's lover.

"That's an interesting analysis. I'm not sure that he is guilty, but I do have some serious reservations after hearing his story about his friendship with Emilia.''

"Roy, there is something about him that really frightens me,'' Keri admitted in earnest. Perhaps Roy could help put Brian in the proper perspective. Maybe she was reading too much into his penetrating gaze.

Roy was interrupted by the waiter, who tempted them with the chef's specialties for the evening. Keri ordered Caesar salad and baked red snapper.

Roy smiled at her. "Don't worry about Brian and don't let him frighten you. After he is free on bail he will settle down and help in his defense.'' A patronizing tone crept into Roy's voice as he filled his wineglass. "Try not to upset him Tuesday.''

"Tuesday?'' She gave him an inquisitive look.

He looked at her in amusement. "You'll be handling the arraignment, so be prepared.''

"Me? Why me?'' Keri's heart pounded and she felt her stomach contract with anxiety and confusion. She'd assumed Roy would be handling the court appearances, not her. She wasn't ready for this.

"You're on the case, remember? And, I have a trial. It should take up all of next week.'' Roy set his wineglass down while the waiter served the salad.

"But I have a preliminary hearing on Monday. It could go into Tuesday,'' Keri protested. She already knew that Michaels wouldn't be released on bail. He would blame her; she was sure of it. How could Roy leave this in her hands, especially when he loved being the center of attention?

"The judge is the Honorable Harry Pennell," Roy advised her. "Try to make it short, for his sake and yours. That case of yours is *pro bono*. Brian Michaels is a paying client. He wants out of jail, so you had better get him out. Don't waste time on guilty clients who can't pay."

"Roy!" Keri looked at him in astonishment. "There's no way he'll be released. You know that."

"Be prepared, Keri. You are going to be spending a lot of time on Brian's case, so clear out your trial calendar. Unless, of course, you're not interested in working with me anymore."

Keri wished she could wipe Roy's smug expression from his handsome face. He knew she wanted this chance and he intended to use her. "Quit playing games, Roy. All you had to do was ask me. I'll be ready for Tuesday's arraignment."

"Good. Oh—" Roy paused, "—Hector Rodriguez will probably be there. He's the homicide detective on the case." Roy reached for the wine bottle again while he watched Keri's reaction.

Keri knew Roy had deliberately kept that information from her. From experience, Keri knew that Rodriguez would be uncooperative. She would have to be one step ahead of him.

The dinner had already taken a turn for the worse, Keri decided. Roy was acting strange and she felt odd—they were like twin engines out of phase. While he was exerting pressure, she was losing control. Between Brian and Roy, her predictable life was coming apart at the seams and she could do nothing about it. Worse, Roy wasn't through with her yet. She had seen him in action before and for some reason, this time she was his target.

"Don't look so down and out." Roy drained his third glass of wine. "A bottle of after-shave lotion with Brian's fingerprints on it is not enough to prove Murder One."

"What?" Keri's eyes widened in surprise. So it was true! Michaels was having an affair with Emilia. Suddenly she was angry. Angry at Roy.

"Finding a bottle of Turbulence in Emilia's cabana bath is merely circumstantial. Don't let it throw you." Roy explained with a trace of laughter in his voice.

Keri shook her head. Roy had contacts in the police station. What else did he know?

"So, what else are you hiding from me?" Keri demanded. "Or do you like doling it out for effect?"

Roy's eyes narrowed. "Nothing. We'll find out the rest Monday."

Keri finished her salad and set her plate to the side. The evidence would be hard to rebut. "I think that we should have Tom Eaton look into Emilia's love life. That's where we'll find the motive."

Roy shifted uncomfortably in his chair. He waited for the waiter to remove the salad plates and place their dinners before them. "It's a delicate situation, Keri. We should be careful not to jump to conclusions. We don't want to smear Emilia's reputation."

"That's not what I meant," Keri answered indignantly. "Our client is charged with Murder One. We have to do our own investigation." Keri stabbed at her snapper filet. Roy was not sounding rational. He knew as well as she did that a thorough investigation was imperative in such an important case. There was a chance Michaels could be innocent and important facts could surface. Let the prosecution worry about what they dug up. The best defense was a good offense.

"Calm down, Keri. All I'm saying is that we don't want to needlessly embarrass her husband, Pablo, or tighten the noose around Brian's neck."

"Sometimes, I just don't understand you," Keri murmured.

"Face it, Keri. It will be much easier to get a witness who saw Brian jogging than to find a murderer." Roy set his fork down.

"What you are really saying, is that in spite of your earlier comments, you think Brian is guilty."

"Yes. If we can't plea bargain, the trial will be one of strategy. The prosecutor must prove guilt beyond a reasonable doubt. All we have to do is establish a reasonable doubt. No more. No less."

Keri toyed with her food. Roy was wrong. They had to find real evidence. They had to go beyond the requirements of the law. They had to go beyond a reasonable doubt.

Chapter Four

It was Tuesday, May 14. Keri had taken special care with her looks today. Her soft blond hair had been carefully worked into a French braid. Instead of a suit, she had chosen a simple short-sleeved black sheath. She had tied a raspberry-colored silk scarf around her neck. Keri knew that she radiated beauty and vitality, and that knowledge gave her confidence.

All weekend Brian Michaels had been the central focus of her thoughts. She had spent long tedious hours at the University of Miami Law Library researching to prepare herself. She was determined to be ready for anything the prosecutor might try. Reluctantly, she had retrieved the scandal sheet and reread every word. The picture had burned an image in her mind of two lovers, oblivious to the rest of the world. How many potential jurors had read the same magazine and followed the gossip? By the end of the weekend, Keri doubted that Michaels could get a fair trial thanks to the recent publicity. Who wouldn't believe that the sexy Emilia Martinez was bedding him?

When Keri climbed the courthouse stairs, she was thirty

minutes early and eager to get the arraignment behind her.
Brian didn't have a chance for bail. She knew it; Roy knew it.
Brian would blame her when he found himself stuck in jail.
And Roy knew that, too. As she reached the head of the stairs
she saw that the press had gathered early, in hope of getting a
scoop from the defense attorney, Roy Foxx. She smiled to
herself. She couldn't believe that Roy had given up this chance
to be in the limelight. She might have anonymity this morning,
but after the arraignment it would be over.

Keri passed the security checkpoint and entered an elevator
ready to make its way to the fifth floor. While she stared at the
floor-indicator lights, her mind raced, anticipating the upcoming
hearing.

"Ms. Adams." A low masculine voice broke her concentration.

Keri looked around to see a finely dressed stranger holding
the elevator door open. He was a tall handsome man with
compelling gray eyes that, at the moment, were filled with
humor.

"I believe you want the fifth floor?" His amused voice
brought a smile to Keri's beautiful lips.

"Yes." She stepped out of the elevator and gave him a
questioning look when he joined her. "Thank you, Mr. . . . ?"

"Matthew West."

"I know that name," Keri said. "You're an investigative
reporter. I've enjoyed reading your stories."

"I'm flattered that you know of me." He spoke quietly
with an air of self-confidence. "May I walk with you to the
courtroom?"

"Of course."

Keri wondered what he was going to ask her, certain that
he was here because of Brian.

"I'm a big fan of Brian Michaels," he said—his voice was
filled with admiration. "I've been following him since he was
in the minor league."

Keri smiled at Matthew. "I'll tell him that you asked about him."

West stopped and turned to her, his eyes dark with concern. "Ms. Adams, I came here for more than just a story. I came here to offer my help."

Keri looked at his earnest, intelligent face with confusion. "I don't understand."

"Brian Michaels is not guilty of killing Emilia Martinez. I would like to help. I have a network of resources at my disposal which I am offering to you."

"And what do you want?" The question was genuine, even if it was blunt.

"To find the real murderer—and an exclusive story."

"I don't know yet what I will be needing, Mr.—"

"Matthew, to you." He smiled deeply into her eyes as he reached into his pocket. "Here is my card. My home telephone number is on the back. I won't print anything without you knowing and I will keep your confidences."

Keri glanced down at the card he handed her. How could a reporter help her? "I don't know, Mr—Matthew."

"Call me anytime. I'll be ready to help."

"Thank you."

"Don't thank me yet." With a quick salute, he turned and entered the courtroom.

Keri paused to look down the hallway in the direction of Prisoner's Walk. Brian would be in a holding room adjoining the courtroom by now. She stuffed the card in the pocket of her briefcase. She needed to concentrate on the hearing and on making sure Brian was released on bail.

Keri inhaled deeply and walked through the courtroom door. In spite of her reservations about the hearing, she was anxious to see Brian. The courtroom was filled to capacity, leaving a standing-room-only crowd. Eager crews were busy setting up TV cameras. The wolves have gathered, she thought, ever ready to feed.

As she stood silently in the back of the courtroom, she sensed an unwelcome presence. She wasn't sure just how she knew. Maybe it was the sense of uneasiness which flooded her body. Or, maybe it was the way her skin crawled for no reason.

She knew he had come to watch her.

Her heart pounded rapidly when his cold dark eyes sought her out and found her. His angry expression sent chills down her spine. Keri knew that here was more than mere opposition; she was faced with a hatred that she did not understand. Her body tensed, as if readying itself for fight.

Keri closed her eyes to block out the courtroom and his haunting eyes. She had to get to the defense table; the deputy was bringing in Brian Michaels. She would need her wits about her to do her best for him. The courtroom fell silent. She opened her eyes and saw Brian at the defense table talking with the bailiff.

She marveled again at how handsome he was. He was dressed in a conservative blue suit and tie, and he seemed to exude a self-confidence that concealed any doubts or fear. His face warmed with a welcoming smile for her. She felt a warm flush and she knew that she would never be the same. This man, killer or not, could touch her innermost depths with just a look. She had to protect him; she had to see him free.

Confidently, she walked to the front of the courtroom, nodding to the prosecutor before standing next to Brian.

"Have you spoken with Roy this morning?" she asked.

"Yes. He told me that the arraignment would be a piece of cake for you."

A piece of cake? How could Roy be so stupid, telling Brian such an outright lie?

"All rise." The bailiff ordered.

Keri motioned for Brian to turn and stand to her left while Judge Pennell, entered the courtroom and settled in at his bench.

"This court is now in session. The Honorable Judge Harry Pennell presiding."

Keri sat down, ignoring the bailiff's routine, and tried to calm her racing emotions. Hector Rodriguez had set her off the moment she stepped into the courtroom with his glances filled with unveiled hostility. Now, next to her sat her client, a man whose presence electrified her, making her acutely aware of his every move and expression. Before her lay the impossible task her client believed was a piece of cake.

"State vs. Brian Michaels." The bailiff called out. "All parties are present, Your Honor."

Judge Pennell studied Keri for a brief moment. She looked lovely today. It would be more enjoyable listening to her than to the arrogant Roy Foxx. "Ms. Adams, are you ready to proceed?"

Keri smiled politely as she stood to answer. "The defense is ready, Your Honor." Her voice, smooth and silky, hid her apprehension.

"Counselor." Judge Pennell nodded to the prosecutor, Louis Garcia, who rose from his chair.

"Your Honor, the State charges the defendant, Brian Michaels, with first degree murder. On May 7, at approximately 2:00 P.M., in the City of Coral Gables, in Dade County, Florida, the prisoner, with premeditation and malice aforethought, murdered Emilia Martinez by choking her until dead. Due to the nature of the crime, the State requests that bail be denied."

"Ms. Adams, how does your client plead?" Judge Pennell's authoritative voice masked his opinions.

"Not guilty, Your Honor." Keri stepped forward focusing on the judge with her intense brown eyes. "The defense requests that bail bond be set at this time."

Judge Pennell turned to the prosecutor. "Mr. Garcia, what does the State have in the way of evidence in this case?"

Louis Garcia scanned his legal pad before answering in a confident tone, "A list of the evidence was given to Your Honor and to defense counsel yesterday. To summarize that list, the State has evidence that places the defendant at the scene of the crime.''

The judge silently studied the list of evidence before him before turning to Keri. ''Ms. Adams?''

''Your Honor, I have reviewed the evidence. It is circumstantial and there is no direct evidence linking Mr. Michaels to this crime.'' Keri felt cold. This was her only good argument, and while she was legally correct, would it be enough to free Brian on bail?

The judge frowned and leaned toward the prosecutor. ''Does the prosecution have any direct evidence placing the defendant at the scene?''

''Not yet, Your Honor.'' Louis hurriedly continued, ''However, the State expects to have a witness who will place the defendant on the scene at the time of the murder. The State also has a possible hair match-up and other trace evidence.''

''Counselor, do you have a witness, someone you can name today, who by his or her testimony will tie the defendant to the crime?'' Judge Pennell's voice was edged with impatience.

''No, sir.'' His eyes narrowed in anger as he glared at the judge.

Judge Pennell leaned back in his chair and rubbed his chin thoughtfully. He studied Brian closely as he made his decision. He liked Michaels. He'd have to be a fool to kill that woman and Michaels didn't strike him as a fool. Besides, as a star baseball player, he wasn't going anywhere.

''Ms. Adams, has Mr. Michaels ever been arrested before?''

Keri's heart began to race with hope. ''No, Your Honor,'' she answered confidently. Keri unconsciously held her breath while she watched the judge deliberate over the issue.

Finally, Judge Pennell looked back at Keri and Louis Garcia. ''I'm not going to keep a man with no prior criminal record in jail on mere circumstantial evidence. Bail is set at $300,000.''

Shouts rang out, cameras flashed, and reporters scurried out the door of the courtroom.

"Order in the court! Bailiff, empty the courtroom if necessary." Judge Pennell pounded his gavel forcefully and motioned to the bailiff. Begrudgingly the unruly audience turned its attention back to the judge.

"May it please the court," Keri raised her voice over the still mumbling crowd. "The defense moves to have the amount of bail lowered."

"Objection." Louis Garcia was indignant.

"Your Honor, Mr. Michaels is a public figure and a well-respected member of the community who has never been in trouble before. By the prosecutor's comments, the State is obviously still fishing for evidence to support its case." Keri glanced at Brian who sat watching her with a relieved expression.

"Mr. Garcia, what's your objection?"

"The prisoner is charged with premeditated murder and the State has solid evidence linking the defendant to the murder. In the interest of the safety of all the State's citizens, the bail should be set high enough to be a deterrent." Louis answered emphatically.

"Well, having heard arguments of both counsel—" Judge Pennell poured himself a glass of water and glanced at Brian. "—bail is lowered to $100,000."

The prosecutor stared at the judge in disbelief and anger.

"Thank you, Your Honor." This time Keri's bright smile was genuine. Relief flooded her. "The defense requests that the prosecution turn over to the defense copies of all lab reports, pictures, descriptions of evidence and police reports by Friday, May 17."

"Ms. Adams, I'm going to enter an order approving your request for information. However, the timing depends on the ability of the prosecution to have it ready." He turned to the prosecutor. "Mr. Garcia?"

"The earliest that we can provide the defense with the information is Monday, June 3, Your Honor."

"Your Honor, I strenuously object. The defense needs time to examine the evidence and hire experts before trial. There won't be enough time."

"Overruled. Mr. Garcia, make sure that the defense receives the requested information by June 3."

"Yes, Your Honor." With an irritated expression Louis glared at Keri as she moved quietly away from the judge's bench and returned to the defense table.

Keri ignored the adjournment proceedings and smiled happily at Brian. He gave her a penetrating look and stood up as she approached. "Am I free to go?"

"Not yet. First we have to arrange bail. There's a bail bondsman that I know here in court," she whispered.

They waited for the judge to leave the courtroom before Keri continued. "You'll be held in the holding room until bail is arranged. It's better for you to stay in there anyway because of the press. We can leave the back way. They don't know my car. I'll be taking you home. We have to talk."

"Okay." The beginning of a smile teased at the corners of his sensuous mouth.

She swallowed hard when his gaze sought out her eyes and lingered there. She lowered her lashes and stepped back as she felt a surge of excitement race through her. "I'll be back shortly," she whispered happily before picking up her briefcase. "Don't make any statements to the press."

Brian grabbed her gently by the arm. *"Like I said, a piece of cake!"*

Chapter Five

The black Porsche roared into the curve as Roy downshifted to hug the road tightly. Keri pushed herself into her black leather seat and shot a glance at him. Should they be meeting Brian tonight in Miami Lakes? Surely their office would be more private. She'd feel more in control and a whole lot safer there, too.

"Too fast for you?"

Keri listened to the throaty purr of the engine while Roy continued to down shift. "No. I was thinking about meeting Brian tonight. We should have waited and talked to him tomorrow in our office."

"Why? The Seventh Inning Club is upscale and relaxing. Besides, it's one of the favorite hangouts for the team." Roy smiled confidently. Keri had done an outstanding job of getting Brian out on bail. Now they needed to pamper their client.

"It's not that." Keri shifted uncomfortably. "Forget it. I'm just overreacting to today." She looked out the window and stared out at the dark shadows cast by trees lining the

street. Why couldn't she get this afternoon out of her mind?
She had taken Brian home. He had been warm and friendly,
but then . . .

"What about today?" Roy shot Keri a keen penetrating look.

Keri shivered. "After I left Brian at his home, I took the
most direct route to Emilia's house. It was a little more than
a mile away."

"So?"

"Brian would have had plenty of time to jog to the house,
kill Emilia, and jog home," Keri answered flatly while she
continued to stare out the window. All afternoon she had been
filled with disappointment. There was nothing unusual about
defending guilty clients, but she desperately wanted to believe
that he was innocent.

"How could you come to that conclusion?" Roy asked impatiently. What the hell was she doing playing detective?

"He said that he went jogging for about an hour—" she
paused, "—long enough to jog around the perimeter of Riviera
Golf Course, which is about two and one-half miles."

"That doesn't make him a killer. Leave the detective work to
our bloodhound and concentrate on his defense." Roy ordered
curtly.

Keri refused to answer his arrogant command. Keri was tired
of Roy's hypocritical behavior. He should save the devil's
advocate line for the courtroom. At this point, it wasn't worth
arguing with him. He would develop a plan of defense soon
enough and then she would have more than enough to analyze,
condense, and prepare.

Roy pulled the Porsche up to the valet's station and muttered
unintelligibly. One of the waiting valets ran to the passenger
side to assist Keri in getting out. Roy handed another valet the
keys with a low command regarding the car's safekeeping. Keri
smiled at the valet and stepped up onto the curb, wishing that
this night was over.

Roy held the door open for her as they entered the Seventh

Inning Club. The reception area resembled an atrium with lush hanging plants and tropical trees. While Roy approached the maître d', Keri stood admiring a fringed orchid bending under the weight of its blossoms.

"You are very beautiful tonight."

Keri turned to see Brian standing behind her. Her voice caught in her throat as he boldly surveyed her sand-washed silk leopard print shirt and black silk slacks gently clinging to her trim body. His eyes lingered on her flowing blond hair, before traveling to her full, firm breasts. Suddenly the fear which had teased her all day became an aphrodisiac, stimulating her and awakening her to his overwhelming sensuality. She could almost taste his mouth upon hers. Her mind reeled with thoughts of his hands caressing her and pulling her close.

Her lips curved into a welcoming smile. "Hello, Brian."

"Brian! It's good to see you. Congratulations!" Roy interrupted, grabbing his hand enthusiastically. "We have a table reserved overlooking the lake."

As they followed the maître d', Keri smiled to herself. She loved coming here. The Club had been built on the edge of a lake, surrounded by a championship golf course. A large, glass sunroom at the rear of the club allowed members to view glorious sunsets and dine under the stars. The maître d' led them inside the sunroom to a round table with an arrangement of orchids and ferns in its center.

While Brian held the chair for her, Keri tried to still her pounding heart. Brian had dressed in black slacks and a beige silk shirt. He had left several buttons near the neck unbuttoned, exposing his muscular neck and fine silky hairs at the top of his chest. Brian's well-defined shoulders strained at the delicate fabric. Could he hear her heart pounding against her breasts like drums from a primitive ritual? What sort of magic did this man have to cast such a spell upon her?

Keri waited impatiently while Roy, sitting across from her, ordered Dom Perignon from the wine steward. She silently scolded herself for succumbing to Brian's magnetism. She knew better than to get involved with a client; it was unethical and unprofessional, *not to mention dangerous*. Why couldn't she stop thinking about his overpowering attractiveness?

"Sorry I'm late." A familiar voice called, breaking the silence that had started to settle around them.

"Hi, Tom." Roy greeted the smiling man with a friendly handshake. "Brian, this is Tom Eaton, our investigator. Have a seat, Tom."

"Thanks. It's a real pleasure to meet you, Brian." Tom reached over the table and shook Brian's hand with sincere enthusiasm before turning to smile at Keri. "How did it go in court today?"

Keri eyed the chunky little man as he adjusted his horn-rimmed glasses. His dark eyes looked past her to Brian while he unconsciously brushed at his receding hairline with his hands. For some reason, he always got on her nerves and she knew that tonight would be no exception.

"It went very well. I won't be getting all of the police information before June 3. However, that shouldn't keep you from finding out all you can." Even though she had turned to look at Tom, Keri could feel Brian's dark mood. Without thinking, she glanced to her right and saw that Brian's eyes were alive with anger. Keri wondered what she had said to cause his quick change.

Roy noticed Brian and turned more toward him. With a cheerful tone Roy attempted to dispel his anger. "Brian, have you talked to Coach Greaton today?"

"Yes, he called this afternoon." Brian paused as the waiter provided them with menus. "I'm not going to be able to play. I've been placed on temporary suspension because the owners are worried about public opinion."

"I can't believe it! The team needs you." Tom declared incredulously.

"That's really tough." Roy rubbed the bridge of his nose. "Maybe I could talk to the owners for you."

"Stay out of this. I'll take care of it," Brian snapped. "Maybe you could start working on my defense as you should have today."

"What's that supposed to mean?"

"I hired you to handle my defense. You should have been at my arraignment today and you weren't." Brian's angry frown deepened.

"Now, just a minute," Roy cautioned. "Keri did a great job today. You're free on bail. What difference does it make whether or not I was there? You still got our best." Roy's soothing tone held a patronizing edge.

Keri watched Brian's face begin to relax. His intense gaze softened while he studied her thoughtfully. Then he leaned back in his chair.

"Brian, don't worry. I'm in charge of your defense. Besides, Judge Pennell likes Keri's style." Roy paused. "Remember, I told you to trust me on this one? Well, you're out of jail tonight. I knew Judge Pennell would side with Keri. She's a real asset to our team."

Before Brian could reply, the waiter arrived to take their orders. Keri felt relieved that the conversation had changed to the more pleasant topic of eating.

Brian lifted his glass to his lips and tasted the light bubbly wine. With an almost wistful expression on his handsome face, he studied Keri's animated features as she discussed the arraignment with Roy. Keri sensed his scrutiny and felt herself responding to his presence. She reluctantly turned her attention back to Roy.

"Did Louis Garcia introduce any evidence?" Roy asked.

"He didn't go into specifics. For some reason he didn't want Rodriguez on the stand." Keri sipped her champagne. "Garcia told the judge that the State expects to have a witness who will place Brian on the scene at the time of the murder. He also alluded to trace evidence.''

"Was Rodriguez there?"

"Yes. He glared at me with such hostility, Roy." Keri paused. "He isn't going to be objective on this case. He seems to have a personal interest which I really don't understand. I'm certain that he has crossed the line of professional conduct and I have absolutely no idea why."

"Perhaps, you are mistaken. You know that the two of you have been at each other's throat for quite some time," Roy commented.

"No, Roy. This is different. I can feel it." The hostility which had emanated from Rodriguez was unmistakable. And the sinister quality of his glances told her that he wanted to do bodily harm. Since childhood she had learned to trust her inner feelings, just as she was trusting them now. Her reactions had convinced her that she could be in danger.

"Well, we'll just have to keep our eyes open." Roy turned to Tom. "Tom, ask around. See what you can dig up on Hector Rodriguez. Find out what he has been up to and why he has a grudge against Keri."

Tom smiled broadly from ear to ear. "The pleasure will be all mine. I've wanted to dig into his background for a long time."

"Roy, did you review the police file?" Brian's voice was edged with impatience.

"Yes, this afternoon." Roy shifted his position in his chair to include Brian in the conversation. "They estimate that the murder occurred in the early afternoon—maybe around two o'clock. As you know, Pablo and Juan Cardera found the body. The police found red marks around her throat. The medical examiner found no water in her lungs. Looks like whoever did it, just wanted to keep her quiet."

"Roy!" Keri stared at him in shocked surprise.

"Why the surprise? Can you think of another reason to kill her in the pool?"

"Maybe the killer threw her in the pool after he choked her to death," Tom offered.

"That's possible." Roy rubbed his chin absentmindedly. "Her bikini was lying on the patio; there was some speculation that it had been ripped off, but the medical examiner didn't find any bruises on her body."

"Anything else?" Tom prodded.

"Yeah. Her suntan lotion had spilled out where the bottle lay on its side."

"Roy, none of this evidence points to Brian." Keri looked puzzled.

"The crime lab did a physical hair match-up. Apparently, they found a comb in the cabana bathroom." Roy looked uneasily at Brian. "The physical characteristics of the hair in the comb match Brian's hair."

"That's ridiculous. It wasn't my comb. My comb was in my locker." His voice, hard and cold, sounded true.

"How could they know who to match it with? They arrested Brian only two days later." Keri hesitated, something was missing.

"The police confiscated the contents of my locker. I'm sure they suspected me because of the argument that I had with Pablo that day. He didn't waste any time accusing me of her murder."

Roy paused to let the waiter serve the entrees. "I agree with you, Brian. But the police would not have arrested you on the argument alone. They have enough trace evidence to be able to charge you. In addition to the comb, the police also found a crumpled piece of paper outside the screen door to the patio. They found another piece in your locker which appears to match the tear pattern."

"What?" Brian gave him a disbelieving look.

"It's true. The crime lab is arranging DNA testing for the

hair and setting up tests for the paper. They are also getting a handwriting expert to testify to the similarities of the handwriting on both pieces of paper.''

''What was on the paper, Roy?'' Keri asked.

''Emilia's number to her cellular telephone.'' Roy's voice was emotionless.

Fear coursed through Keri's veins and she felt herself withdrawing into silence as she tried to reason with herself. There was still no proof that Brian had killed Emilia Martinez, but it sure pointed to him being her lover.

Roy looked up from the remains of his steak and saw Tom making notes. ''Tom, I don't think the police report says it all. There must have been other evidence which they have—maybe can't connect yet—that made them come to the conclusion that Brian killed Emilia.''

''Got to be. Something's missing here.'' Tom looked at Brian. ''Can you think of anything that was in your locker which would have connected you to Emilia Martinez?''

''No.'' Brian appeared stunned, but his voice was firm and confident.

''Tom, get to work right away on the police investigation. Find out what they've got and where they're going.'' Roy directed. ''That should fit in neatly with checking out Hector Rodriguez. I'm willing to bet he's hiding something. He's really clever.''

''He's definitely up to something and I'll find out what,'' Tom answered with assurance.

Roy watched Brian for a brief moment before turning again to Tom. ''Check around and find out what Pablo did after his fight with Brian, too.''

''Do you suspect Pablo of killing Emilia?'' Brian asked.

''Don't you?'' Roy retorted.

''I don't think that Pablo is a killer. We've been over this before.''

"Sorry, Brian. We can't rule him out as a possible suspect, regardless of how you feel about the situation."

Keri reminded Roy, "We still haven't addressed the issue of who the witness might be who saw Brian."

"There can't be any witness, I wasn't there." Brian answered heatedly.

"That's not the issue." Someone could have seen the real killer from a distance, but testify that it was you. It's a dangerous problem. We need to know who the police are referring to as quickly as possible.

"Brian," Keri continued, leaning toward him, "You have had a difficult time. Why don't you—" She turned away from him with a start, as someone touched her arm.

"Murderer!" the angry man screamed at Brian. "You murdered Emilia!"

"Please calm down." Keri scanned the shocked faces. The man's shouts had brought the attention of the whole room to their table.

"You!" the man hissed as he looked to Keri. "Because of *you,* that *murderer* is free." Filled with rage, the strange man glared down at her.

Only then did she realize that he still held her arm. He tightened his grip and with unsuspected strength, yanked her from her seat. Keri cried out in surprise, while desperately trying to keep her balance.

"Pablo, leave her alone!" In one powerful motion, Brian leapt to his feet and lunged at him. But Brian's jump to Keri's defense was blocked by Roy.

Pablo grabbed Keri by the throat. She felt his grip tighten as she stared in horror at his contorted face. "Think about this—" he tightened his grip again, "—when you defend that monster!"

Keri tried to wrench free of Pablo's hold, her eyes wildly, seeking out Roy struggling with Brian, restraining him from coming to her aid. A black void began to close in on her. She

pulled at Pablo's arm, then frantically tried to pry his fingers
loose. She could feel her knees weakening and her chest began
to hurt from lack of oxygen. As the room began to spin, panic
seized her pounding heart. "I can't breathe," her mind cried
out, "I'm going to die!"

Chapter Six

Strong arms caught Keri as she began to sink to the floor. The hands that held her, pulled her close, comforting her. Opening her eyes, she saw several men pulling a struggling Pablo out of the room, but her attention was on the warm sensuous body supporting her. He was strong, he was holding her, and it was wonderful. With her head resting gently against Brian's broad shoulder, Keri felt her breath return in small little gasps.

Gentle fingers explored the soft, bruised skin of her throat. "Are you hurt?" he asked tenderly.

Keri moved to speak, but her voice wouldn't come. His hands caressed her, leaving her body burning with sensation. Confused and disoriented, she didn't understand why she was reacting with such unrestrained sexuality when a man had almost choked her to death. She closed her eyes and concentrated.

Shocked disbelief flooded through her. "Why? Why did Roy try to stop you?" Keri gasped out. Her arms encircled Brian, drawing strength from him.

"We couldn't let Brian get involved, Keri." Roy's voice was filled with indignation. "I don't want him thrown back in jail, so stop feeling sorry for yourself."

Keri felt Brian's arms tighten protectively. "He could have killed her," Brian growled.

"Still think Pablo is innocent?" Roy's sarcastic voice ignited her already volatile temper.

"Roy!" Keri's voice, barely a whisper, strained in censure. She moved away from Brian and glared at Roy.

"See, she's okay." Roy laughed as Brian released Keri and helped her into her chair.

Keri bit her lower lip to keep from venting her anger at Roy. Even though he may have been right about Brian landing back in jail, it didn't help the throbbing in her throat or the angry bruises she knew would be there when she looked in the mirror. She didn't want to think about it. Common sense told her that she should be relieved that she was safe. She should also be angry that Pablo had just tried to kill her. Instead, she found her mind and body alive with thoughts of Brian and his closeness. What was she going to do? She had wanted to cling to him, but with the world looking on, she had no choice but to allow him to let her go. She wanted him so desperately that she was in danger of advertising it in front of everyone.

Shaking her head slightly, Keri focused her attention back on the meal. She motioned the waiter over and let him describe the tantalizing desserts. Finally, she picked a white chocolate mousse in the hopes that it would help soothe her irritated throat and keep her mind off the chemistry that threatened to drive her mad.

"Rodriguez appears to be honing in on a love affair gone bad as a motive for murder." Roy tasted the rich chocolate cake he'd chosen. "So, you will be front-page news as the questions delve deeper. The paper will be full of speculation and your reputation will, unfortunately, never be the same."

"People are going to believe what they want to." Brian

shrugged his shoulders indifferently. ''Emilia and I were friends. I can't deny that.''

''How close?'' Tom demanded.

''We were getting closer. She needed someone to confide in and I think she liked having a man's point of view.'' Brian's vivid blue eyes searched Keri's face.

''Did Pablo know she was confiding in you?'' Roy asked.

''I doubt that he did. He didn't pay much attention to Emilia or her actions. Most of the time he just tuned her out when she tried talking with him.'' Brian settled back in his chair. It was clear that his focus was on Keri and not the conversation at hand.

Tom coughed. ''Brian, are you seeing anyone special right now?'' Tom's eyes were glued to his notes as he waited for Brian to answer.

''Not yet.'' Amusement lurked in Brian's deep blue eyes as he caught Keri's gaze and held it.

She swallowed hard and looked away. What was he implying? How could he joke when his life was at stake?

Roy leaned back in his chair and stretched out his long legs. ''You saw Emilia often?''

Brian shifted his attention back to Roy. ''No, after I moved into my home, I only saw Emilia at social gatherings. She and Pablo used to have me and a few other friends over for dinner and a swim. We would grill steaks on the patio and sometimes watch sports on TV. Otherwise, I saw her at parties.''

''You *never* saw her alone?'' Roy eyed Brian with a suspicious look.

''A couple of times—but it was just to talk.'' Brian ate the last of his Napoleon without any further elaboration on his answer.

''Tell me about the times you saw her alone.''

''There isn't much to tell. She called me once after her lover left and asked me to come over. I did. She looked really bad.

She had a bruise on the side of her face and her wrist was swollen.''

From what Keri could observe, the conversation was beginning to upset Brian. He had been through a lot for one day and needed to relax and rest, not be grilled.

If Roy read Brian's signals, he ignored them. "Did you ever meet her anywhere away from her house? You know, somewhere where you could have been seen. Is there someone out there who could point to you and Emilia?''

"No. I only saw her at her house. Most times that I spoke with her, she called me.'' Brian glanced at Keri.

Roy turned to Tom and spoke to him in muted tones. Tom shook his head negatively and then consulted his notes.

Keri shifted in her chair. She wanted to go home and get away from Roy, this case, and this conversation. Her neck ached and it hurt to swallow. She knew she needed to get to a doctor and then decide what she was going to do about Pablo's assault on her.

As if he had read her mind, Brian stood up and walked to her side. Leaning over her he whispered, "You need to see a doctor. May I drive you to a hospital? You shouldn't let this go overnight. Your throat will swell and it could interfere with your breathing.''

Keri glanced down at her watch. It was eight-thirty. She nodded. "Yes, thank you.'' She found herself becoming lost in his blue eyes.

"Brian! Great to see you!''

Brian straightened and turned to greet a rangy-looking young cowboy with red hair and millions of freckles. His tight pants had a new "just off the designer rack'' look and his crocodile boots had never seen mud or stirrups.

"Hi, buddy.'' Brian's face lit up.

"Keri, this is my friend, Jesse Davis. He's also a baseball player for the Stingrays.'' Brian stepped back so that Jesse could come closer to shake her hand.

"Some guys have all the luck. You get brains and beauty. Honey, you can defend me anytime." Jesse switched his drink to his left hand.

Keri liked him immediately and chuckled as he shook her hand. "Jesse, you can compliment me like that anytime." She motioned to Tom and introduced him.

"Pleasure to meet you. I would have come over sooner, but I figured that you needed to calm down after the show Pablo put on." Jesse stuffed his hand in his back pocket and finished off his drink.

"You saw it?" Brian queried.

"Yeah. I'm sitting over there with some friends. Even though old Pablo is a very jealous husband, I still can't believe he pulled that stunt. Hell, he knew Emilia had affairs. Guess it really shook him up finding out she was getting on with you." With a quick motion he set down his drink and winked at Keri.

"She wasn't!" Brian face reddened.

"Calm down, kid. I didn't know one way or the other. Hell, I fooled around with her myself for a while. She had other ideas though. She dumped me for a cop." His broad grin told Keri that he actually thought that his relationship with her had been a joke.

Keri's eyes widened with surprise. "I would like to talk to you sometime Jesse. Would you mind?"

"Sure, ma'am." Jesse smiled engagingly. "Come by the stadium anytime. You're a darn sight more good-looking than the jocks are!"

Keri laughed, unaware of Roy's icy stare.

At the entrance to Laughing Gull Cove, Brian waited for the guarded gate to open. He eased the Lexus through the gate and picked up speed. Keri directed him down tree-lined brick streets to her luxury townhouse overlooking Biscayne Bay. Keri felt overcome with weariness and fatigue after the trip to the hospital. The doctor had examined her throat and ordered X-rays. The end result was medicine to reduce the inflammation, and strict orders to use compresses regularly for the next few days.

She motioned for Brian to pull over. She sat quietly while he got out and came over to her side to open the door. Keri smiled up at Brian when she got out, grateful for his attentive consideration.

"Thank you, Brian. I really appreciate your help tonight," Keri said sincerely in a strained little voice. His gentle concern for her had reduced her to a state of helplessness. She was ripe for the taking and she wondered if somehow he knew.

"Try not to do any more talking. If you do, I can't be held accountable for my actions."

"What do you mean?" she asked in a frightened whisper.

"Roy kept me from getting to Pablo first. That's why you're hurt. Pablo can't control that nasty temper of his, and I knew you were in real danger. I'd like to wring Roy's neck every time I hear your beautiful voice fail."

They walked to the entrance of her locked courtyard. He gathered her into his arms and held her close. Keri melted as she felt the gentleness of his caress. She looked up when she felt him stir. Brian lightly kissed her lips.

"I'm not a murderer, Keri. Please believe in me."

Her lips tingled. His face was so close, his expression so sincere. How could she resist such a gentle entreaty? She smiled, wanting him to kiss her again. For what seemed to be an eternity she studied his lips, so close, so inviting. Then she looked up into his eyes only to find herself locked in his gaze, lost in an ocean of brilliant blue. She caressed his face before cupping it in her hands and slowly pulling him down to her. His lips claimed hers in a moment of gentle merging before he pressed hard, exploding her body with excitement. A soft moan escaped her lips. Although it was purely sexual, he misunderstood. To her dismay, he straightened and slowly released her.

"Get some rest, Keri," he commanded gently.

Before she could gather her thoughts, he turned and walked away.

Keri tried to call after him, but only the softest of whispers came from her strained throat. Silent tears streamed down her face, releasing the pent-up tension. With a sigh, she unlocked her courtyard gate. Closing it quickly, she turned and found her key to the front door. Remembering his protective embrace, Keri wished that his arms were still around her. They seemed so much more secure and protective than the security system she disengaged upon entering the townhouse.

Keri had thrilled at feeling his strength around her, yet, she was feeling vulnerable and alone. She shook her head, then regretted it as her hand went to her throat. Keri flipped the light on in the kitchen and set about making a cup of hot tea. Settling down, she made her decision. With a determined set to her jaw she reached for the telephone and punched in the number.

Keri listened as she waited for an answer. "I'm glad that I found you in," she whispered hoarsely. "I need your help."

Chapter Seven

Keri slept while danger crept silently, darting behind every dark shadow until it closed in upon her. A strangled cry escaped her lips. She was hot and sticky. Her lungs burned. Engulfed in darkness, she felt his viselike grip around her throat, tightening to slowly deprive her of life.

Keri flailed her arms out into empty space. In a state of confusion and fright, her eyes strained to penetrate the dim bedroom. Shadows slithered across the floor, fleeing her disoriented gaze. Night sounds teased her ears and fanned her rising terror.

"Where is he?" she breathed. She cradled her throat with her hand as it throbbed with pain. She swallowed hard and breathed deep, slowing her racing heart. Another nightmare; if only they would stop and give her peace. Pablo had certainly given her something to think about. This type of fear was new. She didn't know how to cope with it.

Her red silk gown clung to her, damp from perspiration. She pulled it away from her skin and shook it. The motion seemed to release the intensity of the moment. Her thoughts turned to Brian Michaels. The man had shattered her stable life with a smile. She craved him, desired him, dreamed of him and she knew that she couldn't have him—he was a client. More, he could be a murderer. Somehow the danger intrigued her and beckoned her.

A glance at the clock told her it was five-twenty in the morning. It would be useless to try to go back to sleep. She probably wouldn't be able to fall asleep before the alarm went off at six. Feeling around in the dark, Keri found her robe. What she needed was a quick shower and a some hot coffee.

Cold water pelted her burning body, cooling it and sending shivers down Keri's spine. Alive with feeling Keri stepped forward and let the water claim her face and hair for a while. With a quick twist she shut off the shower and stepped out. Still dripping wet, she gathered her robe about her and headed for the kitchen.

While the coffee brewed, she opened her vertical blinds at the bay window in the breakfast area. She looked out over Biscayne Bay to a tiny area of light beginning to define the horizon. How romantic it would be to watch the sunrise with a man, Keri decided. But then she had no one to blame for her solitude but herself. She had been too busy building a career to allow herself to become deeply involved with anyone.

After pouring her coffee, Keri settled into the soft cushions of her wicker chair. The truth was, she told herself, she was too selective. No one had struck the right chord, no one except Brian. And that truth was uncomfortable and unacceptable.

Brian was her client. She had a duty to counsel him and protect him, not to seduce him. It was a confidential relationship that she was in a position to take advantage of. There were cannons of ethics which prohibited personal and sexual relationships with clients. The breach of any one of them could result in her suspension, or worse, she could lose her license to practice law. So far no one suspected her ardent responses to Brian. But she was dangerously close to revealing herself accidently. The mere mention of his name started her heart beating faster. Try as she might, she could not stop herself from indulging in daydreams and fantasies of him. Her first thoughts upon awakening were of Brian. Her last thoughts upon falling asleep were lustful dreams of him.

Keri sipped her coffee. The past two weeks had taught her a lot. She had not realized how lonely her life had been. It had felt wonderful to have Brian want to take up for her when Pablo assaulted her. Keri closed her eyes. She could still feel the hard muscles of his body pressed close to her. She could still feel his passionate kiss when he said good-night.

Desire for Brian gave way to anger as her thoughts turned disturbingly to Roy. She could not accept his explanation for restraining Brian. She felt betrayed by him, a man she thought was her friend. Roy had shown no concern over her injury. He had come into her office and warned her not to allow the incident to be blown out of proportion. She had resented his veiled threat, but had remained quiet. Not wanting to cause Brian more trouble and publicity, she had decided not to press charges against Pablo. Keri wondered, as she had many times during the past few weeks, if Roy was really as indifferent as he appeared.

The coffee took effect. She began to feel alert and anxious to start the day. She wanted to get to the office early, Brian was coming in and she had to prepare him. Lt. Rodriguez wanted to question Brian further and she had forced the lieutenant to come to her. Keri knew that he would be angry, but she felt safer and more in control in her own territory. She sighed unhappily. Roy was tied up in another murder trial and had done virtually no work on Brian's case. She alone had the task of developing Brian's defense.

Keri looked back at the horizon now colored with soft pinks, blues, and purples lighting the sky and heralding the coming of a new day. Keri smiled with renewed hope. Maybe today would be better.

Chapter Eight

A discreet brass sign announced in gothic lettering that the offices of the law firm of Foxx & Adams lay behind the heavy honey-oak doors. Brian paused and straightened his shoulders confidently before crossing the threshold.

The spacious reception room embraced Brian with a relaxing atmosphere not usually found in a business environment. The soft dusty rose-colored walls trimmed with honey oak molding complimented the rose, beige, and tan print sofa and easy chairs. A picture window looked out over a tropical garden below, and an aquarium with brightly colored tropical fish bubbled softly in one corner.

A smiling face surrounded by a mass of tight reddish-brown curls met him at the reception window. "Hi. You must be Mr. Michaels. I'm Jenna, Keri's secretary." She looked at Brian in awe. The expression on her plump face revealed her childlike admiration.

"Hi, Jenna."

"Jenna? Is that Brian?" Keri's voice filtered out from her office.

"Yes, he's here," Jenna answered, her eyes never leaving Brian.

"Please show him to my office."

Jenna's face reddened. "Sorry, Mr. Michaels." She unlocked the door and opened it for him. "We don't often have celebrities come here." Jenna gestured to an open door down the hallway.

"Thanks." Brian smiled again and with a quick stride, headed for Keri's office.

Keri stood behind her desk facing the window. The window, beginning at waist height and towering to the ceiling, stretched the breadth of the room. Morning sunlight flooded in, bathing Keri in a warm glow. Her hair shone as if it were spun gold. Keri turned to meet Brian.

"Good morning, Brian." Keri smiled warmly at him. Darn, he looked good. His baby blue Polo shirt matched his eyes perfectly. Did he wear that just to distract her? His navy shorts fit snugly over his taut muscled thighs and accentuated his lean hips. Keri's heart pounded rapidly forcing her to look away.

"Please sit down." She motioned to a comfortable chair in front of her desk and silently reassured herself that today she would maintain her self-control.

"How's your throat?"

"Better, thanks, but it is still tender. It bothers me mostly at night while I'm sleeping."

"Hopefully, it won't bother you much longer." Brian watched her with concern. "Where's Roy today?"

"Roy has been in trial all week. It's me and you again. I'm sorry." She had expected Roy's absence to be a sore spot with Brian and waited for his reaction.

"Don't apologize for Roy. It's not your fault." Brian leaned back and stretched out his legs. "Roy is definitely not winning points with me. After my conversations with him, I'm surprised he hasn't heeded my wishes."

Keri pressed the intercom. "Jenna, come into my office." She looked back at Brian. "She probably got sidetracked. With you here I don't know how that could have happened. She's a fan."

"I could tell." Brian laughed.

"Did you need me?" Jenna walked in bringing a plate of Danish, croissants, and other pastries. She gingerly placed them on the small round conference table in the rear corner of Keri's office. Coffee cups, silverware, and napkins had been placed there earlier.

"Thank you, Jenna. It looks delicious." Keri smiled at her secretary who stood by the table looking self-conscious in her short black dress and three-inch high heels. "I wanted to finish giving you my instructions before Lt. Rodriguez gets here." Keri gestured for Jenna to take a seat next to Brian.

"Brian, I am going to try to get Rodriguez to agree to let me tape the interview. I believe that by analyzing the tape we can figure out what they are still looking for and possibly their strategy. Rodriguez underestimates me. That makes him careless. So far it hasn't hurt him, but one day it will trip him up."

"Sounds good to me. I won't forget that we are being taped."

"Jenna, even though we are taping, I want you to take notes and type them up for me. It never hurts to have a witness present. When we are through, you will put the tape in the safe deposit box we rented to hold it." Keri hesitated for a brief moment. "No one else including Roy, is to know about this tape or what was said today. Is that clear, Jenna?"

"My lips are sealed." Jenna smiled.

"Good. Why don't you see if the lieutenant has arrived? If he has, give me a minute and then show him in."

Jenna nodded. With one last wishful look at Brian she left the room.

Keri smiled at Brian. "You have won her over."

Brian smiled before a shadow crossed his face. "Keri, I

have a conference with Coach Greaton today at eleven o'clock. There's a general consensus among the team members that I should be allowed to play. Coach Greaton has talked to Pablo about my coming back. Although Pablo doesn't like it, he has agreed to stay away from me and not start any trouble. If the coach can convince the owners to let me play, I will be taken off suspension.''

"Oh, Brian, I hope so. From what I've heard, your team has not been doing very well since you left."

"Part of that is their low morale." Brian frowned. "I hope my coming back will help."

"I'm sure it will. I'll have you out of here in plenty of time to make the appointment." Keri looked past Brian to the doorway where Jenna stood. She rose from her chair and extended her hand. "It's good of you to come over, Lt. Rodriguez."

Hector Rodriguez ignored Keri's extended hand and walked toward Brian. He pushed his jacket away from his belly and shoved his hands deeply into the pockets of his loose-fitting trousers. "Martinez tells me that the owners are going to lift your suspension. Have you heard anything yet?"

"Not yet."

Keri would take a defiant stance. From years of practice, she could hide her thoughts behind a blank expression. Although her heart pounded rapidly, this time it was from anger and suspicion. Rodriguez was a dangerous man. She had already sensed he wanted to harm her. She needed to be cautious until she knew his limits of self-control. Keri motioned to Jenna, who promptly disappeared and then reappeared carrying a pot of hot coffee.

Keri forced a polite smile. "Lt. Rodriguez, would you care for a cup of coffee or *café con leche* before we start. We have been waiting for you before having ours."

"Yes, by all means. Regular coffee will do fine." Rodriguez

turned to the conference table and looked hungrily over the refreshments.

"Please," Keri motioned to Brian. "Let's sit down at the conference table. We can do our talking there."

Keri glanced at Jenna who nodded back discreetly.

After they had been seated, Jenna walked over to the conference table. She smiled at Rodriguez and set a coffee cup in front of him. "May I pour your coffee for you, Lieutenant?" she purred.

The detective smiled back and nodded to her. "I take it black."

Carefully, she poured his coffee. "I recommend the *pastelitos* with guava preserves. I went to the bakery this morning and got them especially for you."

"Of course. They are the best. I shall have to come here more often." Looking very pleased, he grabbed a *pastelito* and took a large bite.

Keri poured Brian's coffee and then her own. Placing the cream pitcher within Brian's reach, she waited for him to take it before serving herself. Silently, she decided how to broach the subject of taping the meeting.

"Would you mind terribly if Jenna stayed and took notes?" Keri looked at Lt. Rodriguez with big innocent eyes.

"She is certainly welcome. I have no objection." He smiled at Jenna who stood in the doorway smiling back.

"She often tapes conferences so that if she misses anything important for her notes she can replay it. Would that be a problem?" Keri asked in her most sincere and innocent voice.

"No. It is not a problem." Rodriguez glanced at Jenna and cleared his throat. "However, you must make the tape available to me if I desire it."

"Certainly. All you need to do is call Jenna and she will provide you with a copy of the tape." Keri tried to hide her elation. He was easier to play than a violin. She was glad she had coached Jenna and encouraged her to dress in such a sexy outfit.

Jenna sat down to the table, placing the tape recorder on the floor and its small microphone inconspicuously on the table.

Keri inhaled deeply. How was she going to pull this off without endangering herself? She had to bait the lieutenant so that he would get angry enough to forget the microphone and say something important. Getting him angry wouldn't be too hard to do. The hostility that he projected toward her was almost tangible. Hopefully, he wouldn't go for the throat!

"Let's get busy. I have a lot of work to do today." Lt. Rodriguez ordered brusquely.

"Fine." Keri smiled politely and placed a legal pad and pen on the table in front of her.

"All right, Michaels," Rodriguez began. "Were you having an affair with Emilia Martinez?"

"No."

"Did you ever have an affair with her?" His question was muffled as he stuffed the last half of another *pastelito* into his mouth.

"Never."

"Do you know of anyone else who was having an affair with her?" He licked his fingers noisily and reached for a pastry.

"No."

As Keri nodded almost imperceptibly, Brian reluctantly continued. "Emilia told me she was having an affair with someone and wanted to break it off. She didn't tell me his name or anything about him."

"Do you know if she had any past lovers?"

"No. I've heard rumors that she did. I personally didn't know of any." Brian studied the detective.

Oblivious to Brian's scrutiny, Lt. Rodriguez watched Jenna taking notes. "How often did you see her?"

"I saw Emilia and Pablo often. They were my friends. We

went to the same parties and we had cookouts on an almost weekly basis.''

''Ever see her alone?''

''A couple of times, for a few minutes. That's when she told me she had a lover she was afraid of.'' Brian sipped his coffee and toyed with the cup, ignoring the detective's watchful eyes.

''Did you see her the afternoon of the murder?''

''No!''

''What did you fight about with Pablo on the day of the murder?''

''I told him that Emilia had a lover that she was afraid of and wanted to break up with. I told him that I knew the man had a violent temper because I had seen bruises on her. That's when he went into a rage. He accused me of having an affair with her under his nose. I kept telling him he was wrong, that she needed his help, that he needed to go home and talk to her.'' Brian put his empty cup down.

''When did you see bruises on her body?'' The lieutenant looked at him in disbelief.

''About a week before she was killed.'' Brian ignored Keri's startled eyes.

''At her house?''

''Yes.''

''Why didn't you tell him the truth? You were having an affair with her and wanted to break it off.''

''No. That's not true.'' Brian clenched his hands into fists.

''When she wouldn't break it off you threatened to go to her husband,'' Rodriguez hissed.

''No. You're twisting it,'' Brian growled in a cold, harsh voice and leaned toward Rodriguez in anger.

''You confronted Pablo and warned him to get her off your back or you'd make trouble for them both.'' Rodriguez was animated now, venting his rage at Brian.

''That's absurd!'' Brian looked incredulously at Rodriguez. ''What are you so hot about?''

"When he got angry and threatened you, you decided to kill her and place the blame on Pablo." The lieutenant's voice had become belligerent, his expression contemptuous.

"No. You're wrong." Brian shouted at him, obviously restraining a desire to go after him.

Keri interrupted, "Lieutenant, you are badgering Mr. Michaels. He has denied killing Mrs. Martinez."

"Stay out of this." Rodriguez demanded. "I can ask him anything I want to."

"Yes, but he doesn't have to answer you."

"Stop pretending to be an attorney and shut up!"

Shocked at his insolence Keri fought to control her anger. "I don't understand your attitude toward me. Why do you dislike me so much? Why are you so hostile?"

Rodriguez laughed defiantly. "You're paranoid. You're imagining something that isn't there. Face it, lady. You're the problem."

Keri slammed her legal pad down on the table. "The interrogation is over. You had better leave. Mr. Michaels will no longer be available for questioning."

"The investigation is over when I say it is. Not before. Brian Michaels is guilty and I am going to prove it." Quickly he turned to Brian and demanded, "Tell me Michaels, what did you do with her rings?"

"What rings?" Keri watched as Brian's face changed from anger to exasperation.

"Don't act like you don't know what I'm talking about. Emilia had lots of little idiosyncrasies. One of them was taking off her wedding rings before she made love."

Keri watched as an incredulous look crossed Brian's face. How would a police detective know something so intimate about Emilia? Keri's eyes fixed on Brian studying Rodriguez; it was as if his blue eyes were attempting to reach past memories.

"I didn't know about her rings. Are they missing?" Brian asked.

"She wasn't wearing any rings." Lt. Rodriguez answered. He suddenly frowned and rose from his chair. "I have another appointment. We'll continue this another day." He nodded to Jenna and walked out, slamming the door behind him.

Jenna shut off the tape recorder and ran out of the office to answer the telephone. Deep in thought Brian failed to notice the troubled look on Keri's face.

Keri closed her eyes, trying to block the image in her mind of Emilia taking off her rings and embracing Brian. Keri felt chilled to the bone as she lost her perspective of time and lingered on the horror brought to life by her imagination.

"You haven't heard a word, have you?" Brian's voice was filled with annoyance. He stood over her, hands on his hips, his face betraying suspicion.

"I'm sorry. What did you say?" Keri managed as she focused on Brian's quick change of attitude.

"I thought that I had run into Rodriguez before Emilia's murder, but I just couldn't place where. Now, I remember seeing him." Brian's eyes narrowed as his steady gaze held Keri's eyes. "I've seen him talking with Emilia at parties; they were close, intimate."

"What are you saying?" Keri felt a surge of excitement and hope.

"I'm saying that he could have been her lover. That might explain his hostility toward you for defending me."

"Brian, he might be her killer," Keri whispered in amazement.

"Just try and prove it," he said sarcastically.

"Keri," Jenna called from the door. "There's a call for you on line two. He wouldn't give me his name." Jenna smiled at Brian and lingered to find out who was calling.

Keri found herself irritated at Jenna's misplaced curiosity. She waved Jenna out of the office.

With her back to Brian, Keri picked up the telephone. "Keri Adams, speaking."

"Fine. How are you doing?" Her face lit up with a smile as she spoke into the receiver softly. "Just name the time and place, and I'll be there."

"Yes, I know it well. See you then." Keri turned and smiled at Brian after hanging up. "Brian, you had better get going if you intend to be on time. Call me here at the office around four o'clock if you are able to. I'd like to hear how your conference works out."

"I'll try," Brian smiled. "Talk to you later." Brian walked to the door and then hesitated, looking back at her with a question in his eyes.

"Bye." Keri called out, anxious for Brian to go. She would give him three minutes, then she would leave unnoticed.

Brian gave her a curious look before exiting the office. Keri felt a pang of guilt. She had practically thrown him out. It didn't matter. He had just enough time to get to his meeting.

Chapter Nine

Cool grey eyes studied Keri appraisingly while she sipped her mandarin orange iced tea. It wasn't every day that she had the attention of such an attractive and intelligent man. Too bad this was business. She looked around the outdoor cafe. Cheerful red and white checked tablecloths adorned the small tables sheltered by gently swaying palms. Luckily they were a little early for the lunch crowd.

Talking with Matthew West reminded her again of the loyalty that Brian inspired in people who had followed him and his career. Maybe it was more than loyalty with Matthew, she thought. He seemed to be very analytical in his thinking. Perhaps he was a good judge of character; knowing people was part of his business and certainly a large part of his success.

"You have a worried look, Keri." Matthew spoke softly. "Apart from the obvious, what is troubling you?"

"I have to be very careful how much I discuss with you. There is an attorney-client privilege that has to be protected. That I can handle. It's the other problems which I really need help with and I'm not sure that you will be able to help.'' Keri frowned, trying to sort out the priorities.

"Try me.'' A confident smile crossed his face. He had done a lot of investigating and double-checking his facts since the night she had called. He had hardly recognized the hoarse little voice on the end of the line. He had wanted to wring Pablo's neck for hurting her. Lucky for Pablo that he hadn't been there.

"It's Hector Rodriguez. Brian thinks that he recognizes him. He remembers seeing him at some parties that Pablo and Emilia attended. Rodriguez was talking with Emilia. Brian said it was intimate. I don't know if he was having an affair with her or not. If he was, that might explain his hostility toward me and Brian. But that doesn't make him Emilia's murderer.'' Keri paused and waited for the waiter to replenish their iced tea.

"Brian is right. Hector Rodriguez was quite intimate with Emilia. I haven't been able to pinpoint when the affair ended, but I can place them having an affair a year ago.'' Matthew watched the surprised expression on Keri's face. "Looks like to me you might have a suspect for murder.''

"Rodriguez is so adamant that Brian killed Emilia. Maybe he was in love with her.'' Keri answered. She looked at Matthew thoughtfully. She was afraid to hope that Lt. Rodriguez might be a suspect. Even knowing that Rodriguez was potentially dangerous, she couldn't imagine him as Emilia's murderer. She bit into a mandarin orange plug she had captured with her fork and watched a couple walking past the cafe. The young woman's head was tilted up and she was smiling. They were clearly in love. Keri felt a pang of envy as the young man laughed and hugged the woman closer. She wished that she had someone holding her, comforting her, loving her.

"You can't ignore the obvious, Keri.'' Matthew warned her. "Rodriguez could have killed her because she wanted to dump him. If he is adamant about Brian being guilty, he may be covering up for his own actions.'' Matthew leaned forward before continuing. "It's an avenue that should be explored. I'll be discreet."

Keri smiled. She was sure that he would be. "What else did you find out Matthew?"

Matthew put his glass down and smiled. "I thought that you would never ask." With a smug look he pulled out his notebook. "Emilia saw several men over the past few years."

"Jesse Davis?" The question was out before Keri could stop it. She shifted in her seat and tried to look unconcerned.

"Yes. How did you know?" Matthew looked up from his notes to give her a questioning gaze.

"He told me that Emilia dumped him for a cop!" Keri's face was alive with excitement.

"Rodriguez?"

"I don't know, but I sure intend to find out!" Keri answered confidently. "I asked him if I could talk to him about Emilia. He seemed very open about it."

"Good. See what you can find out." Matthew studied his notes for a few seconds before looking back to Keri. "I think there's another ball player, but I have to do more investigating. Also, I haven't been able to find anyone in Brian's neighborhood who saw Brian out jogging the day of the murder. I'll keep trying."

"Matthew, ask around in Emilia's neighborhood too," Keri said softly.

"What?" Matthew looked at her, clearly surprised at what she had suggested.

A look of sadness covered her features. She didn't like herself much at the moment. "Emilia lived about a mile from Brian. There was enough time for him to jog to her house, kill her, and jog home, with no one the wiser." Keri stared unseeingly at the few shoppers walking by before placing her hands in her lap. A voice deep within her told her that Brian was guilty and that she was only kidding herself. She had to know for sure.

Matthew took his time answering, preferring to study Keri

thoughtfully. With an odd expression on his face, Matthew broke the silence. "You're a good detective, Keri. You have lots of imagination, but it's only a theory. The nice thing about theories is that it's okay to be wrong. This time you're wrong. He didn't jog down the streets in broad daylight to murder someone. Brian didn't kill Emilia."

"We have to know. I have to be one step ahead of Lt. Rodriguez—especially now." Keri didn't understand the vise that held her heart. Why was it so hard to think of Brian as a killer?

Suddenly, she remembered! "The rings, Matthew, the rings! Rodriguez asked Brian what he had done with them. Rodriguez knew that Emilia always took her rings off before—that is—" Keri stumbled over the words, embarrassed to continue.

"That clinches it!" Excitement filled his voice. "I'll look into that, too."

"We haven't heard from Tom Eaton yet. That's Roy's investigator. He's a big fan of Brian's. As soon as I hear something, I'll call you." Keri smiled at Matthew gratefully.

"Good." Matthew motioned to the waiter to take the check, then looked at Keri and smiled back feeling confident that something would break before long. He wanted this story and he intended to get it. "I have two tickets for the hockey game tonight and one of them has your name on it. Join me Keri; you'll enjoy it."

"Now that's an offer that I can't refuse!" Keri laughed. She felt her emotions lighten beneath Matthew's friendly gaze. He was going to be good for her.

Keri settled back into her plush leather seat and started the ignition. She wasn't ready yet to face her office problems. Happy, she found herself smiling and planning what she was going to wear to the game. Matthew was very well known and she knew that she would be the center of attention. Busy in thought, she drove her car west on Miracle Mile toward the old picturesque neighborhoods that made Coral Gables so popular. After a few winding turns, Keri became aware that she was not far from the Martinez home. Beckoned by an undeniable lure, Keri turned her car toward Emilia's house. Gone were her thoughts of Matthew and her date. They were replaced by a haunting feeling; one that had nagged her relentlessly since she met Brian.

Keri pulled the car over to the curb about fifty feet away from the home and studied the neighborhood. She took her pad from her briefcase and jotted down a few notes. No one appeared to be at home in the neighboring houses. The tree-lined sidewalk with its heavy shrubbery gave excellent cover for anyone walking or jogging. Keri decided that it would have been easy for anyone to come and go unobserved.

A feeling of discouragement crept over her. Motive and opportunity she had already established. Now, she could see how easily he could have done it. Regardless of the attraction and desire she felt for this man, she admitted to herself that Brian could very well be lying. She hoped that Matthew was right. Keri sighed heavily and put her car into gear. The office was only a few minutes away. She had better get back and finish her work so that she could enjoy her date. Tomorrow was Friday and she wanted to be able to leave the office early and enjoy her weekend.

Chapter Ten

The afternoon sun beat down, pushing temperatures into the high eighties. Keri looked out her office window to the garden below. It was only the end of May and already getting hot, she thought unhappily. And it would be hot at the game tonight with Matthew. She quickly made a mental note to wear cool clothes. They would all roast this summer. And it would be humid and sticky.

"Is there anything else that you need?" Jenna called from the door, interrupting Keri's wandering thoughts. "It's four o'clock and I want to wrap everything up soon."

Noticing that Jenna had discarded her three-inch heels and was padding around in her stocking feet, Keri smiled inwardly. "Jenna, I was about to call you. I will need you to work on this tape that I'm dictating." Keri flipped through the papers in front of her.

"Is there anything that has to go out today?" Jenna asked.

"No. But I want it all done tomorrow." Keri looked at Jenna. "Any big plans for the weekend?" Keri wanted to be sure that the work would get out. Jenna was a good one for taking long weekends without giving advance notice.

"Not this one. Don't worry Keri, it will be done." Jenna smiled. "I have some letters and pleadings to copy before doing the mail. Then I'll start on this."

When Jenna turned to go, Keri called to her. "Jenna, wait. Did Brian call in this afternoon?"

"Not yet. Would you like me to try to get him on the telephone for you?" Jenna paused at the doorway to the office.

"No, thanks. He must still be busy." Keri waved Jenna away and sat back down. With a disappointed shrug of her shoulders, Keri closed her eyes. She was tired and wanted to go home. She had wanted to hear from Brian to find out if he would be allowed to play. Apparently he didn't want to talk to her. Maybe it was just as well. She was too attracted to him for her own good. Feeling the need to still her thoughts, she allowed herself to drift quietly for a few minutes.

"Things can't be all that bad!" A low masculine voice chuckled softly.

"Brian!" Keri's surprised voice was barely a whisper.

He stood at the doorway looking sexy and virile. With a confident smile Brian closed the door to her office and walked over to her desk. Keri looked to Brian's handsome face and felt the heaviness of the day lift off her shoulders. Just seeing him, excited her. What was this crazy effect that he had on her?

"Why didn't Jenna call me?" Keri asked breathlessly.

"She didn't know." Brian stood facing her between the visitor's chairs and her desk. "There's no one around. The door was unlocked, so I just came in. That could be dangerous, you know." Brian's voice was light but the warning was clear.

"I know. The inner door to the offices is supposed to be locked at all times." Hiding her excitement, Keri reached for the intercom and punched in Jenna's extension; there was no answer.

Keri stood up and turned off the intercom. She walked around to the front of her desk to go find Jenna before thinking better of it. ''She's probably in the copy area for a minute. She said she had mail to do.'' His nearness was unsettling. She could feel tiny quivers shooting through her, teasing her, unnerving her.

Brian's eager, sparkling eyes captured hers. ''Forget Jenna. I have news.'' A look of happiness crossed his face as his gaze swept over her, disarming her defenses.

Keri felt excitement racing through her. ''What?'' She somehow managed to ask.

''I'm back to playing. I'll be in Sunday's game!''

''Brian, that's great. I'm so happy for you!'' Keri's smile broadened as the realization came to her: the owners believed in him.

Without warning, he reached for her and pulled her to him, circling her with his arms. Her efforts to free herself locked her tighter in his arms. He kissed her gently on her mouth. Keri felt herself sinking beneath the sweetness of his kiss. Hands splayed against his strong, hard chest, she tried to push herself away, fearing that she would lose all of her control. His hands caught her wrists, forcing her arms down and behind her back. One of his hands held her wrists securely behind her back and the other hand found the small of her back and pulled her roughly against him.

Brian held her tightly and reclaimed her mouth, this time with a demanding mastery she had never experienced before. His tongue caressed her full lips before entering her warm mouth. She gasped with desire, her knees weakening as pleasure radiated through her being. Her body arched as his fiery kisses inched down her throat to her breasts. His hand pulled open her blouse, as his eyes, flaming with desire, softly caressed her.

Her soft brown eyes probed his, as if reaching into his soul. Struck by the tenderness and the magnetism she found there, Keri's body shivered with delight and anticipation. She freed her hands and pulled his head down, kissing him with an intensity that shocked her. His hands found her breasts and brushed away the flimsy lace of her decolleté bra.

Fearing her own untamed desires, Keri stepped back gasping for breath. Brian smiled and released her, his eyes smoldering with passion. Keri looked beyond his shoulder and saw her open office door.

"You closed my door when you came in, didn't you?" Keri's ragged voice was edged with suspicion.

"Yes. I closed it all the way. Why?"

When Keri failed to answer, Brian turned to see the open door. "Well, it looks as if someone saw you in my arms. Do you mind?"

Still reeling with excitement, Keri looked at his sensuous face and smiled. "Of course not."

Brian reached out and cupped her breast before he leaned over and kissed her again.

"Keri," Brian spoke softly, "I have to go to practice. I'll call you soon."

Speechless, Keri could only look at him in disbelief. Brian kissed her forehead. "Bye."

"Bye," she whispered, as Brian walked out of the room.

Keri tucked in her blouse and smoothed her hair, regaining as much of her composure as she could. Now she was angry, angry at the intruder who had effectively halted the most exciting moment in her life. Keri walked out of her office and down the hall. After looking for Jenna and Maxine in every conceivable place in the office, she found them in the coffee room.

"Did either of you come to my office while my door was shut?" Keri worded her question carefully. For some reason she didn't think either of them would enter before knocking.

"No." Jenna answered. "I didn't even know your door was shut."

Keri looked at Maxine. "Has Roy been in this afternoon?"

"No. As far as I know, Roy is still in court. He hasn't even called in." Maxine explained.

Convinced they were telling the truth, Keri proceeded to warn them. "The door to the inner offices was unlocked this afternoon and someone opened the door to my office. Please try to remember to lock it. We are all in danger when you forget."

Keri left them with surprised faces. That should give them something to think about, she decided. She was glad that she hadn't lost her temper, as she was inclined to do.

Seated in her office, Keri gazed unseeingly out her window. She wondered who had walked into her office. The logical answer would be Roy, but he was in court. She could read Jenna and Maxine too easily and she knew that neither of them were lying. Try as she might, Keri could come up with no other answer.

Keri's thoughts turned to Brian. She felt her body tremble at the mere thought of him. Her feelings were getting out of hand. She had better start controlling herself. It was undeniable that she was attracted to him, but it was also undeniable that he could be a cold-blooded murderer. Keri sighed and closed her eyes, while she yielded to the overwhelming conflict of emotions raging within her.

Chapter Eleven

Friday morning was just as hectic as Keri had anticipated. Grateful that she had pushed herself the day before, Keri felt confident that she would be able to leave the office early and enjoy her weekend. It would be a nice change. For a moment, she gazed out her window intent on how to plan her free time.

"You have another call from the man who won't leave his name. What a voice!" Jenna stood at the door to her office eager to find out just what Keri was up to.

Keri looked at Jenna for a moment and turned back to her desk. Keri smiled as she picked up the telephone, "Jenna, would you please close the door on your way out?"

"I get the hint. So, you finally got yourself a boyfriend. When do we get to meet him?" Jenna laughed.

"Jenna! Out!" Keri laughed as the door closed behind Jenna.

"Keri Adams." Keri leaned back in her chair and glanced around the room. Her eyes settled on the oak wall clock with roses delicately carved around its border. It was nine-twenty. What did Matthew want this early?

"Hello, Keri, this is Matthew." His cheerful voice lifted Keri's spirits. "Did you really enjoy last night?"

"Of course I did. You just want more compliments for being the perfect date. Plus, you like being right; it was a lot of fun." Warmth and laughter filled her voice. She had enjoyed being with Matthew immensely. Much to her surprise he hadn't made any romantic moves in her direction. As much as she hated to admit it, that disappointed her a little. She wanted a nice strong barrier to put between her and Brian before she lost every vestige of her self-control.

"I have some news for you."

"I can't imagine. Let's hear it," Keri answered enthusiastically.

"This morning I jogged from Brian's house to Emilia's. You were right about the timing." Matthew hesitated when he heard a soft groan from Keri. "I still don't think anyone would jog over. There is too much risk of being seen."

"I don't know, Matthew. It seems like a good way to look innocent." Discouragement flooded Keri's emotions. Brian was guilty and she knew it.

"Keri, I was seen by a lot of people. If someone was killed in the neighborhood, it would be easy to put a strange jogger at the scene," Matthew argued.

"Maybe you are right. But I don't think that we can rule out the possibility yet." Keri wanted to be wrong and Matthew made sense. Maybe she was putting too much emphasis on the short distance between the friends. Still, if Brian was having an affair with Emilia, it would be easy to jog over when Pablo wasn't home. How many people really noticed joggers? She didn't.

"I asked around both neighborhoods. No one remembers seeing him. That's encouraging." Matthew sensed that Keri was waiting for more information. "I'm still trying to find out when Rodriguez stopped seeing Emilia. I'll get back to you when I have something. Have a nice weekend."

"Thank you, Matthew, for working so hard on this. You have a good weekend too."

Keri lowered the receiver and sighed. Well, he didn't ask her out again. Another busy career man. News and sports didn't stop for the weekends. And what about Brian? Truthfully, she didn't know what to think. All that she seemed to be able to focus on today was Brian and his hard lean body, his broad strong shoulders. Most of all though, she felt his kiss on her lips and saw the tenderness in his eyes when he held her.

"Daydreaming again?" Roy walked unannounced into her office and left the door open.

"I thought that you were in trial today." Keri knew that she had not hidden her surprise or her irritation at seeing him.

Roy sat down in one of the rose and beige plaid chairs in front of her desk. He crossed one ankle over his knee and relaxed before answering. "The trial portion was over yesterday and the jury is still deliberating. I went over this morning, but the foreman told the bailiff that it could take all day."

"Did you come by the office yesterday?"

"Yeah. For a short time. I hope you've been busy on the Brian Michaels case?" There was a hint of sarcasm in his voice, but his expression was a mask of innocence.

Keri decided not to take her suspicions further. He would only feign innocence and then demand to know what had been going on. "Yes. As a matter of fact, Hector Rodriguez was here yesterday to interrogate Brian further."

"Here?" Roy gave Keri an incredulous look. "Why would he come here?"

"I asked him to." Keri ignored his questioning gaze and omitted her motives. "He really didn't add anything new," she lied. "From what Brian told me, he asked the same questions again."

"A typical, no-imagination detective." Roy muttered.

Keri thought for a moment, carefully choosing her words. "Brian told me that he recognized the lieutenant from some

of the parties. I presume he means the victory parties for the
ballplayers. He seems to think that Rodriguez could have been
having an affair with Emilia. I think that Tom should look into
this.''

''The hell he will!'' Keri was caught off guard by the belligerent tone in Roy's voice. His lips thinned in anger as he swept
his foot to the floor and leaned toward her. ''I am *not* going
to try to discredit a well-respected police officer. Juries don't
like that!''

''He could be a suspect, Roy. We need to get to the truth.''
Keri argued, her tone rising with her frustration. What was
wrong with him? Couldn't he see that they couldn't just ignore
the relationship between Rodriguez and Emilia?

''Forget truth. Brian killed Emilia. That's truth.'' Roy glared
at Keri aggressively. ''I want to continue practicing in this
town long after this case is over and forgotten. You discredit
a cop and no one forgets. That kind of strategy will backfire
on Brian. A jury will think we're desperate. Back off.'' Roy
stood up, towering over Keri.

Keri bit her lower lip to keep from screaming at Roy. Just
shut up, she told herself, he didn't have to know that she
was investigating Rodriguez. If the evidence turned out to be
worthwhile, then she could fight to get it into the trial.

''Well?'' Roy demanded. ''I want you to back off this ama-
teur investigation of yours and get back to the legal issues.
Defend the defendant! Got that?''

''Got it.'' Keri choked back her words and clenched her
fists.

''Good.'' Roy's lips twisted into a cynical smile. He turned
and walked arrogantly out the door. Stopping in the hallway,
he halfway turned to Keri. ''We'll get together next week.
Right now, I have a trial to worry about.'' Without waiting for
her to comment he disappeared down the hall.

Keri sat stunned. How dare he patronize her so? Keri closed
her eyes and breathed deeply while she leaned back in her

chair. Slowly, she became aware of the extent of her tension. Her clenched hands hurt as her nails dug deeply into her palms. Her jaw ached from where she had gritted her teeth. She unclenched her hands and worked her fingers, thinking how close she had come to telling Roy off. For Brian's sake, she couldn't just drop the case. But as soon as this case was finished, their partnership was over.

Unable to calm herself enough to work, Keri grabbed her purse. She was going to get out of the office and unwind. Ignoring the unfinished work on her desk, she switched off the light and locked her office door. The hallway and secretarial areas were empty. Probably having another coffee klatch, Keri thought angrily. Without a word to anyone, she let herself out of the office and reached her car in the parking garage in record time.

Turning onto the ramp of the expressway, Keri shut off the air conditioning and opened her sunroof. The sunshine felt good and as she accelerated the noise of the rushing air helped drown out her angry thoughts. Halfway home Keri heard her cellular telephone ring and decided that it was probably Jenna wanting the rest of the day off. She grabbed the telephone from her purse and answered.

"Hi, Keri. What's up?" A happy masculine voice caressed her.

"Brian, how did you know how to get in touch with me?"

"I called you at the office and at home. This was my last attempt." Brian hesitated. "You sound tense."

"I just wanted to leave early. I'm going home for a swim." Keri laughed and hoped that she sounded sincere. She needed time to sort it all out. She might have to advise him to find another attorney. He deserved a fair trial with an attorney who would put forth his or her best efforts.

"Well?" Brian asked with laughter in his voice.

"Well, what?" Keri answered, slightly confused.

"Why don't I come join you?"

Surprised by his aggressiveness, she swallowed hard. Her body had already begun to awaken. Little shivers played up and down her back at the thought of being alone with him. Why not? He wouldn't be her client much longer anyway. "Okay, come on over."

Keri turned off her telephone and switched on her turn signal. Leaving the expressway, she headed for home. As she drove the last few blocks to Laughing Gull Cove, she thought about Brian and the attraction between them. He was no longer just a client. The relationship was personal. Finding the truth behind Emilia's murder was suddenly the most important task she had before her.

When she slowed her car to enter the brightly lit underground parking garage, her thoughts were still in turmoil. She carefully parked and hurried up two flights of stairs, ignoring the elevator. Brian would be here soon and she wanted to be relaxed and calm. No more thinking about Roy and the case. This was going to be just for fun. She kicked off her shoes and headed to the bathroom, stripping as she made her way to the shower.

Chap[ter]

Water, cool and refreshing, cascaded over Keri's body. Her anger had dissipated, leaving in its place, an unfamiliar eagerness—an eagerness to be with Brian. Reaching for the faucet, Keri pressed the control slowly toward cold so she could cool her reactions to Brian. Minutes passed and Keri, unable to stand the cold water any longer, stepped out of the shower and allowed herself to drip.

At the door to her bedroom, she studied her reflection in the full-length mirrored door to her closet. Not bad, she admitted to herself. She had piled her hair loosely on top of her head and had scrubbed her face clean. Her complexion was just a little too pale she thought, as she removed the hairpins. Turning to her dresser, she reached for her brush and ran it through her long blond curls.

Keri turned quickly to answer the telephone. After telling the guard to let Brian through, she rummaged through a drawer to find a bathing suit. The first one she came across was her favorite: a Hawaiian print two-piece with a draped sarong front.

                          ...nd stepped into the bottom and
                   ...rbell rang. Grabbing a sheer matching
               ...d down the stairs to the front door.
            Keri greeted him cheerfully and stepped back
      ...im to enter.
   ...i, beautiful." Brian grinned and walked inside. "Skipping
out is out of character for you. Just what are you up to?"

Keri eyed him before answering. She would have to tell him
the truth, but it could wait a little while. Besides, no man should
look as good as he did. He wore a pale green sport shirt and
white slacks. His muscular arms were bare except for a modest
sports watch.

"Did I say something wrong already?" An amused expression spread over his handsome face.

"No. Of course not." Keri groped for words to satisfy him.
Finding none, she promised, "I'll discuss it with you later."

"Okay. It's only ten-thirty. Want to go down to the pool
now before it gets too hot?"

Keri smiled. "I was about to suggest it. Let's go."

Keri grabbed the towels and her keys and locked the door
behind them. Even though she was aware that he was watching
her every move, she led the way down a brick walkway to the
pool. At the edge of the sun deck she paused and looked around.
The pool and sun deck were deserted. She headed for her
favorite spot near the waterfall where thick palms and shrubs
sheltered two chaise longues from the morning sun.

"Do you like it here?" Keri turned to Brian expectantly.
Her heart pounded for no apparent reason.

"It's great." He kicked off his shoes and unbuttoned his
shirt. Looking down at Keri he surveyed her breasts and smiled.
"Can I get you a Coke or an iced tea from the pool bar?"

"Maybe later; it doesn't open for another twenty minutes."
Keri had slipped out of her cover-up and was busy stretching
out on her chaise longue.

Brian looked at her lazily while he took off his shirt and

slacks. Without a word, he stretched out and sighed heavily. It was as if he wished that he could forget for just a few hours that his whole life was threatened, that he was about to be tried for murder.

A gentle breeze stirred, rustling the palm fronds overhead. Brian's tense body began to relax as he breathed deep, inhaling the sweet fragrance of gardenia blossoms. Several minutes passed before Brian broke the silence.

"Thanks for having me over, Keri." Brian's voice was soft and caressing.

"I'm glad you came." A simple statement, but its warmth revealed to Brian much more than Keri intended.

"Do you have family in Miami?"

A broad smile crossed Keri's face and her eyes opened to look at Brian. "No. My mother and dad live in Sarasota. It's just far enough away that I'm not under foot, but they can see me any time they want."

Laughter filled his eyes. "I can't imagine you being under foot." He propped himself on his side to view her better.

"My brother and I probably drove them crazy when we lived at home. We were always finding some mischief to get into. Then Mitch discovered girls." A whimsical expression crossed her face.

"Did you discover boys?" Brian teased.

"No. I was one of those late bloomers. Guess I was just too serious for my own good. Besides, I have a bad temper that men shy away from."

"If they shy away from you, it isn't because of your temper." Brian's vivid blue eyes captured Keri's.

Unable to think of a reply, Keri held his gaze. What did he mean? Was there something undesirable about her? She forgot her inner thoughts as her pulse raced to her throat and her body came alive in response to the sensuous energy passing between them.

Brian broke the contact with a shocked expression. He leaned back onto the chaise and closed his eyes.

"Where is Mitch now?"

"Tampa. He went to medical school and is now an orthopedic surgeon. He lives closer to my parents than I do, so they depend more on him. What about you, Brian? Where's your family?"

"My family lives in Dallas. My sister comes over and stays with me whenever she gets the chance. She teaches first grade, so she has a number of holidays. I fly out about twice a year to see everybody. My mother is afraid to fly so my parents don't get down this way."

"How are they taking the news of the murder?" Keri asked without thinking.

Brian's blue eyes hardened, but not before Keri caught a glimpse of pain. "They haven't said much, but I don't think they believe me. They certainly weren't here when I needed them most. Those five days in jail were the longest days of my life." Bitterness crept into his voice. He sat up and threw his legs over the edge of the chaise.

"Oh, Brian. I'm so sorry to cause you so much pain." Keri hated herself for bringing the subject up.

Brian stood up and placed his hands on his lean hips. He looked down at Keri. "On the contrary. You have never caused me the slightest pain. I'm going for a swim. Care to join me?"

"I thought you would never ask!" Keri jumped up and started toward the pool. "Race you," she cried as she ran and dove in. When Keri felt the cool water, she reveled in her freedom from gravity. She swam close to the bottom of the pool before arching her back upward to surface for air.

Brian's head popped out from beneath the surface a few feet in front of her. He laughed as he sent a wave of water into her face. Sputtering, she reached for him and forced him beneath the surface of the water. Pulling up her knees to her chest she catapulted off of him and swam on her back to the other side of the pool. She tried to pull herself up onto the coping, but he caught her ankles and pulled her back into the pool. He pressed his body against her and trapped her against the side of the pool.

"You wench. You will pay for almost drowning me." Playfully, Brian's right hand slipped to her underarm, the other holding on to the pool's edge.

"No! No! Please don't tickle me," she begged as she squirmed against him. The feel of his smooth skin against hers had to be one of the most sensuous feelings she had ever experienced. Glancing up to his face she saw his eyes sparkling with mischief. But it was his smile that mesmerized her. It was alluring; it was magical; it was just for her. Unconsciously she ran her tongue over her lips as she stared at his beautiful, sensual mouth smiling at her.

"Now you've done it," he moaned as he leaned over and kissed her warm, moist lips. Lighthearted at its start, the kiss became more and more demanding, more and more intense, more and more sexual. He pulled away slightly but she could feel his hot breath against her lips. "Kiss me, Keri." he commanded, "like you did yesterday. Make me feel you that deeply again."

Lured by his soft words, Keri found his lips once more to taste him and experience him. Kissing him passionately, she felt emotions erupting from deep within her. Rational thinking gone, Keri sailed on a sea of passion, wildly kissing him like a sailor whose life depended upon it, believing surely she would drown.

Suddenly she was aroused beyond her own limited experience, a dynamo of sexual energy pressing against his hard, handsome, nearly nude body. Desire raced through her as his hand slipped her shoulder strap down, tugging insistently until her breast emerged free. His firm caresses sent chills through her. Desperately wanting him to taste her, Keri arched her back so that her breast broke the surface of the water. He grinned at her obligingly, then as his tongue licked and teased her, his hand followed the curve of her hip. His fingers slipped beneath the sarong and found the elastic of her briefs. Keri gasped with need and opened her legs to his exploring fingers while her hands grasped his shoulders tightly for support. Feeling wild and wanton, she reminded herself that she didn't care. She had been living for this moment. She wanted him, needed him, and intended to have him.

Keri rested her head back on his left hand which gripped the coping, holding them both to the side of the pool. She closed her eyes and reveled in the feel of his mouth and his fingers as they discovered her bare flesh, gently stroking her, eliciting whimpers of desire from her.

"Brian please . . ." she begged breathlessly as she arched her back still more to bring herself closer to his male hardness. His mouth gave up her breast and passionately took her mouth as his fingers plunged deeply, driving her mindless, pushing her to the point of no return. Beneath smothering kisses she moaned in ecstasy. Surely he was a seer, a sexual magician. He knew her; he knew what she needed. She felt his hard muscles and pressed him closer. Suddenly her mouth was free and she heard his breathing at her ear. His fingers were forcing her toward orgasm.

"No, please, no . . ." she whimpered as the feeling became too intense. She was his now. All her self-control was gone. Desperately gasping for breath, she quivered and shook and came.

Keri moaned softly, realizing that her hands had left his shoulders and were encircling his erection. She wanted to give him the same wild pleasure he had just given her and glanced at him to see if he wanted her to continue. To her surprise, he didn't. Instead he released her hands and in one fluid motion, raised himself onto the coping.

Halter and strap back in place, Keri looked up at Brian from the pool while he straightened his swim suit. His muscles glistened with thousands of droplets of water, accentuating his masculine hardness. Once again she became acutely aware of his unleashed power. She wanted to be in his arms.

Brian looked into her eyes and smiled. He leaned forward and caught her beneath her shoulders. In an effortless motion, he sat her on the coping and released her.

"It's about time for the pool bar to open. Why don't we have a snack?" Brian's voice was filled with laughter.

"Okay." Keri looked at Brian in amazement. How could he think of food at a time like this? Keri pondered the question as he caught her hand and led her over to the pool bar. Patiently they waited, until the bartender opened the shutters from the inside and fastened them back.

"Hi, folks, anything to drink?" The sandy-haired bartender yawned sleepily and smiled.

"Two iced teas, please." Brian seated himself on a bar stool and reached for a menu. "What will you have, princess?"

Keri peered over his arm to the menu. She knew the menu by heart, but it gave her an excuse to be near him. "The tuna salad is fine."

"Make it two," he told the bartender.

Brian sipped his iced tea and studied Keri thoughtfully. Keri returned his look. She felt overwhelmed by him, a man who haunted her dreams and pervaded her thoughts. Brian was the most desirable man she had ever met and she didn't know what to do with him, at least not under these circumstances. It was plain that she couldn't resist him. What was next?

"I have to leave soon. I have practice at the stadium and a dinner conference that I must attend." Brian gave her a passionate look. "I will be free later in the evening, if you would like to meet me at Pelican Bay for dancing and drinks."

Keri's face brightened at the suggestion. "What time?"

"Nine o'clock?" Brian was unable to hide his excitement.

"I'll be there." Her soft voice took on a new warmth as she smiled back at Brian.

Much to Keri's surprise, she found herself talking about

baseball over the rest of lunch. Brian skillfully breathed life into what had always seemed to Keri to be a boring game. For the first time, she actually wanted to see a baseball game.

When they finished lunch, they walked quietly back to the chaise lounges. Brian stepped into his slacks and swung his shirt casually over his bare shoulders. "See you later." A smile crossed his handsome face before turning to walk away.

"Bye." Keri closed her eyes and stretched out lazily in her chaise longue. A feeling of contentment washed over her as the heat began to relax her and lull her into a sleepy state. Within minutes Keri slept.

The breeze picked up, cooling her sleeping body. Clouds, once piles of cotton floating aimlessly through the sky, darkened, weighted down by rain. Keri stirred in her sleep as distant thunder rumbled its warning. Keri broke out in a cold sweat, her sleep becoming fitful. In an instant she shot up from her chaise, torn from sleep by fear. With terror-stricken eyes she viewed her surroundings in confusion. Unsatisfied, Keri grabbed her towels and cover-up and ran to the safety of her townhouse.

Chapter Thirteen

Keri had dressed in a black, halter-neck silk sheath trimmed around the high neck, bodice and low back with ombre flame beading of iridescent hologram sequins which flickered from red to gold to black. She pulled one side of her hair back with an upward sweep and fastened it with a matching comb. She quickly checked her makeup and applied a little cocoa shadow to bring out her large brown eyes. Satisfied with her appearance, Keri dabbed a pale rose lip gloss on her lips and reached for her purse. It was time to go. One last glance in the mirror told her that her look was dramatic. The dress clung to her curves and set off her pale skin and shapely legs. With a smile of self-assurance, Keri set the alarm system and walked downstairs to the parking level beneath the building.

The drive to Coconut Grove was pleasant, but Keri could hardly contain her excitement. Brian would be waiting for her. After her experience with him in the pool she felt both embarrassed and intrigued. Never had a man aroused her so. Yet she still harbored the fear that he was a murderer. The danger was intoxicating; she was playing with fire and she loved it. What magic did he have to make her abandon her ethical principles so willingly? Other attorneys dated clients. They had to avoid the media, whose representatives were not allowed at Pelican Bay.

Pelican Bay had been planned for lovers. The private club occupied the second floor of a glass-faced building which over-looked the Dinner Key Marina. There, every table claimed a panoramic view of the bay, waitresses wore cocktail dresses to lend the club a special ambiance, and couples dined and danced until early morning hours.

Keri pulled up to the valet's station. The valet opened the door and she swung her long legs out. Standing up, Keri quickly smoothed her dress down and reached for her claim ticket. The valet winked and handed her the ticket. Keri laughed to herself. She looked good and she knew it. She stuffed the claim ticket into her purse and grinned at the doorman as she walked in. Once inside she headed for the spiral staircase to the right of the lobby, anxious to see if Brian was already upstairs.

Brian stood in a corner of the lobby watching Keri. She had been so absorbed in her thoughts that she failed to see him waiting for her. As she started her ascent, his eyes followed her, taking in her soft breasts and seductive hips. His breath became short and uneven while he viewed her appreciatively from a distance. With a quick stride, Brian ascended the stairs. He reached the second floor and walked up behind Keri standing at the doorway leading into the dimly lit club.

"Keri?" Brian reached out and placed his hand on her bare shoulder.

"Brian, hi." Keri turned and smiled warmly at him. "The hostess said you were already here. She said she would show me to your table in just a minute."

"We don't have to wait on her. Let's go." Brian slipped his hand to her waist possessively, and asserting a firm pressure, led her to the table. After holding her chair for her, he motioned to the elegant-looking waitress.

"Dom Perignon, please." He looked at Keri waiting for her assent.

Keri nodded, unable to speak. His touch had released her emotions. In his white dinner jacket, he looked virile and self-confident. Her eyes found his and held his gaze. It seemed as if minutes passed while they drank in the energy passing between them.

"Come dance with me." Brian commanded and held out his hand to her. Closing his hand over hers, he led Keri to the dance floor and circled his arms around her. He pulled her close and rested his head against her soft blond hair. "You look very beautiful tonight, Keri." Brian whispered softly when they began to dance slowly to the music.

"Thank you," Keri managed. Brian held her body gently to him while his warm hands caressed her back. Feeling his muscular body moving against hers set her pulses racing wildly. Did he share her same desires? Surely he must, even though he seemed so cool and controlled guiding her over the dance floor. Too quickly, the music came to an end. Brian's hands traced her spine to the small of her back, where he softly brushed her hips and lingered there.

Keri trembled beneath his hands. His magnetism was so compelling that she could only think of her need for him. With a sensual glance, he acknowledged the overwhelming web of desire between them. Reluctantly, Keri drew away, followed Brian back to the table, and sat down. When she lifted her gaze to his eyes, the beginning of a smile teased at the corners of his mouth, but his eyes held a veiled expression, both intriguing and dangerous. Something vague and threatening stirred deep within her. She pushed it away, not wanting to acknowledge it. What was she doing? Brian was still her client—a client accused of murder. Where did she think a relationship with him could go? The trouble was, she wasn't thinking clearly, she was feeling.

Brian handed her a glass of champagne. Lifting his glass to meet hers, Brian offered her a simple toast.

"May your eyes always be filled with the music of your soul."

"How beautiful," Keri said breathlessly.

An amused expression crossed his face. "So are you."

Keri smiled and sipped her champagne, savoring the tingling sensation as it went down. In spite of her reservations, she felt wonderful and wanted more of him.

"Brian, I've heard that you are an artist. What do you enjoy most?"

Surprised, Brian thought before answering. "What I enjoy most is studying my subjects and then capturing their likeness. So, I guess either painting or sculpting would be my answer."

"Who are your subjects?" Keri asked, expecting him to say "women."

With an amused expression, Brian emptied his glass. "I'm a wildlife artist. Animals, birds, and sometimes cowboys and Indians are my subjects." A devilish look flashed in his eyes. "Care to volunteer?" He teased.

Keri felt her cheeks flame at a mental picture of herself in the nude. "No thanks, I don't fit into any of your categories."

Brian laughed. "Let me know if you change your mind. I can always make an exception."

Embarrassed, Keri remained quiet, unsure of herself and uncertain how to answer.

"Finish up, Keri, so we can go dance." Brian's voice, soft and seductive, filled her with a sense of urgency.

Keri set her glass down and stood up. She mentally chided herself for guzzling the champagne. It didn't take much to make her feel lightheaded. Afraid to look his way, she turned and led the way to the dance floor.

Back in Brian's arms, Keri felt herself trembling again. He

responded by holding her closer. Keri pressed herself against his muscular body, overwhelmed by her attraction to his vitality and strength. The champagne began filling her with a warm glow, yet the same threatening sensation that had unnerved her earlier crept back. She fought the realization that she was still very much afraid of him. She desperately wanted him to be innocent. But was he?

Brian relaxed his hold and looked down at Keri. Gazing back into the depths of his intense blue eyes, she found pain, anger and smoldering desire. He lowered his lips to hers and nipped her. A small cry escaped her before he crushed her mouth with his. Her body exploded with rivulets of fire coursing through her veins as she responded to his passionate kiss. Gasping for breath, she pulled away, her eyes dark with erotic promises.

"Come home with me, Keri," he whispered at her ear.

"No," she moaned, "you're my client. We have to be careful." Tears glistened on her dark eyelashes.

"Since when did you start doing reality checks?" he asked with a grin.

"Brian!" Keri protested and laughed. How easily he turned an emotionally changed situation into lighthearted fun. She followed him back to their table, grateful for the end of the dancing. She had almost lost her self-control; she had almost agreed.

Dancing with Brian was dangerous, Keri decided as she sipped another glass of champagne and studied the hors d'oeuvres the waitress had placed before them. She reached for a stuffed mushroom.

"Keri, have you heard from Tom Eaton?"

Keri shook her head while she made a mental note to call him on Monday.

"Then you haven't found out any more about Lt. Rodriguez?"

"Yes, I found out that he was definitely Emilia's lover, for over a year. I'm still trying to find out if he was still seeing her around the time of her death. I don't know if their affair was over.'' She bit into her mushroom, savoring its pleasant taste.

"I'm sure that the affair with Rodriguez was over. Emilia was involved with someone else when she died." Brian placed a few hor d'oeuvres on his plate.

"How can you be sure?"

"Apparently, Emilia was involved with two men about six months before her death. She ended it with one. The other man was the troublesome one, the one that frightened her."

"But how do you know it wasn't Rodriguez?" Keri persisted.

"I stopped seeing him at parties and social events. Besides, he doesn't strike me as being violent." Brian turned his attention to the Swedish meatballs on his plate.

"Violent?"

"Yes, violent." Brian's expression grew resentful. "Emilia told me that her lover had threatened her. She was terrified."

"When did this happen?" Surprised, Keri lifted her lashes to study his face.

"In the morning, the day she was killed. That's why I went to Pablo, to enlist his help. I was sincerely concerned for her safety. She was in danger and needed him." An expression of fury crossed his face.

"You lied to me!" The accusation was out before Keri realized it. "You told us that you didn't talk to her the day of the murder."

"I did not. No one asked me if I spoke to her in the morning. Everyone asked me if I saw her that afternoon!" A warning tone crept into Brian's voice.

"That's begging the question, and you know it!" Keri accused angrily. "Do you have any idea how damaging it would be if the police knew you talked with her the day of the murder?"

"Yes." Brian snapped.

"Were you at her house?"

"Yes. I went over to her house before going to the stadium. Are you satisfied?"

"How dare you? I'm trying to defend you and you're holding out on me." Keri's face paled with fury. "If the police have witnesses placing you there, you could be convicted. These are facts I need to know *now,* not sprung on me at the trial!"

"I thought Roy was defending me."

Stunned and hurt, Keri grabbed her purse. *"In absentia?* Open your eyes, Brian. Better still, go talk to him, see just how he intends to defend you!" Keri said as she stood up to leave.

"What's that supposed to mean?" Brian demanded in a hostile tone.

"He thinks you're guilty. And maybe you are!" Keri accused.

Brian's blue eyes darkened to black as Keri stared at him. For an instant she was frozen with fear. Brian rose, while his cold dark eyes reflected his mounting rage. Keri rushed to the door. She rummaged through her purse for the claim ticket as she hurried down the stairs.

Once outside, she ran to the valet, and begged breathlessly, "Please hurry!"

No one was in sight when she looked over her shoulder at the entrance. How foolish of her to think that he would come after her. She tipped the valet and smiled as he helped her into her car.

Keri drove off faster than usual. She wanted to get home, to security. The evening had gotten out of hand. He didn't deserve to be treated that way. After all, his life was at stake. It would have been normal for him not to trust his attorneys. Why had she overreacted? Her disappointment with Roy was no excuse. She knew that Brian's overwhelming attractiveness unnerved her and that her desire for him made her irrational, but it was more than that. Reluctantly, she admitted that her reservations about him were more than normal concerns. She shivered involuntarily. Facing her emotions was not easy. But she recognized the root of her problem. It was cold-blooded fear.

Still angry with herself and her fear, Keri drove slowly down the brick streets of Laughing Gull Cove. She turned into the entrance of the underground parking garage only to find that one dim light illuminated the way. A sense of foreboding welled within her as she drove through the dark, eerie garage to her parking spaces. She should have just parked on the street for the night instead of trying to park in the dark. She would have to phone the guard and tell him the lights were out. Her headlights reflected off a neighbor's car as she pulled into her parking space next to it. Uncomfortable with the dark garage, Keri hurriedly got out and closed the door. As she set the alarm, Keri heard the sounds of a car in the distance accelerating.

Tomorrow, she thought, she would have to deal with Brian, and apologize for walking out on him. Without looking, Keri started across the drive. Suddenly, she realized that a car was speeding toward her. She ran as the car swerved, missing her by inches. Keri stood shaking. There had been no lights on the car and the garage was practically pitch black. How could the driver be so stupid?

Keri gasped in shock as realization dawned. The driver had been trying to hit her! She spun around and raced to the stairs, avoiding the elevators. The driver could still be around, she thought in panic. Someone else might be lying in wait, too. Holding her breath, she quickly unlocked her door and ran in. Once inside the townhouse, she called the guard and explained what happened.

"No, I didn't get a good look at the car." Keri bit her lip to keep from crying. "Did you let anyone in?" She asked in a shaky voice. "A gold Lexus perhaps?"

"No, ma'am. I've been on duty since six o'clock and we haven't had anything unusual happen or let anyone in who didn't have a reason for being here." The guard answered her confidently.

"Please have the lights fixed."

"Right away. I'll send a patrol to check it out. He'll get back to you tonight."

"Good." With a sense of despair, Keri hung up the telephone.

Who would want to kill her? The question continued to haunt her while she fixed a cup of hot tea. A suspicious voice kept asking her if Brian was angry enough to kill her. I'm being ridiculous, she thought. Besides, he didn't follow me or come into the development. So where did that leave her?

When the doorbell rang, Keri jumped, spilling the tea she had just put to her lips. Shivering involuntarily, she set her cup down and walked to the intercom for the door.

"Yes?"

"It's John Beatty, Ms. Adams."

"One minute." Keri opened her door and walked to the courtyard gate where a tall, slender man in a security uniform patiently waited.

"Good evening, Ms. Adams." The patrolman smiled.

"Hello, John. Did you find anything?"

"No. I've been all over the grounds of the complex. I didn't see anything unusual or suspicious." He shook his head. "Don't worry though. We'll keep an eye on your place tonight."

"Thanks, John." Keri turned and went back inside. From the conversation, she knew he wasn't taking the incident too seriously.

Back in the kitchen, Keri wiped up the hot liquid and sipped at the remaining tea. She reached for the telephone and punched in Brian's number. The telephone rang several times before Keri set her receiver in its cradle. He's just out, she thought. His absence didn't mean that he had tried to run her down. He could be anywhere. Why was she torturing herself?

Keri carefully locked her doors and windows and set her alarm system. Overly cautious and fearful, she left her bathroom door open and quickly showered. After one final check, she slipped into bed.

Sometime during the blackness of the night, Keri woke with a start. For a moment she wondered if her assailant was trying to break in. She listened. Only normal night sounds came to her. Foolish! She reached for the clock and switched the alarm off. Why bother getting up early? Saturdays were great for sleeping. She rolled over and dozed off, satisfied that nothing was wrong.

Ten minutes later, the telephone rang. Half asleep Keri reached for the receiver. "Hello?"

The line was quiet except for the faint sound of breathing.

"Hello—who is this?" Keri felt her fear rising, bringing her to the edge of her bed.

The breathing continued louder. Angry and unnerved, Keri slammed the receiver down. She looked toward the telephone in disbelief. The rotten machine was ringing again. She answered once more only to hear more heavy breathing. "Murderer!" She cried out and ripped the cord from its wall plug.

Keri sat crossed legged in the dark, in the middle of her bed, shivering with fear. What was happening to her? She wondered if the calls were connected to the attempt on her life or just a coincidence. Did someone really try to kill her or was she reading too much into the incident? She clenched her arms tightly around her and fought the tears streaming down her face.

Chapter Fourteen

"I have been trying to reach you all weekend." Roy's angry voice penetrated her sleep. "Why haven't you been answering your telephone?"

Nestled snugly under her pink satin coverlet, Keri vaguely remembered getting up when the alarm rang, plugging the telephone back in, and lying down again for just two more minutes. Not fully awake, she mumbled sleepily into the receiver. "My telephone has been unplugged since Friday. I plugged it back in this morning."

"Why?" he demanded in an irritated tone.

"So I could get calls." Keri blinked and shook her head at his irrational question. Roy could be so difficult. What in the world could he be so aggravated about?

"That's not what I meant," he replied in an exasperated voice. "I meant why did you unplug your telephone!"

"I needed a vacation." Keri offered no further explanation. She resented his nosey interference. Why was he calling anyway?

His voice hardened as he retorted, "Well, the vacation is over! I can't believe it's ten o'clock on Monday morning and you're still in bed!"

"What?" A startled Keri interrupted his tirade. She threw off the coverlet and stared in disbelief at the clock.

"Get over here quick," he demanded. "A package just arrived from the prosecutor's office and I want you here to go over it with me."

"I'll be there shortly." Keri hung up the receiver before she could hear anymore of his arrogant complaining. She dreaded the thought of going in to work today now that she knew Roy was in a foul mood. But she had to go. She was anxious to review the prosecutor's long-awaited evidence.

Keri took a quick shower, then quickly arranged her hair into a French braid, fastened securely at the nape of her neck, and pinned on a large brown silk bow. Ignoring makeup, she went to her closet. Remembering that she was not going to court today, she rejected her suits in favor of a butterscotch silk shirt and a warm brown silk skirt.

Keri was busy with the buttons of her shirt when the telephone rang.

"Hello?" Keri answered tentatively.

"Keri—Matthew here!"

"Hi, Matthew." A warm smile touched her lips.

"Sorry to call so early, but I thought you would want the news." His eager voice aroused her curiosity.

"Of course. What have you found out?"

"Do you know who Donald Reid is—'D.R.' for short?"

"No. Who is he?" She vaguely remembered hearing the name somewhere.

"He's a member of the Miami Stingrays. Overall, he seems to be a pretty nice guy. Anyway, he had an affair with Emilia!" A triumphant note filled his voice.

"You're kidding!" Keri sat down in amazement on the edge of her bed. Her mind reeled with the implications. Was it possible that Brian didn't commit the murder; that one of her paramours did?

"I don't know the exact time frame yet, but it was recent. And I have a witness who is willing to testify, if necessary." Matthew waited before continuing. The sound of pages turning told Keri he was reading his notes. "According to the witness, D.R. took the break up pretty hard. Apparently, he kept bothering her afterwards."

"Matthew, you're great!" She felt her adrenalin surging. There could be hope for Brian. Matthew was such a dear. He had probably spent all weekend investigating.

"Just keep thinking that. By the way, tonight there's a party at the Seventh Inning Club. Come with me?"

"Okay, sounds like fun!" She needed a friend and confidant right now. Matthew would be perfect for the job. Besides, she had to warn him of the possibility that someone was trying to kill her. He could be in danger, too.

Keri felt elated as she finished the call and slipped on her shoes. Deep in thought, she grabbed her purse, set the alarm system, and walked cautiously downstairs to her car. She relaxed when she saw that the garage lights were illuminating the whole area. Had she imagined the car had swerved toward her on Friday night? Maybe her argument with Brian had triggered her imagination. And it was possible that the telephone calls were a coincidence. Perhaps she should think things through before telling anyone.

During her drive to the office, her excitement turned to dismay. What was it about Emilia that men found so fascinating that they couldn't give her up? When no answers came, she switched her thoughts to Roy. She admitted that she didn't know him as well as she had thought. On top of that, she didn't like him anymore. Life was getting complicated and she owed it all to Brian.

Brian was the most exciting, erotic man she had ever met and she wanted a relationship with him. How could she though?

It just wasn't smart and definitely not safe. Then there was Matthew: handsome, witty, and smart. And free. Suddenly her life was full of choices. If she knew what was good for her, she would put all her energies into defending Brian and stop acting like a woman starved for affection. Both men could wait until she got a few issues resolved.

Entering the parking garage, she looked around carefully before pulling her car into its assigned space. Keri sighed when she noticed Jenna's car missing. Out on a Monday morning. She needed to have a talk with her. Still uncomfortable, Keri quickly locked the car and ran to the elevator. Safety was taking on a new meaning.

The conference room was unexpectedly cold when Keri entered. Roy had documents strewn all over the table's oval surface as well as on some of the chairs. He glanced up with an angry look before he leaned over and cleared a chair.

"Sit down." Roy commanded, his mouth twisting disagreeably.

Keri sighed indulgently as she sat down. It was going to be a very unpleasant conference. She looked at the round aquarium in the corner and watched the colorful tropical fish swimming in and out of coral caves. Now, there was an idea for a vacation. She could go to the Bahamas and snorkel among the shallow reefs with the fish, and—

"What took you so long?" He stared at her coldly. "You should have been here an hour ago."

Roy's actions were deliberately designed to start an argument. Keri didn't like being manipulated and she certainly wasn't going to play into his hands. It wouldn't do any good to remind him that an hour ago she was still sleeping. With a little patience, she would discover what he was really angry about. "You're right, Roy. I'm sorry."

Her reply seemed to defuse Roy's mood. A thin smile crossed his lips as he called his secretary over the intercom.

"Tom Eaton will be here soon. Maxine has ordered lunch for us so that we don't have to break."

"Did you need me, Mr. Foxx?" A pretty woman with a heavy Brooklyn accent stood at the door waiting.

Roy's eyes raked over her before he answered her. "Yes, Maxine, when Tom arrives, bring in the coffee and sandwiches."

"Sure." Ignoring his leer, Maxine turned to check the reception area.

Roy rose from his chair and began clearing the conference table and chairs. His eyes narrowed suspiciously as he glanced at her. Keri shifted uncomfortably. He reminded her of a predator stalking its next meal. This cat and mouse game aggravated her and she didn't feel like being patient any longer.

"What's bothering you, Roy?" she asked softly.

"I talked with Brian this weekend." His eyes, hard and cold, peered out from an expressionless face. "He was pretty upset."

"Oh?" Keri feigned innocence, expecting an angry tirade from Roy.

Roy dropped his stack of papers on the table and leaned over her, forcing her to look at him. "What were you trying to do—turn my client against me?" His voice was cold and unyielding.

"I don't know what you mean." Keri attempted to check her growing anger. Brian must have told him everything, even that they had gone to Pelican Bay. Well, that was her business and none of Roy's. She lifted her head defiantly and stared back at him.

Surprisingly, Roy didn't pursue it. He lowered himself into the leather conference chair and leaned back. "Well, you told him the truth. I believe he is guilty. The evidence supports it—as you will see from the reports today. It doesn't matter though. It's all circumstantial and can be easily discredited."

"Mr. Foxx." Maxine stood in the doorway. "Mr. Eaton is here to see you."

"Show him in." Roy rose to greet his friend. "Tom, you are just in time for lunch."

"Good timing." Tom smiled broadly at Keri as he found a chair and sat down. "I parked in a reserved parking space on the second level of the garage. Do you think I'll be towed?"

"Did you notice the number of the space?" Maxine asked, as she carried in a tray of coffee and ham sandwiches.

"Not really. I parked next to a gold Toyota sedan, if that's any help."

"No problem, Mr. Eaton. That's my car. Jenna's out today. You parked in her space." Maxine paused at the door. "If you need anything else, just let me know."

"Maxine, why is Jenna out today?" Keri asked, making a mental note that Jenna had been taking off a lot of time lately.

"She called in sick." Maxine shrugged her shoulders.

"Thanks." Keri turned and waited for Roy to pour the coffee. She reached for a sandwich and removed the wrapper. She'd been too rushed to grab breakfast.

"Tom, you haven't missed anything. I was just about to summarize the evidence for Keri. Since you're here now, why don't you recap your investigation of Hector Rodriguez for us."

"Sounds good to me." Tom leaned toward Roy. "He's clean. I mean really clean." Tom paused while he glanced at Keri then turned his attention back to Roy. "I couldn't find anything damaging about him."

"Did you ask around about his attitude toward Keri?" Roy asked.

"Yeah. He does have a reputation for not liking female attorneys. There doesn't seem to be anything going on that's personal against Keri though." Tom settled back with a satisfied look. "That's about it for Rodriguez."

Roy seemed quite pleased, Keri thought. Even smug. She could feel her chances of bringing in damaging information on Rodriguez lessening by the minute. Roy would throw Tom's investigation up to her and refuse to consider anything else. She was beginning to doubt Tom's ability. Common sense told her that the lieutenant's hostility toward her was personal. Even more, if Matthew knew about his affair with Emilia, surely Tom could have discovered it.

Keri shook her head sadly. Working with Roy on this case would be hypocritical and leaving Roy to his own devices would be unfair to Brian. She wanted out, but Brian should be told first.

"Did you check on Pablo?" Roy looked intently at Tom. "Does he have an alibi for the afternoon of the murder?"

"Yeah. Air-tight. He stayed for practice. He was at the stadium until he left with Juan Cardera around three-twenty." Tom took another bite out of his sandwich. "Roy, I'm still working on motives. Nothing conclusive yet."

"Okay. Keep digging." Roy set his coffee cup down and picked up a photograph. With a sly, slightly amused look, he turned his attention to Keri.

"Remember I told you that Brian pinned fishing lures to his baseball cap for good luck because he enjoyed fishing so much?" Roy waited momentarily for an answer. "Well, the police found a fishing lure on the patio floor near the chaise longue. They believe that it came from Brian's cap. I'm sure the prosecutor will try to make the connection at the trial."

Keri made no comment, but her stomach churned and knotted in pain at the news. She glanced down at the photograph that Roy had tossed arrogantly in front of her. It was a fishing lure. If matched to Brian's cap, it would be extremely damaging. Roy seemed delighted with this turn of events. Oh, how Roy loved being right.

"As we all know," Roy began, "the police also found a comb with light brown hair in the cabana bathroom. A laboratory analysis is being done on it to see if it matches with Brian's."

Tom looked at Keri sadly. "It doesn't look good for Brian."

"It gets worse." Roy scanned Keri's face, finding it devoid of any emotion. "Outside the door to the screen enclosure they found a torn piece of paper with Emilia's cellular telephone number scribbled on it. If you remember, it's being matched up by laboratory analysis to another torn piece of paper found in Brian's locker. If the tear patterns match, that could clinch it."

"What about witnesses?" Keri asked in a subdued tone. Surely, the police had no witnesses. Wouldn't the prosecutor have fought harder at the arraignment to keep Brian in jail?

"A neighbor saw Brian's car leaving Emilia's home the morning of the murder. There's even a partial license number which matches up with Brian's." With a triumphant look he challenged Keri. "Still think Brian is innocent?"

Hiding her conflicting emotions, Keri looked at him squarely. "Yes."

"Then take a look at these photographs taken at the scene." Roy tossed a large brown envelope to her.

Keri sorted out the pictures, studying each one in succession, and comparing each to the list of evidence. Suddenly, she sat up. "Look Roy, in this picture of the cabana bath—there's the bottle of after-shave lotion you told me about. But it's not on their list of evidence!"

Roy looked surprised. "You're right Keri. They probably weren't able to get a clear enough print to submit it as evidence. That's a real break."

Keri stood up and spread out the pertinent photographs of the murder scene on the table so that the three of them could study them. Tom noticed the torn pieces of Emilia's bikini lying haphazardly near an open bottle of suntan lotion. Something he said stopped Keri short. The bikini was obviously torn, but the police report indicated there were no bruises or marks except on her neck. It wasn't possible to tear off clothing without some trauma to the skin.

While the men talked, Keri studied another picture. The

fishing fly was clearly visible, but it was lying close to a chair near the back wall of the patio. Roy had said it was found near the chaise longue. Keri couldn't decide if it made a difference. If it had fallen there on a day when there had been a party, it could make a big difference. She needed to know Brian's habits. When did he wear his lucky baseball cap? It was a little odd that he would wear it over to the house on a day he planned to kill someone. No, Keri decided, the evidence just didn't add up right. Maybe he really was framed.

"The prosecutor only has circumstantial evidence, no motive." Roy sounded pleased.

Tom stood up and stretched. "You know me, Roy. I hate to disagree with you, but the prosecutor is going to have the testimony of Pablo Martinez, who has accused Brian of having an affair with Emilia. Crime of passion is what they'll say."

"The State has no witnesses who know first hand that Brian was having an affair. In addition, Tom, there is no evidence here that will prove premeditation." Roy smiled and began gathering the photographs.

"Roy, this evidence is damaging." Keri's tone hardened as she realized how good the case was against Brian.

"Look, Keri, the State cannot prove beyond a reasonable doubt that Brian killed Emilia Martinez!"

"I truly believe that you have made an inaccurate assessment of the evidence and that you have underestimated the ability of the prosecutor to prove up his case." Keri watched Roy's smug expression turn to anger.

Ignoring the warning look on his angry face, Keri continued. "We do not have enough favorable facts here to establish a reasonable doubt. I suggest that we investigate Donald Reid and Jesse Davis. There we might find some motives for killing her."

Roy's curt voice lashed out at her. "You are the one who has made an inaccurate assessment. You don't have the experience to analyze such a high profile case."

"That's not true. I know conclusive evidence when I see it."

"You're emotionally involved with Brian and you are not being objective." Roy mocked. "Stop trying to grab for straws and face reality."

Keri searched the faces of the two men. Neither one of them had grasped the intricacies of this case. Either they were exceptionally dense or they just didn't care. In either case, they both were impossible to deal with. Tom's investigations were all but useless and Roy's attitude could land Brian in the electric chair. She had to talk to Brian.

Keri leaned over the chair and grabbed her purse. Without a word, she hurried out the door, ignoring Roy's impatient calls. Her heart pounded rapidly as she ran to her car and got in. Roy's ego was unbelievable. He was good, but not good enough to establish reasonable doubt when he was unable to refute the evidence.

Stopped for a red light, Keri reached for her cellular telephone. Brian had to be home. She had to talk to him. Relief filled her when he answered.

"Brian, this is Keri. I'm a few minutes from your house. I need to talk to you about your case."

"Come over. I'll be here a while."

Keri tossed the telephone back in her purse and concentrated on keeping her speed within the posted limits. Adrenaline flooded through her, throwing her nerves into overdrive. She had to get to Brian before Roy did.

Chapter Fifteen

Brian stood in the doorway, casually leaning against the doorframe, when Keri drove up. Her eyes froze on his lean body. She knew by his damp swim trunks that he had been in the pool. The muscles of his bare arms and chest glistened with moisture.

Keri got out of her car. Brian looked good—too good. Once again her body betrayed her and trembled in anticipation. In an effort to still her heart, Keri walked slowly to the door, aware of Brian's compelling blue eyes watching her.

For a moment, he studied her eyes, then a look of understanding covered his face and a smile tipped the corners of his mouth. Keri felt lost in his magnetism. Brian circled her in his arms while he kissed her full on the mouth.

Keri trembled a moment with excitement, then fear. Not wanting to offend him again, Keri looked up and smiled warmly. He smiled and released her, stepping back to allow her to enter his home.

"Roy called after you did. He wanted to know if you were here or if I had heard from you."

"Did you tell him that I was coming over?" Keri's tone was guarded. Her anger surged at the thought that Roy would call Brian to find her. How presumptuous! How arrogant!

"No. I told him that I hadn't heard from you." Brian looked at her squarely. "Why would he think that you would be with me?"

"We had a fight. I walked out on him after he told me that I was not being objective about your case." Keri left out Roy's accusation that she had become too involved with Brian.

As they walked through the house to the lanai, Keri realized how beautiful and peaceful it was. The rooms were light and airy. Vaulted ceilings lent the spacious rooms an air of elegance. From what she could tell, the home was a U-shape with most of the rooms opening onto the patio, pool area.

Keri assessed the lanai as she sat down on a plush-cushioned wicker chair. The pinks, peaches and soft mint greens of the wallpaper and vertical blinds were repeated in the hibiscus-patterned fabric of the wicker furniture. Small palm trees in decorator pots were placed throughout the lanai and patio.

"Like the house, so far?" Brian asked in an amused tone as he set two iced teas with lime down on a small table between them.

"Yes. It's magnificent!" Keri changed the subject back to Roy. She had to know what Brian had told him.

"Did you tell Roy that we went to Pelican Bay?"

"Of course not. It's none of his business." Brian quietly explained. "I called Roy on Saturday and told him that after one of our conversations, I came away with the impression that he believed that I was guilty."

Brian sipped at his iced tea. He leaned back in his chair and stretched his long legs out in front of him. "Then I told him that I wanted to come into the office to see him. I told him he would have to explain to me what he had done on my case and what he intended to do. If it met with my approval, I wouldn't change attorneys.''

Keri's laugh sounded hollow. ''No wonder he was angry with me this morning.'' She turned to Brian in earnest. ''Luckily, you are way ahead of me. I came over today to give you my analysis of your case and to tell you that I am withdrawing. I won't work with Roy any longer. I'm breaking up the partnership.''

As Keri looked away, a sense of desperation swept through her at the finality of her words.

''Have you told Roy?'' Brian asked.

''Not yet.'' Keri avoided his questioning eyes. ''I wanted to talk to you first.''

Brian jumped up. ''Do you have a bathing suit in your car?''

''No.'' Keri looked up into his mischievous face.

He grabbed her arms and pulled her from the chair. ''Come with me. My sister leaves her suits here and she is about your size.''

Brian led her into a bright, roomy bedroom. He motioned to a pale yellow chest with hand-painted blue flowers. ''Look through there. You'll find at least one that fits. I'll be on the patio.''

Speechless, Keri stood in the center of the bedroom. She couldn't let her fear overwhelm her. She had no proof that Brian was anywhere near her home on Friday night. Even if he had killed Emilia, he had no reason to kill her. With trembling hands, she searched the first two drawers before she found a suitable two-piece bathing suit in ice blue satin latex. She tossed the suit on the bed and began taking off her clothes.

Keri admired the soft yellow bedroom. Sheer embroidered panels hung in soft folds from the windows. Pastel paintings of seascapes and flowers and framed photographs had been carefully arranged on the walls. Keri studied the photographs. Brian and a beautiful woman smiled in happiness. The woman had to be his sister, the resemblance was unmistakable.

''Keri.'' Brian called. ''Did you find a bathing suit?''

"Yes." Keri finished putting on the suit and slipped out the French doors onto the patio. She spotted Brian near the spa carrying iced tea glasses. "We're going in the spa?"

"You need to relax. Afterwards, you can go swimming." Brian set down the glasses and walked over to the wet bar to retrieve the cordless telephone.

Keri paused at the top step of the spa testing the water. Satisfied that it wasn't too hot, she walked down the steps and gingerly sat down. She glanced up, to see Brian following her down the stairs. He settled down across from her and handed her a fresh glass of iced tea.

"You look lovely in that suit," he commented before he turned and reached for the controls. The spa turned into a pool of motion as air raced through the jets and immersed them in a sea of bubbles.

"This is wonderful!" Keri exclaimed. She could feel her tense body start to relax. Leaning her head back and resting it against the edge, she noticed Brian studying her intently through narrowed eyes. An odd sensation flooded her senses, something akin to fear. She felt as if her breath had been stolen from her. Brian grabbed her shoulders and pulled her forward. Keri gasped in shock and panic as Brian's hand went to the back of her neck.

"You forgot to take off your bow," he said, releasing her and proudly displaying it. "The chlorine water would ruin the silk. And are they expensive! I should know—I've bought enough replacements for my sister." Brian smiled and tossed the bow to safety.

Her face flushed with embarrassment as she mumbled a thank you. Silently, she scolded herself for panicking and reminded herself that Brian had never done anything to hurt or threaten her. Brian was busy drinking his tea and seemed oblivious to her maverick emotions. She leaned back again and rested her head. Although her body relaxed easily, her mind and emotions remained dangerously tense.

Brian set his tea on the coping and settled further into the water. "What kind of evidence am I going to be looking at this afternoon? It's better that I hear it from you. I don't need any surprises."

"Most of it you already know about. First, there's the comb that was found in the cabana bath. The hairs found in the teeth are being compared with samples from your hair. There's no report from the lab yet, so we don't know if there will be a match-up."

"Count on it matching."

Keri glanced at Brian with a puzzled look. "Why?"

"I kept a comb in my locker at the stadium. About four days before the murder, I missed the comb. I figured that I had dropped it somewhere in the locker area. Now it looks as if someone took it."

Keri sighed heavily. It was possible that he was telling the truth about being framed and she wanted to believe him. Without commenting she continued. "The second piece of evidence is the paper with Emilia's telephone number on it. The lab is analyzing the handwriting and the tear patterns. Nothing is back on that yet either."

"I'm sure it will match the tear pattern of the paper they found in my locker. Emilia had just changed the number to her cellular telephone the week before so that her lover couldn't call her. When she called me at the stadium one day, I scribbled it down. Right about the same time that I missed the comb, I noticed that the number, but not her name, had been torn off my pad. Even though I didn't remember tearing it off, I dismissed it as unimportant."

"So, you are very confident that the paper will be a match?"

"If my theory that someone is trying to frame me is correct, then it will be a match." Brian sat up and reached for his tea. "What else?"

"A neighbor saw your car in Emilia's driveway on the morning of the murder and was able to get a partial license number.

It's been matched to yours.'' Keri swallowed hard, the next one wouldn't be easy.

A disgusted look crossed Brian's face. ''She had a jealous neighbor. Anyway, it doesn't prove that I killed her.''

''None of it does, but taken together, it creates a presumption.'' Keri sat up straight. ''Brian, think carefully. Did you tell the police that you did not go to Emilia's house on the day of the murder?''

''No. They only asked if I was there on the afternoon of the murder. I'm sure of it.''

Keri picked up her tea. She sipped at it while trying to decide how to approach him. ''Brian, when do you wear your baseball cap?''

''During the games. Why?''

Brian's innocent look made Keri feel guilty, but she had to find out if he was telling the truth. ''Do you wear it on fishing trips?''

''No. Just during the ball games.''

Keri smiled and returned her glass to the coping. ''Did you ever wear it to Emilia and Pablo's home?''

''No. Never.'' A cold tone had crept into Brian's voice.

''Are you absolutely sure that you did not wear it to Emilia's house the day of the murder?'' Keri clenched her hands nervously beneath the surface of the water.

''I am absolutely sure. How many different ways are you going to ask me the same question? You sound just like the cops interrogating me.'' Anger flashed in his vivid blue eyes.

''I'm sorry, Brian. Did any of them ever ask you those questions?''

''No. Now tell me why you are asking me about my cap. The police confiscated it and I have a right to know why!''

''The police found a fishing lure on the patio the day of the murder. They are trying to match it to your cap.''

For a moment Brian sat in silence, stunned by Keri's news. He set his glass on the coping and ran his fingers through his hair. Sadness settled over them as they looked at each other in earnest.

"Things are looking really grim." Brian said in a whisper.

A knot rose in her throat as Keri summoned the courage to ask, "Did you have an affair with Emilia?"

"No," he responded hoarsely. "Never!"

Keri studied his face silently for what seemed to be minutes. A sense of strength and power flowed through to her, not the anger or guilt she had been expecting.

I can't give up on him, she thought. No one believes him. She picked up her tea again and began to sip it. "Did Emilia tell you anything unusual about the man she was afraid of? Anything at all?"

Brian sat back and thought for a moment, before shaking his head. "She called him a fish freak."

"A what?" Keri asked incredulously.

"A fish freak. I guess he likes fish." Brian laughed. "If that's the case, I guess I'm one, too. I love to fish and I love to eat fish."

"Did she ever call you a fish freak?"

"No."

"Then I doubt that she meant it the way you took it. I'll have to give that one some thought." Keri smiled to herself. Now she had a clue. A ridiculous clue! What in the world did she think that she could do with it?

"Remember anything else?"

"No. If I come up with anything else, I'll let you know."

"I'm withdrawing, remember?" Keri toyed with her glass before setting it back down. She glanced back in time to see Brian's disappointed face.

"Keri, what's the big problem between you and Roy?"

"He doesn't seem to be putting energy into building a solid defense for you. I mentioned what you told me about Lt. Rodriguez and he became incensed at the thought of trying to discredit him. He was more concerned about his ability to practice and his reputation after your trial is over with, than he was in finding out the truth.''

"I can understand his point of view, Keri. Especially since he believes that I am guilty.'' Brian commented quietly. "What else?''

"I believe that we need to talk to Donald Reid and Jesse Davis. They may have valuable information which would help us. Someone had to have a motive to kill her. We need to find out who. Roy won't try and has ordered me not to try. He keeps telling me to stop looking for a murderer and to defend the defendant.'' An angry tone filled her voice.

"Ask Tom Eaton to do it.'' Brian suggested.

"Tom's investigations have been worthless so far,'' Keri replied curtly. "I don't trust Roy's judgment. That's the major problem. I want to be sure that you have a competent attorney who cares about you.''

"I do!'' Brian smiled deeply into her eyes.

"What?'' Keri asked softly, afraid that she had misunderstood him.

"I have you,'' he said simply.

"Roy is really angry. I'm sure he intends to take me off the case.''

"Keri, if you are willing to fight for me, the only attorney removed from the case will be Roy. As long as he works, he can stay, otherwise, he's history.''

"I'm willing.'' Excitement gave her a warm glow of satisfaction. He respected her ability. Unbelievable!

"Come by tomorrow and we'll go over to the stadium together. We'll talk to D.R. and Jesse. Afterwards, you can watch the game in my friend's skybox.''

"Brian, there's something else . . .'' Caught in midsentence, Keri's voice froze. A wave of apprehension flowed through her. Mesmerized by a look of steel determination in his eyes, Keri stared in surprise as he reached out and grabbed her.

"It can wait!''

Chapter Sixteen

Brian pulled her gently to him and settled her halfway lying on his lap. As he bent over, his sensuous lips parted and claimed hers. Skillfully, he kissed her, breaking down her defenses. When Keri moaned, he trailed his kisses down her neck. Placing his arms beneath her, he shifted her body so that her shoulders and breasts broke the surface of the water. Holding her securely with one arm, he traced with his free hand the curve of her neck and slowly caressed down to her breast.

An undeniable sense of urgency exploded within Keri. She arched her back and pulled his head close to hers. Her full lips ached for his kiss. Seductively, his lips teased hers, tracing their soft fullness. Brian groaned as he heard the telephone ring. He reluctantly helped her up and reached for the cordless telephone next to the coping.

"Brian Michaels." He gave Keri a conspiratorial wink and continued.

"No, Roy, I haven't heard from her." He paused to listen. "Yes, that would be better for me."

Brian turned off the telephone and set it back on the coping. Brian turned to Keri. "It looks like you got a reprieve. Roy has an emergency to take care of this afternoon and wants me to come by now."

Keri watched him stand on the top step, allowing the excess water to drip off. He leaned over and offered her his hand. Keri stood up and climbed the stairs holding his hand. "What time shall I come by tomorrow?"

"Ten o'clock would be good. I'll get things set up this afternoon."

Their eyes met for one last moment, before Brian handed her a large fluffy towel. Disappointed, Keri wrapped the towel around herself and walked back to the bedroom. Peeling off her wet bathing suit, she walked to the adjoining bathroom to towel herself dry. What was she going to do? She had been powerless to resist him. Her body craved him and his tender touch, short-circuiting her natural defenses. She still had doubts about his innocence, but she intended to do her best to defend him.

Carefully, she hung the two-piece suit over the free-standing towel rack next to the sunken bathtub. Only then did she notice the men's toiletries on the vanity. Her inspection revealed a bottle of Paul Sebastian after-shave lotion. Color mounted her face as she realized with embarrassment that she had wandered into the wrong bedroom. This was the master bathroom!

Keri ran from the bathroom and grabbed her towel from the bed. She turned to see Brian standing at the open French doors with an amused expression on his face. Holding the towel tightly to her chest, she attempted to explain.

"I accidentally came into the wrong room!" Her heart pounded in her throat when she saw an invitation leap from the depths of his sparkling blue eyes.

"You've pushed your luck too far, Princess."

Keri gasped as he started toward her with a look of unveiled passion. Stepping back, her leg hit the bed. She realized there was no place to run. She was trapped, trapped by her own wild desires.

"No, Brian," she whispered.

Fear and need ran rampant through her. She watched as he stopped inches from her, forcing her to look up into his face. His eyes were deep blue pools of mystery, luring her into their depths, inviting her to taste him. *And she knew she wanted to.*

Brian held her face in his hands for a moment before lowering his mouth to hers. He kissed her again and again, demanding more and more from her. She gave more and more, helplessly caught in a tidal wave of desire. She knew she couldn't stop even if she had wanted to. Her body demanded satisfaction—nothing less would do.

With one hand he ripped the offending towel from her and pulled her hard against his wet body. Keri gasped with pleasure at the feel of his sensuous body pressed against hers. His arousal was unmistakable, his passion undeniable. *And she had no intention of denying him now.*

His arms found their way around her as he continued to kiss her with unrestrained desire. His hands caressed her back and her bottom. When he squeezed, Keri cried out in sheer pleasure. With wild abandon she rubbed her abdomen against him while she returned his passionate kisses.

Brian shifted his weight aggressively and forced her to fall back on the bed. He grabbed her legs behind her knees and forced her legs apart. Positioning himself between her legs, he leaned over her and raked her body with his smoldering eyes. Keri moaned. She was helpless and vulnerable and exposed, and she knew it. *That too excited her!*

"Brian . . ." Keri whispered his name as if calling out to a saint. She had lost almost all rational thought. All she wanted was Brian: Brian to kiss her, Brian to send her to the outer corners of the universe to satisfy her insatiable hunger for him. She quivered beneath his hot kisses. Somewhere, somehow, it registered that her breasts were being caressed and that wet, erotic kisses were traveling down her abdomen.

She felt his fingers exploring, stroking, evoking moans and groans of pleasure from her. She quivered and squirmed and lifted her hips from the bed. When was he going to satisfy her? She seemed forever to teeter on the edge of ecstasy, trembling and burning, waiting for oneness with him.

The wetness of his mouth seemed to engulf her, sending her to new heights of awareness. The moment that she grabbed at his hair, his tongue entered her. She screamed with passion and excitement, losing the last vestiges of control. She shivered and quaked and lost all sense of reality. She came, again and again, pulsating and throbbing, bringing her to tears of joy.

Exhaustion claimed her and she slept. When she woke, Brian had left. She found herself covered and tucked in beneath the coverlet of his bed. His note lay next to her, reassuring her: *Until tomorrow, my sleeping princess.*

Chapter Seventeen

The gold Lexus was a lot like Brian, Keri decided: refined strength and elegance. And very responsive, Keri added when Brian accelerated to pass a slower-moving car in the fast lane of the expressway. Amused at her simile, she began to smile, easing the tension building up within her. She looked down at her cream-colored raw silk slacks and her soft pink Polo shirt, hoping that she had made an appropriate choice. Nervously she swept back her long blond hair and secured it with two mother-of-pearl combs to keep it out of her way. Oh, stop worrying, she chided herself, they were only going to the stadium.

She looked at Brian. His pale aqua sport shirt fit loosely over his strong broad shoulders and narrowed slightly at the waist and hips. How he had managed to tuck the shirt into his snug jeans was beyond Keri's comprehension. Just taking in his lean body made her adrenaline flow. Never in her wildest dreams had she imagined she would meet a wonderful, sexy man who could take her to such ecstasy with his kisses.

''Brian, how did your meeting with Roy turn out yesterday?''

"Better than I anticipated." Brian stole a quick glance her way before turning his concentration back to his driving. "Roy was relaxed and friendly. He voiced the same opinion that you mentioned. He believes that no one can place me at the scene of the murder in the afternoon. He thinks the fact that I was over at Emilia's in the morning could work in my favor to discredit the physical evidence. You know—I dropped the paper in the morning, not the afternoon. I left my comb in the morning, not the afternoon. I must say, he is very convincing."

"How do you feel about that?" Keri asked in a defensive tone.

"I don't like it, but I won't be testifying. He can get up and argue all sorts of things to a jury if it will help." A hint of desperation crept into his voice. "What kind of defense do I have Keri? I've been framed. Even you don't believe me."

Keri felt like a traitor. Brian was right; she didn't believe him. Nobody did. Nobody but Matthew. How could she tell him about Matthew? The party last night had been fun and Matthew delightful. Only, she had been on pins and needles the whole evening worrying that Brian might show up and see them together. She had to tell Brian that he was working to help him. The rest could wait. After all, she hadn't made any commitments to Brian and he hadn't asked for any.

"I want to believe you, Brian. I want to help you." With a look of sadness, Keri studied her hands folded in her lap. "That's why I'm here."

"I know," he answered in a low, husky voice.

"Brian, do you know who Matthew West is?" Keri intertwined her fingers nervously, hoping that he wouldn't be angry with her for involving a reporter.

"Sure. He's an investigative reporter and a sports buff. I've talked with him a couple of times—he's a great guy. Very competent. Very ethical." For a brief moment Brian looked at Keri. "Why do you ask?"

"He approached me getting out of the elevator the morning

of your arraignment.'' Keri bit her lower lip, afraid to continue. ''He offered to help. He believes that you are innocent, adamant about it, in fact.''

''That's impressive! What did you do?''

''I took his card. His home telephone number was on the back.'' She hesitated, deciding how much to tell him. ''That night when Pablo attacked me—I was pretty upset. I was unhappy with Roy and I didn't have any confidence in Tom. I thought you needed more help than you were getting. I called him and asked him to help. I called him after you took me home.''

''Good girl.'' Brian looked pleased.

''You're not angry with me?'' Keri asked in a soft voice.

''Of course not. You did the right thing. Right now, I need all the help I can get. I'm not going to fry for something that I didn't do. Anytime that you want the three of us to meet, set it up. I'll be there.''

''Great.''

''Does Roy know?''

Keri shook her head and then realized he couldn't watch her and the road, too. ''No. I've kept him from finding out. Whenever I mention the information that Matthew gave me, he flies into a rage. Pretty much what I told you yesterday.''

''Interesting.'' For a moment Brian appeared deep in thought. ''I can't say that I like Roy much, but he is supposed to be an excellent criminal attorney. So far, I'm not impressed. I will probably have to ride him to keep him moving on the case. Unfortunately, given the facts of my case, I'm not convinced that I would fare any better with another attorney.''

''Did Roy ask you about me?''

''Not a word.''

Keri settled deeper into her seat and moved her legs to get more comfortable. Roy was an enigma. When the partnership began, he seemed uncomplicated and straight forward. After three years, she felt like he was a stranger. ''I have found Roy to be very vindictive. If he doesn't attempt to throw me off the case, he will find some other way to punish me for telling you.''

''Let me know if he tries.'' A warning tone filled his voice.

''Are you sure you don't want to hire another attorney? There are other high profile attorneys in the area.''

''Not unless circumstances force me to. I have my reasons for wanting to wait.'' Brian's hands tightened on the wheel. ''There was something else that I missed from my locker that no one has mentioned yet.''

''What?''

''An old bottle of after-shave lotion that Pablo gave me. I never liked it, so I never used it. I was going to throw it away, but it disappeared on its own. I thought maybe Pablo borrowed it, since he used it all the time.''

''Pablo uses Turbulence?'' Keri stared at him in astonishment.

''You knew?'' Brian asked, as he gave Keri a troubled look. ''What's going on? How could you know?''

''The evening that I met you, Roy told me the police had a bottle of Turbulence with your fingerprints on it. They found it in the cabana bath.'' ''I saw the bottle in the pictures the prosecutor sent over, but it wasn't on their list of evidence.''

''What did Roy have to say about that?'' Brian slowed the car and turned onto the off ramp.

''He said that the police probably couldn't get a clear enough print. He dropped it, unconcerned.'' Keri shrugged. Roy couldn't have cared less.

Brian flipped on his turn signal and turned onto a street leading to the stadium. ''I would like to know how he knew about the bottle in the first place.''

''From someone in the homicide department. He has his sneaks. He has gotten information ahead of time on more than one occasion.'' Keri cringed at her own words. Why hadn't these little quirks of Roy's bothered her before?

Brian pulled into a special area designated for the players and parked the Lexus. ''Forget Roy. We have more important work ahead of us. When we get to the locker room, I'll show you around. You can give me your opinion of the area.'' His eyes, alive with controlled passion, sought her out.

Keri's breath caught when she saw the expression of desire smoldering in his eyes. She watched, mesmerized, while he flipped off his seat belt and reached for hers. Skillful fingers released her belt before he pulled her close to him. Gently and slowly his mouth closed over hers and kissed her deeply.

With a sigh of resignation, he broke the kiss, lifted her hand to his lips and kissed her palm before smiling at her with a look of an apology. ''We have to go. This place is much too public for what we want.''

Keri smiled back. She could wait until there were no prying eyes to see them.

Chapter Eighteen

Judging from the layout, it would have been easy for anyone to come into the locker room unobserved, Keri decided. She looked around the huge locker room several times. Lockers ran parallel to the front and back wall with benches in between. A narrow walkway ran down one side of the room and led past the rows of lockers to the showers and first aid area where she smelled soap and the antiseptic odor of the cleaners used to keep the room well scrubbed.

There was only one way in and one way out. However, the door was not clearly visible from most areas of the locker room. For a long time, Keri stood staring at the entrance. Brian was right. Anyone could have come in here. His story was not so incredible after all. She retraced her steps back to his locker. It afforded more privacy than many of the others. Someone could hide in the corner between the locker and the wall for a short time, if they had to. She became angry with herself that she hadn't done her job fully. She should have come before now and checked everything out.

"Brian, in my opinion, it would be extremely easy for anyone to come in here and not be observed. The fact is, though, it wasn't just anyone. It had to have been someone who knows both you and Emilia."

Brian looked at her determined face in surprise. "Are you actually beginning to believe me?"

As their eyes met, Keri's mood turned buoyant. "Brian, when did you notice that your locker had been broken into?"

"I didn't. There was no forced entry. The entry had to have been done while I was around. We all get a little careless about locking up when we're at the stadium all day."

"Leave Emilia out of this question. Is there anyone you know who doesn't like you or has a grudge against you?"

"Sure, there are team members that don't particularly like me. I haven't had any arguments or fights with anybody though. As far as grudges go, I'm not aware of any."

"Jealousy creates and sustains grudges."

"True, but I'm not aware of any jealousy." Brian walked over to her and caressed her shoulders with his hands. "What else?"

"That leaves us back where we started. Who had a motive to kill Emilia? Maybe you were just someone convenient to pin it on."

"I have already come to that conclusion, Keri." Brian pulled her to him and brushed his lips against hers before lifting her off the floor and laying her on the bench in front of his locker. Keri looked up in surprise as he swung his leg over and straddled both her and the bench.

"You're driving me crazy, Keri," he breathed.

Erotic thoughts flashed through her mind while her breath became heavy. Aching with desire for him, she lost her sense of time and space. Her hands found their way slowly up his steel thighs. His eyes darkened with desire, as she pulled herself up against him to press her parted mouth against the bulge beneath his zipper. His strong hands eased her back down on the bench before he loosened his belt, but her fingers fumbled with his zipper and freed him.

"I swear you delight in tormenting me!" Brian's voice was low and husky.

He pulled her shirt out from her pants and pushed it up, then unhooked her bra and pushed it aside. He caressed her breasts with skilled movements that made her cry out. Keri could only moan helplessly when he leaned over and sucked each breast in turn. No one had ever made her feel so alive, so vital, so passionate.

Filled with impatience, she squirmed loose and caught him with her hands. She pulled him to her gently; she wanted to taste him, to feel her mouth on him. Her tongue teased him and her teeth nipped at him, forcing him to become her willing slave. She consumed him with her erotic kisses, until his heightened desire forced him over the edge. In fierce labored silence, he found release.

Keri groaned softly when he lowered his body on top of her and pinned her down. Tired as he was, he kissed her breast. Her nails dug into his back as her body, aching to accept him, arched upward. He lifted himself enough to loosen her slacks and pull her pants down past her hips.

"We need a bed," he muttered.

"I don't care," she whispered while he gently parted her legs.

Sitting up and straddling her, he gently stroked her. She realized that she was trapped and couldn't move. She could only lie back and allow him to caress her intimately until her body, begging for the feel of him could stand no more. She cried out as his fingers teased and explored until she thought surely she would go out of her mind. Then, when she was beyond thought, her body exploded, sending spasms through her, releasing her from her torment.

A smile crossed her lips as she caught him watching her intently. She closed her eyes and felt Brian lift himself off. She listened to the rustle of clothing while he straightened his shirt and pants, then with a little moan she sat up and began to dress. What in the world had possessed them? Anyone could have come in that open door. As she straightened her mussed hair, Brian leaned over and kissed her neck. Keri pulled away and whispered. "I heard a noise outside."

They quickly made their way to the shaded entrance where a figure stood in the shadows. "Who's there? Keri called out.

"Hey, Keri, Brian. Good to see you." With a big smile, Jesse Davis stepped through the doorway into the locker room. "Sorry I'm late. I wasn't sure you were in here."

"Good to see you, too." Brian shook his hand. "Why don't we sit outside in the bleachers?"

"Yeah. It's a beautiful morning. The breeze has picked up, so it won't be too hot." Jesse led the way to a nearby bleacher in the shade.

Experience told Keri to position herself in the middle of the two men to keep from being shut out of the conversation. When Jesse straightened his shirt before sitting down, Keri maneuvered herself between them and sat down.

"Jesse," Keri began, "I really appreciate you taking the time out to talk with us." She hoped he wouldn't be able to tell they had just made love.

Jesse settled down beside her. "No problem ma'am. Brian here is my friend."

Keri smiled at his simple statement. "Do you know of anyone who is out to get Brian?"

"No. Can't say that I do. Everybody on the team respects him." Jesse tilted the visor of his baseball cap back and glanced at Brian.

Brian studied Jesse's face thoughtfully. "What about Emilia? Did she have any enemies?"

"Oh, yeah!" Jesse leaned slightly toward Brian. "She was a tease. You know. She was getting restless and was looking to replace Pablo. I reckon some of the jocks didn't like rejection."

"You mentioned that she dumped you for a cop?" Brian tried to sound casual.

"Yeah. Some big guy. Older. Guess he was willing to spend some bucks on her." He gave Keri a wink. "She liked to spend money, lots of it. She was too much like my wife. They were friends, you know, her and Janet."

"Do you know the cop's name?" Brian asked.

"No. But I sure saw him around. He was at a lot of our parties, hanging around Emilia while Pablo was off gabbing or the like."

"Would you recognize him if I could show you a picture?" Keri asked.

"Yeah. No problem."

"You said Emilia liked to spend money?" Keri was curious. Money was always suspect when it came to crime.

"Emilia was looking for a big spender, and that sure ain't me. Just ask Janet. I know she spends more than I give her." He laughed and adjusted his cap again. "Sometimes I think she's got a job, 'cause I sure don't know where she has been coming up with the money lately." Jesse uncrossed his legs in an effort to get more comfortable on the hard bench. "Janet always manages. Emilia didn't. She was always asking me for money. Her spending caused her big problems with Pablo."

"They fought over money?" Brian asked.

"All the time. Last I heard she wanted a pond in the back yard with these big Chinese goldfish. Pablo was screaming about it."

"That's not unusual for South Florida, Jesse." Keri commented.

"I know, but it was something different every week. Pablo was constantly complaining about all the money she spent."

Keri turned to Brian. "Did you know all this?"

"No. I stay to myself. The guys don't confide in me like they do Jesse. He knows everything about everybody." He flashed Jesse a smile.

"Jesse, would you mind telling me where you were on the morning of the murder?" Keri kept her tone light. She didn't want to offend him.

"I was right here at the stadium. As a matter of fact, I was here all day."

"Did you see Brian?"

"Yeah. He was here. I saw him and Pablo go into the locker room, but I didn't hear anything."

"Did you notice anything strange? Did you notice anyone near Brian's locker?"

"Can't say that I saw anything strange. As for the lockers, I don't remember seeing anyone near his locker when I was around."

"How about a few days before? Did you see anyone that didn't belong, or anyone near his locker?"

"Nope."

Keri bit her lower lip in frustration. They weren't getting anywhere with him. She turned and looked at Brian with a silent plea. What did she need to ask Jesse? What was she missing?

Brian leaned toward Jesse. "Has Pablo mentioned that Emilia's wedding rings were missing? The pictures of the body show she wasn't wearing any."

"He never said a word, but I'll find out for you." He looked earnestly at Brian before speaking. "Brian, Pablo was no angel. When we had out-of-town games, he was always looking for company. He wanted out of the marriage. He's told me that himself. I sure don't know why he's so angry with you."

"He thinks that I killed Emilia."

For a moment no one spoke, then Keri asked, "Jesse, what kind of car do you drive?"

"Me? A black Oldsmobile." Jesse stood up and stretched. "I've gotta meet with Coach Greaton. If you need me for anything else, just give me a call."

Brian stood up. "Thanks Jesse. See you later."

"Bye, Jesse." Keri smiled as Jesse waved good-bye.

Brian stood quietly next to her, hands on hips, staring down intently at Keri. She leaned back, to gaze into his bright blue eyes. She was startled by the look of disappointment and pain that she found there. She rose and gently touched him.

"Brian?"

"We didn't find out much, did we?" His voice was rough with suppressed anxiety.

"Everything will fall into place, Brian. It always does." Keri tried to reassure him. How could she promise him everything would work out when she was not certain it would? Something had to happen. There had to be a decent clue somewhere.

"Okay, Princess. Let's take a walk over to the skybox. I told D.R. to meet us there." Brian forced a cheerful smile as they began to walk.

"How did you come by a skybox?

"Jordan McDaniel. We went to college together and then he came to Miami to start a business."

"I could sure use a soda right now." Keri pulled out the combs and let the breeze flow through her hair. "It's hot!"

"If you think that it's hot here, you should try Fort Worth in the summertime."

"Fort Worth?"

"Dallas/Fort Worth. We're going to be flying out to Arlington to play the Texas Rangers soon."

"Sounds like fun."

"It will be." Brian smiled mischievously and led her into the building. At the elevator he turned to her and teased, "What you need is a vacation."

"I know. I've been wanting one. I just can't figure out where to go." Keri said.

"Maybe I can help." Brian chuckled and held the elevator door for Keri. "People are already starting to fill the stadium for the game. We had better get this over with fast."

Chapter Nineteen

Ice rattled noisily inside the glasses as Brian dropped the cubes in. He popped open the sodas and poured. Nothing like a little healthy jealousy to prep him up before a game, he thought sarcastically. His gaze was glued to D.R., who was busily appraising Keri with lust in his eyes. He watched as Keri's animated face lit up with a smile at one of D.R.'s jokes. He'd never figured out what women saw in the man.

"D.R., here's the sodas." Brian called.

With an arrogant stride, D.R. walked over to pick them up from the wet bar. "What's up, Brian?"

Brian picked up his drink and walked over to a chair next to Keri as D.R. handed her a soda. "We wanted to talk to you about the murder. We thought you might know something without realizing it."

"Shoot." D.R. pulled a chair around to face them and sat, straddling it.

"Does Brian have any enemies on the team?" Keri asked.

"Not one. They all like him, or, if they don't, they don't say anything."

"How about Emilia?" Brian set his soda down and stretched out his legs.

"She was a flirt, but I don't think she had any real enemies, not on the team."

"Did you know she was having problems with Pablo?" Brian watched his face hoping to catch any change in his expression.

"No. Pablo and I stay away from each other. I think he knew that Emilia flirted with me for a while." He looked at Keri. "I'd be the last one Pablo would confide in."

Keri thought for a minute. He seemed to know less than Jesse. Maybe he had seen something. "Did you see anyone around the locker room who didn't belong there on the day of the murder?"

"No. No one."

"How about a few days before the murder?" Keri looked at Brian sadly. This was hopeless.

D.R. put his hands on his thighs and thought. "Yeah. I did. I saw this guy leave the locker room a couple of days before the murder. I figured he was just a fan trying to find somebody."

Brian sat up. "Do you remember what he looked like?"

"I never saw his face. I really didn't pay too much attention to him." D.R. gazed at Brian sheepishly. "Sorry, Brian."

"How did you happen to remember him?"

"He had on a Dodgers cap and we weren't playing the Dodgers that day." He nodded to Keri. "What are you two up to?"

"Someone went into Brian's locker. We're trying to find out who it was."

"Security is real loose. Anyone could have gone in." He shook his head slowly. "That's going to be a tough one."

"We know."

Keri stared off into space as Brian questioned D.R. further.

She half heard the questions and knew the answers by heart. All they had was a man wearing a Dodgers baseball cap who liked fish and had a bad temper. If it wasn't so tragic, she would be laughing.

"D.R., what kind of car do you drive?" Keri asked.

"None." He laughed and turned to Keri. "I drive a little red pickup truck. Want to go on a date with me?"

Keri laughed. "Not until after this case is over, thank you." Keri shot a glance at Brian to see if he was jealous. Keri couldn't tell. "Thanks for talking with us D.R."

"Yes, D.R., thanks." Brian jumped up from his chair, now anxious to get rid of him.

"Anytime. Sorry that I wasn't more help."

Keri studied her hands until she heard the door close. Looking up, she found Brian watching her with a mischievous look in his eyes.

"There's a couch. Want to try again?"

"Brian, you're incorrigible," Keri protested.

Brian laughed. "Nothing ventured . . ."

"Forget it, sailor!"

Jordan McDaniel smiled warmly at Keri who stood at the window watching the crowds gather for the game. Keri had liked him from the minute he and his friends walked into the skybox. One glance and she knew he was the leader. He was tall and solid with a rugged handsomeness. He had welcomed her with a sincerity and friendliness that surprised her. Was it because he thought she was Brian's girlfriend? Whatever the reason, he had readily accepted her into his circle of friends.

Keri watched as Jordan and Brian walked over to join her by the window.

"Keri, I have to go. We've got a game to play. When the game is over, go with Jordan. I'll catch up with everybody later."

"Okay." Keri smiled at Brian.

Brian glanced at Jordan and winked. "Jordan, take care of Keri for me."

"Glad to do it!"

Brian grabbed her by the shoulders, pulled her to him, and lightly kissed her sweet full lips. Keri glowed with happiness.

"Wish me luck!"

"Good luck." Her voice, soft and warm floated after him.

Jordan motioned to an easy chair near him. Keri settled herself in its deep plush cushion, then leaned back to watch the game.

"Keri," Jordan leaned toward her. "I'm throwing a victory celebration tonight at the Seventh Inning Club. You'll be coming with us."

"You're that sure they are going to win?"

"Absolutely sure! I'll drop you off at your house to change. You'll need to be ready about seven-thirty. We're having a buffet dinner."

"Great! I'll be ready."

Much to Keri's surprise, she found the game exciting. She watched in awe as Brian came up to the plate. With a crack of the bat, he sent the ball flying out of the stadium. The team went wild! They skipped and danced and walked on their hands around the bases. What a show! Keri could hardly contain her excitement. No wonder everyone loved Brian!

Chapter Twenty

The black limousine pulled up to the entrance of the Seventh Inning Club. The chauffeur climbed out and with the help of the valets, opened the doors for Jordan and his friends to climb out. Jordan reached back in and grabbed Keri's hand to help her out.

With an agile movement, Keri emerged dressed in a red satin cocktail dress with a sweetheart neckline and puffed sleeves trimmed in iridescent beading. Jordan openly admired her trim body and long legs.

"You look even more beautiful tonight than you did this afternoon. Brian is a very lucky man."

Keri chuckled at his assessment. "Thank you, kind sir."

They turned and walked slowly into the club, talking and laughing, unaware of covetous glances from others. Before she had a chance to look for Brian, Jordan maneuvered her to the dance floor.

"I won't have time for another dance tonight. I have to play host all evening." Jordan explained with a warm smile.

"It looks like it will be a good party, Jordan. Look at the turnout." Keri's eyes covered the crowded dance floor with amazement. How many did he invite?

"Most of the invited guests haven't come yet." Jordan remarked, practically reading her mind. "It might pay you to eat early before all the favorite foods run out.

She laughed lightly. She doubted that a man of his stature would allow any of the food to run out. If it did, somebody's head would roll. She was sure of that.

"Thanks for the tip. Do you think that Brian is here yet?"

"No chance. He would have found you already and staked his claim." Jordan laughed as the dance came to an end. He turned to the tap on his shoulder.

"Willing to give the pretty lady up?" D.R.'s eyes undressed her.

Keri watched Jordan's expression change from enjoyment to displeasure before he answered. "Keri, I'll send Brian over." He nodded quickly to D.R. and crossed the dance floor.

"What's eating him?" D.R. asked as he grabbed Keri and pulled her close to dance.

She stumbled and withdrew a short distance from him. "I really don't think anything is bothering him. He has to host the party all night and I suspect he is in a hurry to get started instead of entertaining me."

"I doubt that." D.R. responded in a sarcastic tone. "I'll be glad to entertain you. How would you like to leave the party and find something more exciting?" His hand slipped down to the cheek of her bottom and pulled her close.

"Get your hand off me," Keri demanded. She struggled to free herself from his grasp.

"You don't know what you're missing. I can show you a real good time." His voice dripped with suggestion. "Besides, dressed like that, you are asking for it."

"No thanks." Keri answered coldly. She feverishly hoped

the dance would soon be over. To her relief, D.R. pushed her away with an insulted look and walked away.

Left alone on the dance floor, Keri decided the best move would be to take Jordan's advice and find the buffet. She made her way off the crowded dance floor and wandered around the club for a few minutes before realizing the buffet was in the sunroom. Smiling to herself, she headed for the buffet.

Everything looks wonderful, she thought, as she piled her plate high with expensive hors d'oeuvres. The only thing missing was Brian. She found a small table in a corner beneath the curve of the glass roof and sat down to eat. The waiter walked by with a silver coffee decanter and poured her coffee. The party was truly elegant and well planned. She must remember to send Jordan a thank-you note for inviting her.

"Ready for the main course?"

"Brian!" A welcoming smile crossed Keri's face and her eyes brightened with pleasure. He held two plates with thinly carved roast beef, potato puffs and French-style green beans with almonds.

"I hope you like my choices." He set a plate down in front of her. "There's plenty more if you don't."

"I see you are definitely a meat-and-potatoes man," Keri observed with a hint of amusement in her voice.

"Getting to know all my secrets, are you?" He looked up from his plate, his eyes filled with happiness.

"Hardly!" Keri sampled a potato puff which promptly melted in her mouth. "This is delicious," she moaned.

"I know. Whenever Jordan throws a party, it's first class all the way."

"That was a great game you played Brian. I was very impressed, only—" Keri's voice faded off.

"Only what?" Brian demanded anxiously.

"Only, I didn't know that you could do back flips!" Keri's serious face turned to delight as she chuckled.

"Very funny, Princess." Brian motioned for the waiter to

bring coffee and turned back to Keri. "Have you seen anyone that you know tonight?"

"Just Jordan's friends from the skybox and D.R." Keri sighed. "I'm afraid that I insulted D.R. tonight."

"How?"

"He wanted me to leave with him so that he could show me a good time. He told me that I didn't know what I was missing. I turned him down and he left me standing on the dance floor." Keri laughed.

Anger hardened Brian's features as a blush crept up his neck. "I'll beat that little runt to a pulp!"

"Calm down. I didn't tell you that to make you angry. It really is comical. Forget it, Brian. There wasn't any harm done."

"He's not going to talk to you that way and get away with it!" Brian rose from his chair and caught Keri's hand. "Come on. It's time for a dance."

She followed him to the dance floor. The music was intoxicating as they swayed together gently.

"Come with me, Keri, when I go to Dallas to play the Texas Rangers." His seductive voice coaxed her gently.

"Brian, I can't. I have a case to work on. Besides, it's too soon for us. I'm your attorney. We have to maintain a professional relationship." Keri tried to make her voice sound firm.

Brian lowered his lips to hers and kissed her, leaving her mouth anxious for more. "This is professional?"

Brian's hands caressed her shoulders and coaxed her again. "You have to come. I've already reserved a table in your name at the Front Row Sports Grill at the stadium. You'll have a tremendous view overlooking right field."

"You certainly were sure of me." Keri whispered softly.

"No, but it's the best seat in the restaurant. You can sit right in front of a big picture window and eat, drink, and enjoy the game. You can even color in the cartoon characters on the table covers!"

"Are you crazy?"

"Yes." Brian captured her eyes with his passionate gaze.

Keri's body ached with desire for him. It sounded like so much fun, like today. She knew she couldn't go. He was her client and possibly a murderer. She just couldn't let herself be lulled into a false sense of security. Not now.

"No way!" Keri laughed. "I have work to do."

"Fine. I'm keeping the reservations just in case you decide at the last minute to drop in unannounced."

"Never!" Keri smiled and looked away. When she glanced back, his attention was on someone in the distance. Her eyes followed his gaze, coming to rest on Roy Foxx talking with some of the ball players.

"They don't care who they let in, do they?"

"No." Keri answered. "I guess not. Hector Rodriguez is here, too."

Brian brushed Keri's forehead with his lips and led her to a table away from the dance floor. "I have to make a call. Order a drink when the waiter comes by."

Keri watched Brian walk away toward the bank of telephones. D.R. approached him before he was able to make his call. They spoke for a moment and walked off together into the crowd.

"Hello, beautiful." A strong husky voice called out to her.

"Matthew!" Keri smiled with pleasure as he walked over to her table. Darn, he looked handsome.

"Dance with me?"

Keri nodded and led the way to the dance floor. After making her way to the center, she turned and stepped into his waiting arms. Hopefully, Brian wouldn't see her this far into the crowd. "Working tonight?"

"Absolutely. The parties are the perks of the job." His admiring eyes swept over her quickly. "And you are definitely in the perk category."

Keri laughed. Matthew always made her feel good about

herself. "I'll bet there's lots of women here drooling over you," she offered.

"Maybe one or two." He winked.

They both laughed. Out of the corner of her eye she saw Brian watching her. What was she going to say to him? She felt uneasy knowing that she was being observed. She turned to look at him, but he wasn't there. Maybe seeing him had been her imagination. With a sigh, she tried to focus on her conversation with Matthew, but her heart wasn't in it. When the dance was over, Matthew escorted her back to the table. Luckily he hadn't noticed her change of mood.

"How's Brian doing?" Matthew asked in a low voice.

"He has been in good spirits, considering the problems he is having," she replied while she adjusted her sleeves. Matthew was such a dear. He always expressed his concern.

"Going back to work has probably helped considerably, not to mention winning tonight's game."

"It may not last, the Yankees are hard to beat," Keri answered.

Matthew looked at her intently for a moment then gently placed his hand over hers. "Keri," he hesitated before continuing in an apologetic tone. "I'm leaving Thursday for Dallas to see the games and relax a little. I'll try to do all that I can on the case while I'm there."

"I know that you are doing everything you can for Brian." Keri leaned forward and patted his hand reassuringly. "Don't worry. Just enjoy yourself and get the job done."

"It's a rough job." Matthew laughed and looked past her into the crowd. "I thought that I saw Brian coming this way, but I must have been mistaken."

Matthew rose from the chair and bent to kiss Keri lightly on her forehead. "You'll hear from me before I leave."

Keri looked up and smiled. "Okay. See you later."

Keri watched as he walked off. After she lost sight of him, she turned to motion to the waiter. She gave her order for a cocktail, propped her head in her hand, and gazed curiously around the room. With the thought of Matthew being out of town, the familiar feelings of fear surfaced to haunt her. Someone in this club was a murderer. She was sure of it. Had that same someone tried to run her down? Was it her imagination? Could it have been just a reckless driver? The only answer that came was disconcerting: If the murderer had tried to kill her once, he would try again.

Chapter Twenty-One

Light flashed as a school of pearl gourami navigated through the water to feed near the bubbles pushing up from the floor of the aquarium. The sound of bubbles hitting the surface accentuated the silence of Roy's office. Deep in her own private thoughts, Keri stared unseeingly at the tiny world beneath the surface of the water.

Tomorrow it would be three weeks since the incident in the parking garage. Keri was no closer to the driver's identity than she had been that night. She still was unwilling to tell Roy, Brian or the police because she couldn't overcome her doubts about the deliberateness of the driver's actions. Now she regretted that she had not confided in Matthew. He was always so rational and objective. His personality seemed to have such a stabilizing effect on hers. The fact that he would be gone was disturbing. She needed his friendship more than she had realized.

Keri shifted in her seat and glanced across the table to Roy. She felt her mood turn to anger as she watched Roy and Lt.

Rodriguez going over a list of evidence and making notes. Secretly, she suspected that Roy had taken great pleasure in overruling her decision not to allow Rodriguez to question Brian again. She could feel Brian's tension mounting while he waited quietly next to her.

Roy was always cool and calm, but today he seemed apathetic. It matched his unkempt appearance. Roy had offered no resistance to any of the lieutenant's questions, nor had he instructed Brian not to answer. What was he thinking? Keri was getting tired and she knew Brian was. Did Roy think that Rodriguez was going to give up? It was clear that the lieutenant's only purpose was to try to push Brian into changing his story. If Roy didn't put a stop to his harassment of Brian soon, she would. She found Rodriguez and his crude, obnoxious behavior very offensive and she was having a hard time concealing her repulsion.

"Keri," Jenna called from the doorway. "You have a call from Janet Davis."

Keri glanced up, reached across the table, and picked up the telephone.

"Keri Adams speaking." What could Janet Davis want? She listened intently as the woman, asked her to meet her.

"Yes. Of course. Yes, five-thirty would be fine. No. It's not out of the way. I can stop by on my way home."

Keri reached for her pad and jotted down Janet's address. "Good. See you then." Keri replaced the receiver and turned to Rodriguez.

"You need to finish, Lieutenant. Mr. Michaels has other appointments."

Rodriguez gave her an insolent look before taking up where he had left off. "What time did you get up on the day of the murder?"

"You've asked me that five times today."

"So?"

"So, I'm not answering any more questions." Brian said through gritted teeth.

Rodriguez scowled at him. "We'll end this session when I say so, you loudmouthed jock. All I've heard from your mouth are lies!"

Brian jumped from his seat. Keri grabbed his arm in warning.

"That is quite enough, Lieutenant. You are harassing Mr. Michaels. This meeting is over." Keri turned to Roy for support, but one look told her not to expect it.

For a moment Rodriguez stared at Brian, obviously caught off guard. Regaining his composure, he puffed up his chest and straightened his tie. With a menacing look he leaned forward. "Go ahead and grab me, jock, so I can throw you back in the slammer!"

"I said, get out!" Scorn filled Keri's voice as she stood up.

Slowly, the lieutenant raised himself out of the chair and reached for his jacket. As he made his way around the table, his gaze fixed on Keri. "That's the trouble with women. They have no objectivity."

Rodriguez shook his head and smiled viciously. "The jock has you suckered, Baby! He's romancing you the same way he did Emilia Martinez."

Keri could feel Brian's arm tense as his hands closed into fists. "Get off it, Lieutenant." Brian's voice held a clear warning tone.

"We've been following you, jock. You're good. I'll have to admit it!"

"Get out before I throw you out!" Brian demanded.

"Careful who you threaten, jock!" Rodriguez struggled into his jacket as he glared at Brian.

Keri knew she had to stop this fight. That's what Rodriguez wanted. He was deliberately baiting Brian. Worse yet, Roy was letting him get away with it.

"Brian, please," Keri pleaded. "Please go." She tightened her grip on his arm. "Please, don't start a fight."

Their eyes met, and in that silence Brian made his decision. Without a word, he nodded to her and walked out the door.

Keri spun around and confronted Rodriguez. "I've had quite enough. I don't approve of your crude display of police tactics. Don't bother asking for any more time with Mr. Michaels because you won't get any!"

She crossed to Roy's desk and picked up the telephone. "Jenna, please show Lt. Rodriguez out. He is leaving now." Keri hung up the telephone and raised her chin defiantly while she watched his cold calculating expression.

With an unconscious smirk, Rodriguez walked to the door. He turned. His eyes, black with anger, raked her. He didn't miss a detail, from her navy blue double breasted jacket to her oyster-colored blouse and skirt. Even her navy pumps didn't miss his scrutiny. Slowly his eyes inched up her lithe body to her face. Finally, after a moment, he gave Keri an odd look. "Be careful, Ms. Adams, or you may end up like Emilia Martinez."

"Is that a threat, Lieutenant?" Chills crept up her spine and splayed out in all directions. This man was deadly serious.

Rodriguez ignored the question and turned to follow Jenna out of the office.

Still shaking with anger, Keri turned to Roy. "Why do you want your client to go back to jail?"

The question hung in the silence of the office. Keri stood in the center of the room, hands on hips, glaring angrily at Roy. She intended to get answers. His erratic and unpredictable behavior was totally unacceptable.

Roy rose from his chair and walked casually over to the aquarium. "I'm worried about you, Keri. You're letting your imagination get out of hand," he laughed.

"That's just not good enough, Roy!" Keri watched him with an incredulous expression. How like him to shift the blame to her.

"After his violent display today, there shouldn't be any doubt in your mind that he is guilty."

"Well, there is!" she said indignantly.

"Keri, he got violent over words. You saw how he looked. You don't go beating up people or killing people over words."

"That's a sorry excuse for not defending your client today." Keri fumed.

"He killed once, he will kill again." Roy's voice was filled with conviction. "Unfortunately, Rodriguez was right this time. You could end up just like Emilia."

"How can you say that?" Keri felt uneasy. How could he be so sure Brian was the killer?

"Temper, Keri. His temper," Roy answered confidently.

"Roy, *I* have a temper."

"Yes. But you use your head. You don't go around beating up people because they make you angry." He walked back to the table and began picking up his papers.

"There are times that I would like to!" Like right now, Keri thought.

"But you don't." His voice hardened.

Could Roy actually be concerned about her safety? Not likely, she thought. "Roy, regardless of how you feel about Brian, you should have stood up for him today. You let Rodriguez harass and insult your client. I've never seen you do that before."

"If you remember, *you* have been handling his defense, so I left it up to you. Poor job, I might add." Roy smiled vindictively.

"What?" That comment threw her off guard.

"You allowed Rodriguez to make a circus out of today's conference. You're a lousy lawyer, Keri!"

Stunned by his words, Keri struggled to make her thoughts coherent. "I thought when you got this case that you would work hard to clear Brian. I was wrong. From the very beginning you have failed to investigate, ignored the importance of the prosecutor's evidence, and have thwarted my efforts to develop a good defense. You are not even trying to defend Brian."

Keri watched his expression change from mockery to anger. Cold deliberate anger. But there was something more in his eyes. A wave of apprehension swept through her as she tried to understand its meaning.

Roy walked toward her. "I've told you before, lay off the police. I want to continue practicing law in this town."

"I don't understand you," she said in a deceptively calm voice. "This is Murder One. No one would fault you for defending him with zeal."

"I keep telling you the evidence is on our side." Roy stood a few feet from her, studying her face.

"I keep telling you that I don't agree." Keri stayed calm, refusing to let him read her conflicting emotions.

"The lieutenant is right. You are not being objective, Keri." His patronizing tone was like a slap in the face. "You have allowed yourself to become emotionally involved with a criminal."

"He's *not* a criminal!" she denied.

"Face it, Keri. Brian is guilty. Guilty as sin. Your judgment is impaired. I'm not sure now that you should be working on the case."

"You can't throw me off the case. Brian wants me on it." Keri straightened her shoulders and met his harsh angry gaze.

"Then stick to the defense as I have determined and stop grabbing at straws." A warning edged his voice.

"That's just the point, Roy, I don't know what your defense *is*. Is it lie down and die and argue a little to the jury? Or, maybe it's the 'well someone else did it, we don't know who and we didn't try to find out, but please believe us' routine?"

Roy looked at her in disbelief. "Can you really be so stupid? Haven't you understood anything I've said to you?"

Speechless, Keri could only look at Roy. She could see that his anger was mounting rapidly.

"What do I have to do to get through to you before I lose my temper?" Pale and deliberate, Roy tried again. "Keri, all we have to establish is reasonable doubt. Don't go making a big thing out of this. We have enough evidence for reasonable doubt.''

''I don't believe that he killed Emilia Martinez. I have to prove that he didn't. I have to know the real facts.''

''Stop trying to solve a murder that has already been solved. We'll get him off. What you're trying to do is personal. As his attorney you only have to prove reasonable doubt, not innocence. You know that. My patience with you has reached its limit. Back off and follow my lead. It is the only way.''

''God, Roy! Where's your integrity?''

Hot with rage, he grabbed her arm and pulled her toward him. ''Don't push me, Keri!''

''Roy,'' Keri screamed, ''you're hurting me.''

Roy dropped her arm. ''Back off, Keri,'' he demanded furiously, his gaze wild and menacing. ''Get out from under Michaels and get back to the business of practicing law. Now, get out of my office!''

Shocked by his hostile behavior, Keri grabbed her notes and walked out, careful not to look back. She walked down the hall to her office wondering what had just happened. Something was wrong. Was she championing a murderer? How could Roy be so sure that Brian had killed Emilia?

Emotions in turmoil, she sat at her desk and turned to the window. It wasn't just Roy and Rodriguez. She had been on the receiving end of anger and jealousy many times. For better or worse, she didn't have a neutral effect on men. The problem lay in the response that they wanted or needed from her. Did she threaten men or their self-images? She would have to watch herself.

Turning back to her desk, she pushed herself to concentrate. She had work to do. Leaving every time that she got upset was getting to be a habit.

The afternoon passed quickly. The slant of the rays from the afternoon sun told her it was time to get ready to leave the office. She had to pick up some dry cleaning and meet with Janet Davis. She still felt unnerved by her earlier confrontations with Roy and Hector Rodriguez. Thank goodness tomorrow was Friday. It had been a rough week.

Perhaps she was reading too much into the lieutenant's comments. While she didn't credit him with much, it was possible that he was trying to warn her for her own safety. If Rodriguez was Emilia's killer, she doubted that he would dare to threaten her in front of Roy. After all, he was a policeman. If he wasn't threatening her, then he believed that Brian might try to kill her. Roy had implied that Brian had killed once and would kill again. What did they see in Brian that she couldn't?

Confusion overwhelmed her. Tomorrow the team would be flying to Dallas for a week. Maybe she would have time to sort all of this out. Keri realized it was getting late. She grabbed her purse and locked her desk and office door. Where was everybody? She called out, but no one answered. Why hadn't Jenna told her she was leaving early? Irritated, she turned off the copy machine and office lights before locking up for the day.

Suddenly, she felt all alone and vulnerable. The thought of walking to her car through the cold, grey parking garage was overwhelming. Danger seemed to lurk behind every dark shadow. Somehow, she had to stabilize her runaway emotions. She hurried toward her car, anxious to lock herself in and leave. Listening carefully, she heard only the sounds of her own footsteps on the hard concrete floor. With a sigh of relief, she reached her car without incident. Feeling foolish, she started the car and backed out. What made her act as if someone was after her? She had no proof, only a suspicion. It was time to get back to practicing law and stop letting her imagination run away with her.

Chapter Twenty-Two

Keri walked out of the dry cleaners carrying her cleaning for the week. She slipped it onto the back seat of the car, forsaking the small clothing hooks at the edge of the header. She was right on time. In a few minutes she would be in Coconut Grove talking with Janet Davis. Keri turned her car onto LeJeune Road and settled back to enjoy the drive.

As much as she hated to admit it, Roy had been right. She had allowed herself to become involved with a client. It was true, Keri admitted to herself, she was not being objective. So what? She wasn't sure that not being objective had any significance. She had always been passionate about issues. It made her a good attorney. She believed that Brian should be given the best defense possible.

What Roy didn't know, what no one knew, was her fear. She covered it, disguised it, obscured it, but the fear was always with her, just beneath the surface. It arose when she least expected it and embarrassed her. Her fear that Brian could be the murderer woke her up every night. More important, it seemed to undermine everything she did. Now she questioned her every decision, even her sanity. She had become afraid of walking to her car, or grocery shopping alone at night. She needed time to get more facts, time to sort things out.

Suddenly, her car swerved. She held tightly to the wheel and braked. When the car came to an abrupt stop, she realized that a rear tire had blown out. After checking for traffic, she drove the car over to the shoulder of the road. Disgusted, she reached for her cellular telephone and called road service. When she finished her call, she tried reaching Janet Davis, but after four rings, the woman's answering machine clicked on.

"Mrs. Davis, this is Keri Adams. I have a problem with my car. I would like to change our appointment to seven-thirty this evening. See you then." With a heavy sigh, Keri turned off the telephone, got out of the car and waited for the road service to come.

Her wait was short. She walked to the service truck as the driver, a rangy-looking man with a heart tattoo on his left forearm, got out and smiled.

"I'll have you out of here in no time, ma'am," he drawled softly.

Keri smiled and walked back to her car with him. As he examined her flat an odd look crossed his face. Without comment, he circled the car, examining each tire as he went. He dug his hands into his pockets and shook his head before walking over to Keri.

"Ma'am, I can't fix your tire. I'm going to have to call for a flat-bed truck and have your car taken back to the shop."

"Why?" A look of dismay crossed Keri's face. "I have a spare."

A look of apology crossed his weathered face. "One spare won't do you any good, ma'am. All four of your tires have been slashed. It's a good thing you weren't on the expressway. You'd be dead."

The blood drained from Keri's face and her knees almost gave out from under her. Who could have slashed her tires? Rodriguez? Brian? Someone else? Was it coincidence that she'd thrown Rodriguez out today?

"You okay, ma'am?" The mechanic grabbed her arm to steady her.

"No. I need to sit down." She opened the car door and slumped inside holding her head with her hands. "Call the Mercedes dealership in Coral Gables," she requested. "They will pick up the car and provide me with a loaner."

"Sure, ma'am." He turned back before he reached the pickup truck. "You need a doctor?"

"No." Keri hesitated. "Thanks for asking."

This time, Keri waited in the car. Shaking, she tried to still her runaway thoughts. Maybe her fears weren't so irrational after all. Now she was completely convinced that someone was trying to kill her. Her life had certainly taken on a new dimension.

"Can I help you, miss?" A clean-shaven young man stood outside the window. A glance at his shirt pocket told her that he was from the Mercedes dealer. He reached for the handle and pulled the door open for her.

She had been so engrossed in thought that she hadn't noticed him park the tow truck behind her. So much for being observant. Next time her life might depend on it.

"Yes, thanks." She handed him the car keys and explained her dilemma.

Within an hour, Keri was driving her loaner car to *La Tratto-ria*, a small gourmet restaurant on the edge of Coconut Grove. She had checked and rechecked her rear-view mirror to assure herself that she had not been followed. Satisfied that she was completely alone, she pulled up to the restaurant and gave the valet the keys.

Keri entered the restaurant and allowed the maître d' to seat her. It was early and, with the exception of her waiter, she was alone in the dining room.

"Pasta primavera, please and a glass of white Zinfandel."

For a moment Keri watched the waiter head for the kitchen to fill her order. Turning back to the table, she reached with trembling hands for a garlic roll which had been generously coated with Parmesan cheese. As she bit into the warm tasty bread, she wondered if her dinner would upset her churning stomach.

After picking up her loaner car, she had come here to relax and eat before seeing Janet Davis. If she didn't calm down and think coherently, Janet would change her mind about talking to her. What did the woman want? Janet had told her it was extremely important; she had information on Emilia's murder. Why hadn't she followed up when Jesse told her that Emilia and Janet were friends? She shook her head sadly and wondered if there were other leads that she had missed.

Keri glanced up just as the waiter leaned over and placed the glass of wine in front of her. "Thank you," she murmured.

"Your salad will be out momentarily." Noticing she had only taken one bite of her roll, he asked, "Is there a problem with the rolls?"

"No. Everything's fine." Keri waved him away and picked up her wine. She took a few sips, enjoying its soothing mild taste.

Driving over to Janet's house this evening might be futile, but it had to be done, she thought. She had tried calling several more times, but had gotten no answer. Hopefully, Janet was there waiting and just not answering her telephone. The woman had sounded rather mysterious, and Keri wished she had been able to take a break and immediately talk with her.

Keri reached over for her telephone and tried the number again. Still, no answer. Slightly annoyed, Keri wondered why the woman would ask her to come over and then not be there.

She put the telephone back in her purse and glanced down at the salad the waiter was placing in front of her. Better to eat in peace, she decided. She would have plenty of time for worrying later.

Chapter Twenty-Three

Keri's heart sank as she pulled the black Mercedes over onto the shoulder of the road in front of the Davis residence. The driveway was filled with police cars and a crime lab van. What had happened? Trembling, she parked the car and got out. Calm down, she told herself, there's no need to panic. Slowly, she walked to the entrance and stepped inside.

"Halt!" A loud voice called out.

Keri froze. A grim-faced detective in loose grey slacks and a Hawaiian print shirt made his way over to her. His eyes studied her intently and took in every curve before he asked, "What's your business here?"

"I have an appointment with Janet Davis." Keri answered. She was getting tired of all the scrutiny she had gotten from men today. Didn't they have something better to do than to study her body in detail?

His face relaxed. "Oh, you must be Keri Adams?"

"Yes." Keri wondered how he knew.

"Hey, Lieutenant. Ms. Adams is here." The detective looked

around to see if he had been heard. "Wait here," he ordered and crossed the living room before disappearing.

"Ms. Adams?" A familiar voice called out to her.

It was Lt. Rodriguez. Keri felt a pang of despair. Rodriguez was here. That could only mean one thing. Someone was dead and he was investigating it as a potential homicide. "Lieutenant?"

"Come this way, Keri." Rodriguez disappeared from her view.

It was the first time that he had ever addressed her by her first name. Was he human after all? Keri rushed out of the living room and onto the patio to catch up with him.

Keri stopped suddenly and looked in horror at the patio floor. A body covered by a white sheet lay not ten feet from her. "Who?" Biting her bottom lip hard to keep from breaking down, Keri looked around to find Rodriguez behind her. Her eyes widened with surprise as he searched her face with a questioning look in his eyes.

"It's Janet Davis. We pulled her body out of the pool about twenty minutes ago." True to character, his voice was cold and unemotional. Apparently, he had seen too much death in his lifetime.

"Oh, no!" Nausea spread through her stomach. "How did it happen?"

"Drowned, we think. She was fully clothed so she wasn't taking an afternoon swim.

"Do you think she was murdered?" Keri asked. Why would anyone want to kill Jesse's wife? No wonder the poor woman hadn't answered the telephone. She might have walked in and found her at the bottom of the pool. The thought made her head swim. That would have been more than she could take in one day.

"We don't know yet." Rodriguez gave her a cold hard look, his eyes narrowing suspiciously. "I thought your appointment with her was earlier."

BEYOND A REASONABLE DOUBT   173

"It was. I changed the time later." Keri wondered why she deliberately avoided telling him what had happened. She pondered the possibility of Rodriguez being her killer. He knew Janet wanted to talk to her. "How long has she been dead?"

"We won't know until we get the medical examiner's report."

"Where is Jesse? Has he been told?"

"He's under sedation. He's the one who found her."

His cold manner irritated Keri. She was becoming increasingly uncomfortable in his presence. "I have to go, Lieutenant." Keri forced a smile and turned to leave. When she reached the door, Rodriguez called after her.

"Looks like your jock got to her before you did!"

Keri felt her face drain of all of its color. "You're just guessing." She wanted to get away from this place and from him.

"No. Not really. A witness saw a gold Lexus in the driveway, a little before four o'clock. Your jock still drives a gold Lexus, doesn't he?" His malicious laugh followed Keri out to the car.

"Come in for questioning tomorrow morning. I'll be needing a statement from you," he ordered.

Keri turned and nodded. She hated his arrogance! Keri slipped behind the wheel and started the ignition. Could she possibly drive? Tears spilled over onto her cheeks. There was certainly no one here to help her.

Cautiously, Keri put her trembling hands on the steering wheel and pulled the sleek sedan onto the road. As she drove off, she pulled the visor down and opened the vanity mirror. Her day had not gone well, she thought, as she glanced at her tear-stained reflection. Then she noticed a movement in the mirror. She closed the vanity and threw the visor up. Her eyes were fixed on her rear-view mirror. A car had pulled out from a side street and appeared to be following her!

In the dim evening light, the colorless car looked like a Lexus, but she couldn't be sure. Was it her imagination that it was following her? Keri put her turn signal on. There was only one way to find out. Turning the car, she headed for Coral Gables. She made several more turns along the way and the car stayed behind her. Keri felt a surge of panic when the distance between them began to narrow. Without a second thought, she hit the accelerator and sped toward the Coral Gables police station.

She lost the car. But then, what difference did it make? Everyone knew where she lived. Maybe her home wasn't so safe after all; there was only one way in and one way out. That thought tormented her the rest of the night. It nagged at her in the parking garage and in the shower. It was her last thought before drifting off to sleep.

The telephone rang several times that night, but Keri refused to answer it. Early the next morning, it rang again and again before Keri roused herself to answer it. Who could be calling at six-thirty on a Friday morning? She met silence on the line. She put the receiver back and sleepily sat up. Did the telephone ring, or had she dreamed it? Stretching and yawning she climbed out of bed.

When she headed toward the bathroom, it rang again, stopping her dead in her tracks. An uneasy feeling settled over her. Should she answer it? Good grief, what was wrong with her? She crossed the room and picked up the receiver.

''Hello?'' Keri waited for an answer that did not come. ''Hello!''

No answer. She dropped the receiver. With trembling hands she reached for it and set it in its cradle. Sitting on the edge of her bed she put her face in her hands. She couldn't believe this was happening. Calming herself as best she could, she picked up her robe and wrapped it around herself. What she needed was a cup of hot tea. Quickly, she ran the brush through her hair and headed for the kitchen.

After heating some water in the microwave, Keri sat down at the breakfast table and fixed her tea. She leaned toward the window and opened the vertical blinds. The sun had already broken through the horizon, lighting the sky. Keri sighed and tried to clear her mind of sleep.

Sipping her tea, she couldn't help but think about yesterday's events. The car last night had followed her through a number of meaningless turns, but when she sped up, the car had fallen back and turned off. She had headed home by a route different from her usual one. Constantly checking her rear-view mirror, Keri had realized that she was no longer being followed. She knew that it really didn't make much difference whether or not the killer followed her home. He obviously knew where she lived. The real question was what could she do about it?

She walked over to the counter and picked up the telephone. Glancing down at the notepad, she punched in the number.

"This is Keri Adams. Yesterday, I made reservations on Flight 413 to Dallas/Fort Worth leaving today at eleven-thirty. I want to know if I can take an earlier flight."

Keri emptied her cup and slipped it into the dishwasher while she waited. Now she was glad that she hadn't told anyone where she was going, not even Brian. "Yes, I could make that. Flight 226 at eight-thirty. Thank you."

Keri hung up and turned on her answering machine. Already packed, she only needed to shower and dress. That wouldn't take much time. Feeling confident about her decision, she headed to the bedroom. She needed to talk to Brian right away. She needed to confront him. This was one time that she would have to be objective and not let her feelings intervene.

When Keri stepped out of the shower, it was seven o'clock and the telephone was ringing again. When she reached the answering machine, there was no message, only a menacing silence and then a dial tone.

Chapter Twenty-Four

"Fort Worth is where the West begins," the taxi driver proudly informed Keri as they neared the hotel. "It used to be an army outpost at the fork of Trinity River. Sure has changed since then."

"I thought that it started out as a cowtown! Didn't Butch Cassidy and the Sundance Kid hide out this way?"

The driver glanced into the rear-view mirror and smiled. "Sure they did, but that was after the railroad came in. Long before that, trail drivers stopped off here to load up on provisions and such before driving the cattle to Dodge City."

"You seem to know a lot about Fort Worth." Keri observed as he turned into the historic district, with its brick streets and restored buildings.

"Yep. I've lived here all my life. Staying long?"

"Just a few days. How far is the Sundance Hotel?"

"Couple of blocks. You sure picked a good one. It's right in the heart of the stockyards. You'll be right in the middle of shopping, honky-tonks and saloons. You'll have plenty of nightlife there.''

"Sounds good!"

"Last stop before hitting the Chisolm Trail, ma'am," the taxi drawled in his soft Western accent, as he pulled up to the front of the hotel.

Keri's eyes traveled over the facade admiring the authentic Western style. "Here, keep the change." Keri handed the driver several bills and climbed out with her flight bag.

Excitement raced through her as she entered the hotel. She felt like she had stepped back into another century, to a time of real-life cowboys, cattle barons, and oil magnates. The Sundance Hotel was an authentic Wild West hotel, lavishly decorated in authentic Wild West motifs and hand-rubbed, custom-made oak furnishings, with twelve-foot-high pressed tin ceilings and classic brass appointments. Everywhere she looked, she saw Western art reminiscent of Remington and Russell, cowhide chair-cushions, and American Indian rugs.

The desk clerk watched her approach from beneath heavy dark eyebrows. "Howdy, ma'am. You from these parts?"

Could he be for real? "I'm Keri Adams. I have a reservation."

"Yes, ma'am, we're expecting you. Take a look here at our picture album and see what room theme you would like."

Keri browsed through the pictures, quickly rejecting the rugged mountain man and the charming Victorian themes. "Either the cowboy or the American Indian would be fine."

The clerk looked at her with a dubious expression. "Well, we've got a couple of rooms left in both, but you might want to try our Bonnie and Clyde room. It's said to be the actual room the couple stayed in during the summer of 1933!"

Keri cringed inwardly. She wanted to escape murder not sleep in the middle of it. "No, thanks. I'll take the American Indian motif."

Check-in went quickly and Keri found herself settled comfortably in her room. She unpacked her flight bag. With her clothes in the armoire, she viewed the room with curiosity. The room was airy, light, and roomy, complete with a queen-size bed covered with Indian blankets. Suspended above the head of the bed was an imitation buffalo skull trimmed with leather, feathers and beads. On the adjacent wall hung a brightly colored ceremonial mandala. Pleased with her choice of rooms she relaxed on the bed, and for a few minutes watched the slow revolutions of the ceiling fan, while she relived the events from the day before.

Keri wondered if confronting Brian face to face would make any real difference. Logic told her that Brian would not slash her tires and then go kill Janet. It was too out of character. When he was with her, he was warm and caring. More than once he had come to her defense and his reactions had been more protective than violent. Could a man change so quickly? Could an angry encounter with Rodriguez trigger some sort of violent reaction? Rodriguez could have slashed her tires when he left. Why not blame him? His hostility was blatant.

Keri realized that she was assuming that her tires were slashed after the conference in Roy's office. That, she thought, could be a serious flaw in her analysis. After all, the car had been in the parking garage all day. So, where did that leave her? She could no longer ignore the fact that someone was trying to kill her. She knew only too well how close she would have come to serious injury or death had she just taken the expressway home instead of going to Janet's. The appointment with Janet had saved her life.

She still had no answers and she didn't intend to leave until she got some. Her fear of Brian was controlling her life and making her miserable. Could the story about a gold Lexus in Janet's driveway be true or did Rodriguez fabricate it to cover himself? She saw the car that followed her. From a distance it looked like a Lexus. Keri fought back tears which had welled up at the thought of Brian trying to kill her. It didn't make sense. There had been plenty of opportunities for him. She could not go another day without talking to him. She *had* to know.

She picked up the telephone. ''The Hilton in Arlington, please.''

Keri waited for the Hilton clerk to answer. ''Could you tell me if Brian Michaels has checked in?'' Keri wondered how was he going to react when he found out that she was in town. ''Good. Would you please ring his room for me.''

Brian was out. She felt a flood of disappointment. What had she expected? He was probably at practice. After giving her telephone number to the clerk, she hung up with a sigh. There was nothing to do but wait until it was time to leave for the game. She might as well call room service and then take a nap. A shower and a rest would certainly help the fatigue that she felt catching up with her.

Keri peeled off her shirt and jeans, tossed them aside, and slipped out of her silk bra and panties. While the warm water pelted downward, beating her thirsty skin, Keri rinsed the shampoo from her hair. In no hurry to bring the shower to an end, she turned the hot water to a higher temperature and allowed it to massage the aching muscles of her back. By the time she finally decided to get out, everything in the bathroom was covered with mist. Keri laughed and traced a heart in the mirror while she brushed her teeth.

Still dripping, she padded out into the bedroom to discover that room service had left her deli sandwich and soda on the table. Delighted at the timing, she grabbed a towel, threw it into the chair to sit on, and began to devour her sandwich. When she finished, Keri placed the tray outside her door. The aroma of pastrami and corned beef lingered in the room. She padded over to her bed and slowly stretched out hoping to fall asleep.

Instead, she found herself pondering her reactions to Brian. It was amazing and wonderful that he could arouse her by just being in the same room. She remembered each time she had been with him. His gentleness and kindness seemed to dominate her thoughts. No murderer could be so sweet and compassionate. A feeling of peace settled over her.

Roy's harsh words came back to her. Keri knew that once again Roy was trying to manipulate her in some way. But how? He had been adamant about keeping her on the team and had thrown all the real work her way. Would he have done that if he thought she was a lousy lawyer? Roy had seemed to enjoy Brian's confrontation with Rodriguez. Was Roy still angry at Brian for exercising his authority over him? That seemed the most logical answer. Roy had to be in control; it was a thing with him. And Brian had too strong a personality for Roy to manipulate.

Keri didn't know how long she had been napping when the telephone rang. She was confused by her surroundings, and her heart skipped a beat as her hand brushed across her naked body. Memory flooded in—it had to be Brian. Keri grabbed the receiver. How was she going to explain her unexpected presence? In a voice barely above a whisper, Keri said. "Hello." Panic grab at her throat, choking off any further response. Her body trembled, as she waited for a reply.

"I'm really glad you came." Brian's voice, low and confident, sent shivers of anticipation through her. "You *are* coming to the game tonight? It starts at seven."

"Yes. I'll definitely be there." Somehow she would find the courage to see this night through.

"Take a taxi. Tell the driver you're going to the Ballpark at Arlington for the game and that you need the entrance for the Front Row Sports Grill. After you get your ticket, just go up to the second floor. They will have a front-row table, reserved and paid for, in your name. Dinner and beer come with the table."

"You didn't give up, did you?" Keri laughed. Would he make love to her tonight? she wondered.

"No. There's always hope." Brian chuckled. "Wait there for me after the game."

"Okay. Do you want me to wait and have dinner with you?"

"No. Don't wait. I can always get something later." After an awkward silence, Brian's voice filled with anxiety. "Have you heard about Jesse's wife?"

Keri's heart skipped a beat. Surprised that he brought the subject up, she tried to remain calm. "Yes, of course." Her voice wavered as her suspicions took hold. "Brian, we have to talk."

"Keri, I didn't kill her. When I left your office, I went straight to the airport."

"Why?" Anxious for his explanation, she almost forgot to breathe.

"I flew in yesterday, a day ahead of the team. That was Coach Greaton's idea. I've talked to Jesse and he knows that I didn't kill Janet. I don't know how he knows, but I couldn't press him. He was angry and upset when I talked to him."

"Will he be playing tonight?"

"No. He stayed in Miami." Brian waited for a moment before continuing. "Keri, there's a knock at my door—probably Coach Greaton. I'll see you after the game tonight."

"Good luck." Keri lowered the receiver thinking about what Brian said. She desperately wanted to believe him. His story could be substantiated once she knew the time of his flight, but she couldn't be sure until after the coroner determined the time of Janet's death.

Chapter Twenty-Five

The Ballpark at Arlington loomed in the distance; a brick fortress with huge globe lights painted like baseballs, evenly spaced above its parapet walls. As the taxi drew closer, Keri could see the well-manicured lawns surrounding the building. Inside this formidable structure, Keri reminded herself, was a state-of-the-art-stadium, and just for her—just for tonight, a table with a view of right field.

Getting her ticket, her table, and her dinner was the easy part. Figuring out what was going on in the game without Jordan McDaniel sitting next to her was the hard part. The crowd roared as Brian came up to bat. The bases were loaded and the Miami Stingrays desperately needed a home run. After two balls, Brian obliged. The crowd cheered wildly as the ball ripped into the stands. Her fears long since forgotten, an excited Keri applauded enthusiastically, before returning to her dinner.

Sitting in front of a full-length glass window, Keri had a full view of the playing field. Off to her left was a video game room and a bar with a skybox for the local radio station. Definitely made for the fans in mind, she thought. When she first sat down, the waiter had told her the restaurant had seventy-five TVs for the patrons to watch who didn't have a front row seat. It must have been difficult for Brian to get this table. Keri reached for her glass and motioned to the waiter that she needed a refill.

She felt vibrantly alive and sexy tonight. She glanced down at the pale blue silk sweater that curved over her breasts. Her matching silk slacks, though loose enough to be comfortable, clung to her. Not bad, she thought. Her attention was drawn suddenly to the table next to hers.

"Well, I really don't care!" An indignant woman's voice exclaimed. "I want to know why he was allowed to come to Dallas with the rest of the team. He should have been arrested!"

"Shana, why do you already have Brian Michaels tried and convicted? Do you really think that he killed Janet?" The woman looked at Shana in amazement.

"Oh Judi, of course I do! He murdered Emilia, didn't he?" Her voice held a hint of exasperation.

"Everyone says he did. I heard that Janet's death might have been an accident. The police haven't said it was murder yet." The woman called Judi gazed at Keri, but there was no look of recognition in her eyes.

"You're being naive, Judi. As wives of the players, we are all in danger. Who is going to be his next victim?"

"Maybe it will be Rebecca Lawrence. I hear she's back in town." Judi laughed. "As I heard it, he was angry enough to kill her when she dumped him."

Anger coursed through Keri. How could they talk so callously about Brian? The trial hadn't even started and they were convinced he was guilty. They didn't even know what the evidence was! And what did she mean Rebecca Lawrence was back in town?

"Ladies, let's don't quarrel." Another woman's voice said. "Emilia was seeing a cop for a while. She dumped him because he didn't have enough money to satisfy her. She got herself another boyfriend, and I hear that it wasn't Michaels."

"Well, who was it?" Shana demanded.

"I don't know, but I heard that he had plenty of money."

Keri couldn't help but stare. Could this be the lead she had been looking for? She wanted to memorize every one of the woman's features so that she could recognize her later.

"Then you don't think Brian killed Emilia?" The tone of Shana's voice sounded like a dare.

"No. He's a nice guy." The woman brushed back her soft brown hair and crossed her legs.

"Katie, that's the most ridiculous reason that I have ever heard!" Shana exclaimed. "Next you'll be saying that he didn't have an affair with her."

"I don't think that he did. You're just bitter because he turned you down."

Keri failed to hear Shana's reply. The waiter set another glass of lite beer in front of Keri and scanned her empty plate.

"Is there anything else that I could get for you?"

"Chips and salsa, mild, please." Keri smiled unseeingly at the waiter. She wanted to hear the rest of the women's conversation.

". . . and that's not all." Judi paused for a drink. She turned to face Katie before she continued. "I hear she wants him back and I mean really wants him, if you get my drift."

Katie leaned over and whispered something. It must have been good, Keri thought, when they broke out in peals of laughter. Keri wished that she could have heard the rest. They had finished talking and were sitting back watching the game. Keri grabbed a crayon and began coloring in some of the characters on her paper tablecloth while she mulled over the conversation. She wanted to talk to Katie and find out where she had gotten her information. However, this wasn't the proper place and her timing couldn't be worse. The sooner this game was over, the better. Even with Brian's efforts, the team was losing badly tonight.

Just as she expected, the Texas Rangers won. Maybe the next game would be better, Keri thought, as she watched the wives and fans filter out of the restaurant. Sitting alone, Keri picked up the *Front Row* newspaper and scanned its advertisements. The place served over one hundred different kinds of beer. Who in the world would like beer that much?

"Well, howdy, ma'am. Is this seat taken?"

"Matthew! What a nice surprise." Keri motioned to Matthew to sit down.

"What are you doing here," Matthew asked, "besides the obvious?" He sat down and motioned to the waiter. "Can I buy you a drink?"

"Thanks, but drinks are included with the table. How about if I order you one?" Keri smiled at his friendly face. To her surprise, he graciously accepted and ordered one of the most obscure kinds of beer on the menu. She hoped he knew what he was ordering.

Too soon, her lightheartedness came to an end.

"Keri," Matthew started, "I'm beginning to question my judgment. I believed that Brian was innocent. Now with Janet Davis' death, I'm not so sure. The police haven't called it a homicide yet, but it's probably a matter of time. It really came at a bad time Keri. I had called her to try to get her to talk to me, but she was very evasive about setting up a time. Now I can't."

"He says that he didn't kill her and that he can prove it." Keri offered. "Please don't quit trying to help." His lack of confidence in Brian worried her, much more than her own. "Tonight, I heard some of the wives talking. One of them, Katie, seemed to know a lot about Emilia and Janet. And she appeared to know something about Emilia's lover."

"It might help if I talked with her." Matthew leaned toward her. "How long will you be in town?"

"I planned to be here just for the weekend. I had to see Brian and clear the air about Janet. It's the only way to be one step ahead of Rodriguez." She leaned toward him. "I have to talk to you about Janet and me. But not here, it isn't private enough. I don't want to be overheard."

"Is next week soon enough?"

"Yes. I think so." Keri didn't think he was any real danger yet. As much as she wanted to tell him, Brian would be showing up any minute.

Matthew held her hands between his. "Keri, stop worrying so much. I won't quit trying to help. You should know that."

"I do," she whispered.

For a moment he hesitated, as if deciding what to say. "Rebecca Lawrence is back in Fort Worth. Rumor has it that she's hot for Brian. Watch your step with him," he warned.

She looked up into his cool, grey eyes and realized what a friend he was. "Thanks." They looked at each other without speaking, prolonging their moment of understanding.

"Enjoy the game?" A low, masculine voice said.

Keri looked up to see Brian smiling down at her. She felt a warm flush ease its way over her body.

"Yes. I was rooting for the Stingrays."

"It's okay. There's always another game. Hello, Matthew." Brian held out his hand to Matthew forcing him to relinquish his hold on Keri's hands.

While Brian and Matthew engaged in an easy conversation about the game, Keri wondered how Rebecca Lawrence fit into her already too complicated life. Brain would be crazy to want her back. Unless, of course, he had never gotten over her. Or, maybe he might be interested in revenge. She smiled. He wasn't the revenge type, of that she was sure.

If he was angry with Matthew for holding her hands, no one would be able to tell, Keri decided. She knew it had been a rather personal scene that he had encountered, and she felt a little disappointed that he wasn't jealous. Shouldn't it be normal to be jealous after the intimacies they had shared?

Glancing over at both of them, she marveled at her luck. Two gorgeous men and they both liked her. Matthew sat in his tailored grey business suit looking like an affluent executive and Brian looked like a cowboy out on the town. Brian had on boots, jeans and a Western shirt in shades of brown and tan. The colors set off the glow of his skin and sunlight of his hair. The more that she knew of him, the more difficult it was not to think of him as hers.

"Keri and I are going out for drinks. Won't you join us, Matthew?" Brian looked to Keri for confirmation.

"I can't, tonight. But thanks for the invitation." Matthew rose to leave. "I have to meet a friend. Have a good night." He smiled at Keri and shook Brian's hand before leaving.

Keri hated to see him go. Now she was alone with Brian and had to face some unpleasant topics with him.

Brian caught her hand. "If you are ready, let's go grab a cab to Fort Worth."

"Fort Worth?"

"I'm checking in at the Sundance Hotel. It's better for me right now to be some distance from the team. My luggage is with the maître d'."

Keri searched his earnest face for a motive and came up empty-handed. Whatever she had been expecting, it wasn't this. What was she going to do? She wanted to be with him, but she was still afraid of him. Knowing that he would be staying at her hotel was just too unnerving after all that had happened to her. She felt a sense of panic race through her as she felt more of her control slipping away.

Brian stood up and pulled her to him. He looked down into her troubled eyes and lowered his head to kiss her. "It has been much too long since I kissed you," he whispered.

Keri couldn't think of anything to say, nor could she take her eyes off his lips. They tilted upward in a sexy smile that melted her heart. Then they were claiming hers as his own. He tasted of mint and beer and smelled of after-shave lotion. Her head whirled. Suddenly, her doubts were gone.

Chapter Twenty-Six

Keri waited impatiently in the hotel lobby for Brian to come down. He had checked into the Penthouse Suite, complete with a wet bar, fireplace, and outdoor Jacuzzi. Just what could be keeping him? She had gone to her room and freshened up. Certainly, she had given him plenty of time. Restless, she glanced at the Western art displayed in the lobby of the hotel. The work was good, but she didn't recognize any names. Then she eyed a lone Indian warrior on his horse. It was striking in its simplicity and it reached out to the viewer to tell of their hardships and isolation. Impressed, Keri leaned over to read the artist's name. She straightened quickly, stunned to find the name of Brian Michaels. It was a magnificent work. No wonder the hotel manager had come out and given Brian their best suite.

"Like it?" Brian stood beside her.

"I'm overwhelmed!" Keri answered honestly.

"Good. I hope to keep you that way." He laughed and grabbed her hand. "Let's go to the Gunslinger Saloon."

He led her through a connecting door to the lobby and into the saloon. "Let's have a drink at the bar."

"You're kidding!" Keri eyed the odd barstools suspiciously. The tops of the barstools were saddles, real saddles!

Brian laughed and led her to the bar. "Need help getting on?"

"I'm not getting on that!" Keri gave him an incredulous look. Somehow she couldn't imagine herself straddling a saddle in a bar.

His hands shot to her waist. He lifted her up in one easy motion and placed her upon the saddle. "So ride sidesaddle, if you want to."

How did he know what was bothering her? Just to prove him wrong, she threw her right leg over to the other side and straddled the saddle. There! That should undermine his confidence a little. Keri watched as Brian climbed into the saddle on her right. His eyes caught hers in a moment of childish delight. Keri laughed. He really was fun to be with.

"Howdy, Partner. What can I get you and your lady friend?" The bartender looked like he had just come off the range.

"Gin and tonic for both." Brian answered, his gaze never leaving Keri until the bartender returned. He picked up both drinks and handed her one.

"Will you join me for dinner tomorrow night?" Brian asked.

"Yes. I would like that."

"Good. I need to get some rest tonight. It hasn't been a good week." Brian smiled.

"I know." She answered softly and sipped at her drink. "Brian, which team member has a wife named Katie?"

"I don't know of any. Why do you ask?"

"Some of the team wives were sitting at the table next to me. The only names that I caught were Katie, Shana, and Judi." Keri sipped her drink, trying to decide how much to tell him. Leaving out the worst part of the conversation, she continued. "I overheard part of their conversation. It seems that Katie heard from someone that Emilia was seeing someone with lots of money. The waiter came over and I lost the rest of the conversation.''

''Don't worry about it tonight. I'll ask around. It really doesn't surprise me. I have a couple of hunches that I have to look into.''

Why was Brian acting so mysterious? He should tell her. After all, she was his attorney. ''Tell me about them.''

Brian finished his drink as he studied her lovely face. ''Not now. Maybe later. You know how hunches are. Sometimes they are like a psychic knowing and other times an elusive thought that falls short of its mark.''

Keri nodded. She knew he didn't want to be pushed—and truthfully, she didn't feel like pushing. In fact, she felt fatigued. Keri watched as Brian tossed a twenty on the bar and hauled his big frame out of the saddle. He turned to her and with his hands on her waist, gently kissed her.

''Let's go.'' He whispered.

Keri slipped out of the saddle and followed him to the elevators. He accompanied her to her room, pausing at the door.

''The game is at one o'clock tomorrow. I'll come by your room about six-thirty. Dress casually—jeans, if you like.'' His face broke into a warm smile. ''If you didn't bring a bathing suit, pick one up and we'll try out the Jacuzzi.'' Brian unlocked the door for her and handed her back her key.

''Good luck tomorrow.'' Was he really ending their night?

''Thanks.'' Brian's eyes smoldered with unspoken passion. He bent to kiss her cheek, but Keri turned her lips to meet his. He crushed her to him, thrilling her with the strong hardness of his body. Gently he backed her inside the room and shut the door behind them.

Suddenly, she was hot. All she could think of was his hands doing delightful things to her. ''Oh, Brian,'' she whispered.

With a low groan he pushed himself away and gazed down into her soft brown eyes. ''Sleep well. See you tomorrow.''

"Good night." Keri smiled at him as he left her room. She closed her door and leaned against it. Waves of disappointment crashed over her, stripping her of her defenses. She knew now that she was falling in love with him and that it was too late to turn away. For better or worse, she intended to see this through. Filled with resolve, she promised herself that she would fight for him, fight like she had never fought before!

Chapter Twenty-Seven

Black lace, lined with pink satin clung to her firm round breasts, barely covering them. The moderate cut bottom of the bikini set off her shapely hips and narrow waist. Keri turned in front of the full-length mirror and admired the suit. It was devastating and she fully intended it to be so. She had no intention of being pushed aside tonight. If this didn't break through Brian's iron will, nothing would.

"You look lovely!" The saleslady smiled knowingly. "We have a matching cover-up."

"I'll take both." Keri laughed as she headed for the dressing room. Why not? She didn't have anything like it. All of her suits were modest and proper. This one was a shocker.

Fully dressed, Keri gathered her packages, from her long day of sight-seeing and shopping. Satisfied that she had made the best choice, Keri headed for the counter to pay for it.

Outside the store, Keri hailed a cab. She settled into the back seat with her packages and rested her head. Her tension had eased considerably with all the exercise she had gotten today.

Keri decided that she had just enough time for a quick nap before getting ready.

Did the boots go over the jeans or under them? Exasperated, Keri tucked the jeans into her boots and looked at her reflection in the mirror to assess her Western-style silk shirt in the palest of pinks, tight-fitting dusty rose jeans, soft suede boots and matching belt. Her reflection was cool, calm, and poised—but she knew better. It was getting harder and harder for her to control her desire for Brian. He haunted her days and nights.

A soft tap at the door told her that Brian had arrived. When she opened the door, her breath caught. Leaning against the doorframe he looked like the healthy, virile athlete that he was, his black jeans snug against his hard muscular thighs, and his white silk shirt setting off his golden tan and vivid blue eyes. The cocky grin on his face told her that he knew he was running late and didn't care.

"Would you like to come in?"

"No. Let's get going. I'm a hungry man."

Keri grabbed her purse and locked the room. Rustler's Steak House was only a short walk from the hotel. They were taken immediately to their table.

Seated next to a hearth, Keri and Brian relaxed in silence while they waited for their dinner to be served. Keri was feeling overwhelmed with anticipation. Did he feel the same urgent desire as she? The depths of his blue eyes failed to give her a clue. They seemed to be shrouded.

"You look lovely tonight, Keri."

"Thank you." Keri smiled, trying not to reveal her excitement.

"You said that you wanted to talk. This would be a good time." He leaned back and studied her.

Keri breathed deeply. So this was why he had been so silent. Even though she was disappointed, he was right. They needed to get the issues out of the way. She decided to begin with Janet.

"I made an appointment to see Janet on Thursday afternoon, after work." She hesitated for a moment before deciding to bait him a little.

"I remember." His matter-of-fact tone told her nothing.

"Well, I had to call her back and reschedule for later. She was out when I called, so I left a message on her machine. When I arrived, I found Lt. Rodriguez and the crime lab van at her house. He called me out to the patio where her body was lying."

"Rodriguez, again!" Suspicion clouded his eyes. "What time did you call her?"

"Around four-thirty." That was the best estimate that she could give him. Why was the time so important to him?

"She could have been dead when you called." A deep crease cut into Brian's brow.

Keri's voice wavered. "Lt. Rodriguez told me that a neighbor saw a gold Lexus in her driveway a little before four o'clock." Keri leaned forward and lowered her voice. "He says that there isn't enough evidence yet to classify her death as a murder, but he is sure that you killed her!"

Keri watched the range of emotions cross Brian's face. Although his eyes had narrowed in anger and hostility, his voice was deceptively calm.

"I don't know why that should surprise me. Everyone one else suspects me, including you."

"That's not true. It's just that so many terrible things have happened that I'm wary of my own judgments," Keri admitted.

Brian searched the depths of her eyes. "You are questioning your own judgments? By now you should have realized that I could not murder innocent women."

All it took was a smile. It was a little smile, but it warmed her soul.

"I can prove that I didn't kill Janet. I parked my car in the airport parking garage and waited at the gate for my flight."

"Brian, we will have to have concrete proof to convince the police."

"Don't worry. I can give it to them."

"Good." She was beginning to feel more confident.

"Believe me?" His gut twisted painfully as he waited for her answer.

Keri had to be honest with him. She plunged deeply into her very being and allowed her subconscious to answer.

"I believe you," she answered with confidence.

Brian studied her quietly, as if trying to decide whether or not he believed her answer. His hand reached out and found hers.

"Here comes our food." Keri smiled. She was hungry tonight.

The waitress set their steaks in front of them and proceeded to bring a fresh basket of hot bread. Brian motioned to their glasses, indicating that they needed a refill on their iced tea.

"Why would anyone want to kill Janet?" Keri asked. It didn't really make any sense.

"Janet may have been able to identify Emilia's killer." Brian swallowed the last of his iced tea.

"How could you come to such a conclusion?"

"Janet was Emilia's best friend. She probably confided something to Janet that was damaging. I can't think of any other reason."

Keri felt a warm glow of embarrassment cover her face. "I didn't think of it in that way," she admitted. "Janet's murder was only two days ago, but I felt it was related to Emilia's."

Keri waited while the waitress filled their glasses with fresh ice and tea. "She told me over the telephone that she needed to talk to me, that it was extremely important. She said she had information on Emilia's murder." Keri sighed. "I wondered if she had found out something about her husband."

"I really doubt that Jesse is involved, Keri." Brian's matter-of-fact tone told Keri that he had other ideas.

"You've talked to him again, haven't you?"

"Yes. I see him every day, Keri."

"That's not what I meant and you know it. What are you doing that I should know about?" If he knew something, he should tell her. How could she give him the best defense if he was still keeping secrets from her?

"It's only a hunch. When it's more, I'll tell you." He smiled, but his eyes were hard and stubborn.

Keri wanted to argue, then thought better of it. There were other ways to get information out of him. Demanding obviously wasn't one of them.

"There's a rodeo at the Cowtown Coliseum tonight. We can just make it after dinner. Want to go?" His face lit up with a boyish expression.

"Sounds like fun. Let's go." Keri was only too glad to abandon the unpleasant conversation and enjoy the evening with Brian.

"Great. Billy Bob's is just around the corner from the Coliseum. It's really wild on Saturday night if you want to go dancing after the rodeo."

"I don't know how to two-step or any of the other Western moves."

Brian laughed. "I don't either, but we could try our hand at bull riding."

Keri flashed him a dubious look. "I don't think so."

"Where's your sense of adventure?" Brian teased as his eyes filled with amusement.

"I came to Fort Worth, didn't I. That's enough adventure for me." Keri reached for her tea. Some of Brian's earlier coolness had worn off. Whatever was bothering him, she would find out later. His smile warmed her, and for now, she wanted to enjoy it.

Chapter Twenty-Eight

Keri looked out over the private terrace of Brian's suite as she waited for him to change into his suit. All night her body had ached with desire for him. Those tight jeans clinging to his hips had wreaked havoc with her resolve to keep her hands off and let him come after her. Actually, he had pulled her close to him as they walked back from Billy Bob's. But something was wrong, he had been too cool, too impersonal, and too distant. Maybe he didn't want to make love to her; maybe Rebecca Lawrence was back in the picture.

At the sound of Brian's approach, she turned to him. His breath caught as he stood, stunned by her appearance. Keri's new black lace bikini and cover-up had produced the effect she'd wanted.

"Champagne?" he asked in a soft husky voice.

"Yes. Thank you." Keri followed him back into the suite and over to the wet bar. She couldn't take her eyes off of him in his black swim trunks.

Brian handed her a glass and wandered over to the couch.

"A toast, Keri, to fear, an incredibly strong and irrational emotion."

"That's not a toast." Keri felt a surge of hot anger. "I won't drink to that." She walked to the couch and set her glass down on the cocktail table. "What is wrong with you tonight?"

"How long are you going to continue being afraid of me?" Brian's voice hardened. "What will it take? What will I have to do to prove to you that I'm not going to hurt you?"

Keri flushed with embarrassment. What could she say? She *was* afraid of him. "I don't know," she stammered.

Brian emptied his glass. "Do I act like a murderer?" he demanded, furious with her.

Keri choked back a sob. "No." Tears welled in her eyes and threatened to spill down her cheeks.

Brian stood over her: tall, powerful, and angry. Then gently, he brushed back her hair and kissed her eyes. "Don't cry Keri. I'm sorry."

"It's okay, Brian."

He picked up his glass. "I need a refill. Why don't you go get into the Jacuzzi? I'll bring our glasses."

"Okay." Keri was thankful for the few moments to compose herself. She found her way out to the terrace and lowered herself down into the tub.

Brian set the champagne bottle and glasses down on the coping and stepped into the Jacuzzi. Deliberately placing himself directly across from Keri, he switched on the controls before sitting down. He leaned back and closed his eyes, relaxing in the hot, foaming water. When he opened his eyes again, Keri had moved next to him.

"Champagne?" Keri sipped the last of her champagne and with a grandiose swing of her arm, handed her glass to him.

Brian looked at her mischievously while filling her glass. "You're full of surprises."

"Am I?" Keri moved closer to him. When he failed to

respond, she took one last sip of champagne before setting down her glass.

Entranced, Brian watched Keri, as her need drove her to him. Her hands found his broad, wet chest and caressed him. Her body tingled from the contact. Suddenly, she was beyond fear, logic, or reason. Only her passionate desire for him remained.

Brian gazed deeply into her brown eyes. He leaned closer, his eyes filled with arousal. "Are you sure this is what you want?"

A hot fire possessed her voice and her body. Unable to answer, she brushed his lips with hers. Slipping her hands down his chest to his abdomen, she caressed him boldly and intimately. A soft cry escaped her lips when his arms circled around her. She wanted to taste him, to feel him, to possess him as she knew he possessed her. He kissed her passionately, draining her breath from her.

Keri moaned softly beneath Brian's hot, demanding kiss. Quickly, he released her mouth, leaving her lips tingling with pleasure. His hands, firmly holding her waist, lifted and turned her so that he cradled her in his lap. One strong muscular arm supported her as she settled against him, reveling in the feel of his nearness.

His eyes sought her in a moment of shared intimacy. Looking up, Keri saw that his clear, blue eyes mirrored all of the passion and desire that surged through her. As he moved to reclaim her mouth, she pulled his head slowly down to her breasts.

Brian's mouth found her soft curves straining against the confining fabric of her suit. Strong and firm, his hand cupped her breast sending ripples of excitement through her. His lips and tongue slowly teased a path along the edges of her black lace bra. Slowly, he eased aside the lace on each breast before capturing her in his mouth. Keri cried out in delight.

His hand caressed her as it traveled down the flat plane of

her abdomen, beneath her bikini bottom. In a deft motion, he slid the bikini from her hips and down her thighs.

"You are so sexy, Keri." Brian's husky voice was barely above a whisper. His eyes traveled over her to drink in the beauty of her half-nude body.

"Do you realize what you are doing to me?" Keri asked breathlessly. Her fully exposed breasts were still framed by her black lace bra, her hips were bare but her thighs were trapped by her bikini panties. She bent her knees and struggled to free herself completely of them.

"Tell me, Princess; tell me what I'm doing to you," he demanded softly. He kissed her mouth and reached for the warm soft swells of her inner thigh. "Tell me."

She couldn't. His gentle stroking sent currents of erotic desire through her. "Please, Brian. Please," Keri whispered.

Suddenly, her head began to swim from the champagne. She grasped his shoulders wildly to stabilize herself, but it didn't work. She had lost her sense of direction. She cried out as his fingers tickled and pinched, invading her privacy and discovering every sensitive spot on her body until her body exploded with sensation. Her head fell back and her nails dug into his shoulders. She writhed wildly, but her legs were still confined by the bikini bottom.

"Take my panties off," she begged breathlessly.

A mischievous grin crossed his face while his fingers slithered sensuously down the inside of her legs to her ankles, and freed her. When he released her to slip out of his own suit, she pushed herself away from him. Smiling at his surprised face, Keri laughed. "This time, it's my way."

Keri stood up and allowed the water to run off her voluptuous curves while Brian waited for her next move, perfectly willing to let her take charge. She could hear his heavy breathing as she stood with her legs invitingly spread apart. She inched her way toward him, prolonging his agony and hers. When she reached him, she slipped easily over him and straddled him.

Fire, white hot and explosive coursed through her body as his mouth, tongue, and hands caressed her. Nothing mattered except Brian. She wanted to surround him, to grab him and force him as deep as he could go. This single act of possession was all she lived for.

"Easy, Keri," he whispered in a husky voice as he pushed deeper into her. His hands pulled her hips down on him and rocked her back and forth. She screamed with pleasure as he drove her to the limits of sensation where she collapsed in his arms.

Keri gasped for breath and rested her head against his shoulder. She could still feel him throbbing inside of her. His breathing was labored as he lifted her hips and slipped out of her. For a few minutes they rested with the water swirling wildly around them.

"Now, it's my turn." Brian grinned and picked her up.

"What?" Keri looked at him in confusion.

"It's bedtime, Princess," he whispered while carrying her into the bedroom. "And the night is still young."

Keri barely noticed when he pulled back the covers and laid her on the bed. With her eyes closed she luxuriated in the feel of the cool satin sheets beneath her damp skin. Not until she felt him straddle her and grab her breasts did she open her eyes and wonder just what he intended to do.

"I'm dead," she offered tentatively.

"Not a chance, Princess." He gave her a mocking smile. "It's time for you to find out what your body can really do."

Stunned by his answer, she didn't object when he lowered his mouth to her neck and trailed kisses up to her ear, across her eyes, and down to her mouth. The kiss was deep and long. His hands massaged her breasts. Without warning, her body quivered with need and desire. What the hell was he doing?

His hands left her breasts to caress her shoulders and his mouth smothered her breasts with hot, wet kisses. Her body trembled as his hands traveled down her arms to her hands.

With a deft motion, he caught her wrists and forced her arms under her where he trapped them with one hand.

"Brian!" she protested.

Ignoring her objection, Brian nudged her legs apart and lowered himself between them while she squirmed. Still holding her captive, he trailed kisses down her abdomen to her inner thigh.

Keri cried out with pleasure. How could he do this to her? Waves of desire swept through her washing away rational thinking as his fingers stroked her intimately, going beyond her ability to endure.

"Brian, please," she begged.

"You are so hot, Keri," he breathed. "You are driving me out of my mind."

"Now, Brian, please!" she whimpered.

He lowered his body and stretched out his long legs between hers. Just the feel of him sent her body into spasms.

Whining and whimpering as if her life depended on it, Keri pressed against him. This time he wasn't as gentle. Her hips lifted to his rhythm and she writhed and squirmed and cried. Once again she felt herself on the brink of a climax. Once again, he withdrew.

"No, no, don't!" she moaned. How could he? How could he leave her like this? She was completely at his mercy, a willing victim to his sexual mastery. She had to have him, totally and completely. How could she make him understand?

She looked up into his eyes, dark with passion, and saw the look of pleasure upon his face. His breathing was rapid and heavy, his body shivering with desire.

"Tell me you're mine, Princess. All mine," his voice, rasped under the strain of his self-control. "Tell me!"

"Yes, oh, yes!" Her legs tightened about him. "Make me all yours, Brian. Now!"

He willingly obliged. Keri screamed, a raw, primitive scream as her quaking body grabbed at him, possessing him, as he possessed her. Silently, he came with her, pushed over the edge by her carnal responses.

Brian kissed her gently and fell back on the bed. He pulled her to him and cradled her in his arms. Keri had never gone to such great heights of passion nor had she ever felt so satisfied. She smiled at him and closed her eyes. Spent with exhaustion, they fell asleep.

Chapter Twenty-Nine

The first rays of the sun danced upon the curtains drawn across the open windows of the bedroom. The sheers fluttered in the soft breeze that stirred Keri from her sleep. Smiling to herself, Keri listened to the quiet breathing of the handsome man sleeping next to her. She relived his gentle touches and tender kisses. Her face grew warm at her thoughts of their passion. Where would their actions lead them? Keri knew that Brian had not intended to make love to her; his actions had told her that. She had deliberately set out to seduce him.

Now, she had to face an even greater reality. In the midst of her bold actions, she had been forced to recognize that her feelings for him ran much deeper than she had been willing to admit. If she was going to try to make this man a permanent part of her life, she had better start by trusting him.

"Don't go home today, Keri. Stay here with me."

She glanced over at Brian to find him smiling at her contentedly. She turned on her side and faced him, touching his lips with her delicate fingers.

"Brian, I have to go. I have to prepare for the pretrial hearing which is coming up July 6. That is, if I'm still on the case."

"What's that supposed to mean?" Brian pulled her into the circle of his protective arms and pulled her close.

Keri was having trouble keeping her mind centered on the conversation with his hard, lean body pressed against hers. "Roy and I had a fight after you and Rodriguez left the office Thursday."

"Why?" He seemed more interested in caressing her rump than he did in the conversation.

"I asked him why he wanted you to go back to jail." Keri looked at Brian earnestly. "Brian, he didn't deny it. In fact, he told me that you were guilty and that he didn't want me to end up like Emilia. That's why he didn't try to stop Rodriguez from harassing you."

Brian's eyes smoldered with anger. "Was he implying that I would kill you?"

Keri slipped her arm around his shoulder and smoothed the sheet around him. "Yes. After that we got into the argument that we've had before about his lack of interest in defending you. Then, it got nasty. I asked him where his integrity was, and he grabbed me."

"He what?" With a look of surprise, Brian pressed himself up and leaned on his elbow, while he studied her intently.

"When I told him he was hurting me, he let go and threw me out of his office." Keri looked at Brian's face. He was angry; she was sure of that. But he was also lost in thought. What trouble had she just started?

"Brian?" Keri whispered.

Brian gave her a look of reassurance. "When I get back, I'll talk to him. In the meantime, stay away from him."

"That's going to be difficult!" Keri sighed. When Roy came looking for trouble, he usually found it. She was good at standing her ground. Now she would have to avoid confrontations with him.

"Call me if he gives you any problems or threatens you."
Brian settled back onto his pillow and slowly caressed her face
and hair while he gathered his thoughts.

"Keri, when you said that you were wary of your own
judgments because so many terrible things had happened, I
sensed that you were referring to more than the murders of
Emilia and Janet. Am I right?"

"I believe that someone is trying to kill me."

"Who?"

"I don't know. I think it's Emilia's killer."

"Why didn't you tell me?" Brian's voice was filled with
concern.

"I wasn't sure until Thursday." She gazed into his eyes and
wondered how she could have believed that he would hurt her.

"Tell me."

"The night that we met at Pelican Bay—" Keri hesitated.

"Yes. Go on." Brian closed his hand over hers and raised
it to brush his lips against her palm.

"When I got back to Laughing Gull Cove, there was only
one light on in the parking garage. I didn't think too much of
it. I parked my car, got out, and started toward the elevators.
A car with no lights came speeding toward me and missed me
by inches." Keri felt Brian's body tense.

"Then at two in the morning my telephone rang and no
one answered. I heard heavy breathing, so I hung up." She
shuddered. "Later, I tried to tell myself that it was my imagination."

"Didn't you call the police or the security guard?"

"I called the security guard. He couldn't find anything
unusual, so I didn't bother with the police." Keri breathed
deeply in a futile attempt to calm her racing heart. She didn't
want him to see how afraid she had become.

"Nothing happened again until this past Thursday. I left the
office around four o'clock. On the way over to Janet's, I had
a flat tire. I called for road service and then left a message on

Janet's answering machine that I was changing our appointment to seven-thirty. When road service arrived, the driver told me that he would have to call a flat-bed truck for me.''

"For a flat tire?''

Keri's breath caught in her throat and her voice betrayed her fears as she tried to continue. "All four of my tires had been slashed.''

Brian stared at her; a stunned expression covered his face. "Princess," he breathed, as he gazed tenderly into her eyes and pulled her close. "You could have been killed!''

"The driver told me that if I had been on the expressway, I would be dead. But Brian, it wouldn't have just been me. The car would have gone out of control and caused serious injury or death to others, too.''

"True, but it didn't happen." He looked at her in amazement. "It's unbelievable that you still went to see Janet.''

"I had to. You're depending upon me to defend you. I had to know what she wanted." Keri closed her eyes. "Unfortunately, I was too late.''

"What did Rodriguez say about your tires?''

Keri looked up at him. "Nothing. I didn't tell him. When I threw him out of the office Thursday, he warned me to be careful or I might end up like Emilia. I thought that he might be threatening me. I still suspect him, Brian.''

"Oh?" His anxious eyes studied her intently.

"It was dusk when I left Janet's house. A car pulled out from a side street and followed me. It could have been the police, but the car looked like a Lexus. It pulled off when I got to Coral Gables. Why would Rodriguez leave the scene of a crime and follow me?''

"Maybe he thought you were going somewhere to meet me," Brian offered.

"I never thought of that." Keri hesitated, testing the idea.

"The telephone calls started again early Friday morning, so I changed my flight out here to an earlier flight.''

"You had reservations before all this happened?" A smile teased at his lips.

"Yes," Keri continued, not noticing his change of mood. "And I didn't tell anyone that I would be out of town."

Brian gazed deeply into Keri's troubled eyes. He traced her cheek with his fingers, trailing them down her neck and across her collarbone to her shoulder, where they rested for a moment. "Obviously, you are striking a nerve with all your questions."

"Brian, we still don't have any answers!" Keri's voice was filled with frustration.

"Then it's just a matter of time. You must be making someone uncomfortable. When I get back, we need to go over what you have done and discuss what we still need."

"You think that it will lead us to the murderer?"

"Yes. I'm convinced now that whoever killed Emilia also killed Janet. I'm also convinced that you are in real danger. Don't do any more investigating without me."

Tears welled up in Keri's eyes and threatened to spill over onto her pillow. Brian nuzzled her before finding her lips and kissing them gently. "Princess, don't cry." He turned her over on her back and caressed her delicate curves as his lips began a slow tantalizing journey to her breasts.

Brian's skillful kisses drained her of her fears and anxiety. She was barely aware that the horror faded like a thief in the night, leaving behind an intoxicating warmth. Pleasure filled her senses. Consumed with desire, Keri reached for Brian, eager to thrill him as he thrilled her. He raised no objection, returning her passion fully.

Chapter Thirty

Arrogant and angry, Roy glared at Keri from the entrance to her office. It was getting increasingly difficult to deal with her, he thought. She was stubborn and clever, too clever. He wanted to know why she hadn't shown up for work on Friday. Something had happened for her to disappear for three days without a word to anyone.

"Keri!" Roy called out. "You had everyone worried Friday. After hearing about Janet's death, we were all on edge."

Keri looked up from the open file on her desk. "I took the day off."

"Obviously," he replied sarcastically. "Unplug your telephone again?"

"My answering machine was on." Her matter-of-fact tone told Roy she didn't intend to pursue the conversation.

Roy's eyes narrowed. "Your behavior has been very inconsiderate lately."

Keri ignored his comment. Brian didn't want her to fight with him, but it was such a temptation. She knew he would continue to needle her until she got angry. Then he would move in for the kill. She had his *modus operandi* down pat.

Roy stepped into her office. "I want to know where you were," he insisted with grim determination.

"That's my business Roy, not yours." She gazed at him with a cold penetrating look. "I'm not your employee."

"It is my business," he countered. "Brian is my client."

"Why bring Brian into this?" Keri asked. "I took the day off—what's that got to do with Brian?"

"You're supposed to be working on his case." Roy leaned forward and grabbed the back of a chair in front of her desk. His angry eyes bored into hers. She was starting to get on his nerves.

"Every waking minute?" A smile tipped the corners of her mouth, a smile that didn't reach her eyes.

"Where were you?"

Keri fought to control the anger flaring within her. It would be so easy to lash out at him. She had to hide her emotions so he could not use her anger to manipulate her. Keri watched as a look of disbelief crossed his face, followed quickly by a sadistic expression.

"Brian killed Janet Davis!" Roy straightened up and waited for the shock and tirade he was sure would come.

"Has he been charged?"

"No, but it's just a matter of time before formal charges will be filed," he answered confidently.

Keri eyed him curiously. "Have the police questioned Brian yet?"

"No. They want to interrogate him when the team gets back in town on Thursday." With an air of impatience, he shifted his weight.

"Here?"

"I don't know. I put in a call to Lt. Rodriguez, but he hasn't called back."

Keri watched as Roy shrugged and walked back to the door.

His comments didn't ring true. What could he gain by lying, other than to antagonize her? Her thoughts were interrupted when he stopped at the door and turned to face her.

Roy gazed at her. "When will you be getting your car back?"

"I don't know." Keri leaned back in her chair. She wished he would leave so that she could call Rodriguez.

"Try to get it before Friday. Set up an appointment with Brian to come in to discuss the pretrial hearing with us. Friday is a good day for me." Roy walked away before she could comment.

Keri wondered how he always knew what was going on? Did he know that she had been in Fort Worth. Keri threw down her pencil and turned her chair to face the window. In the street, she saw Maxine's gold Toyota turning into the parking garage. "Bankers' hours," she muttered and turned back to her desk to reach for the telephone.

The voice on the line was cool and crisp. "Homicide. Lt. Rodriguez speaking."

"This is Keri Adams, Lieutenant."

"Feeling better?"

"Yes. Thank you." Keri hesitated. His question took her by surprise. Since when did he care how she felt? "I wanted to let you know that I will be representing Brian Michaels when you question him regarding the murder of Janet Davis."

"We haven't conclusively found that it was a murder," he stated flatly.

"Then you're not planning to charge my client?"

"No." His voice hardened with contempt. "I do want to talk to him though. Call me when Michaels gets back in town and the three of us will go over his story."

"Fine."

"Your office?"

"Yes. It would be better. Thanks." Keri hung up the telephone and turned back to the window. That was unusual. He wanted to come to her office. Maybe she had Jenna to thank for that and possibly the *pastelitos*. Keri stared unseeingly out the window as her thoughts turned to Roy. He had lied. Why? He knew she would find out the truth. There was the possibility that Rodriguez had some strategy going so that Brian would be caught off guard. Well she didn't trust either one of them.

Keri sighed and checked her watch. It was past time for Matthew to be here. She hoped that he remembered the appointment after his weekend of partying. It was time to take action and she needed his advice. Somewhere out there was a murderer who wanted her dead, someone who would try again.

"Sorry I'm late."

The timbre of Matthew's low voice warmed her. She turned to see him standing at the entrance to her office, alert and smiling, obviously enjoying seeing her. Why couldn't it be you, she thought, instead of Brian? Life would be so much less complicated. While she knew Matthew was pursued by many women, she was sure he was interested in her. But she wanted Brian. Brian excited her, Brian made her ache with just a kiss. Who could explain the chemistry that brought lovers together?

"Come in, Matthew. Did you enjoy your weekend?"

"Immensely!" He didn't explain.

Keri waved him to a chair, while she walked over to the door. After checking the hall for signs of people, she shut the door and locked it. Unexpected interruptions and ears were not on her agenda today. What she had to tell Matthew could affect both their lives and she had no intention of broadcasting, like her errant secretary, Jenna. She returned to her desk feeling grim.

"What's bothering you?" he asked.

"Someone is trying to kill me. I didn't know for sure until last Thursday when I was forced off the road with a flat. Only it wasn't a flat, all four of the tires on my car had been slashed. I didn't tell anyone. I needed to talk to Brian first. My suspicions were haunting me and I had to get everything out in the open."

His face registered shock. Keri continued, her words spilling out faster and faster. "Your life may be in danger if the murderer finds out that you are helping me. So far, only Brian knows. Whatever it is that I'm doing is making the murderer very nervous. If you don't want to work on the case anymore, I'll understand.''

''You couldn't pry me off,'' he answered. His voice and expression had changed to hardened steel.

Relieved, Keri smiled at him. ''You don't know how much it means to me to have a friend like you. Just knowing you and your strength are there gives me a great deal of confidence.'' She wanted to kiss his cheek affectionately, but thought better of it. ''Brian has ordered me not to do anymore investigating before he gets back. Then we'll go over what has been done and what needs to be done.'' She leaned toward Matthew. ''Time is running out. The trial will be on us soon, and we still don't have an adequate defense.''

''Something is bound to break, Keri. It always does.''

''That's what I keep telling myself.'' Keri pushed her chair away from the desk and turned it to look out the window. ''It's a beautiful day. Funny how simple pleasures get taken for granted until there is a danger of losing them.''

''Keri, stop worrying. I have some leads to check out before Brian gets back. In the meantime, how about a movie tonight?'' Matthew stood up and stretched his tall frame.

''Thanks. That sounds like a good idea.'' Keri walked to the door to open it for him.

''We'll go to an early movie and have a late dinner.'' Matthew suggested.

''That's a perfect prescription for gaining weight!'' Keri laughed. Seeing the look of mock hurt on his face, she gave in. ''Okay. You win. Pick me up around six.''

''See you then.'' He leaned over and lightly kissed her lips before turning to go.

Keri watched him walk to the reception area, then quietly closed her door.

Chapter Thirty-One

"Lt. Rodriguez, would you summarize for Mr. Michaels and me, the circumstances surrounding the death of Janet Davis."

Keri didn't like appointments on Friday afternoon, and this was no exception. In fact, she had set up this conference at Roy's insistence and now he was nowhere to be seen. Gazing at the stoic detective, she managed a cool smile. She might as well be civil, after all, her testy mood wasn't his fault.

The lieutenant flipped open the file resting on the conference table in front of him and scanned a few pages before responding. "Mrs. Davis was found floating in the family swimming pool by her husband about seven o'clock on the evening of her death. He called us. When we arrived, he was in shock and was taken to Doctor's Hospital."

"How did she die, Lieutenant?" Brian asked.

"The medical examiner determined that she drowned."

Common sense told Keri that there was more to Janet's death than just drowning. Unfortunately, he wasn't willing to volunteer the details. She was going to have to drag it out of him. "Were there signs of a struggle?"

Keeping his eyes fixed on Brian, he answered her in a caustic tone. "There was a blow to her right temple."

Keri knew that Lt. Rodriguez was indirectly accusing Brian of killing Janet Davis and baiting him to see what his reaction would be. When Brian's face tightened, his jaw clenched, and his eyes narrowing at the arrogant cop, she quickly tried to defuse the situation. "Has the medical examiner determined whether or not she could have sustained the blow by a fall?"

Begrudgingly, the lieutenant turned to Keri. "Yeah. He says she could have fallen and hit her head on the coping. But that's not the way it happened. Somebody hit her and threw her into the pool while she was unconscious. That's my guess."

"What was the time of death?" Brian asked.

"About four o'clock."

Brian leaned back in his chair and crossed his legs. "When I left our conference last week, I went straight to the airport, parked my car, and waited at the gate for the flight."

"Long wait." Rodriguez dripped with sarcasm.

"Not really. I didn't fly with the rest of the team. Coach Greaton asked me to leave a day early, so I took a flight at four-fifteen." Brian leaned back further in his chair and clasped his hands behind his head.

Keri wondered what would it take to convince this man that Brian couldn't possibly be Janet's killer? She wanted to give him whatever proof they had and get him off Brian's back. One murder was enough to worry about; he didn't need two.

The detective's eyes narrowed. "Who knew about this?"

"Just me and Coach Greaton. No one else knew, not even my attorneys."

"Here is his copy of the airline ticket." Keri reached over the conference table and handed it to Rodriguez. "Jenna can photocopy it for you if you want a copy."

"Yeah. It's not conclusive, you know." He studied the ticket stub with indifference.

"I have a receipt from the parking concession." Brian tossed the receipt to him.

"This only shows the total number of hours. It doesn't show when you were in or out." Rodriguez smirked. "You'll have to do better than that."

Brian set his chair down and leaned toward Rodriguez. He smiled confidently and tossed another paper to him. "We anticipated your objection. I kept the time-stamped parking stub." Brian's tone issued a challenge to Rodriguez to disprove him.

Rodriguez picked up the parking stub and stared at what seemed to be an airtight alibi.

"Lt. Rodriguez?" He looked up to see Jenna smiling down at him. "May I take those to photocopy for you?"

"Yeah. Thanks." He watched her walk out of the conference room before he addressed Brian. "The day of Emilia's murder, when you were in the neighborhood, did you see a red pickup truck in Emilia's driveway or parked across the street?"

"No. Why?"

Jenna entered the conference room with copies for the Lieutenant. "Here you are Lt. Rodriguez. Mr. Michaels, these are yours."

The lieutenant's eyes raked her body with interest. "Thanks. I've got another appointment this afternoon." Rodriguez turned to Keri. "Give me a call next week, Ms. Adams."

Keri stood up and faced him. "Lt. Rodriguez, do you have immediate plans of charging my client with murder?"

Rodriguez frowned as he glanced at Brian, who sat across from Keri with a stunned expression on his face. "No. None. I thought I made it clear that, based upon the evidence, we have not determined there was a murder." He started for the door, then turned again to her with a cold, calculating look in his eyes. "I am certain that your client murdered her. Sooner or later, I'll prove it."

Keri ignored him and waited for him to leave. After Jenna followed him out, Keri settled back down into her chair and reached for the intercom button.

"Keri, what was that all about?" Brian looked at her keenly.

"I can't tell you now. We'll discuss it later." She flashed him a smile, turned to the intercom and asked Maxine if she had heard from Roy.

"Sure. He called to find out if Brian had come in. He said he'd be in soon, so I expect him any minute."

"Thanks." Keri turned off the intercom and leaned back to relax. "Want a soda?"

"Sounds good." Brian flashed a bright smile.

Keri felt excitement surge within her. An urgent need filled her, reminding her that it had been four days since she had seen him. Maybe that was why she had been so crabby. "Jenna," she called into the intercom, "bring us some sodas."

"You look lovely today, Ms. Counselor," Brian teased.

She could tell he liked the way she was dressed today. Instead of one of her more conservative suits, Keri had chosen a pale pink and cream plaid. It made her look soft and approachable. That's what she wanted. She needed to feel him next to her. With an intimate look, she communicated her desire to him.

Recognition flashed in his blue eyes, then expectation, and a promise of unspeakable pleasure.

Keri's heart pounded hard and fast. He was entirely too sensual for his own good, she decided. One more look like that and she would rush into his arms and kiss him passionately.

"Am I interrupting?" A satirical voice, broke through their impassioned silence.

"We're waiting for you." Brian answered.

Keri was speechless. When had he come in? Neither of them had noticed. Roy leaning against the doorframe. Keri felt anger stir beneath her cool exterior.

"Oh, Roy. I didn't know you were here, too." Jenna entered the room to deliver the sodas. "Can I get you something?"

"No!"

"Thanks, Jenna. That's all for now." Keri dismissed her with a quick smile. There was no need for Roy to be rude to her.

"Did Keri go over the evidence with you?" Roy walked over and lowered himself into the chair vacated by Lt. Rodriguez.

"You and I discussed it several weeks ago." Brian took the glass of soda Keri handed him and settled back.

"I had hoped that she would go over it with you again." He shot a disgusted look at Keri before continuing. "We both agree that the prosecutor's evidence is very damaging."

"So?"

"Tom has worked very hard to find witnesses who saw you out jogging the day of Emilia's murder. He hasn't been able to find one person to corroborate your story. If we can't go forward with our own evidence, then we have to attack the prosecutor's."

"I would expect nothing less," he commented drily.

"And so you should." Roy loosened his tie and unbuttoned the neck of his shirt. "Their evidence is circumstantial, but it points directly to you. You could be convicted on that evidence alone."

"I'm aware of that." Cool and detached, Brian studied Roy.

"I don't think that you are. The charge is Murder One and you're facing a death penalty." Roy's voice filled with impatience.

"That is precisely why I hired you, Roy. You came highly recommended. You are supposed to know how to handle the case and to put all of your time and effort into defending me."

"I have done just that," he answered in an arrogant tone.

"No, you have not!"

"You're paying me big bucks to make decisions and represent you. You need to trust my judgment." Roy's face flushed with anger.

"What is that supposed to mean?"

"I'm good in the courtroom, Brian. Really good. I can probably establish reasonable doubt in the minds of the jurors. However, by basing your defense on my being able to establish
reasonable doubt, you would be taking a big chance, one that
I don't think you should take."

"I agree." Brian's expression was impenetrable.

"Just what are you getting at Roy?" Keri choked back her
anger. She knew exactly what he was selling—and she wasn't
buying. How could Brian just sit there and agree with his
warped assessments?

"The pretrial hearing is July 6. Next Wednesday, Judge
Pennell is going to pressure both the prosecution and the defense
to come to an agreement on the evidence and the issues at the
hearing. You know that, Keri. That's the way it's done."

Brian studied Roy thoughtfully. "You are recommending
that I agree to let you plea bargain?"

"Never!" Keri glared at Roy. He knew how Brian felt. Why
was he bringing this up again?

"That's exactly what I recommend. Your best bet to stay
alive under the circumstances is to plead to a lesser charge,
serve some time, and get out on parole. Then you can get on
with your life." Roy glanced at Keri with a smug look.

"Pay no attention to Keri, Brian. Women are so often stupid
in their decision making. When the chips are down, men make
logical decisions, not emotional ones. Women are incapable of
being objective, There is just no place in the law for them."

"You have seemed anxious from the beginning to have me
plea bargain. Why?"

"Because of the evidence. It's too risky to go to trial."

"I won't be able to play baseball if I plea," he responded
matter-of-factly.

Roy smiled mockingly at Brian. "You won't be able to play
baseball if you're dead!"

Brian rose to his feet and smiled down at Keri who sat filled
with shock and fury. "Well, it's settled then. I agree with

you, Roy.'' He walked to Keri's chair and stepped behind her, caressing her shoulders. ''It would be too risky for me to trust you to establish reasonable doubt. That's why Keri will be representing me in the courtroom.''

''What!'' Roy jumped to his feet, his face red with anger.

''You heard me. You have done an extremely poor job of representing me from the very beginning. I'm not at all impressed with you or your advice. I've made it clear to you from day one that I don't intend to plea bargain.''

Roy's laugh was hollow. ''It's a little late to fire me, Brian, but if you want to, go ahead.''

''I just did.''

Roy glared down at Keri. ''You've worked against me from the very beginning. You deliberately turned my client against me.'' He turned and walked to the door.

Outraged, Keri rose from her chair. ''That's not true.'' She moved toward Roy, but Brian caught her.

Roy paused at the door and smirked. Keri could only stare at him in disbelief. He actually looked amused.

''Wake up, Brian. If you weren't so busy bedding her, you would see that she has a lousy track record. She's no prize attorney.'' He leaned one hand above him on the doorframe and shoved the other in his pocket. ''Be sure and pay my bill; I don't want to have to collect from your estate.''

Keri felt stunned. She saw his laughing eyes as he turned and walked to his office. He was actually happy that he was off the case!

''Brian, no!'' Keri caught his arm as he walked menacingly to the door. ''Let him alone!''

Brian grabbed her and pulled her to him. ''Keri,'' he said softly. ''He *wanted* me to fire him.''

''I know,'' Keri whispered. ''He expects us to lose!''

Chapter Thirty-Two

Keri slipped into a strapless sheath of royal blue silk and cautiously zipped up the back. Three rows of rhinestones bordering the edges of the bodice and hem sparkled with her every movement. Keri glanced at the clock. Brian was picking her up at eight and she was running late. Hurrying to find her matching shoes and handbag, she assured herself that she would have a good time tonight. It had been a rough day with Roy and Rodriguez back to back and she really didn't feel like going out.

Keri headed downstairs to the kitchen holding her handbag and jewelry. At the edge of the counter she stopped to answer the telephone. It must be the guard, ready to let Brian in.

"Hello." There was no answer. Keri listened intently. There was someone holding the line open. She could hear breathing. Shaken, she hung up. With trembling hands she tried and failed to secure the clasps to her jewelry. She gave up and settled down in the living room to wait for Brian.

The knock at the door finally came. Keri made her way to

the door and peered through the peep hole. It was Brian. Relieved, she decided that it must have been the guard calling. He is incredibly handsome, Keri thought as she opened the door and smiled at him.

"Hi, beautiful." Brian looked her over approvingly before leaning over to kiss her cheek. "You're a knockout tonight."

"Thanks." Keri led the way into the living room. "Could you help me with my bracelet and necklace? I seem to be having a hard time with the fasteners."

"Yes. Bracelet first?"

Keri handed him her diamond bracelet and held out her right hand so that he could fasten it around her wrist. He snapped the lock into place and lifted her hand to his mouth. He slowly kissed the back of her hand then turned it to place a kiss in the center of her palm. His kiss was explosive. Currents of excitement raced through her body, forcing her to step back in surprise.

"Where's your necklace?"

She picked up a delicate chain from the cushion of the couch and handed it to him. A blue topaz pendant surrounded by diamonds hung from the center.

"That's a beautiful pendant."

Keri turned and lifted her flowing blond hair. "Thank you."

Brian fastened the chain securely and slipped his arms around her. He gently kissed the back of her neck and shoulder, sending chills through her body. When his hands grasped her breasts from behind, a cry of surprise and delight rose in her throat. Her head fell back on his shoulder and she offered her neck to him. His mouth trailed down her throat, kissing and licking.

Feeling his hard arousal against her, she pressed back against him, causing him to groan with desire. His hands left her breasts and trailed down to her thighs, lifting her skirt. His hands caressed her intimately, through the sheer fabric of her panty-hose, until her legs trembled and weakened. His fingers roamed upward and slipped inside the elastic waistband. With a skillful motion, he eased the pantyhose over her hips and slipped them down her legs, and off one foot, leaving her bare.

Keri stood holding her dress at her hips, feeling deliciously sexy, while he ripped open his fly. Still behind her, his nimble fingers unzipped her dress, letting it fall softly to the floor.

Burning fire coursed through her veins. A strange cry escaped her lips as he turned her and forced himself between her legs. With fingers twined behind his neck, she closed her eyes, letting her head fall back as he lifted her off the floor.

Suddenly, he was in her, pressing upward. Gently, he found his way to the floor and leaned back against the couch, allowing her to straddle him. He pulled her head down to his and captured her mouth, kissing her deeply, passionately and throughly. When she came, he was there with her—two lovers, joined in time and space, and spirit.

Long blond curls fell from her shoulders, and she brushed back one side with her hand. "Hi, cowboy," she whispered softly.

"Hi." A mischievous look crossed his handsome face. "Want to have a party here?"

Keri laughed. "You promised me dancing, so let's go."

Brian smiled back at her. "Next time I'll be more careful what I promise."

Chapter Thirty-Three

"I could hold you like this all night." Brian whispered into Keri's ear. He held her gently, pressing her soft body close against him as they danced. The music was slow and sensual, lulling them both into a false sense of security.

"Me, too." Keri sighed, overwhelmed by his nearness. She could feel his strength and warmth radiating through her, caressing her, protecting her. Somehow she had to find a way to clear Brian. She would not be able to face the pain she knew would come if he were found guilty of murdering Emilia.

As if he sensed her fears, Brian moved away, forcing her to look up at him. His eyes smiled deeply into hers and warmed her soul. Gently, his mouth captured hers. Keri came alive with emotion. She knew then that she didn't want to spend another night without him.

Keri groaned inwardly as the slow music ended and a fast tempo came on. "Let's sit this one out." Keri turned and led the way off the dance floor and back to their table.

Brian signaled the waiter to bring new hors d'oeuvres over

to the table. "I haven't had a chance to talk with you since I came back from Texas."

"True." Keri sipped the last of her champagne and handed Brian her glass.

Brian poured more champagne while the waiter set a medley of delights on the table.

"Keri, have there been any more incidents or threats that I should know about?"

"I'm not sure. There were some calls over the weekend on the answering machine. Just heavy breathing, like before. During the week there haven't been any." Keri helped herself to a cheese puff, savoring its mellow taste.

He didn't want to frighten her, but she had to be told. "You're not safe at home. I know how the phantom car got in. Tonight, to prove a point, I tailgated a resident right past the guard. By just smiling and waving as I went by, the guard didn't realize what I was doing."

"Oh, no, no!" Keri looked at him horrified.

"What's wrong?"

"Right before you came to the door, I got another one of those telephone calls. When you knocked, I dismissed it as being the guard with a bad connection." Suddenly, she felt foolish. How easily she had deceived herself. The guard would not have been breathing heavily in her ear. Embarrassed, she glanced at Brian and looked away.

Was it the killer or was it merely a coincidence? Brian's concern deepened as he thought of ways to protect her. "Call the telephone company next week. You can add Caller I.D. service that tells you the number the call is coming from. Maybe we can track down who is doing it."

"That's a great idea." Keri sighed. Why hadn't she thought of that? "I'll call Tuesday and set it up."

Brian helped himself to the hors d'oeuvres. "Now tell me what's going on with Hector Rodriguez. What was it that you didn't want to talk about at the office?"

"It wasn't about Rodriguez; it was about Roy." Keri sipped at her champagne. "Monday, Roy was furious with me for disappearing. He got even angrier when I wouldn't tell him where I was."

"It's none of his business."

"I know. That's what I told him." Keri lowered her voice and leaned toward Brian. "He got this odd look on his face and told me that you killed Janet Davis. Then he just stood there waiting to see how I would react. He said it would be just a matter of time before the police arrested you. The way that he said it implied that it would be immediate."

"That's why you questioned Rodriguez the way you did?"

"Yes. Roy also told me that he called Lt. Rodriguez to set up a conference, but that he hadn't returned his call."

"You didn't believe him, I take it."

Keri's eyes widened in earnest. "Not for a minute. Rodriguez is a stickler for returning telephone calls. He never misses."

"That's interesting. Why would he lie?"

"I don't know." Keri reached for a Swedish meatball. "There's something else that bothers me. Roy always seems to know what's going on. He knew about the loaner car, but he didn't ask me where my car was. He couldn't have cared less."

"How would he know?"

"I guess he saw the black Mercedes in the parking garage at the office. I sure didn't tell him." She picked up her glass and glanced back at Brian. "Roy is a manipulator. Everything he does is designed to get people to do what he wants them to do. I assume that he has been trying all this time to convince me that we should plea bargain."

"I agree. Maybe he really does believe that the evidence is overwhelming. He was certainly trying to build a case for plea bargaining today. We've known all along that he believes I killed Emilia." Brian reached for her hand and held it tight.

"Keri, I don't care how overwhelming the evidence is, I won't agree to a lesser charge. I am *not* guilty!"

"I believe you," Keri whispered. "The fact that someone is guilty has never stopped Roy from litigating before. Now with the whole country looking on, you would think that he would want all the attention."

"Unless he thinks that he can't win." Brian suggested.

"I don't think so. People forget details, but they remember the name and the face. It's great publicity for him, win or lose."

"You could be right." He released her hand and rubbed his chin thoughtfully. "What really has me stumped is the question Rodriguez asked about the red pickup truck. I think that he deliberately avoided answering me."

"I'm sure of it." Keri hesitated. "Brian, didn't D.R. say that he drove a red pickup truck?"

"Yes. I'd like to know what the connection is."

"I'll call Lt. Rodriguez next week and see what he will tell me. Maybe we should call Matthew, too."

"Good idea." Brian stood up and held out his hand. "Let's dance."

Once on the dance floor, Brian pulled Keri into the circle of his arms. "Let's don't talk about murder anymore. We could use some comfort and peace." Gently, he held her in silence, slowly moving to the rhythm of the music.

Keri pressed herself against him while she rested her head against his chest. She could hear the rhythmic sound of his heartbeat against her ear. Her body ached for the fulfillment that only he could give, but common sense told her they would have to be cautious.

"Come home with me, Keri. Spend the night with me." Brian's whisper stirred the primitive urges within her.

Desperation filled her. No matter how much she wanted him, he was still her client and it was just too risky. Above all else, she had to protect him. "No, Brian. Lt. Rodriguez is having us followed. It could be extremely prejudicial to you in court.'' Even as she denied him, the rejection tore at her heart.

"If I'm convicted, we won't have any time together." His voice was rough with emotion.

"Brian!" Keri protested. "You shouldn't talk that way. Besides, it will give me someone to visit while the case is on appeal."

Dumfounded, Brian stopped in the middle of the dance floor. He studied her face and saw the laughter in her eyes. "Very funny, Princess." Quickly, his lips found hers. His demanding kiss threatened to overwhelm her. When he felt her respond, he released her. "How about your place then?"

Keri laughed. "You don't give up do you?"

"I've heard that before." Brian looked at her mischievously. "We can fool them. We can cruise up the coastline, come into the bay at Haulover Inlet and moor at Laughing Gull Cove. No one would know."

Keri realized that he was quite serious. Then it hit her. "You have a sport fishing yacht docked at Dinner Key Marina, don't you?"

"Yes. The *Misty II.*"

"You certainly have a clever mind." Keri answered.

Brian moved his hands slowly down her back and pressed her hips to his. His lips slowly met hers before giving way to a fiery intensity. He released her mouth long enough to whisper to her. "A moonlight boat ride would be romantic." Again, he claimed her lips, sending waves of desire over her.

Keri moaned her assent and allowed herself to be led off the dance floor.

Chapter Thirty-Four

"Are you lost?" Her words hung silently in the air as Brian checked the rear-view mirror. She had thought that it was rather odd that he was taking such a circuitous route to the expressway, but he knew this area well, so she hadn't questioned him.

"No." He finally answered. "I thought that we were being followed, but the lights turned off about a block back."

Keri shuddered. "I didn't think to notice when we left the club. At first, I thought you were headed for Dinner Key a new way. Why didn't you say something?"

"I didn't want to alarm you." Brian checked the rear-view mirror again. "We were definitely being followed. I noticed car lights following us from the Seventh Inning Club. That's when I decided to take some of the winding streets of Miami Lakes. When it became obvious to the driver that I was deliberately going in circles, the lights turned off."

"Do you want to take me home?" Keri was worried. He couldn't stand bad press right now. News of an affair with his attorney would destroy their credibility. That would be the end of her ability to establish reasonable doubt.

"No!" Brian glanced at her quickly as he turned the car onto the Palmetto Expressway. His voice softened before he added, "I'm looking forward to my romantic boat ride."

"Me, too." Keri sighed and settled back. She just hoped that they weren't still being followed. It would have to be the press or the police, more likely the police, because the press was more insistent.

"I think that I will go a different route." Brian glanced over at Keri and smiled reassuringly. "We'll take the Okeechobee Road exit to Miami. It's a good short cut."

"Doesn't Okeechobee Road parallel Miami River?"

"Only to the airport. I'll cut off there and head for Coconut Grove." Brian reached for her hand and held it gently. "I want to make this a special night for you. Out on the water, no one will be able to bother us. We'll be able to forget, even if just for a few hours."

Keri turned and smiled brightly. "It already has been a special night for me." Nothing could compare to the sweetness of his kiss, the gentleness of his caresses, or the consideration he constantly showed to her. Then there was the passion, the unbelievable passion that made her feel alive, really alive.

A pleased look crossed over Brian's face as he checked the rear-view mirror. Brian flipped on the turn signal and turned the Lexus onto the off ramp at the Okeechobee Road exit. At the light he released Keri's hand and checked the rear-view mirror once again. He noticed several trucks entering the off ramp—nothing more. When the traffic light turned to green, he turned onto Okeechobee Road and positioned the car in the far right lane.

"Could we stop somewhere and buy some snacks and sodas to take with us?" Keri asked. After all they had eaten—but then, she always got hungry out on the water.

"Sure. I'll get a bag of ice, too." Brian turned to smile at Keri. "There's a grocery near the Marina."

"Brian! Look out!" Keri screamed as a red pickup truck attempted to sideswipe the Lexus.

Keri listened for a sickening crash of metal against metal, but Brian swerved the car off the pavement, avoiding impact. The Lexus careened wildly toward the river as Brian fought for control. With a quick twist to the steering wheel, Brian spun the car around, barely missing the water's edge.

When the engine stalled, Brian jammed on the emergency brake, jumped out of the car, and ran up the shoulder of the road to find their assailant. An empty road lay ahead of him. When he saw no one, not even a witness, he turned with a shrug and headed for the car.

Brian threw open the passenger door and pulled Keri out. "Are you hurt?"

Keri grabbed Brian and held him tightly. "No. Just scared." Her heart pounded rapidly and her knees gave way beneath her.

Brian lifted her and placed her gently back in the car. "I should take you to the hospital, you've been under too much stress lately."

"No. Let's go. We have a boat to catch." Keri breathed deeply, trying to calm her racing heart. Don't think about it, she told herself. We're safe.

"Don't you want me to call the police?"

"And tell them what? We don't have any proof. They would just suspect us of setting it up." A bitter tone crept into her voice. "The newspapers would get the story and blow it up into the news of the year. Once I am linked to you romantically, my ability to establish reasonable doubt is gone. Without that, I won't be able to give you an effective defense. Forget it, Brian. It could only hurt us."

Brian stared down at Keri. "Sometimes you surprise me with your insight. You're right, the chance of the police believing me and looking for an assailant is slim to none. Rodriguez will be involved and he's hostile toward both of us.'' He shut the door and walked to the driver's side. ''We need to get away from the river fast, before we attract attention.

Keri sighed with relief when he pulled the Lexus back onto the street. Did the killer intend to continue stalking them or had he fled? She would have to be more observant. She should have paid attention tonight; she knew better. Assuming that being with someone would insure her safety was naive. Apparently, it didn't matter to the killer whether or not she was alone. To make matters worse, she suspected that he had been looking for the chance to find them both together. Shaking her head slightly, she realized that she was also assuming the killer was a man. Well, she had no reason to think otherwise.

''Forget it, Keri, we have a good night ahead of us.''

''I can't forget. It was a red pickup truck, but I missed the make and the license tag. You know what kind of truck D.R. has. Was it his? Did you see him? Why would he want to kill us?''

''The truck was the same make and model as the one D.R. owns. But it didn't have a tag. That's an indication that the truck could be stolen. Someone could be trying to frame D.R. or could be just trying to cast suspicion his way.'' With a grim set to his face, he pulled into the parking lot of a small food market and parked the car.

''Well, it also could be him, not wanting to be identified.'' Keri climbed out of the car and headed for the door. Brian locked the car and joined her. When the cold air hit her bare shoulders, she remembered she was dressed in a strapless cocktail dress and he in a white dinner jacket. They definitely looked out of place.

Keri was relieved that there were no other customers at the all-night market. She picked out some snacks and sodas and motioned to Brian. All she wanted was to get on the boat. She was going to be edgy until they put out to sea. There they could get lost fast. The killer wouldn't be expecting them to be taking a midnight boat ride.

This time they both watched the road, to the front, to the rear, and to the sides, as they entered Coconut Grove. Nothing looked suspicious when Brian parked in the private, gated parking lot of the marina. The lot was concealed from the road by man-made knolls. From the street, no one would be able to see Brian's car. Thank goodness, she breathed, safety was only a few hundred yards away.

Chapter Thirty-Five

Misty II bounced lazily against the dock, ricocheting off the protective bumpers only to be returned again by the restraining ropes. One look at her long sleek hull and Keri knew that *Misty II* was a high-performance vessel.

"She's beautiful, Brian!"

"Built for pleasure," he whispered in her ear.

Keri flamed. Did he mean her or the boat? She hadn't been expecting a double entendre from him. When she finally thought of a good retort, Brian had already boarded and flipped on all of the lights.

"Welcome aboard, Princess." Brian held out his hands and helped Keri onto the deck. She slipped off her shoes and followed him into the main salon.

"Take a look around. After I put away the groceries, I have to check out the boat." He looked at her in subtle amusement. "Make yourself at home. The master stateroom is on the port side at the foot of the galley steps."

"Thanks." Keri decided to look around. The spacious air-conditioned interior was painted a soft cream, with upholstery in pale lavender. White ash replaced the traditional teak trim and cabinetry throughout. Instead of the standard plush carpeting found in yachts of its class, the carpet was a lavender and cream-flecked berber. There was a built-in stereo system and TV. The spacious bedrooms were decorated in soft tones of blue and lavender. The crowning touch was the rod and reel locker the size of a large closet. Inside was the most amazing collection of tackle that she had ever seen. It fit the owner like a glove, Keri decided.

She knew they were about to put out to sea. Keri noticed the absence of the sounds of bumping against the dock. The boat came to life with a throaty roar. The engines were a powerhouse beneath a luxury finish.

Keri returned to the master cabin. It was spacious and had a pleasing masculine ambiance. On impulse, she removed her cellular telephone from her purse and placed it on the console near the bed. Anxious to find something more seaworthy to change into, Keri opened the closet door and browsed through Brian's clothes. A pair of white cotton shorts and a rayon seersucker sport shirt in a pale green color looked promising. She slipped off her dress and pantyhose and placed them in an empty drawer with her jewelry. She put her shoes and purse in another drawer. That should protect them, she decided. Clad only in bikini panties, Keri took Brian's clothes over to the bed and put them on.

The white shorts were a loose fit with the waistband settling at her hips, but they were comfortable. Brian's weight must be in those powerful shoulders of his, Keri thought, as she pulled the big shirt up over her shoulders and tied its front tails tightly at her waist. Her fingers found a few buttons to fasten, but none of them went high enough to keep her breasts securely covered. Well, she sighed, it would just have to do.

Keri mounted the stairs to the galley and grabbed two glasses for ginger ale. A little more rummaging resulted in the soda and some ice. Glasses in hand, she found the stairs leading up to the flybridge where Brian sat at the steering station.

"Ginger ale?" Keri asked, handing him a glass.

"Great." Brian's gaze traveled over her appreciatively as she stood next to him. "I never knew my clothes could look so good."

"You don't mind do you?" Keri looked up at him with an impish smile.

"Not if I can have them back later." His voice held a decidedly suggestive meaning. He glanced at her long legs before returning his attention to the dark waters and flashing buoys ahead of them.

The breeze off the water was intoxicating. Keri gloried in the feel of its cooling fingers teasing her hair and lifting her shirt away from her skin. She closed her eyes and sipped the last of her ginger ale. She wanted to drink it all in, the cool of the evening, the rush of the breeze over her body, the thrill of Brian next to her.

Keri looked around the wide and roomy flybridge. There was seating forward of the console for guests. "You must do a lot of entertaining."

His quiet laugh rippled across the water. "Sometimes. The seats accommodate about ten people. Guests who are not fishing have a grandstand view of the action without interfering with the helmsman or crew. It's a great way to relax."

"You've got a wet bar and an icemaker up here." Keri's smile broadened in approval. At first she had thought that only the electronics were installed in the console.

"There's a stereo sound system in there, too. Flip it on."

Gentle music caressed her as she settled comfortably on the soft padded bench seat, ready to enjoy the cruise. Slowly, fatigue crept over her. Her head nodded sleepily. She pulled her legs up and stretched out. If she could rest for just a few moments . . .

Sheer physical desire surged within Brian, threatening to

snap his iron will. Every fiber of his being wanted her. His eyes traveled languorously over her. She looked lovely napping across from him in his big shirt. It fluttered in the wind, exposing her tantalizing breasts intermittently. It was all he could do to keep his mind on piloting the boat instead of pressing his mouth against her soft, firm breasts, and tasting her satin skin.

Brian walked over and kissed her forehead before shifting his gaze back over the channel. Soon he would be out of the channel and into deep ocean water. Then, the cruise would be safe and uneventful. Tonight had been a close call for them. Did she realize how close they came to being at the bottom of Miami River? He was angry with himself for not being more observant. Truthfully, he hadn't been expecting a truck to be a source of danger. Whoever the killer was, he was devious. Brian recalled the incident over and over again, trying to remember a clue, no matter how insignificant. Finally, he rested his thoughts and pushed in the throttle, anxious to reach the boat's thirty knot cruising speed.

The ocean was calm as the yacht made its way up the coastline. Brian set the controls on automatic pilot and lowered himself onto the bench after gathering a sleeping Keri in his arms. While his head rested gently against hers, he breathed in the faint scent of perfume in her hair. His lips brushed her cheeks gently as he cuddled her closer. Keri stirred.

"Guess I dropped off to sleep." What a romantic feeling, waking up in Brian's arms, feeling the cool ocean breezes, and smelling the fresh salt air. She knew she must be dreaming, but what a dream.

"Guess you did." He smiled that wonderful smile and she melted. Surely she had found heaven. She caressed his face with her hand and traced his smiling, tender lips with her fingers.

"We'll be at Laughing Gull Cove soon."

Keri laughed softly. "Are you telling me to behave myself?"

"No, but we don't have time to finish anything you start."

"I start?" Keri looked at him incredulously. "I can't believe you said that! If I remember correctly, you have been the one pursuing me. Who invited me to Fort Worth?"

Brian grinned. "A mere technicality."

"Technicality?" Keri squirmed out of his hold and jumped up. "Who invited me on this moonlight cruise anyway?" Happiness welled inside of her as she watched his eyes sparkling with mischief.

"I did." Without further comment, he grabbed her hips, pulled her to him, and kissed the top of her bare tummy.

"Hey, you're tickling me!" Keri laughed with pleasure. What kind of madness was this that only a kiss could excite her so? She could feel his hands grasping her bottom, as if he would never let her go. He was going to make her crazy and they didn't have time.

Brian kissed her tummy once more then looked up into her smoldering eyes. "I brought you back something from Fort Worth?"

"Really? What?"

After running his hands down the back of her legs, he released her and stood up. "You'll have to open it." He reached for a package sitting on the console, wrapped in white paper with blue ribbon and a big floppy bow.

Eagerly, Keri tore open the package and pulled out a delicate macramé hoop covered with beads and feathers and streamers. "It's beautiful," she whispered.

"It's an authentic dreamcatcher. The Indians believe that if you hang a dreamcatcher above your bed at night that it will catch all the nightmares in the webbing and only allow the good dreams through. I figured that if I gave you one, you would stop having nightmares and only dream about me."

"Oh, Brian." Tears filled her dark eyes. "It's a lovely gift."

She kissed him sweetly on the lips and laid her head against his chest. He caressed her gently and held her close. "We're coming up on the inlet now. Sorry, but I've got to play captain."

"I'll go put this away and then come help." She turned and made her way down the stairs.

Brian's eyes followed Keri down the stairs and out of his sight. What a night. It had all started out so innocently. Without warning, the red truck flashed in his mind. And a face. Had he seen the driver's profile or was it his imagination? Unbelievable, he thought. What possible motive could there be? There was no evidence that would connect the driver to either murder. If his suspicions were correct, he would have to find a way to prove them.

Chapter Thirty-Six

Anchored safely at Laughing Gull Cove, *Misty II* swayed gently with the early morning swells of Biscayne Bay. The sun inched over the horizon to cast its rays over the water. The sounds of water lapping against the sides of the hull woke Brian. He looked at Keri sleeping peacefully next to him on the bed and decided not to wake her. With more than a little effort, he showered, shaved, and slipped on a blue bikini bathing suit. Taking one last look at Keri, he went upstairs to fix breakfast.

Awakened by the smell of bacon, Keri stretched sleepily. The feel of the sheets next to her skin told her that she had no memory of coming to the cabin or taking her clothes off. One thing she was sure of; they hadn't made love; she would definitely remember that. She made her way to the shower, where the cold water stole the last vestiges of sleep from her. She slipped into the shorts and shirt from the night before. The shirt clung to her skin where droplets of water remained after the shower. Old habits die hard, she thought, realizing she should have dried off first.

Keri ran her brush through her tangled hair, forcing it to fall softly into place. Barefoot, she headed for the galley, eager for breakfast and Brian.

"So, you cook, too?" Keri smiled at Brian. "I like my eggs sunny side up."

"Your wish is my command, Princess." Brian's bright blue eyes flashed with humor and happiness, as they fixed on the wet shirt clinging to her breasts.

Keri studied him while he stood cooking their eggs and buttering their toast. If she hadn't been so hungry, she would have run to him, caressing and kissing every inch of him.

With breakfasts in hand, he crossed the galley to the dinette. His laughing eyes caught hers in a moment of pure pleasure. He knows how much I want him, Keri thought in amazement, while he poured the coffee for them. When he finally came to the table to eat, he pulled her up from her seat to kiss her deeply.

Keri settled back down into her seat while Brian searched for the sugar. Her eyes were riveted to him, his passion unmistakably evident. "I fell asleep on our romantic evening, didn't I?" Her husky voice betrayed her arousal.

"It doesn't matter. We both had a rough day." He grabbed the sugar and sat down. "How about tonight? Same time, same place?"

Her brazen eyes raked him, while she recklessly invited, "How about after breakfast?"

He grabbed her hand and nibbled each finger seductively before he decided. "You have a date!"

They laughed together. "We need to go ashore and pack your bags for the weekend," Brian said.

"Where are we going?" Keri asked eagerly. She didn't care; not as long as she was with him.

"Key Largo. Since it's the Fourth of July weekend, everyone

will be out on the water. If you've never seen it before, it's quite a sight. Thousands of boats migrate down to the keys for the holiday. It's like being in a regatta.''

"Wonderful. We'll have to shop for food though.''

"No. Last night we just picked up snacks. I had already stocked up for the weekend.'' He flashed a confident smile.

"You were that confident that I would come with you?'' Keri felt mildly embarrassed.

"Not at all. I planned to spend the weekend out on the water and I hoped that you would want to join me. So, I shopped for two.'' His expression grew serious. "You do want to come, don't you?''

Keri brightened. "Of course I do.''

She reached for the jam and spooned a healthy amount onto her toast. For some reason she was ravenous. Must be the great sex! Keri chuckled softly and took a bite out of her toast. It was going to be a great weekend, she decided.

"So let me in on the joke.''

Keri smiled. "No joke. Honest. I was just enjoying the breakfast. I'll probably gain at least five pounds on this trip, if not more.''

"Maybe not. There are ways to stay trim.'' Looking pleased with himself, Brian replenished his coffee. "You're going to have to fish to earn your keep.''

"Really. That's great! Only . . .''

"Only what?''

With a look of feigned terror, Keri whispered, "I don't know how.''

"Then I guess that I will just have to teach you.'' Brian grinned. "Think you can stand it?''

"Maybe,'' she answered in a noncommittal voice. "Roy told me that he went down to the keys with you and some of the team members once. Did you have to teach him?''

"No, Roy knows how to fish. He's been on this boat more

than once.'' Brian gave her a penetrating look. "What else did
he tell you?''

"That he had a great time.'' Keri sensed that his mood was
turning to serious. What had she said to cause such a quick
change? Maybe she could get him to open up and confide in
her. There were so many things about him that she wanted to
know and some things she absolutely had to know. Like what
brand of toothpaste does he use? Is he big on pizza and beer
and football games? Does he shave on weekends? Not to mention, was Rebecca Lawrence back in his life? More important,
how does he feel about her?

"And?''

"He assured me that you didn't throw any wild parties while
he was on board, nor did you invite any women. As a matter
of fact, he told me that there were no women in your life and
that you kept a low profile.''

"Did you believe that?'' A smile teased at the corners of
his lips as he placed a sweet roll in front of her.

"Absolutely not! I saw all those pictures of you in the scandal
sheets. You were with Emilia Martinez at some wild parties.
I thought for sure you were a party animal and a womanizer
to boot.'' There she had said it. How would he take it? She
held her breath, half afraid that he would get angry.

Looking a little dumbfounded, Brian stirred his coffee. "I've
been accused of worse. Is there anything else he told you that
you care to repeat?''

"Aren't you going to deny any of it?''

"Not yet.''

Should she take the plunge? Should she tell him that she
knew about Rebecca Lawrence and chance losing him? If he
cared about her, surely he would give her some explanation.
Matthew had gone out of his way to warn her to be careful
and so far, she had totally ignored the warning. Better to find
out now than halfway down to Key Largo.

"Well, he told me that you had been engaged to Rebecca

Lawrence and that she dumped you for a title̲
was of the opinion that because of the pain and em̲
Rebecca caused you, that you would not allow yo̲
become involved with a woman again.'' Keri watched a̲
tions played across his face. Filled with regret, she reached
his hand and held it gently.

"So far, I can't take offense to anything he has said. I'm
rather amazed that he told you all that and yet he is still convinced that I had an affair with Emilia.'' He looked out over
the bay, avoiding Keri's gaze.

"It's the evidence. It's very damaging. Apparently, he
decided he was wrong about you. Having an affair with a
married woman is a good way to avoid commitments. He knows
that.''

"Well, I didn't have an affair with Emilia.'' He turned back
to Keri and reached for his coffee.

"What about Rebecca Lawrence, Brian?'' Keri lifted her
cup to her lips. Was it possible to find out how he felt without
alienating him?

"What about her?'' Angry sparks lit in his eyes as he
answered her in a guarded tone.

"I heard that she came back to Fort Worth and that she
wants you.'' Her chest tightened, anticipating his answer. In
just a few months he had become such an important part of
her life that she couldn't stand the thought of losing him now.

Brian leaned back and sighed. "You've got some interesting
sources. I guess I have Matthew to thank for that?'' A smirk
crossed his face as he gazed at her.

"You haven't answered me.'' Keri searched his face for
some emotion that she could identify. What was he thinking?
Her heart sank. Apparently Matthew had been right and she
had disregarded his warning, recklessly jumping headlong into
a consuming relationship with a man she hardly knew, a man
charged with murder.

"Rebecca came back to Fort Worth to spend some time with

parents. She is divorced and as far as I can tell, has a
mber of men interested in her. While I was in Fort Worth,
e looked me up and invited me to have dinner with her and
er family. I didn't turn her down.'' His steady eyes met hers.
''Anything else you want to know?''

''Yes.'' Keri's heart pounded in her throat. She had to ask.
''Do you still love her?''

''I don't know how I feel.'' Brian rose and headed for the
refrigerator. ''Want a soda?'' When she nodded, he brought
the soda to the table and returned for the glasses and ice. ''What
I do know is that until the trial is over, my emotions will
be in a constant state of turmoil. I can't make promises or
commitments. I can't make plans for the future. What have I
got to offer any woman right now?''

Keri felt his pain as deeply as she felt her own. She watched
him as he returned to the table and poured a bubbling, cold
soda for her. So she was reckless, she thought. It made her feel
alive. No one could have brought her out of her shell the way
Brian did. She knew that he had gambled on her; now it was
time to gamble on him.

''A weekend of fishing in the keys?'' she answered.

''You still want to go with me?'' He looked at her in disbelief.

''If you still want me.''

Powerful hands and arms pulled her from her seat and pressed
her hard against him. His mouth crushed hers with a relentless
intensity, robbing her of her doubts, her fears, and her self-
control.

''I want you,'' he whispered savagely in her ear. His hot
breath traveled across her skin before he captured her mouth
again. It was a long, compelling kiss, promising her wild,
passionate love. She moaned beneath his ardent fury. Desire
flashed through her.

''Last chance to change your mind, Princess,'' he breathed
heavily. His hands caressed her breasts through her thin seersucker shirt while he waited for an answer.

Was he crazy? Change her mind? Her pulse pounded wildly. She lived for his touch and she wasn't about to give it up without giving it her best shot. Damn Rebecca Lawrence. There must be some way to make him forget her and she was game to try. "Last chance to change *yours,* cowboy!"

"Grab the glasses, we're going downstairs." He picked up the sodas and headed for the master cabin.

By the time Keri reached the cabin, he had ripped off his bathing suit. "Lie down, he commanded."

She settled in the middle of the bed and had barely unzipped her shorts when he yanked them off and spread her legs. Caught by surprise, she gasped when he positioned himself between her legs and lowered his body. He unbuttoned her shirt and eased it back around her shoulders, pinning her arms down. "What are you doing?"

"Worried, Princess?"

"Not a chance."

"Good."

In an act of naked possession he trapped her mouth with his and shoved his tongue deep inside her. She tasted him, consuming him with her own fathomless heat. She felt herself spiraling toward a dark abyss of sheer passion. Lifting his lips to allow her to breathe, Brian's eyes sought out hers, filling her with expectations of rapturous pleasure. Breathless, she begged him. "Now, Brian, now."

"Not a chance," he teased. Laughing softly, he explored her with his fingers. She squirmed and tried to free herself, but his weight was too much for her. Fighting for self-control, he nudged himself inside her, gently at first, then wildly. His body shivered and shook as he came, pressing deep into her center, bringing cries of joy from the very depth of her being.

When he rolled off, Keri snuggled against him, content in the warmth of his arms. I love him, she thought as she drifted off to sleep. *I really love him.*

Chapter Thirty-Seven

"Your reel is singing!" Brian shouted. "Keep it taut."

Filled with excitement, Keri allowed the fish more line, then began reeling in to set up tension. Her rod began bending as the fish fought the drag. "How am I doing?" Keri looked up eagerly while she hung on tight.

"Great. Don't go slack. Keep the tension. Good girl."

Clad only in bathing suits, they had trolled most of the morning, catching fish along the way. She was finally getting the hang of it, thanks to Brian's patient tutoring. This one, though, was getting harder to handle than the rest. It must be a bigger fish.

"He's really fighting you, look at your rod!" Brian grabbed her rod from behind her and helped her hold on as it bent and shook from the strain. "Start reeling it in. Slowly."

Suddenly, the fish broke water.

"Look! It's a sailfish!" Keri quickly reeled in the slack resulting from the jump.

"You're working it good. It will be a while before it tires." Brian let go and returned to his chair.

For the next half hour Keri worked, reeling in, letting out, keeping the line just taut enough to keep the sailfish hooked, never enough for the line to break. The sun burned clear and hot. Sweat trickled down her face. Her hands hurt, her back ached. She stayed with her fish.

"I don't think it's fighting as much now." Keri glanced at Brian for instruction.

"Go ahead and try to bring him in." Brian moved close to her, ready to help, while Keri worked it in.

Light flashed off the silver blue body of the sailfish as Brian hauled it into the boat. "Hold on to it a minute. It could jump out."

Brian grabbed his camera and aimed. Keri laughed and looked up proudly while her hands clutched her catch tightly.

"Time to throw it back." With a quick economical motion, Brian removed the hook and returned the sailfish to the ocean. "Welcome to sport fishing. You did a great job!"

"I'm exhausted."

"Want a cold drink?"

Too tired to answer, Keri nodded. What fun! She had no idea! After he brought her a soda, he pulled a red snapper from their cache and began to clean and filet it.

"Could that be our dinner?" Keri asked hopefully.

"As a matter of fact, it is." Brian threw the scrapes into the bait box.

"Why, Mr. Michaels—" Keri teased. "—I just love a man who cooks."

He gave her a penetrating look. "Then I'm in good shape, wouldn't you say?"

Keri smiled, confident that he couldn't see her blush under her already flushed face, reddened by the salt air, sun, and heat of the day. She wasn't going to tip her hand so soon. Tired of being sticky and grubby, she rushed down to the cabin to take a quick shower and change. She pulled out a pair of denim shorts and a pale blue cotton knit pullover to put on. Within a few minutes, she was dressed and ready for lunch. She dashed up the stairs and peered up at Brian on the flybridge.

"Hi, cowboy. Ready for lunch?"

"I fixed it while you were in the shower. Come up and join me."

When she climbed up, his arm circled her shoulders. "Look out there. You can see the boats making their way down the keys. It will get even better later. We'll watch them after lunch."

It was a spectacular view; boats were in every direction, as far as the eye could see! Whitewater wakes stretched out behind each boat as their hulls pierced the water. Keri lowered the camera and settled back. They had spent the last hour on the flybridge watching the regatta-like formations heading south.

Shaded by the canopy, Keri thrilled at the wind in her face. Her skin tingled with salt from the day's accumulation of sea spray. Being outdoors always increased her appetite. She couldn't wait for Brian to cook. "When's dinner?"

An amused grin warmed his chiseled features. "Around six. We're near Key Largo where we'll stay for the night. One of my favorite spots is just up ahead. After we anchor, I'll fix coffee and we can have a snack."

"Sounds good." Keri got up and stretched. "I'm going to go shower off."

"Want company?" Brian teased.

"There isn't enough room." Keri smiled brightly and climbed down the stairs. The main salon was cool and inviting, offering instant relief from the heat. Brian cut back the engines as she reached the galley stairs. The bow came around and headed for a small channel between distant mangroves. Brian was a lot like nature, Keri reflected. There was something untamed in his eyes, his lovemaking. It frightened her and intrigued her, and she wanted more of it.

By the time she had finished her shower, the boat was anchored in a hidden cove. Keri slipped on her Hawaiian swim suit and wrapped her sarong skirt around her hips. She brushed her hair back and fastened it with a mother-of-pearl clip decorated with a matching silk hibiscus. As she reached for her perfume, strong arms encircled her waist and pulled her back against him.

"You look lovely," Brian whispered softly as he nuzzled her ear.

Chills ricocheted up and down her spine. Without a word, she leaned her head back and captured his mouth. She kissed him with passion, teasing him and finally denying him.

"Princess," he moaned huskily. "Wait for me. I need a fast shower." He backed away, stripping off his clothes as he headed for the shower.

The cellular telephone which Keri had taken from her purse lay on the console next to the bed. She reached for it and dialed her answering machine. The third message made her heart skip a beat. It was only heavy breathing. The fourth message brought a cry of horror.

"You're next!" A muffled voice rasped. "You're next!"

"Oh, no!" Keri choked back a sob. Who was doing this to her? Why did he want to kill her? A sense of panic engulfed her as she realized he wanted to kill Brian too.

"Keri, what's wrong?" Brian, alarmed by her outcry, stood before her, poised for action.

With a shaken voice she tried to explain. "He called, Brian. He says that I'm next." She gazed into his eyes in desperation. "Oh, Brian—if we don't catch him, he's going to kill us." Tremors shook her body. She rushed into his arms, pressing his wet body against hers.

Silently, they stood holding each other. Brian gently caressed her, calming her, reassuring her. He determined to find enough evidence to connect the killer to the murders. Their lives now depended on it.

"Keri, relax. No one knows where we are. This is our weekend to forget. Remember?" His voice coaxed and soothed her. He cupped her face in his hands and kissed her gently, erasing her fears.

"I remember." She kissed him, running her hands down his back, enjoying the feel of his soft, wet skin beneath her fingertips. "Make love to me Brian," she whispered. She wanted him, all of him, as often as she could.

Obliging hands helped her out of her bathing suit and led her up the stairs to the main salon.

"Where are you going?"

"*We* are going skinny-dipping. Come on." He caught her in his arms before she could protest and carried her out the door onto the deck where he dropped her feet. "Just climb over the side where I set up the steps. I'll be right behind you."

"No. There might be sharks."

"The only nipping you'll be feeling will be me, so get going."

"You're not very reassuring, Brian," Keri commented drily. One strong arm still encircled her waist. She weighed the possibility of escaping and decided against it. She was sure that he would just catch her and throw her in. She mounted the stairs and climbed down to the water's edge. Testing it with her toe surprised her. It was warm and clear. She lowered slowly in and pushed off with her feet. From her vantage point, she watched Brian jump in with a splash.

"Well, you just scared all the fish away," she teased.

"More than likely, I just attracted them."

"Very funny." Keri wondered if this wasn't a little too wild for her. Brian was wild enough for both of them. She looked at the beautiful, unspoiled scene. The sun was hanging in the West, casting shadows across the cove and turning the blue sky to pink, purple, and orange. A seagull flew over eyeing them as if they were potential food. A fish jumped in the distance. Maybe after a quick swim she could coax him back into the boat.

A half hour later they were still swimming and playing around the boat and Keri luxuriated in the feel of the water giving her a new sense of freedom. Keri made her way back to the stairs at the side of the boat. She was relaxed and in the mood for Brian's lovemaking. As if he sensed her mood, Brian's head popped up next to her.

"Ready to quit?" His bright eyes danced.

"Mmm." Keri nodded and turned to the stairs to climb up, but his strong hands grabbed her breasts and pulled her back against him.

"Not so fast," he teased. "Want me to make love to you?"

"While we tread water? No, thanks." Keri laughed, but something told her that he was serious.

"Where's your sense of adventure?"

"Haven't I heard that line before? Sure I did, in Fort Worth." Keri held on tightly to the stairs. "If you want sex, you'd better find a bed. I don't intend on drowning when you go wild!"

"Me? Go wild? Sure you have the right man?" Brian laughed and released her.

"Absolutely," she teased and pulled herself up the stairs. Seeing Brian's determined look, she ran into the main salon, past the galley, and down the stairs. He caught her at the edge of the bed in the master cabin and pushed her down, falling on top of her back.

"Maybe I won't make love to you. Maybe I'll go get dinner started," he threatened.

Keri giggled. "You couldn't stop now if you wanted to."

"Is that so?" His hands slid under her and grabbed her

breasts, caressing them with an urgency that sent her reeling. "Can *you* stop, Princess?"

"Yes," she lied with an unsteady breath.

"The hell you can!" He kissed her again, slowly, thoroughly, and passionately. Their lovemaking was resumed.

Chapter Thirty-Eight

"You look tremendous!" Jenna looked Keri over from the tip of her gleaming blond hair, down her beautifully tailored creme suit and soft pink blouse, to the pale creme pumps on her feet. Her weekend tan made her skin glow with vitality and health. "What have you done?"

"I spent the last three days swimming and eating to my heart's content. I also totally ignored anything remotely connected to work." Keri laughed. That was as close to the truth as she could comfortably get. Jenna meant well, but she had a big mouth. Keri glanced at the pastries Jenna held in her hands. "Is it that time already?"

"It's almost ten o'clock. Mr. Michaels and Mr. West are due here any minute. I have to go get the coffee before they come in. See ya."

Jenna placed the pastries on Keri's work table and left the room in a bundle of energy. Keri wondered if Jenna's excitement was due to Brian coming in. She understood the magnetism that Brian radiated. It was hard to resist.

Keri crossed the room to her desk and stared out the window. Images of Pablo with his hands around her throat, strangling her, still haunted her. Granted, he was hotheaded, but was he a crazed killer? She couldn't imagine him being cold and calculating enough to plan the accidents that had happened. More likely, he would react in the heat of the moment, just exactly the way he did at the Seventh Inning Club. With the exception of Rodriguez, he was the only one that Keri could think of who was angry enough at her to harm her. Yet, he had an alibi for the time of his wife's death. And what about the red truck? Would D.R. be so stupid as to try to run them down in his bright, easily identifiable, red truck? She doubted it. Still, angry people often committed crimes in the heat of passion.

Despite her restful weekend, Keri was worried. Tomorrow was the pre-trial hearing. Judge Pennell would also hear Roy's Motion to Withdraw as counsel for Brian. Would he let Roy withdraw this late into the proceedings? She had filed a Motion for Continuance to buy time. Time to convince Brian that he needed to hire big name counsel. Just yesterday, trolling back to Miami, she had warned him that he was taking a big chance using her. With a set to his jaw, he had told her that he didn't need dirty tricks; he only needed a jury who would believe him.

Keri closed her eyes and bit her lower lip, trying to hold back the flood of emotions which welled within her every time she thought about losing Brian. If he was convicted, she didn't think that she would be able to stand the pain it would cause her, not to mention the guilt that she would suffer. She couldn't give in to her feelings of anxiety, otherwise, her abilities would be compromised and she would not be able to give him the best defense possible.

''Hello, Princess.'' A husky voice caressed her from the doorway.

She spun around and flashed him a bright smile. His commanding presence and rugged good looks made him more virile than she thought possible. She gazed into his compelling eyes and felt excitement surge within her. Slowly, his seductive gaze changed to tenderness as he walked over and gathered her in his arms. Softly, he kissed her, gently tasting her, as if it were the first time. Keri pressed her warm moist lips against him, savoring the moment. The intimacy of their kiss left her radiating with pleasure.

"I missed you this morning." Keri gave him an impish look. "I had to cook my own breakfast."

Brian laughed. "I doubt you had any breakfast." He released her and walked over to the work table.

How did he know? She wasn't about to tell him that he was right. Anyway, it was time to quit playing and get down to business, if she could. His kiss had left her practically breathless and longing for more.

"Good morning." Matthew walked from the doorway over to Brian and shook his hand.

"Thanks for coming on such short notice." Brian motioned for Keri to come over.

"Hi, Matthew." Keri smiled. She had forgotten how handsome he really was. He looked impressive this morning in his navy blue suit—much like an entrepreneur about to start an important investment meeting. She laughed at herself before realizing that he wasn't as relaxed or friendly as he usually was. His clear gray eyes studied her intently while she sat down and faced him. Did he have bad news?

"Matthew, is there anything new on Emilia's murder?" Keri asked as she sat down.

Matthew pulled out a chair across from her. "I haven't been able to find anyone who could identify Brian out jogging on the day of Emilia's murder. Since no one has come forward, I doubt that we will get anywhere on that."

"I agree." Keri had anticipated his answer. "Anything else?"

"Well, I narrowed down the time frames on Emilia's paramours."

"Great. Let's have them." Keri reached for her legal pad and pen.

"About two years ago Donald Reid got involved with Emilia. That didn't last too long. He was arrogant and demanding. She wanted someone who was going to lavish her with money and gifts, and he didn't. In about six months, she dropped him and started seeing Jesse Davis. He gave her more attention than Reid, but he refused to spend a lot of money on her. Reid took the breakup hard. It was a blow when she broke up with him. He kept trying to see her, but she rejected him."

Keri glanced to Brian. She knew that he had never considered D.R. a suspect, but she had. Would this change his mind? She desperately wanted to find the killer before he found them. The trial would be coming up soon and surely, the killer would have to make his move before then. What would be next? What devious mind was working overtime, planning to kill them and make it look like an accident?

Matthew looked to see if Keri needed more time to jot down her notes. "Ready?" When Keri nodded, he continued. "Emilia's relationship with Jesse lasted about six months. She met Hector Rodriguez at a party about a year ago and dumped Jesse cold. Rodriguez was quite smitten with Emilia and they seemed to be a good match. The main problem was that his salary didn't go far. He was spending everything he had on her. Three months later she started seeing a younger man without telling Rodriguez. Apparently, this one had money to burn. She finally gave up Rodriguez four months later."

Rodriguez got dumped for a younger man with money. No wonder he was bitter. But why would he hate her? Keri drew a time line on her pad and scribbled in the important points.

"Where is that in terms of time?" Keri asked.

"It's about five months before her murder."

Brian looked at Matthew thoughtfully for a moment. "Did Rodriguez know about the new lover?"

"I'm certain that he did, but I don't have solid information." Matthew answered. "If I'm correct, that might explain his hostility toward you and Keri."

"Right. I was thinking that. If he didn't kill her, then he probably does believe that I did." Brian leaned back in this chair and glanced at Keri. Their eyes met and held for a quiet moment.

Did he really believe that Rodriguez killed Emilia? They both knew the problems with that theory. Keri wondered how she could turn this information to their advantage in the courtroom. With a surge of excitement, Keri smiled at Brian. His erotic gaze told her what she was aching to know. Keri felt her temperature rise and her heart begin to race. With him around it was hard to keep her mind on business. She had to keep pressing forward. There might be a clue, something they had missed, or something new that Matthew might say, that would give them the ammunition they needed to fight.

Keri turned and studied Matthew's face. He had been true to his word. Nothing he had found out or that she had told him had been printed in the paper. Should she take a chance and include him in the defense strategy? If she did, he would have to know more.

"Brian," Keri began in a low voice, "we're at a decision point. If we go further with Matthew on the facts and analysis, he will be privy to sensitive information. He won't have the attorney-client privilege to protect him."

Keri was sure that Brian knew what she meant. She was asking him if he wanted to take a chance on Matthew and his integrity. Right now, Brian felt as if he had nothing to lose, so she doubted that he would object.

"Go for it."

"Matthew, I want you to listen to a tape. Then we'll discuss it." Keri rose to go find Jenna. Jenna had forgotten their coffee and she wanted to retrieve the tape.

After she left the room, Brian turned to Matthew. "Did you enjoy the games at Arlington while you were there? I didn't have a chance to talk with you."

Matthew laughed. "I had a great time. Apparently, so did you. I saw you at one of the victory parties with Rebecca. I hear she's back to stay."

A smirk teased at the corner of Brian's lips. "Time will tell."

"She told me that she would be flying in today to be with you. Seems that she is outraged that you have not received any support from your own family." Matthew paused and looked at Brian's brooding expression. "Try to forgive her; she was young and foolish."

"Yeah."

"It's hard facing life-and-death situations alone." Matthew cleared his throat before continuing. "I want you to know, Brian, that I'm with you all the way." Matthew held out his hand solemnly. "I know that you have been framed."

With a cynical smile, Brian shook his hand. "I'm well aware that you are the only one who has believed in me from the beginning; not even my attorney believed me."

"Don't be too hard on Keri," Matthew said. "She lives in a world of lies and deception. Sometimes it's hard to recognize a simple truth. Especially when a rather ingenious mind has framed you."

"She is a good attorney. It's part of her training to be suspicious."

Matthew grinned. "She has a reputation as one of the best. She's very desirable. I should know, I've been dating her. Looks like she is starting to like sports. Someday she might even like baseball."

Brian's eyes flashed with surprise for a split second before a calm settled over his features. His mouth tightened as he sat waiting for Matthew to finish.

"Hot coffee coming up!" Jenna called as she crossed the room and set the coffee on the table. "Keri will be back in a minute. We have to go through certain procedures with the tape. It's evidence, you know." She smiled engagingly at the two bachelors before she left the room.

Brian was busy pouring the coffee when Keri returned. "Coffee?"

"Yes, thanks." Busy with her task, Keri sat down with the cassette and player, unaware that Brian's mood had darkened. "Help yourselves to the pastries while we're listening." Wasting no time, Keri turned on the machine and regulated the volume. She studied Matthew's face intently while he listened.

When the tape was finished, Matthew sat back in his chair and shook his head. "Wow!" He looked over at Brian. "He was hot!"

"That's the day that I recognized him. I remembered seeing him with Emilia. A very angry man, I might add." Brian avoided eye contact with Keri and casually poured himself another cup of coffee.

"I hear that Lt. Rodriguez is a very vindictive man. Looks like to me that even if he didn't kill Emilia, he wants revenge on the killer and anyone who champions him." Matthew glanced at Keri with a look of concern.

"I agree," Keri said. "What do you think of his accusations about the rings?"

"He had obviously been quite intimate with her. Were the rings really an issue?"

"In his mind they were," Brian answered. "Jesse looked into it for me. Pablo told him the rings weren't missing. They were locked in his safe."

Keri sipped her coffee before commenting. "Matthew corroborated his story. I need to know if the police checked into this. I don't want them to know that I see it as an issue, since the rings are part of my defense strategy.''

"No problem." Matthew tossed his pen on the table and beamed at Keri.

Keri smiled back, warmed by the close friendship they shared. She glanced at Brian, who was looking over some of Matthew's notes. A dark expression had settled over his features. Sensing her scrutiny, he looked up. For an instant, his eyes flashed with a look of pain, before an impenetrable shroud covered them. Keri wanted to reach out and comfort him, to ease his pain, and reassure him. But how? She couldn't lie and tell him that everything would fall into place. It just wasn't happening. She didn't have a good grip on this case and the identity of the murderer eluded them.

"What we know about the killer can be easily summarized," Keri began. "He has a very intelligent, devious mind and a violent temper. We know he wears a Dodgers baseball cap and has a hobby that involves fish. The killer is a risk taker. I suspect he enjoys the thrill of it. He has tried to run me over. My tires were slashed the day of Janet's murder, and now, he is leaving threatening messages on my answering machine." She turned to Matthew. "We had a near miss since I saw you last week. He tried to sideswipe Brian's Lexus and run us off the road and into the Miami River."

Matthew sat dumbfounded for a minute. "Did either of you get a good look at him when he tried to force you into the river?"

"No," Keri answered. "We did see that he was driving a red pickup truck. I don't know if it's a coincidence or not, but D.R. told me that he drives a red pickup truck. Then, last Friday, Rodriguez asked Brian if he saw a red pickup truck in Emilia's driveway on the day of the murder."

"Do you think that D.R. is the killer?" Matthew frowned as he studied Keri.

"I don't know what to think," Keri answered honestly. "I'm

suspicious of him, I'm suspicious of Pablo, and I'm suspicious of Rodriguez.''

Matthew turned to Brian. "I can certainly look into that if you want me to."

Brian nodded. "I want to know why Rodriguez is connecting the red pickup truck to Emilia's murder. When I asked him, he evaded answering me."

"Oh!" Keri remembered her last straw of hope. "Remember that I asked you to talk to Katie? Have you had a chance yet?"

"Not yet, but I'll get on it." Matthew made some notes and reached for the coffee.

Keri watched as Brian stretched and got up. The trial was coming up and nothing seemed to help his defense. Ordinarily, he didn't allow his feelings to show, but today he had been looking unusually worried. Keri grabbed her cup. Brian could very easily be convicted of a crime that he didn't commit.

Keri looked at Matthew over her cup. "Is there anything new on the death of Janet Davis?"

"Well, the police have been unable to come up with any clues so far. They did check out Brian's story and they have confirmed it. I think Rodriguez realizes that Brian couldn't possibly have been involved."

"Are they calling it a murder yet?" Brian walked to the window and stared unseeingly into the garden below. Like a pro with years of practice, he masked his inner turmoil and concentrated on Matthew.

"So far all they will say is that she died under 'suspicious circumstances.' "

Keri brushed back her hair and smiled at Brian. Then she turned to Matthew. "We have to find something common between the two women. Janet had information on Emilia's death and died before she could tell me."

Brian's eyes sharpened. "Do you think that you can get your hands on their telephone records?"

"Cellular?" Matthew asked.

''Yes. Not the monthly air time, but the actual telephone numbers that they called?''

''Wow. That's a hard one. I can try.'' Matthew jotted down a few notes.

''While you are at it, can you get credit card records and bank records for five months before Emilia's death and a couple of months before Janet's?'' Keri looked at the incredulous expression on Matthew's face. Excitement flowed through her. ''With some clever coaxing, Pablo might give them to you and I'm quite sure that Jesse will.'' Keri smiled before she turned to Brian. ''Remember Jesse Davis said that his wife spent a lot of money he didn't have? Well, its worth looking into.''

Brian gave an impatient shrug and glanced down at his watch. ''Well, keep me informed, you two.'' With an arrogant air of authority, he walked to the door. ''I have to pick up Rebecca at the airport.''

Keri sat in stunned disbelief as he turned and left the office without another word. Finally realizing that her mouth had dropped open in surprise, she clamped her jaw tightly shut and swallowed hard. Remember to breathe, dummy, she told herself, and inhaled deeply. What had just happened? Why did he leave so angry? Why was he picking up Rebecca?

''Keri.'' Matthew's soft call broke her trance.

She turned to him. She tried to speak, but couldn't.

''Keri, I'm sorry. I spoke with Rebecca at a victory party she attended with Brian last week. She told me that she was flying here to be with him during the trial, since none of his family had shown him any support.'' He reached for her hand and held it gently.

''I see,'' she whispered. She hoped Matthew didn't see her pain.

''I tried to discuss it with him when you were out of the room. He didn't have anything to add, nor did he deny it. I let him know that I had been dating you some. Perhaps I went too far.''

Keri looked at his face and saw he was sincerely sorry. Secretly, she knew that he had been trying to protect her, just as any friend would have done. He obviously thought that Brian was deceiving her, and obviously, he was right. Keri felt numb, but a gentle smile curved her lips. "No, Matthew, you didn't." She held his hand tightly. "Please, take me to dinner tonight. I don't want to be alone."

Matthew released her hand, stood up, and walked over to her. With his hands on her shoulders, he eased her out of her chair. "I'll pick you up at seven. We'll have dinner and go dancing."

Keri looked into his clear grey eyes and smiled. "Thanks, Matthew, that sounds like fun."

Chapter Thirty-Nine

The judge's chambers were hot and stuffy. Law books were piled haphazardly in open piles on tables where young part-time law clerks pored over them in the afternoons. The huge conference table where Keri and Brian sat was filled at one end with papers strewn in disarray. The Prosecutor, Louis Garcia, sat across from them watching Roy Foxx addressing the judge, who sat at the head of the table.

Keri was on edge and conscious of the tall man sitting next to her. Brian had dressed in a black suit and a black silk shirt which he had left open at the throat. The look accentuated his commanding presence. He had been cool toward her, leaving her frustrated. Luckily, she hadn't had the time to feel sorry for herself since he walked out of her office yesterday to go pick up Rebecca Lawrence at the airport. She wanted an explanation, and she intended to get one, but it would have to wait until the hearing was over.

Judge Pennell took a drink of his ice water while he listened to Roy Foxx explain why he was bailing out of Brian Michaels' defense. He didn't like Foxx much. He was arrogant and shrewd, always looking for a technicality or a minor error to take advantage of. Even if the errors weren't prejudicial, Foxx always managed to twist them enough to make them so. What was he up to this time? Surely, he realized how difficult he would be making it on Ms. Adams and Michaels by withdrawing at the last minute.

". . . and in conclusion, Your Honor, allowing me to withdraw will not, in any way, be prejudicial to the defendant. In fact, Mr. Michaels has fired me from the case." Roy Foxx glanced at Brian with a shrewd expression on his face.

Judge Pennell looked shocked. If Michaels had fired him, something was going on. He turned to Brian and addressed him. "Mr. Michaels, is it true that you have fired Mr. Foxx?"

"Yes." Angry and deliberate, Brian's icy blue eyes fixed on Roy.

Judge Pennell rubbed his chin thoughtfully. Foxx had never shown up in court to defend Michaels and all of the defense pleadings and motions had been signed by Keri Adams. "Would you please explain why?"

Brian turned to face the judge with an air of self-confidence. "He hasn't put any time or effort into my defense. In fact, I believe that he has done quite a bit to hinder it."

At Brian's comment, color stole over Roy's face, but he remained silent.

"Mr. Foxx?"

"That's his opinion, Your Honor."

"Ordinarily, I don't allow attorneys to withdraw from capital punishment crimes at the last minute. However, it does seem that an exception should be made in this case." Judge Pennell looked at Keri. "Do you have any objection, Ms. Adams?"

"None, Your Honor."

"Very well. Your motion is granted, Mr. Foxx. Submit an order to me." He opened the case file in front of him and glanced over the motions.

"Excuse me, Your Honor, there is a matter of fees," Roy pressed arrogantly.

"That, Your Honor, I would object to!" Keri glared at Roy. How dare he!

"Yes, Ms. Adams, you are quite right." The judge looked over his glasses at Roy. "Mr. Foxx, you should know by now that you must schedule a separate hearing on the issue of fees."

"Your Honor," Keri interrupted. "Now that Mr. Foxx no longer represents Mr. Michaels, I request that he be excluded from chambers."

"Mr. Foxx?"

Roy seethed with mounting rage. His face conveyed hate and fury as he glared at Keri. Then he quickly regained control. With a sardonic look at Keri, Roy rose from his chair, hurried across the room, and slammed the door behind him.

Judge Pennell coughed. "Yes, well . . ." A satisfied smirk crossed his face. That felt good, real good! But now, he had a murder to listen to. "Ms. Adams, I believe you have a motion to be heard?"

"Yes, a Motion for Continuance." Keri's heart was still beating rapidly from her encounter with Roy. She needed to calm down and keep her wits about her. Maybe if she didn't look at Brian, she could get through this hearing without exposing her frayed nerves and hurt pride. It was hard to keep her mind on her arguments, when all she wanted was to know why he had walked out on her.

"Mr. Foxx was lead counsel for Mr. Michaels' defense. Mr. Foxx failed to participate in the preparation of Mr. Michaels' defense and prohibited me from investigating avenues which we believe would have helped him. Mr. Michaels has been grossly prejudiced by the failure of Mr. Foxx to actively participate in his defense. I request a continuance so that Mr. Michaels will be able to secure competent, experienced counsel to defend him."

Judge Pennell smiled at Keri. She may not be as flamboyant

as Foxx, but in his opinion, she was way ahead of him in skill and ability. She had graced his courtroom many times, and he knew from experience that she would be completely prepared. She would be doing her client a disservice by getting a lead attorney other than herself.

"You seem to have been doing just fine without Mr. Foxx. Are you ready to go to trial?"

"We are still involved in our own investigation, Your Honor." He wasn't going to buy her arguments.

"Motion denied. Counselor, I think that it is refreshing to see modesty coming from such a good attorney. I can assure you that Mr. Michaels will get a fair and impartial trial."

Keri heart sank. What could she do except appeal his decision? There was nothing she could do. Brian was going to trial soon and she couldn't postpone it. She was afraid to look at Brian. Facing his disdain was more than she could take.

After another drink of cold water, Judge Pennell turned to the State's Prosecutor, Louis Garcia. "The defendant has been charged with Murder One. Does the evidence support the charge?"

"Yes, Your Honor. The court has been given a list of the trace evidence that the State will submit to the court. The State will have testimony on the physical elements of the evidence."

Judge Pennell perused the exhibit list, without comment. It was a short list, but it looked damaging. It looked like Keri Adams had her work cut out for her. "What's the motive, Counselor?"

"A crime of passion." His eyes watched Brian for any reaction. "The State will show that the defendant was having an affair with Emilia Martinez. She became fearful of his violent temper and tried to break up with him. The State will prove that he murdered her and that it was an act of revenge."

"Ms. Adams?"

"Your Honor, the defense is prepared to refute the evidence and show, beyond a reasonable doubt, that Mr. Michaels was

not having an affair with Mrs. Martinez, nor did he kill her.''
Keri wondered just how she was going to pull that one off. So
far, Brian had remained cool and quiet. He had leaned back in
his chair with a casual movement, looking deceptively relaxed.

"If I may, Your Honor," Garcia interrupted. "The State
will have witnesses to prove that he was having an affair with
her. Also, these witnesses can place the defendant at the scene
at the time of the murder. It's all there in the State's Pre-Trial
Memorandum and Exhibits.''

Once again the judge scanned the exhibits before commenting. "Ms. Adams, the evidence in this case appears persuasive.
I am sure that you have considered your alternatives.''

"Yes.'' If Brian was innocent, they had no alternative, but
she knew that the judge would press for a plea so that the case
could be settled. Most of the criminals were guilty and didn't
want to go to trial. Brian was no criminal.

The judge turned back to the prosecutor. "Mr. Garcia, have
you considered a lesser charge?''

"I did have some conversations with Mr. Foxx. He indicated
to me that the defendant would be willing to plea to a lesser
charge. He suggested Murder Three or possibly Accidental
Homicide. They both carry substantially reduced sentences,
Your Honor.''

"Ms. Adams?'' Judge Pennell peered over his glasses inquis-
itively.

It was Keri's turn to be furious. Roy's manipulations had
been carefully orchestrated. If Brian thought that he had no
defense, he would be forced to plea to a lesser charge.

She answered in anger, her voice strained under her professional poise. "May I remind Mr. Garcia that Mr. Foxx no
longer represents Mr. Michaels. Mr. Michaels is innocent of
the charges brought against him and he will not agree to a
lesser charge for something that he did not do.''

"The State would accept a plea of Accidental Homicide. I

am correct, Mr. Garcia?'' Judge Pennell opted for the charge with the most lenient sentence.

"Yes, sir.'' Garcia answered in petulant voice, annoyed that the judge was twisting his arm. He had wanted to negotiate a stiffer plea.

"Defense is not willing to plea bargain,'' Keri answered flatly, trying to keep tight control over her temper.

"Ms. Adams, I would be willing to postpone this pre-trial to next week in order for you to confer with your client.''

Even though Judge Pennell was trying to help her, this was one time she had to refuse. "Thank you for your consideration, Judge Pennell. Our position has already been thoroughly discussed with Mr. Michaels and he understands its implications. The defense does not wish to plea bargain.''

"Very well, Counselor.'' He studied his calendar before turning to the prosecutor. "How many days do you anticipate you will need, Mr. Garcia?''

"Three days.''

"Ms. Adams?''

"One and one-half days.''

"I am setting the trial for July 29, which is three weeks hence. There will be no continuances. The trial will start at ten-thirty.''

Keri's mind cut off the conversation that followed. How could she possibly analyze and develop a defense for Brian in just three weeks? She went through the rest of the hearing feeling numb. She was too emotionally involved to be doing this trial. She had compromised everything that she stood for in order to taste this man's love. Ultimately, it had cost her, just as it would cost him. She knew she had no business defending Brian; she was thinking with her heart and not her logical analytical mind. Roy had been right; she was not being objective. In the long run, it was going to hurt Brian.

Outside chambers, Keri stood quietly. Brian had gone to

check out the coffee shop. She shifted her weight to her other foot and looked down the long corridor. Roy turned the corner and hurried toward her. Apprehension rushed through her as she steeled herself to face him.

Chapter Forty

"Before you say anything, I'm not angry." Roy held up his hands in mock self-defense. "Really, I'm not!"

"Well, you did a good job of fooling me," Keri replied, wondering what he was up to now.

"Keri, you just don't understand me. I see this case differently. Brian doesn't have any defense and you know it." He looked at her in earnest. "I only wanted to keep him alive."

"I don't believe you, Roy." Keri answered. "You wouldn't let me investigate."

"Investigate what? So what if Rodriguez had an affair with Emilia? You still don't have a motive for murder."

"Maybe."

"Keri, I'm experienced. I have a feel for these cases. You can't win this one. Brian is going to fry!" A worried frown deepened the faint lines on his face.

"Roy! That's a terrible thing to say." Keri felt her heart pound in fear. She wanted to cry out in protest and in pain, yet he was voicing her own inner doubts and insecurities.

"Remember the first day that I told you about him? You were the one who pointed out to me that he was the type women would die for." He studied her face for a moment. "How about it, Keri? Two women have died for him. Are you willing to be the third?"

Keri unconsciously reached for her throat. "What do you mean?"

"Assume you get him off. How long before he tires of you?" Roy's expression filled with concern. "He will kill again. Think Keri. He doesn't have a defense because he is guilty."

"No. You're wrong," she said with more confidence than she felt. His logic was confusing. Of course, Brian could have been behind all of the accidents if he had been clever or devious enough, but she knew better. She knew what was in his heart, at least she thought she did. After yesterday's events, she could be wrong.

"He's a charmer. Look how the women in the office fall all over him. Keri, I like Brian. I want to keep him alive. That's why I wanted to plea bargain. Think, Keri! You must know me by now. I always do what I think is best for my client. When was the last time you heard of anyone getting an airtight Murder One felon, a plea of accidental homicide?"

She shook her head. She couldn't remember. It was a rather amazing plea, she had to admit.

"Keri, you want to try this case. In doing so, you're risking a man's life. This isn't just any man—it's someone that you care for. I didn't want to risk his life. I wanted to keep him alive."

"You make me sound selfish," she protested.

"Keri, I'm sorry everything happened the way it did. For Brian's sake, get him to plea; don't let him die. He'll be in jail a few years—long enough to cool off, and then he'll be back out, alive."

"He says that he didn't do it." Keri whispered.

"You believe him?" Roy raised his brows in surprise.

"Think it over objectively. Better still, talk to Rebecca Lawrence. I'll bet she can give you a new insight into him. Get her to talk to him. He might listen to her now that they are back together. I have to go, Keri. Remember, if he fries, it will be your fault. Can you live with that?"

Roy nodded to Keri and walked to the elevators leaving Keri standing in a state of shock and confusion. Roy could be so convincing. That's what made him such a good trial attorney. This time he seemed so sincere. Roy was right about one thing, Keri thought. Winning this case would be hard. Brian had no defense.

On top of that, even he knew that Brian and Rebecca Lawrence were back together. She had ignored Matthew's warnings and now she felt like a fool. How could she have fallen for him? Her face burned at the thought of their lovemaking while he still loved another woman.

"What did he want?" Matthew appeared from behind. He rested his arm gently around her shoulders and searched her face for an answer.

Keri looked up and smiled. His strength gave her comfort. He believed in Brian's innocence even if he didn't approve of his duplicity with women. "He wanted to explain his position to me. Unfortunately, today he made sense. As for the plea bargaining, he said that he only wanted to keep Brian alive. He seemed sincere enough."

"No doubt he is sincere about thinking Brian's best chance to stay alive is to plea bargain. The problem is that innocent people don't want to go to prison for a crime that they didn't commit." Matthew lowered his head and kissed her forehead. "How about dinner tonight?"

"Thanks, that would be great." Keri smiled up at him appreciatively. What would she do without his loyal friendship?

"See you at seven. I've got to make some calls." He waved as he turned and walked down the corridor the way Roy had gone.

"Bye." Keri called softly after him.

"So what did Roy Foxx want with you?" An angry voice growled at her.

Keri glanced up into Brian's angry face. She hadn't heard him come up. Too bad he had seen Roy talking with her. How long had he been watching her? He must have seen Matthew kiss her. "Let's go to the coffee shop and then we'll talk." Keri wanted to regain her composure before answering Brian's questions.

"The coffee shop is full and I want an answer now!"

Keri looked at him in amazement. He had never spoken to her that way before and she didn't like it. Since she didn't want to have a fight in the hall, she decided to pacify him. "He wanted to explain to me what his position was on your case."

"We already knew what his position was. Why were you talking to him?" His brilliant blue eyes shot her a possessive look.

"Because I wanted to." Keri's temper flashed. He had no right to question her this way. She wasn't his subordinate.

"He told you that I was guilty and you believed him!" Brian accused.

"It wasn't like that. He was explaining why he wanted to plea bargain." Not wanting to argue, she tried again. "Brian, he wanted to keep you alive."

"I can't believe what I'm hearing." Brian's face hardened with a look of betrayal. "I gave you credit for having more sense. You couldn't be objective if your life depended on it."

"Objective?" Anger swept through her. Almost every man she had talked to on this case had accused her of not being objective. "You men are all the same! When a man doesn't like the way a woman acts or doesn't like her opinion, she's accused of not being objective. It's a 'catch twenty-two.' If that's supposed to mean emotional, you're right, I'm emotional! I'm not changing for you."

"You're begging the question."

Her eyes bored into his. "I think it's time you found another attorney." Keri turned to leave, but he caught her.

"You heard the judge. I'm stuck with you; you can't quit." Brian grabbed her shoulders and turned her around, forcing her to face him. "What else did he say?"

Keri choked back a sob. So he was stuck with her, was he? A whole spectrum of emotions pelted her at the same time: anger, humiliation, embarrassment, hate. All she had to do was pick one and go with it. "He said you and Rebecca Lawrence were back together. Are you?" As hard as she tried, she couldn't hide the anger and disappointment in her voice.

"I haven't asked you about Matthew, have I? What's he to you?" Jealousy and outrage flashed in his eyes, but Keri was too distraught to see them.

"He's my friend. Now answer me," she demanded in a breathless voice.

"She's here. I told you that she was coming in yesterday," Brian answered. He didn't intend to explain her presence or his feelings.

A calmness settled over Keri as she glared at Brian. "I don't like the way you have been acting. You owe me an explanation. How dare you make love to me and then treat me with such indifference? I think that it's time you realized that I don't intend to allow you or any man to boss me around or mistreat me."

"Boss you around? Mistreat you? Are you crazy?"

"I mean it Brian. I'm not taking it, now or ever!"

"Fine." The tone of his voice was edged with an odd finality. "You won't be hard to replace!" Brian turned in a blind fury and walked off, oblivious to the pain on Keri's face.

Chapter Forty-One

From the bay window of her breakfast area, Keri gazed toward Biscayne Bay. It was Saturday morning and pouring. Rain splattered in torrential currents over the window panes, obliterating her view. For a long time she stared unseeingly at the weather before turning to sip her hot tea. Her eyes filled with unshed tears. It had been close to three weeks since she had seen Brian. She had worked long hard hours on his defense and now she was ready. Unable to face him, she had asked Jenna to call and tell him to be in court Monday morning at ten o'clock.

She had fully expected him to take her off the case and hire another attorney to represent him. Instead, all she had gotten from him was silence. Too busy to spend time brooding, Keri had managed not to think about their quarrel. Now it was the weekend before the trial and she had time on her hands.

Images of Brian filled her mind, reminding her of his lithe powerful body, his savage lovemaking and his vibrant personality, filled with humor. The time she had spent with him had been wonderful and she ached to be with him again. Never had she felt more confident and self-assured. Never had she felt so close to another human being. Never had she traveled to such great heights of ecstasy, . . . and never had she felt so rejected.

She glanced down at the newest tabloid. On the front cover, in full color, were Brian and the very beautiful Rebecca Lawrence. Since the auburn-haired siren had flown into town, the news media had been filled with spicy gossip of their affair and the trial. Brian had said that he didn't know if he loved Rebecca or not. It was very obvious to everyone that he did. They showed up in all the best places, arm in arm, smiling as if they had no problems or worries and no trial hanging over their heads. The hardest part for her was trying not to think of them in bed, laughing together, teasing and tormenting each other. She could easily imagine him possessing Rebecca with his skillful mastery, his hands on her breasts, kissing her intimately, driving her mad.

Keri covered her face with her hands. The thoughts were just too much for her to bear. How could he be so insensitive and cruel to her? She had never seen Brian act the way he did. Common sense told her that he wasn't jealous of Roy or Matthew. Over and over again, Keri thought about his actions and kept coming back to the same conclusion. He had wanted to pick a fight in order to get rid of her.

Her anger at Brian had quickly dissipated, but the pain from his parting words remained. So, she wouldn't be hard to replace? Tears spilled down her cheeks. He had certainly let her know that she wasn't anything special—just a good time and easy to forget. All Rebecca Lawrence had to do was show up in Miami and he was ready to dump her. One thing was sure: Their romance was over, almost before it started.

She couldn't blame him, she thought. She had seduced him. He didn't know how much she loved him. Keri would never reveal herself to him. The trial dictated that she do her best for him. After that, each would go their own way. He had given her the choice of going with him for the weekend. She had no one to blame but herself.

Matthew had been wonderful. He had made sure that her nights were filled with lighthearted pleasure. There had been dinners and movies and dancing. They had taken water taxis and gone to hockey games. He had even convinced her to go ice skating one night. Why couldn't he be the one to make her heart lose control? He was witty, intelligent, and handsome. Everywhere they went, women watched him with eyes filled with interest and desire. She was exceptionally fond of him, but she still loved Brian.

Silently, she sipped her tea. She had said she wanted Brian regardless of the consequences and she didn't regret her love for him or her time with him. The days ahead, though, promised pain. She would need a time for healing. After the trial she really would take that vacation she had been wanting and get away from it all.

Keri took her tea over to the microwave to reheat it. She glanced down at the counter to the cruise brochure she had picked up on her way home the day before. It was time to take care of herself, she decided. She flipped through the brochure one last time. A Caribbean cruise sounded wonderful. After the trial was over she would have peace and two weeks at sea.

Chapter Forty-Two

Sounds reverberated through the courtroom as reporters and TV cameramen waited impatiently in the press box. About sixty seats in the two-hundred-seat courtroom had been reserved for the media. The courtroom had filled fast after the last hearing. Curiosity seekers and friends rushed for the remaining seats. Keri stood at the defense table looking around uneasily. There was no sign of Brian or Matthew. The noisy courtroom was packed except for a few reserved seats in the first row behind her and ten rows reserved for the prospective jurors who would be waiting to go through the selection process.

Keri had Jenna with her to help her stay organized during the trial and to take notes on the jurors and their answers. She chided herself for not picking Brian up this morning, because the crowds outside may have been too much for him. Shouts rang out and light bulbs flashed. Keri gasped. Matthew had just come into the courtroom with Rebecca Lawrence at his side. She could only stare in disbelief as they made their way to the front-row seats reserved for them. It only took a moment for her to realize how uncomfortable she would be during this trial with Brian at her side and his paramour behind them.

Matthew smiled and waved her over. Hiding her sigh of exasperation, Keri held out her hand to the auburn-haired beauty Matthew was introducing. To her surprise, Rebecca grabbed her hand and shook it enthusiastically.

"It is such a pleasure to meet you. Both Brian and Matthew have spoken so highly of you. If there is any way that I can help you, I will. I'll be right here in Brian's cheering section through the whole trial." She smiled at Matthew before confiding, "He needs all the support we can give him."

Keri felt faint color creep over her. Not only was this woman beautiful, she was sweet. There was nothing there to hate. It just wasn't fair; she had pictured her as a grasping, fortune-hunting siren, sophisticated and shallow. She had been wrong, dead wrong.

Then silence crept over the courtroom. Keri wheeled around to see Brian walking to the front. His face wore a fathomless expression as his eyes fixed on her. Suddenly, everyone seemed to be shouting at Brian. He pushed his way through a crowd of reporters and TV cameras to the table where he stood towering over her.

"I'm here." His confident tone surprised Keri.

"Good. Sit down between us." She swallowed tightly and motioned to the chair next to Jenna, hoping that he wouldn't see her nervousness. Keri felt her heart pounding fiercely. She was acutely aware that her breathing had become shallow. What if the jury found Brian guilty? It would be her fault! She had to stop thinking the worst and believe they could win. But her emotions defied logic, as fear reached out with icy fingers and grabbed her.

Ignoring Keri, Brian turned to Rebecca and Matthew. He leaned over and kissed Rebecca's cheek and shook Matthew's hand. They said a few words, but Keri couldn't make them out. Instead, her mind was reeling with thoughts of her strategy, Rebecca's presence, and his kiss.

"All rise," the bailiff said.

Keri bit her bottom lip hard. Seeing Brian had opened a floodgate of pent-up emotions. She couldn't panic now, not in front of him. She reminded herself not to let Rebecca Lawrence, the crowds, and her own doubts intimidate her. This was only the jury selection. By the time the trial started, she would have her emotions under control.

"This court is now in session. The Honorable Harry Pennell presiding."

Keri glanced at Brian. He sat calm, cool and expressionless. Then it hit her. He was used to crowds and attention. She was not. She felt panicky. She dug her nails into her hands and stood up to face the judge. If this was jury selection, she wondered, how could she face the trial of the man she loved?

Keri relaxed some after the questioning began. Then it became routine. Jenna proved invaluable, taking notes, reminding Keri, never missing a cue. Brian conferred with Keri over prospective jurors and their answers, his observations astute. Even Matthew and Rebecca got into the act. By the end of the day, they were exhausted, but satisfied with their selection of jurors. Only one more day of jury selection and the trial would begin.

Keri and Jenna finally packed up for the day and headed back to the office. It was after hours when they arrived. Keri unlocked the door and crossed the room, anxious to get to her office. She didn't intend to work tonight. Instead, she was going to take a cool shower and go to bed early.

"Keri, here's a note from Maxine." Jenna scanned the note before walking over to Keri and offering it to her.

Keri had no intention of putting her files down to read the note. She would only have to pick them up again. "What does it say?"

"I put a floral arrangement in your office. It was in the hall when I arrived at the office today. Hope everything went well.'' Jenna tossed the note on her desk as they passed, heading for Keri's office.

Lighthearted and anxious, Keri walked toward her office with an eager smile. Brian must have sent her flowers. Had he been disappointed that she had failed to thank him? Apparently, she and Jenna had left for the courthouse before the flowers were delivered. She would have to explain in the morning.

She rushed into her office, then stopped abruptly. She held her breath. Blood drained from her face. Chills ricocheted up and down her spine, while her skin crawled with reaction.

''Keri, what's wrong?'' Jenna glanced at the flowers and back to Keri. She had never seen Keri so distraught.

''I see you haven't been to many funerals.'' Keri's voice rasped as she strained to speak. She swallowed hard and bit her lip. Fear held her heart in its cruel grip.

''What?'' Jenna looked at her in confusion and then back to the flowers. They were beautiful white lilies with a strange haunting odor. In fact, Keri's office was filled with their sweetness.

''It's a funeral wreath,'' Keri breathed. Keri knew the murderer was closing in for the kill. When would he make his move? She had expected it before now, but nothing had come except those threatening telephone calls.

Stunned by Keri's answer, Jenna walked over to the arrangement and examined it. With a trembling hand, she pulled out the card. ''Do you want me to read this to you?''

''It doesn't matter.'' Keri's voice quivered. ''I already know what it says.''

''Really?'' Jenna looked puzzled. ''What does it say?''

Keri inhaled sharply. She had heard the words so many times before. ''It says, 'You're next!' ''

Chapter Forty-Three

Keri had spent a restless night worrying about how well the trial would go and when the real murderer would tip his hand and try to kill her. After finding the flowers, her nerves had been totally shot. Jenna had looked at her in disbelief, with tears in her eyes, forcing Keri to explain to her that she had been receiving a number of threats and that the flowers were just one more. Common sense told her that the murderer was trying to keep her upset and off balance. If she didn't calm down, she would fail at defending Brian. She knew that she was not matching wits with the prosecutor, Louis Garcia, she was fighting a hidden brilliant and devious mind. It was as if the killer knew her every move, thought, emotion. The fear undermined her self-confidence. She had better try to focus on the trial which had just started.

Keri straightened in her seat and rested her hands on the edges of the defense table while she listened to Louis Garcia addressing the bench. Brian sat next to her, dressed in a conservative suit, looking handsome and serious. Rebecca sat behind him next to Matthew. Brian had said very little to them or to Keri when he came in. Keri closed her eyes, but it didn't block out the pain from Brian's coldness toward her. Perhaps it was the trial and all of the tension. She should expect Brian to be hard to deal with. Her thoughts raced before they began to fade, allowing her attention to focus on the trial.

The prosecution's first witness was homicide detective, Lt. Hector Rodriguez. Keri listened intently as Lt. Rodriguez described the procedures used by his investigative team in gathering the evidence. His emotionless eyes never left the jury. Keri sighed heavily. It was a great technique; a technique she often used.

One by one the prosecutor entered pictures taken by the crime lab into evidence. Some of the jurors cringed at the pictures of Emilia's lifeless body lying on the patio floor. As each picture was passed around the jury box, Lt. Rodriguez explained what the evidence was, its location, and a summary of any lab reports. Then he explained the significance of the evidence to the jury in a matter-of-fact manner.

Louis Garcia, pleased with the testimony of Lt. Rodriguez, turned to the jury. "In your opinion, Lieutenant, who committed this heinous crime?"

"In my opinion, the murder was committed by the defendant, Brian Michaels." Rodriguez smirked as he stole a glance at Keri.

"No further questions."

Judge Pennell peered at Keri over his wire rimmed glasses. "Ms. Adams, you may cross examine."

Keri rose and moved from behind the defense table. "Thank you, Your Honor." Confidently, she squared her shoulders and walked purposefully over to the jury. Today her height was an advantage. Dressed in a simple black suit with a plain white blouse, she commanded respect. She looked at each juror to insure the attention of each one before beginning her cross examination.

She turned slightly, so that she could see the detective and motioned to the tables in front of the judge where the evidence lay in plain view. In an innocent voice, she asked, "Lt. Rodriguez, what has been admitted into evidence which will place Mr. Michaels at the home of Emilia Martinez on the day of the murder?"

"The physical evidence. The fishing fly found on the patio, the comb with the defendant's hair found in the cabana bath, and the torn paper in the defendant's handwriting." His voice adopted a patronizing tone.

Keri spun around and faced him, incredulous at such a ridiculous statement. "Let's start with the fishing fly, Lieutenant. What reports do you have from the crime lab that conclusively state the fishing fly was dropped on the patio the day of the murder?"

Rodriguez shifted uncomfortably in his chair, a look of hate crossing over his face.

"Well, Lieutenant?"

"None."

Keri looked back at the jury, noting the frowns on the faces of several jurors. Great! They were getting the message loud and clear. "Are there any reports from the crime lab that would lead you to believe that the comb or the torn paper ended up in their respective locations on the day of the murder?"

"No," he growled.

Keri carefully articulated her next question, so that the jury would understand her emphasis. "Could the evidence that we just discussed, the fishing fly, the comb, the paper, have fallen there on the day before the murder?"

Keri saw the lieutenant's jaw clench tight. He sat mutely, refusing to answer before her soft voice prodded him. "Lieutenant, answer the question."

"Yes," he hissed through gritted teeth.

"How about the week before?"

"Yes."

"The month before?"

"Maybe."

Keri smiled at the jury. "Lieutenant, why did you tell us in so many words that the evidence indicated the date of the murder?"

"It was my opinion," he answered arrogantly.

Keri's eyebrow shot up in surprise. "Based on what?"

"Emilia Martinez was an immaculate housekeeper."

Keri was dumbfounded. She quickly hid her reaction under her professional mask and turned to the judge. "Your Honor, I will have more questions for this witness later in the trial. I am reserving the right to continue my cross later."

"Very well, Ms. Adams. The witness will make himself available." Judge Pennell made a note to himself. She was starting out well he thought. Just as he expected.

Keri had no questions for the prosecutor's next witness, the Medical Examiner, Stephen Pozner. She stipulated to the entry of the medical report and photographs into evidence. As she expected, he testified that the time of death was approximately two o'clock in the afternoon and that Emilia had died of strangulation. He did not have any testimony that would directly connect Brian to the crime.

Then, Pablo Martinez took the stand. As Keri listened to the prosecutor's preliminary questions, she felt the tension mount. He would start improper questioning, she thought.

"Do you know the defendant, Brian Michaels?" Garcia asked.

"Yes. He is a member of the Miami Stingrays, just as I am." Pablo glared angrily at Brian, ignoring the jury.

"How did you know Brian Michaels was having an affair with your wife?"

"Objection. Counsel is leading the witness!" Keri rose to her feet, ready to battle. Anger triggered a rush of adrenaline.

She wasn't going to let Garcia get away with his line of questioning.

"Sustained."

"I'll rephrase the question, Your Honor," Garcia said with a smile. "Tell me about the relationship between Mrs. Martinez and Brian Michaels."

"They were having an affair!" Pablo continued to stare at Brian.

"Did you argue about this?"

"Yes, that morning before he killed her."

"Objection!" Keri shouted. "The witness doesn't know who killed her."

Judge Pennell looked at the jury wondering just how much damage Pablo had done. "Sustained. The jury will disregard that last answer."

Garcia moved closer to Pablo. "Tell the jury about the argument."

Pablo focused instead on Keri. "He told me that he was having an affair with my wife. We argued."

"Did you know prior to this time about the affair?"

"No, never!" Pablo hesitated before he glared back at Brian. "He was my friend."

"No further questions." Garcia walked to his table and sat down.

Keri rose from her chair, but stood in place behind the defense table. "Mr. Martinez, other than the argument that you had with Mr. Michaels, do you have any proof that Mr. Michaels and your wife were having an affair?"

"No. I don't."

Keri looked at Judge Pennell. "Your Honor, the defense reserves the right to recall this witness to the stand. I have no further questions at this time."

Pablo looked confused as he stepped down from the witness stand. He had expected more of a fight. Apparently, so had the spectators. A low mumble filled the courtroom, echoing off the bare walls.

Judge Pennell pounded his gravel loudly. "Order! Order in the court!" He waited for the talking to die down. "We will break for lunch. This trial will resume at two o'clock sharp."

Chapter Forty-Four

It's a lethal weapon, she thought, a veritable time bomb. Last night she had eyed the ringing telephone suspiciously, as if it might explode at any minute. Caller I.D. hadn't helped a bit. The killer had either an electronic code block or caller I.D. block hardware on his line. His midnight calls were getting more and more frequent. She hadn't wanted to turn the bell off, just in case Brian decided to call. With a sigh of resignation, she had flipped the ringer switch into the off position and tried to sleep.

Stifling a yawn, Keri stole a quick glance at Brian sitting next to her at the defense table. The day before, Brian had been cool watching her cross examine witnesses. After a few comments, he had slipped out, missing the reporters.

Today, Brian was tense. Keri wanted to reach out to him, but there was no warmth in his eyes. He had preferred to smile and chat before trial with Rebecca and Matthew. Hurt by his indifference, she turned to listen to another witness for the prosecution.

Beatrice Suarez, Emilia's neighbor, was testifying that she saw a Gold Lexus in the driveway of the Martinez home the morning of the murder and again in the afternoon. She had even taken down a partial license tag number.

Keri rose to cross examine her. "Mrs. Suarez, what time did you first see the car in the Martinez driveway?"

"About ten o'clock," Mrs. Suarez fluffed her hair and fingered a gold loop earring.

"Is that when you took down the license tag number?"

"Yes." Still fingering the earring, she tilted her chin up and stared at Keri.

"What time did you see the car again in the Martinez driveway?"

"It was around four o'clock," she said confidently.

"Did you write down the license tag again?"

"No, I didn't have to."

"Why not?"

"Because I already had it." Mrs. Suarez straightened her skirt with an indignant gesture as a slight scowl made its way over her features.

"Did you look at the license number that afternoon?"

"No! I didn't need to."

"So, you don't know if the license tag numbers were the same, do you?" Keri's voice was edged with irritation at the indignant woman.

"Of course, they were!"

"You said that you didn't look at the license in the afternoon. How do you know?" Keri walked over to the exhibit table with an air of self-confidence and faced the jury.

"I don't."

"Mrs. Suarez, can you identify a Lexus from other makes of cars?"

"Yes, I can," she answered.

Keri picked up some photographs off the exhibit table. "These pictures are identified as defendant's Exhibit A. Please look at this first photograph and tell me what you see.'' Keri handed her a photograph.

''It's a gold car; a Lexus.''

''And the three remaining photographs?'' Keri handed them to her one at a time to look at.

''They all look alike.'' Her voice filled with hostility.

''You said that you could identify a Lexus from other makes of cars. Please identify the Lexus in those photographs.'' Keri ordered firmly.

''Here.'' She handed Keri a photograph. ''It's this one.''

Keri handed the photograph to the clerk. ''Let the record reflect that the witness failed to correctly identify the automobile in the photograph. It is, in fact, a Toyota.''

Keri walked confidently over to the jury box. Without taking her eyes off the jurors, she asked, ''Are you willing to testify now that the car you saw in the morning was the same car that you saw in the afternoon?''

Beatrice Suarez stared out over the courtroom, her mouth open in silent protest.

''Answer the question!'' Keri commanded in an agitated tone.

''No . . .''

''No further questions, Your Honor.'' Keri returned to the defense table. She knew she should feel good about the way she had been handling the witnesses for the prosecution. But she didn't. Each time she discredited testimony she felt like a tiny drop of water, wearing away at a stone. If she persisted, sooner or later, the dam would break and a reasonable doubt would be established in the minds of the jurors.

As the trial continued, Keri felt her energy heighten. Her control had intensified. The spectators sat in awe as she frustrated witnesses, discredited testimony and angered the prosecutor. She was making headlines. Yet Brian remained cool and aloof.

Keri watched as the prosecutor called Mike Beatty to the

stand. Beatty, another neighbor of Emilia Martinez, testified that he had often seen Brian's Lexus in the driveway of the Martinez home. Keri listened intently as he testified that he saw the car in the driveway on May 6, the Friday before the murder, at two o'clock.

Once again Keri approached the jury, not the witness, to begin her cross examination. "You've told the court that you have seen Mr. Michaels' Lexus in the Martinez driveway often. What dates are you talking about?"

Beatty glowered at her. "I can't give you dates. I just know that I saw it a lot."

Keri straightened with a sigh, then softly asked, "Do you work Mr. Beatty?"

"Yes! I already stated that for the record." His arrogant tone annoyed Keri, but she quietly responded.

"Tell me again."

A sneer crossed his face. "I work for the Sybonex Corporation."

Keri ignored his demeanor and continued. "What do you do there?"

"I'm a computer analyst." He pulled his shoulders back.

"What do you do as a computer analyst?" Keri asked.

"I keep the computers running smoothly."

"What are your normal working hours?" Keri stepped away from the witness and faced the jury.

"Eight to four-thirty, Monday through Friday." Beatty answered.

Keri turned to look at him. "Does that vary?"

"No."

"No shift work?"

Garcia jumped to his feet. "I object, Your Honor, I fail to see the relevance of this line of questioning and I have been more than patient with defense."

Judge Pennell smiled knowingly at Keri. "Ms. Adams?"

"I'm almost there." Keri answered.

"Overruled. Ms. Adams, you may continue."

Keri walked over to the stand and positioned herself so that her voice projected directly to the jury. "Answer the question, sir."

"I don't do shift work."

"Then tell me how you could have seen a gold Lexus in the driveway as frequently as you would have us believe." Keri demanded.

Silence blanketed the courtroom.

"Well?"

"I see it when I'm off."

"Evenings and weekends?" Keri prompted.

"For the most part, yes."

"Normal hours, when Pablo Martinez is home?" Keri asked in a loud voice.

"Objection!" Garcia bellowed.

"Sustained." Judge Pennell ruled.

"No further questions." Keri walked back to the jury smiling brightly.

Still standing, the prosecutor glared angrily at Keri. "Your Honor, the prosecution rests."

Keri turned quickly to Judge Pennell. "Your Honor, I would like to recall Pablo Martinez to finish my cross examination."

"You will have to finish your cross in the morning, Ms. Adams. I'm inclined to adjourn for the day." Judge Pennell turned to the bailiff and motioned for him to come over.

Keri was both disappointed and relieved. She was beginning to feel tired and she really wanted to finish her cross of Martinez and Rodriguez with everyone fresh and attentive. Brian looked exhausted and Matthew looked worried. Unfortunately, Rebecca looked great sitting there in her royal blue chemise smiling at Brian, while Jenna looked like she was falling apart at the seams with her mussed hair, wrinkled suit, and pale face.

Keri walked back to the defense table and sat next to Brian.

"Brian, you look tired. Try to get some rest tonight. Tomorrow will be a big day for us."

Brian looked into her eyes, sending tremors of anticipation through her. When he finally spoke, his voice was rough with emotion. "I'm not going to make it, am I?"

Her mind raced. Where were the words to reassure him? He needed them now, from her. Finally, from the depths of her subconscious mind her answer came, painfully honest, and definitely not comforting.

"It's too soon to tell."

Chapter Forty-Five

Brian must have had a long sleepless night. His face was beginning to show the strain of the trial. Yet, in spite of it all, he looked deliciously handsome. Keri studied Brian beneath half-closed eyes, while he talked to Matthew, Rebecca and a few other friends. Every morning the courtroom was full of Brian's friends, but never a member of his family. Could that be one reason for his coolness? He wasn't confiding in her. In fact, he must have forgotten that just a short time ago they were lovers. But he had been invaluable during the trial. His comments and observations had helped in dealing with witnesses.

Unfortunately, Keri couldn't forget that they had been lovers. Every night she relived the passion they had shared and the looks of tenderness that he had given her. The lovely dream-catcher that she had hung from her bedroom ceiling fan must be working overtime. All her dreams were of Brian and his strong lithe body close to her. She longed for him, but more than anything, she wanted to see him free. Even though she

wanted him, heart, body and soul, she could live with knowing
that she had done her best to defend him and that he was free.

Still deep in thought, Keri turned to face the bench. Court
had been called to order and she was about to be center stage.
If she failed to elicit the right information out of the next two
witnesses, it would be all over for Brian. They were her only
hope.

Keri rose and addressed Judge Pennell. "Your Honor, at this
time, I would like to recall Pablo Martinez in order to finish
my cross examination of this witness."

"Very well. Bailiff call Mr. Martinez to the stand." The
judge leaned back and rubbed his chin thoughtfully as he
watched Martinez enter. "Mr. Martinez, you are still under
oath."

Martinez nodded to the judge and glanced at Keri. She was
quickly scanning her notes with her back to him. Across the
table sat Michaels, staring at him, a look of betrayal in his
eyes. Martinez looked away guiltily.

Keri turned to Martinez, but remained standing at the defense
table. "Please tell the Court how you got to the Stadium on
Friday, May 6."

When her answer met with no response, Keri prodded him
gently. "Mr. Martinez?"

"Brian Michaels took me. My car was in the shop."

"What time did Mr. Michaels arrive at your house?" Keri
asked.

"Around two o'clock."

"You were home?"

"Yeah."

"Is your schedule at work pretty much like Mr. Michaels'?
Do you have practice and games at the same time he does?"
Keri queried him firmly.

"Yeah." Martinez looked at her with a confused expression
on his face.

"So, he's got free time at the same time you do?"

"Yes."

Keri dropped her notes on the table and began walking to the witness stand. She cupped her hands together behind her back and stood looking at him silently for a moment. "Mr. Martinez, was your wife a good housekeeper?"

"Sure. She had a maid."

"Was there anything remarkable about the way she kept house?" Keri watched his face for any telltale sign.

"She liked things in place. I guess she went overboard about that."

"Were other people aware of this?"

"I doubt it."

"Did you ever tell anyone about it or joke about it?"

"No."

"How about the police?"

"No. Definitely not." A frown crossed his brow as he became even more confused by her questions.

Keri approached the evidence table and picked up a picture. Thinking better of it, she dropped it back down and turned back to Martinez. "When I looked at the pictures of your wife's body, I noticed that she wasn't wearing any wedding rings. For that matter, she wasn't wearing any jewelry. Do you know where your wife's rings are?"

"Yeah. They're in my safe." His voice took on a defensive tone.

"How and when did they get in there?" Keri repositioned herself so that she could look at him and face the jury.

"She asked me to put them away for her a few days before she was murdered, and I did," he answered warily.

"Did you discuss the rings with the police?"

"No. They didn't ask."

"Lt. Rodriguez didn't ask about them?" Keri asked softly, as if the question was an afterthought.

"No. He never mentioned them."

"Thank you, Mr. Martinez. Now, one last question." Keri

squared her shoulders. If only he would tell the truth. "When you and Mr. Michaels argued, did he actually say that he was having an affair with your wife, or did you understand it from the content of the conversation?"

Pablo stared at Brian in silence. A look of consternation crossed his face as he tried to decide how to answer.

"Mr. Martinez?" Keri prodded gently.

"I guess that I understood it from what he was saying." Pablo mumbled uncomfortably.

"Then he didn't actually say that he was having an affair with your wife?" Keri held her breath. Why had Pablo changed his story?

"No. He said someone else was. You know how people are. When they want to take the heat off themselves, they manufacture someone else to place the blame on," he answered in an unsteady breath.

A rumble of voices vibrated through the courtroom as the surprised crowd began to recognize the significance of what Pablo had just said. Garcia looked shocked as he sat in angry silence.

"Order!" The judge pounded his gavel until silence fell over the room once again.

"Would you please tell us what he did say?" Keri stepped back forcing him to look directly at the jury.

"He said that Emilia wanted to break up with her lover, but that she was afraid of him because he was violent. When he told me that he had seen bruises on her about a week before, I thought he was lying and just covering up for himself. Then when I got home and found her body, I knew he had killed her so that she couldn't tell me the truth."

Keri ignored his accusation and continued her questions. "To your knowledge, is Mr. Michaels violent?"

"I never thought that he was, until now."

"Had your wife ever had lovers before this incident?" Keri asked innocently.

Martinez thought for a long time before answering. This time, Keri didn't prod him. The long silence was very effective as an admission.

"Yeah."

"Did you know who with?"

"No." Martinez looked down at his hands, shaking his head.

"No further questions."

Keri walked to the defense table and searched Brian's face. He seemed pleased, but angry. She knew that he felt betrayed. Once again she quickly scanned her notes. She motioned to Jenna and turned to the judge. The testimony of the next witness was crucial. "Your Honor, at this time, I would like to call Lt. Rodriguez back, in order to finish my cross."

The courtroom buzzed as Hector Rodriguez entered and walked to the front. Oddly enough, he didn't glare at Keri. Instead, he smiled faintly and with a confident set to his shoulders, sat down at the witness stand. While the judge reminded the detective that he was still under oath, Keri made her way to the jury box. "Lt. Rodriguez, during a conference that you had with Mr. Michaels, you asked him if he had seen a red truck in the driveway of the Martinez home. Why?"

Rodriguez gazed at her with an insolent expression. "I was merely trying to be thorough. I had a hunch."

"Please explain." Keri commanded.

Rodriguez looked to Garcia, expecting Garcia to object, but no objection came.

"I heard that she had an old boyfriend who drove a red pickup truck. I asked around, but nobody had seen one in the neighborhood for months. After that, I dismissed it."

Keri shot her next question at him quickly. "How did you know that Mrs. Martinez was, in your words, an immaculate housekeeper?"

"My opinion," he stated flatly.

"Did you know Emilia Martinez?"

Rodriguez hesitated, then glanced at Brian. With a trapped

look, he responded. "I talked to her at several victory parties for the team that I went to."

Keri heard whispers coming from the crowd. "At another conference with Mr. Michaels in my office, you asked Mr. Michaels what he did with her wedding rings. Why did you ask?"

"She didn't have any rings on when her body was found," he replied in an antagonistic tone.

Keri walked over to Jenna and waited patiently as Jenna handed her a cassette tape. She tapped the cassette tape against the palm of her other hand. "Please tell this court what you told Mr. Michaels about some of the idiosyncrasies of Mrs. Martinez."

"I don't know what you are talking about." Rodriguez hissed.

Keri walked toward him with the tape. "Don't try to snow me; it won't work. What did you say about her rings?" Keri demanded.

"I said she always took them off before she made love."

"How did you know that?"

"Her husband told me," he said triumphantly.

Keri smiled at him confidently. This time she had him, but good! "The testimony of Mr. Martinez is that he never discussed the rings with you."

"Then he's lying!" Rodriguez shouted angrily.

"Isn't it true that you had an affair with Emilia Martinez?" Keri shouted back.

"I talked to her at parties!"

"A yes or no, Lt. Rodriguez!" Keri demanded.

Rodriguez sat fuming as his face turned a deep red. He clenched his fists as if to strike. He turned to Garcia who sat silently with an incredulous look on his face.

"Answer the question!" Keri insisted.

"Yes!" He glared angrily at her.

"You spent a lot of money on her?"

"Yeah."

"Then she stopped seeing you a few months before her death?" Keri walked over to the jury box and waited for him to answer.

"Yeah, I guess that's right," he answered sullenly.

"Did that make you angry?"

"Yes."

"Angry enough to kill her?"

Keri didn't wait for an answer. Shouts filled the courtroom as it erupted in mass confusion. Reporters dashed out of the courtroom to the telephones. Aisles jammed with spectators. TV cameras zoomed in for close ups. Judge Pennell pounded his gavel to no avail.

Keri was only peripherally aware of the noisy courtroom. She turned and faced Brian, studying his emotionless face. His smoldering eyes captured hers. Her heart skipped a beat as she wondered why he was so angry with her. What else could she have done? Finally, she turned to the judge while he sequestered the jury for the weekend. Court was adjourned until Monday morning.

Chapter Forty-Six

It was unusual for the courthouse coffee shop to be so crowded on a Wednesday at three in the afternoon. It could be any day, Keri thought, except she had never waited for jury deliberations before as if her own life depended on it. Monday, she had presented her defense, short and sweet. The jury had the evidence, the testimony, and the judge's instructions. After two days, they were still deliberating. She had avoided the speculation on TV and in the newspapers, for fear that she would build her hopes too high.

Slowly, Keri sipped her soda. She hated waiting for Brian's fate. Brian had kept his comments to her completely impersonal throughout his trial. She had noticed a few unguarded looks of pain. Otherwise, he had been cool and composed. He had volunteered the points that he had wanted her to make with different witnesses. Then, he had left her to her own devices. Rebecca and Matthew had been trying to keep her spirits up as well as Brian's. She had come to like Rebecca, to her surprise. Obviously, Matthew had, too.

As she put her glass down, she sensed Brian's presence in the coffee shop. Before she had a chance to turn to the entrance, he stood by her side, smiling down at her. She noticed the loud talking had become subdued before he settled into the chair across from her. Dressed in a classic navy blue suit, he looked like a successful businessman ready to make a deal. Keri smiled to herself. She would never tire of being with him. The mere sight of him caused her heart to pound with anticipation and her body to flush with a warm glow.

"I thought that I would stop by today. Surely, they can't stay out much longer."

Keri looked at him, hiding her pleasure at seeing him. "I hope not."

Brian's eyes sparkled with emotion. "I was very impressed with your closing arguments to the jury. You summed it up very well."

"Thank you." Keri smiled tentatively while she wondered if he could sense the intensity of her feelings for him.

"I wanted to talk to you before the verdict came in." His face clouded as he searched for the right words. "I wanted you to know that, regardless of the outcome, I believe that you did an excellent job. I couldn't have gotten a better defense."

"Thank you." Keri managed to answer. She was glad he felt that way, even if she didn't.

"I have put all of my business in order and I am here today, ready to be taken into custody."

"You don't have much hope do you?" Keri asked, her eyes filled with unshed tears.

"No."

"Have you had anymore accidents?" Keri needed to stop thinking about what would happen if he were found guilty. It would destroy her. If he went to prison for a crime he didn't commit, she would blame herself and be forced to live with a guilt that would be too great for her to bear. He was now a part of her, for now, forever.

"No, I haven't. Have you?"

Keri looked away, afraid to answer. What difference would it make? She didn't want his sympathy and she didn't want to endanger him. She fully intended to deal with the threats after the trial.

"Earth to Keri," Brian called softly. "Well, have you?"

"Someone sent me a funeral arrangement with a card saying 'You're next' on it," Keri whispered.

"When?"

"The first day of jury selection. Since then, I have gotten several calls with choking sounds left on my answering machine."

"You should have told me!"

"Why? You had enough to worry about with this trial. Besides, I didn't want to involve you."

"Well, I am involved!" Brian snapped.

They sat staring incredulously at one another. Keri pulled her eyes away when she heard noises down the hall. A loud voice pierced the silence of the coffee shop. "The jury is coming in!"

Forty-five minutes later the jury filed into the packed courtroom. Brian sat calmly watching the faces of each person as he or she sat down. Keri focused her attention straight ahead at Judge Pennell. She knew that he wanted her to win. He had been lenient with her leading questions, her baiting, and her improper questions. However, he had been fair and had applied the law consistently. It wasn't her fault if the prosecutor just wasn't sharp enough to catch what she was doing.

When the judge cleared his throat, the courtroom became so silent that Keri was convinced she would be able to hear a pin drop. "Foreman of the jury, have you reached a verdict?"

"Yes, we have," the foreman answered.

"Give your results to the bailiff." Judge Pennell reached out eagerly for the verdict the bailiff handed to him.

"The defendant will rise," the bailiff called out.

Judge Pennell read over the verdict with an emotionless expression on his face. "Mr. Michaels, you have been charged with Murder One under the criminal statutes of the State of Florida." The judge paused and looked at Brian before glancing over to Keri standing by his side. "Mr. Michaels, the jury finds you not guilty. You are free to go."

Brian grabbed Keri and hugged her. They had done it! He was free! Her heart pounded. The feel of his body crushed against her sent charges of electricity up and down her spine. Excitement poured into her as her knees weakened and her body trembled. Brian kissed her quickly, before turning to Matthew. Reporters swamped them, flashes seemed to go off in every direction, microphones were shoved past Keri toward Brian. Friends and well wishers crowded around Brian, moving him away from her and the defense table. The noise was maddening. Keri found herself alone at the defense table, picking up her papers and feeling isolated. With tears flooding her eyes, she grabbed her briefcase, and with one last look at the crowd, left by a back entrance.

Chapter Forty-Seven

Rodriguez sat in his office mulling over the trial of the week before. Any day now he expected to be suspended for his indiscretions with Emilia Martinez. He should have taken himself off the case, but it had been vitally important for him to have control of the investigation. Emilia had been his lover, his confidant, his friend. He had been crazy with love for her. What man wouldn't love such a fiery passionate beauty? If he could just touch her and kiss her one more time . . .

His fist came down upon his desk with a resounding crash. Money! With her it had always been money. She loved him; she had shown him that. It was just that she needed money to be happy. He had scraped together everything he had to give her expensive gifts. He had even borrowed beyond his limit. Hell, it would take years to pay off his debts. He didn't begrudge her the money; he just didn't have enough to satisfy her. A woman like that had to be pampered and taken care of. She was used to affluence, being around all those rich ball players. She needed things that he just couldn't give her.

He glanced around the small government office. The grey walls were dingy, the furniture was old, and the carpet stained from years of use and abuse. The office was bleak and bare, just like his life had been until Emilia brightened it with her flamboyance and beauty. Suddenly, his cold uneventful life had found meaning. He had lived for the stolen moments that the two of them had shared. Now she was dead. Everything good about his life had gone with her.

With elbows propped solidly upon the desktop, he covered his face with his hands. He remembered their breakup vividly, as if it had happened just yesterday. His heart still stung from the pain of finding out she that was involved with someone else. When he demanded to know her new lover's name, she became evasive. A pang of a guilt shot through him as he remembered the way he grabbed her, and the bruises . . . the bruises he had made on her delicate skin. Weeks later, he knew her new lover was Michaels. Michaels was too attentive and always around. The way she hung on Michaels' arm at parties had driven him wild with jealousy. Finally, filled with rage, he had vowed revenge on both of them.

When Keri Adams entered the picture, he wasn't sure just what to expect. Granted she had a good reputation and was a fighter, but he hadn't expected her to hang in with such tenacity. That was a mistake on his part. From past experience with her, he should have known and been more careful. He had resented her trial tactics for quite some time. She had been like a thorn in his side, questioning him relentlessly on the witness stand. But it was his comment about the rings that had been his downfall. He made it when he was furious with Michaels. Rodriguez didn't like excuses, even his own. He should have realized Adams would grab onto that comment and check it out.

It had been quite obvious that Michaels was romancing Adams just as he had romanced Emilia. Women just didn't listen. Perhaps they liked courting danger and found it exciting.

He tried to warn her, but she had paid no attention. Why the newspapers never picked up on their romance was beyond him. They must have been extremely careful. Even he could only place them together alone a couple of times. Having Michaels followed had been his idea, but it hadn't accomplished much. Finally, he had given it up.

Now, thanks to Keri Adams and her clever cross examation, reporters haunted him, following him everywhere, trying to get a statement. Real bad press. Day and night her words tormented him: "Angry enough to kill her?" Hell, yes! And he was angry enough to kill Keri Adams, too!

He was going to get Keri Adams for the humiliation she had caused. Strange that he enjoyed the fact that his friends and co-workers knew that he had been with a woman as beautiful as his lovely Emilia. Damn. The lousy telephone was ringing. With an angry scowl he reached over and answered the telephone.

"Rodriguez speaking."

"Janet Davis was murdered," a male voice whispered, "and you know it."

"Hey, who is this?" Rodriguez swung his chair around. His caller had his full attention now.

"She knew the identity of Emilia's killer!" the voice rasped, "that's why she was killed. What do you think, cop? Should I go to the police?"

"Who are you? How do you know?" Rodriguez shouted.

"You're in hot water, cop. Come to the locker room at the stadium tonight. Ten forty-five. Don't be late."

At the sound of the dial tone, Rodriguez slammed the receiver down. Fury raked his body while chills permeated him. Now what?

Chapter Forty-Eight

Across the city, Keri watched the bubbles gently struggle to the surface of the aquarium. Matthew sat next to her at the conference table going over the records he had managed to get from Pablo and Jesse. While Matthew finished up on the bank account records, Keri tried to sort through all of the past events, trying to find another clue to the identity of the killer. So far, their efforts had produced nothing but frustration.

Keri rose and grabbed their coffee cups. "More coffee?"

"Sounds good," he murmured, deep in thought. "How about another pastry, too?"

She walked over to the credenza where Jenna had set up a tray of coffee and pastries. The cherry-filled pastries were her favorite next to the guava-filled *pastelitos*. She picked out a couple and put them on a dessert plate to wait while she fixed their coffee. This was definitely fattening work they were doing. Unfortunately, she had been unable to exercise lately due to the demands of the trial. It was time to get back to exercising, or she wouldn't be able to fit into any of her clothes; they were already starting to pinch at her waist. She carried the coffee and pastries over to the conference table and sat down across from Matthew. As always, he looked lean and handsome. Maybe they should get out tonight, go to dinner and maybe dancing, just for a break.

"I talked to a neighbor of Janet's. She said that she saw a gold car parked in the Davis driveway on the day of Janet's death." Matthew's voice broke into her distant thoughts.

"Did she say what time?" Keri asked while she fidgeted with the waistband of her skirt.

"Around four." Grey eyes studied her as apprehension crossed her features.

"That must have been the same car that followed me when I left Janet's house that evening." Keri shuddered. "Did you get to talk to Katie?"

"Yes. Apparently, Janet was her source of information. She wasn't very cooperative." He leaned back in his chair and looked at her evenly. "She told me that she didn't want to get involved."

Keri's heart sank. Another dead end. Poor Matthew, after all the work and effort he had put into this, it still wasn't falling together the way it should. Could the murderer have been so clever as to conceal his every trail? She'd give up, but she feared for her life. The threatening telephone calls had stopped, but her fear and anxiety had not. Someone was out to get her and biding his time. Every dark shadow was a potential danger; every glance from a stranger was a threat. Parking garages worried her and she constantly checked her rear-view mirror everywhere she went. This was no way to live.

"What are you doing in here? Beating a dead horse?" Roy stood in the doorway in his tailored blue suit studying Matthew intently. A mocking smile crossed his face when he glanced at Keri. Keri wondered how long he had been there listening to their conversation. She couldn't tell from his dark brooding eyes, how he was reacting.

"Looking for evidence that will point to the killer of Emilia and Janet," Matthew answered enthusiastically. "Brian already knows who the killer is, but he needs some hard evidence to back him up before going to the D.A."

"Brian?" Roy shook his head in disbelief and leaned his shoulders against the doorframe. "He doesn't know when to give up does he?"

"Did he tell you who it is?" Keri asked, trying to hide the hurt that she felt from being excluded. Why hadn't Matthew told her? It might make looking through the records and the evidence a whole lot easier, not to mention that it just might save her life. Keri bit her lips and tried to force back the flow of tears that threatened to betray her.

"No. Not yet. He wants me to come by the stadium tonight at eleven. I'm going to get the scoop of the year! By tomorrow the headlines will be screaming the name of the murderer."

"Don't tell me he didn't tell you!" Roy laughed when he saw the shock and disappointment on Keri's face.

"No. I haven't talked to Brian since the trial," she admitted, desperately trying to keep the hurt and embarrassment from creeping in. She wouldn't let him gloat; she couldn't.

"Maybe you will believe me now. He was just using you all along. You did a tremendous job of getting him off and he's dumped you. I know him, remember? He can have any woman he wants and it certainly isn't a naive little attorney. I heard that he dumped you before the trial. You'll have to admit Keri, that's real nerve!"

Matthew looked at Keri with an odd expression. "You should stay away from Brian, Keri. He doesn't want you around."

Keri struggled to maintain her poise. If it had just been Roy—but it was Matthew, too, warning her, telling her Brian didn't want her. She glanced down at the notes in front of her, blinded by tears. She wouldn't let them see her pain; she couldn't!

"Keri, I have another case that I want you to work on with me. Let's talk about it tomorrow."

Keri nodded, afraid that if she spoke she would cry.

"I'm on my way to court. See you around, West." Roy turned and left the conference room.

Regaining her composure, Keri sighed. Nothing was working out right. Brian thought that he knew who killed Emilia and Janet, but she doubted it. Surely, she would be able to see it clearly, if he had. Still, the facts were not coming together. From the records, she and Matthew had decided that Janet had been blackmailing someone. That was something that she had suspected all along. Janet paid all of her personal bills in cash—large sums of cash. Nothing came out of the checking accounts. Where else would she get so much cash?

Keri glanced at Matthew. What she really wanted was some information on Brian. What was going on in his life? Why hadn't he called her? Where was Rebecca? She was making herself miserable, she knew. Pride was in her way. She couldn't call him, he might realize that she loved him, and that would be too much for her to bear. If she was going to look foolish, it would only be in her eyes and not his. She didn't want his sympathy or his gratitude. She wanted what she knew she couldn't have, his love.

"Matthew, did Rebecca Lawrence fly back to Fort Worth? I would have liked to say good-bye. You know, she turned out to be a very nice person." Keri bit into her pastry and savored its sweetness. Thank goodness for food.

"You ended up liking her, didn't you?" Matthew asked softly.

"Yes," Keri answered honestly, "I can see why Brian loved her."

"Me, too." Matthew glanced at her with a mischievous gleam in his eyes. "She's still here. As a matter of fact, I'm taking her to dinner tonight."

Keri looked at him in surprise. "I thought you were going to the game!"

"Later. Much later." A happy grin teased at the corners of his mouth. "I met Rebecca when I went to Fort Worth for the games this summer. She loves sports."

"Then why don't you take her to tonight's game?" Keri felt a pang of jealousy. She had wanted to be with Matthew tonight. He was up to something. She knew it; she felt it.

"Not tonight, it's much too dangerous." He paused and studied her intently. "You should stay away, too. You could be in serious danger. Trust me, Keri."

"Don't worry, Matthew, I don't have any reason to go to the baseball game. You told me yourself that Brian didn't want me around. I guess you know by now, I'm not crazy about sports." Keri laughed to hide her pain. She wasn't going to wear her heart around on her sleeve for people to see, and that included Matthew.

To her surprise, he drank the last of his coffee and got up from his chair. "Keri, I hate to leave, but I do have another appointment to make."

"It's okay Matthew, the only records left to look at are the telephone calls. If I find anything interesting, I'll let you know. I'll read the papers in the morning. I suspect that you are going to be disappointed tonight."

He smiled but didn't answer. With a quick kiss on her cheek, he turned and walked for the door. As she watched him leave the room, she decided to pack up and go back to her office. There was no use staying in the large conference room. Slowly, she gathered the records and her notes from the conference table and headed back to her office.

"Would you mind terribly if I left early today? I need to take Maxine home and I would like to avoid the rush hour traffic." Jenna's voice followed her into the office.

"I saw Maxine's car this morning. What happened?" Keri gave her an exasperated look. She was tired of Jenna skipping out on work. Although she had proved valuable at the trial, she didn't have much sense of responsibility.

"Roy borrowed Maxine's car to go to court. He has a problem with his." Jenna explained.

"Oh, all right!" Keri voiced her frustration. "I'm leaving now. Be sure and lock up."

"Okay."

Keri gathered her files and purse and headed for the door. She didn't think she could handle being alone in the office today. At least at home she could kick off her shoes, throw on her jeans and a loose shirt, and relax with no Jennas, no Maxines, and no Roys to aggravate her.

All the way home she thought about her conversation with Matthew. How could Brian possibly know who the murderer was? How could he not tell her? Brian knew of the threats upon her life, just as Matthew did. There was something about Matthew's demeanor that told her that he hadn't told her the truth. The more that she thought about it, the more concerned she became. Had she been too quick to trust Matthew? She hadn't known him before the murder. As a matter of fact, she actually knew very little about him. Maybe Roy was right, after all. She was beginning to see how very naive she really was.

So, where did that leave her? There was no reason to think that Matthew was a killer. As far as she knew, he had never met Emilia, and there were no clues to connect him to her. Better for her to stop worrying, she thought, while she opened the door to her townhouse. She was losing touch with reality.

Since Keri loved to watch the sunlight playing on the water, she decided that her breakfast nook was the perfect place for her to work and relax. Roy's words kept coming back to her, like echos in a dark lonely canyon. True, Brian could have any woman he wanted, and for a short while, he had wanted her. He told her that he didn't know how he felt and that he could make no promises. She had accepted him. How deeply she loved him now. She had known that her relationship with Brian was over, but it hurt terribly to have Roy rub it in. Matthew had confirmed Brian didn't want her. Stay away, he had said, you could be in danger. She already had a broken heart. Keri blinked away tears and tried to make some sense out of the telephone records laying in front of her.

She sipped her hot tea. As she scanned Emilia's telephone records, one number jumped out at her. She felt as though a vise held her heart. She dropped the records and reached for Janet's. To her dismay, the number started showing up on Janet's records after Emilia's death. Keri leaned back and thought about past events. Could he have really killed Emilia and Janet? If so, it was clear to her that he would *have* to kill her. Was there anything else that she could point to? One by one the pieces fell together. Disappointment clouded her expression. Blood drained from her face, leaving her a chalky white. Her body shivered with icy chills. "Oh, no," she whispered to herself, "it just can't be."

Keri rose shakily and made her way over to the telephone. Silently, she punched in Brian's number as tears streamed down her face. Finally, she hung up; no one was home. For a moment she wondered what she needed to do. There was only one way. She had a baseball game to go to.

Chapter Forty-Nine

The Miami Stingrays won! The aisles filled with cheering fans in no particular hurry to leave. The team would be showering off and leaving soon for a victory party. She wanted to speak to Brian before Matthew got there. Trying to make her way through the crowds, Keri felt herself being jostled and pushed in the wrong direction. Between dirty looks and cryptic remarks she realized that there must be a better way than going against the crowd. Wearily, she sat down on a bench to let the traffic go by. When it started to thin out, she got up and ran to the locker room.

Short of breath, she opened the door and called out. "Brian. Are you here?" There was no answer. The lights were still on, but Keri couldn't hear anyone talking. She strained to hear any noise, but was met with only quiet. Once more she tried, calling his name softly.

"What do you want?" An angry hostile voice pierced the silence.

Startled, Keri whirled around, her eyes filled with fear.

"Brian! I thought you were inside." Even with the distant lights from the field, she could barely make out his form. Dressed in black jeans and a black pullover, he blended into the night. What was going on?

"You thought wrong." He stared at her with cold hard eyes. "I asked you what you were doing here."

"Could we talk inside?" Keri asked hoarsely. She turned and stepped inside, hurt by his rejection.

"Keri, I don't want to talk to you now." His voice followed her inside the locker room. He towered over her, forcing her to look up to see his ashen face.

"Brian, we have to talk. It's important." Keri looked around to be sure that they were alone. Why was he being so difficult? Matthew wasn't here yet.

"I don't want to talk to you. Now leave." His voice was emotionless and uncompromising. He grabbed her by the shoulders, ready to force her out. Keri struggled to free herself and found herself crushed against him, his mouth on hers. She could feel his heart pounding heavily in his chest.

Fire raged within her, sending sparks coursing through her veins. She wanted him, but not this way. Gasping for breath, she wrenched herself free and glared up into his smoldering eyes.

"Are you crazy?" Keri stepped back, just out of his reach. "How could you?"

Keri watched his labored breathing as he glowered at her. His nostrils flared in anger. The wrath in his eyes was unmistakable. Keri felt her heart shatter, but she continued. "I came here to talk to you. Brian, I know who killed Emilia and Janet."

"Then start by telling me." Jesse Davis stepped from around a row of lockers and walked over to her with a slight swagger. As his eyes bore into hers, she was sure she smelled liquor.

"I thought that we were alone." Keri looked into Brian's unforgiving face.

"Obviously," Jesse said drily.

Brian's eyes flashed with hostility. "Get out of here, Keri," he commanded.

Jesse held Keri's arm. "No. I think it's time we got this out in the open, don't you?"

Keri nodded. Her thoughts spun violently in a web of confusion. Just one look from Brian and she was rendered speechless.

"Did those telephone records tell you anything?" Jesse refused to relinquish Keri's arm. Instead, he stepped closer, intent on discovering his wife's killer.

"It was the combination of Emilia's and Janet's that clenched it for me," Keri managed, hypnotized by Brian's unreadable eyes.

Suddenly, the door opened and Roy stepped inside. "Well, well, the gang's all here." His tall frame loomed just inside the doorway.

Jesse looked confused. "Why are you here?" he asked.

"I came to find Emilia's murderer, of course." Roy stepped toward Keri. "You just couldn't take my advice, could you?" He shook his head. "But then, you never could. I should have known when I went into partnership with you that you were too stubborn to keep around."

Keri's eyes widened in surprise. He looked like an ordinary fan, in his baseball cap and satin sport jacket. Obviously, he had watched the game and had a few beers. "Well, I was just leaving." She needed to call the police. Keri stepped toward the door, expecting Roy to move, to let her by. When he failed to do so, she glanced at Brian's anxious face. He knew!

"Let her go, Roy. This is just between us." Brian's voice was low and commanding.

Roy pushed the visor of his Dodgers cap up higher. "I don't think so. This is even better. The killer and his lover have a quarrel; friend gets caught in the crossfire." With a sadistic smile, Roy eased a handgun from his pocket.

"Hey, what is going on here?" A deep frown cut into Jesse's face. "What are you doing with a gun?"

"I'm going to kill the three of you, stupid! Now, shut up!"
Roy swung the gun around, fanning it at them. "Back up and
sit down on the bench over there."

They backed toward the bench. She had been too late to save
Brian. Surely there was something they could do to stop him.

"Before you kill us, you should tell us how you managed
to frame me." Brian asked.

"You were easy. My secretary has a gold Toyota. Just by
switching her license plate for a stolen one, I could come and
go as I pleased. If someone saw the car at Emilia's, they thought
it was you." Roy laughed.

"But why did you kill Emilia?" Keri asked, stalling for
time. She knew he wouldn't be able to resist bragging.

"She was going to dump me, just like all the others. Nobody
dumps me. She wanted to go back to that stupid detective.
'Love,' she said." With a disgusted look, he looked at Keri.
"You should have taken my advice. I framed Michaels good.
If the verdict had come back guilty, we would all be happy
and alive. He would do a few years and get out."

"You're crazy!" Keri glared at him.

"Maybe. Maybe not." His mouth twisted in a cynical smile.
"I thought that you would screw up defending him. I underestimated you, Keri."

She held her voice steady, buying time. "Why did you want
to kill me, if you wanted me to handle the case?"

"At first, I just wanted to scare you. Then when I walked
in on you two embracing, I knew you were getting too close
to Michaels. I sensed early on that he suspected me. Right,
Michaels?" Roy glanced at Brian with hate in his eyes.

"Right!" His tone assured Keri that Brian wouldn't die
without a fight.

Roy was too engrossed to notice they had stopped backing
up. Slowly, he inched forward, as he explained. "You were
too smart for your own good. With Brian knowing my identity,

I knew it would be just a matter of time before you figured it out, too.''

''Why did you kill Janet?'' Jesse asked.

Roy swung the gun toward him and hissed in anger. ''She was blackmailing me. When she wanted to tell Keri, I had to stop her.''

No one spoke. They looked at Roy, realizing that the man truly intended to kill them.

A loud noise broke the silence of the locker room. Roy jerked and fired in the direction of the noise. As Jesse doubled over in pain, Brian grabbed a baseball bat and swung it at Roy, his powerful shoulders and arms delivering a blow to the head, that sent Roy flying into the wall. Brian dragged him up by the shirt, but his body was limp. Without further examination, Brian slammed him back against the wall.

''Jesse!'' Brian shouted and ran over to him.

''He grazed my head, Brian.'' Jesse sat up holding his head with bloody fingers.

''Stay here. I'll get help.'' Brian looked around. For the first time, he seemed to notice Keri standing there in stunned silence. ''For once, do as you are told and sit down!'' he ordered.

With a resounding bang, the door flew open and Rodriguez jumped in, his gun aimed and ready for action. ''What the hell is going on?'' He looked down at the unconscious body of Roy and then to Brian. ''Is he dead?''

''Not yet.'' Brian straightened his strong body. ''He was going to kill us. I hit him with a baseball bat.'' He motioned to Jesse. ''We need to get help for Jesse. Roy shot him.''

''Why?'' Dumbfounded, Rodriguez lowered his gun and clicked on the safety.

''Because we figured out that he killed Emilia and Janet.'' Brian helped Jesse to the bench and steadied him. ''There's a first-aid kit around here some place,'' he muttered under his breath and wandered off to find it.

''That's right, Lieutenant, and I have his confession here on tape.'' Matthew West walked in from the back of the locker room limping. ''Sorry, I fell off the top of the locker.''

Brian returned with the first-aid kit. ''No apology necessary. It was just the diversion that we needed.'' He pulled out bandages for Jesse's head.

''You set him up,'' Keri breathed, looking from Brian to Matthew and back again. ''You knew he would be here!'' she accused.

''Well, we hoped he would come,'' Brian admitted with a wry smile.

Thoughts reeled in Keri's mind. But one stood out from the rest. He had known the identity of the killer, and he had not told her. She felt betrayed by his silence. What if Roy had decided to stop playing games and kill her. She had been a captive victim at the office almost every day. Suddenly, she felt as if her very life was being drained from her.

Keri turned to the lieutenant. ''I'm going home. You may come by to question me. Please call first.''

Lt. Rodriguez nodded. She looked shaken and he had enough here to keep him busy all night.

''Brian, I came here to warn you, but I see you didn't need me.'' Tears filled Keri's eyes. ''It's too bad that you didn't think it important enough to warn me.''

''It was better that you didn't know.'' He stood up and faced her. ''You would have tipped Roy off in some way and we would never have caught him red-handed.

Keri stared at him in disbelief. She felt too numb to even be angry at this arrogant creature. ''You think a lot of your own opinion, don't you. Well, I almost ended up dead tonight, thanks to you.'' She held up her hand as he stepped forward to touch her.

''Don't ever touch me again.'' Keri gazed at him through eyes glazed with pain. ''I don't want you.''

Chapter Fifty

Calypso music drifted over from poolside. Keri turned over in her chaise longue and fluffed her towel into a more comfortable pillow. From her shaded domain, she motioned to the waiter to bring over a Bahama Mama. When he arrived, Keri flashed him a bright smile and sat up. He smiled back cheerfully and he handed her the cool drink.

Keri was glad now that she had finished off the week tieing up loose ends, ensuring that Roy's clients got proper representation, and organizing her own work so that she could leave it for a while. When Saturday arrived and she still hadn't heard from Brian, she figured that he was in no hurry to talk to her. No doubt he was still angry with her for showing up at the stadium and throwing a wrench into his plans. Not that she had cared; she was still quite angry herself. She had turned off the bell to her telephone, turned off the answering machine, and stopped her daily papers. The ship sailed at five o'clock and she would be incommunicado for two wonderful weeks.

The August cruise had been a perfect break. From the

moment she boarded the five-star ship, she had been pampered and catered to by a friendly staff. Through each day, she exercised, swam and relaxed. At night, after dinner and a show, she danced and visited the midnight buffet. So far, the ports had been interesting and the shopping fun. She had even purchased a couple of disposable cameras and played tourist. Keeping busy and exercising was the right prescription for heartbreak, she had decided.

Through it all, nothing took away the empty feeling that she kept suppressed beneath the surface of her subconscious mind. As the days passed, she was finally able to separate herself from her problems and put them into a better perspective. She loved Brian with all her heart and soul. She wanted the best for him. If his happiness pinned itself on Rebecca Lawrence, then so be it. It hurt at the very essence of her being, but a new awareness had blossomed within her of an inner strength that would carry her through life. Love had transformed her. She had learned not only how to feel, but how to truly give.

Now she knew that she didn't need a mentor, or partner, or friend to help her pave the way. She no longer had to take the abuse that men like Patrick or Roy dished out. Brian had made her recognize her own self-worth. He had given so much more than he had taken. While she still didn't understand his actions, she had faith that in time she would.

Keri finished her drink and settled back for a short nap. She looked out over the calm ocean. When her cruise was over, she would have to face a whole battery of new decisions. She stretched lazily. It was a beautiful day, Brian was alive and free, and she was the hottest attorney in South Florida right now. She laughed at her modesty. Notoriety would bring changes and she would be ready for them.

Chapter Fifty-One

September brought cooler winds and a southern sun. Soon tourists would pour into South Florida. New yachts would be moored at the docks. Invitations to go boating would fill Keri's date book. Keri stretched lazily and glanced over at the clock. It was six o'clock. If she really wanted to watch the sunrise, she still had time. Without turning on a light, she crawled out of bed and headed for the shower.

After a leisurely shower and still dripping, Keri threw on an oversized T-shirt and headed for the kitchen. No sooner had she flipped on a light when the telephone rang. Surprised, Keri picked up the receiver. "Hello?"

"Hi, Princess." A soft masculine voice sent shivers through her body. "Will you join me for breakfast?"

Keri was stunned. "No. I don't think so." Her heart pounded rapidly. Why was he calling her after almost four weeks of silence?

"I'm a good cook. You didn't have any complaints before," he coaxed.

"That was before you dumped me," Keri whispered, trying to steel herself against his charm. Did he think he could walk into her life and start where they left off? He was crazy!

"I what?"

He sounds surprised, Keri thought. A good actor, but I'm not buying.

"Keri, look outside your window. I'm dockside waiting for you." His voice was warm and coaxing. "We have to talk."

"I don't want to talk." Keri forced a tone of indifference into her voice. She hoped the retort sounded familiar.

"Okay, then let's make love." He chuckled softly.

Keri's face went hot. How could he make her feel this way? She thought that she had control over her wild emotions, but apparently she didn't. Anxiety seized her. She didn't want to love him, to feel the pain of losing him again. She had to make him leave her alone.

"Well?" he prodded.

"I don't want you," she said huskily.

"Say it to my face; then I'll believe you." His voice gently mocked her.

"No." Keri felt a sense of panic set in. She had no intention of seeing him this morning. What did he think he was doing? There was no response, but the line was still open.

"Brian?" Keri called into the receiver. No answer. She hung up and rushed over to the window. Sure enough, the *Misty II* was dockside, bobbing gently. How long had he been there?

There was a loud pounding at the door. "Keri let me in."

Keri ran to the front door. "Go away!" She peered through the peephole. At the sight of him, her heart twisted. He stood waiting for her to open the door, telephone in hand. Had he been there all this time?

"Keri," he called out. "Please."

Keri stood watching him, her eyes filled with unshed tears. "Go away," she whispered inaudibly. "Go away."

"Please, Keri."

Slowly, she disengaged the alarm system and opened the door, stepping back to allow him to walk through. He followed her in silence to the kitchen and set the telephone on the counter. Then his eyes traveled languorously over her body. Her damp shirt clung to her. When Brian reached for her she tried to back away, but he pulled her close and held her tightly against him.

"No, Brian," she said firmly as she pressed her palms hard against his chest in a futile attempt to separate herself from him.

He tilted her head back and smothered her mouth with his. His skillful kiss left her mouth burning and aching for more. Slowly, he planted kisses down her neck. His hands caressed her gently, destroying her defenses. Her body trembled with desire and apprehension beneath his touch.

Lifting his head to look deeply into her eyes, he asked seductively, "You're not afraid of me, are you?"

Keri lowered her long lashes, refusing to look at him or to answer. Instead, she squirmed to get away from him.

"Keri, listen to me!" Brian held her firmly as she struggled. "I didn't dump you."

"I don't want to discuss it. Go away!"

With a frustrated sigh, Brian picked her up and carried her to the bedroom. Keri shivered as he slipped off her T-shirt and gently placed her in the middle of the bed. He pulled off his shirt and cast it aside, his eyes never leaving her. She lay quietly as he stripped off his shorts and briefs with one quick motion.

Brian stretched out beside her and gathered her close in his arms. "Why did you tell me to find someone else?"

"What?" Keri looked at him in surprise. "If you remember correctly, you got angry with me for talking to Roy."

"I knew he was the killer; I just couldn't figure out how to prove it. I thought that you still didn't believe in me when I saw the way you were acting. I'm sorry Keri, but it hurt."

"How did you know that Roy was the killer?" she asked.

"I started suspecting him from the beginning, but there were no clues to tie him to Emilia's murder. It was little things at first: the way he handled the case and tried to manipulate you, the bottle of Turbulence that the police missed, maintaining three aquariums at the office. I also vaguely remembered that he wore a Dodgers cap on a fishing trip with some of us to the Keys. Then, the night he tried to run us into the river, I thought that I saw his profile, but I wasn't sure.''

Keri choked back a sob. ''Why didn't you warn me? He was trying to kill me.''

''In the beginning, he was trying to make you think that I was trying to kill you. That way, you would believe that I was guilty and would plea bargain. I would be blamed for the crime and no one would be the wiser. Then, when Janet called, he slashed your tires to delay you, giving him time to silence her. He didn't count on my being out of town at the time of the murder.''

''You still haven't said why you didn't warn me.'' Keri blinked back tears.

''Because I thought that you would give it away. I was afraid that you might indirectly communicate to him that you knew he was the killer. Then he would kill you for sure.'' Brian caressed her trembling body as he explained. ''He wanted you to defend me. He was sure that you would fail miserably in court since he had refused to allow you to develop any type of defense. He was actually happy when he was taken off the case.''

''You said I would be easy to replace.'' Her breath caught. ''You dumped me!''

''Keri, that's not true. I could never replace you. You told me to find someone else. You made me believe that you didn't want me. I was furious, but I left you alone to try to protect you. I hoped Roy would believe that we had broken up. After the trial, he was getting nervous. He knew that I suspected him.''

''How did he know?''

"I gave it away during one of our conferences. He picked up on it fast. After the trial, he started to get nervous. I asked Matthew to help me set him up. It was the only way. I was afraid that he would decide that he had to kill us before we could get solid evidence."

"What about Rebecca?"

"She came to Miami to be with me during the trial not only because she felt bad for me, but because she wanted Matthew."

"Matthew?" Keri looked at him with a stunned expression. Did she dare believe him?

"They met in Fort Worth. It was love at first sight. She begged me to let her come to Miami and give her a chance to be near him. I thought it would be a great idea to pretend that we were still involved. I realize now that I was wrong, but I thought it would shift Roy's attention away from you. Then Matthew didn't show any real interest in her at first. In fact, he told me he was dating you and intimated that it was serious. I got angry and jealous. I was on trial for my life, I was hurting, and I loved you so much that I couldn't stand the thought of you being with another man. It ate at me the whole time."

"You loved me?" Keri managed breathlessly.

"I've loved you from the moment I saw those beautiful brown eyes of yours. One look and I was doomed." Brian chuckled.

"Thanks a lot," Keri answered drily.

"What made you suspicious of Roy?" Brian kissed the tip of her nose.

"Everything fell into place at once. I was reviewing Emilia's telephone records and saw a lot of calls to our office. Then after Emilia's death, Janet started making calls to our office and I knew that I wasn't talking to her. Roy borrowed Maxine's car that same day. It looks just like a Lexus. That and the three aquariums made me realize he had to be the killer. Then I remembered how indifferent he was about my welfare and he always seemed to know things in advance, like the after-shave lotion and the loaner car." Keri paused for breath. "I tried to call you to warn you. That's why I went to the stadium."

"I knew you were in danger," he said gently. "That's why I tried so hard to get rid of you. I was afraid he might kill you, and I wasn't willing to risk that."

"You should have told me, Brian. I think you underestimated me." Keri wondered if she would ever forgive him.

"You are right. I should have warned you, but I never underestimated you. Remember, I knew that I had accidentally tipped my hand. Even if I was wrong about you, I did try to protect you."

"Why? Why did you wait so long to talk to me?" Keri asked. She was close to not caring anymore. The feel of him next to her was sending hot, irresistible urges running through her.

"I needed to straighten out some of the problems in my life. Don't forget, you jumped on the first outward-bound ship and left me stranded." Before she could protest, he continued. "There were a lot of doubts and ill feelings among the team members. I had to know if I was staying with the team and where I was going before I asked you to marry me. It gave everything time to settle down so that we wouldn't be front-page gossip."

"Matthew got his scoop, didn't he?" Keri smiled, thrilled at his words.

"Yes, and he got Rebecca. They are front page news right now." Brian didn't want to talk anymore; he wanted her. He kissed her mouth, warm and yielding, then began exploring her delicate curves. He burned with desire and need. When he heard her soft moan, he moved his body to cover hers. "Keri, I'm sorry that I hurt you. Please forgive me."

Keri caught his head and pulled him down. She kissed him deeply and sensuously. "I forgive you."

"Well, you still haven't said yes." He whispered passionately into her ear. She felt his hot breath on her cheek and sensed his impatience.

"Yes, to what?" she teased.

"Marry me?" His soft tender voice caressed her and enveloped her in a blanket of warmth and security.

"Yes, I'll marry you!" She kissed him again and thrilled at the feel of him becoming one with her.

"Tell me," he demanded hoarsely.

Her heart sang from the depth of her emotions. "I love you, Brian. I love you!"

THE MYSTERIES OF MARY ROBERTS RINEHART

THE AFTER HOUSE   (0-8217-4246-6, $3.99/$4.99)

THE CIRCULAR STAIRCASE   (0-8217-3528-4, $3.95/$4.95)

THE DOOR   (0-8217-3526-8, $3.95/$4.95)

THE FRIGHTENED WIFE   (0-8217-3494-6, $3.95/$4.95)

A LIGHT IN THE WINDOW   (0-8217-4021-0, $3.99/$4.99)

THE STATE VS.   (0-8217-2412-6, $3.50/$4.50)
ELINOR NORTON

THE SWIMMING POOL   (0-8217-3679-5, $3.95/$4.95)

THE WALL   (0-8217-4017-2, $3.99/$4.99)

THE WINDOW AT THE WHITE CAT
                                   (0-8217-4246-9, $3.99/$4.99)

THREE COMPLETE NOVELS: THE BAT, THE HAUNTED
LADY, THE YELLOW ROOM
                                   (0-8217-114-4, $13.00/$16.00)